EVERYMAN, I will go with thee,

and be thy guide,

In thy most need to go by thy side

ALEXANDER PUSHKIN

Born at Moscow in 1799 and educated at Tsarskoe Selo. In 1817 was attached to the Ministry of Foreign Affairs, being sent to the south of Russia in 1820. He settled in St Petersburg in 1830, and was fatally wounded in a duel in 1837.

ALEXANDER PUSHKIN

The Captain's Daughter

AND OTHER STORIES

The Queen of Spades   Dubrovsky
Peter the Great's Negro   The Station-master
The Snowstorm

TRANSLATED WITH
AN INTRODUCTION BY
NATALIE DUDDINGTON

DENT: LONDON, MELBOURNE AND TORONTO
EVERYMAN'S LIBRARY
DUTTON: NEW YORK

© Translation 'The Snowstorm', J. M. Dent & Sons Ltd, 1961
All rights reserved
Printed in Great Britain by
Biddles Ltd, Guildford, Surrey
and bound at the
Aldine Press · Letchworth · Herts
for
J. M. DENT & SONS LTD
Aldine House · Albemarle Street · London
This edition was first published in
Everyman's Library in 1933
Last reprinted 1978

Published in the U.S.A. by arrangement
with J. M. Dent & Sons Ltd

No. 898 Hardback ISBN 0 460 00898 6
No. 1898 Paperback ISBN 0 460 01898 1

INTRODUCTION

PUSHKIN is the greatest of Russian poets, and Russian literature is truly said to begin with him. The national genius found in him its first adequate expression, and his influence determined its subsequent development. His poetry has set a standard of beauty that has never been surpassed; his prose tales established the literary tradition followed by the great novelists that came after him. The realism so characteristic of Pushkin's writing is the key-note of Russian literature as a whole. As a poet Pushkin is untranslatable: the exquisite beauty and the austere simplicity of his verse cannot be rendered into a foreign tongue. Every word of his poetry is so perfect in its context that it is impossible to replace it by any other. But his prose has none of this poetic quality and loses but little in translation. It is vigorous and straight-forward, and sounds as simple and natural to-day as it did a hundred years ago. Prose was not Pushkin's instinctive medium, and it was only after 1830 that he turned his attention to it. The tales in the present volume are among the best known of his prose works.

Pushkin was born in Moscow on 26th May 1799, of an old noble family. His parents were people in good society and led a fashionable life, troubling themselves little with the bringing up of their children who were left to the care of foreign tutors. Pushkin's father was interested in literature, received in his house the intellectual *élite* of the day, and had an excellent French library where the boy could help himself to any book he liked. He early developed a passion for reading and acquired a mastery of the French language. The Russian influences in his childhood came from his grandmother and his nurse Rodionovna, to whom he owed his knowledge of Russian folk-lore. The affection of these two excellent women made up for his mother's neglect, and had a profound influence on Pushkin's mind and character.

At the age of twelve he was sent to the Lyceum at Tsarskoe Selo, an aristocratic boarding-school for boys opened in that year under the special patronage of the Emperor Alexander I. Pushkin was very happy there, and the memory of his school years remained sacred to him throughout life; some of his best poems are inspired by it. It was at the Lyceum that Pushkin began to write poetry, the quality of which was recognized by his teachers and schoolfellows.

On leaving school he threw himself into a life of pleasure which did not, however, prevent him from working hard at his writing. He did not take his duties seriously at the Foreign Office where he had some small post, but he never trifled with his art, and spent a great deal of care on the lightest of his poems. In 1820 he published *Ruslan and Ludmilla*, a fantastic narrative poem which made his name famous throughout Russia: such charming and graceful poetry had never been written in Russian before. In the same year Pushkin aroused the anger of Alexander I by his *Ode to Liberty*. He was banished from Petersburg to the south of Russia; his recklessness and defiance of conventions made him fresh enemies among the governing class, and in 1824 he was ordered to settle permanently on his estate Mihailovskoe in the Province of Pskov. The years of exile provided Pushkin with plenty of new impressions, and it was during this period that he wrote *The Prisoner of the Caucasus*, *The Gipsies*, *The Fountain of Bahchisarai*, the early chapters of *Yevgeni Onyegin*, and a number of beautiful short poems. After the death of Alexander I and the mutiny of 14th December 1825, in which many of Pushkin's friends were implicated, he was sent for by the new emperor, Nicholas I. Nicholas asked Pushkin if he would have taken part in the rebellion had he been in Petersburg; Pushkin answered in the affirmative. The Tsar, impressed by his sincerity, granted him a complete pardon and promised to be his special patron and only censor; Pushkin went away captivated by the tsar's generosity. But Nicholas proved to be far less lenient as censor than the poet had hoped and, what was worse, passed on the supervision of Pushkin's writings to the chief of the gendarmes, Count Benckendorff, a stupid and spiteful man. As time went on, Pushkin came to resent bitterly the restrictions placed on his work.

His marriage in 1831 to a young society beauty, Natalya Nicolaevna Goncharov, made life still more difficult. He was deeply in love with his wife, but they had very little in common. She had no intellectual interests, and was incapable of appreciating her husband's genius; she liked fashionable society, and enjoyed the court atmosphere which Pushkin found so irksome. For her sake he put up with a style of living that was distasteful to him and that he could ill afford. The smart people with whom they associated looked down upon Pushkin for being poor and of low rank in the service; they thought nothing of his greatness as a poet. Pushkin, proud and sensitive, suffered keenly from the contempt of his intellectual inferiors, and retaliated by bitter sarcasms and epigrams which made him many enemies. He felt more and more isolated, and often thought of retiring to the country where, free from perpetual money worries, and the silly trivialities of fashionable life, he could devote himself entirely to writing. But meanwhile a vile campaign of slander was launched against him by a group of men who particularly disliked him for his proud and independent spirit; he was pestered by anonymous letters, reflecting on his wife's honour, and was goaded at last into fighting a duel with Baron Georges d'Anthès, a French royalist in the Russian service. Pushkin was fatally wounded and died three days after, on 29th January 1837. His death was mourned throughout Russia as a national disaster. Succeeding generations have recognized even more clearly the significance of his work, and the cult of Pushkin has become the spiritual heritage of every educated Russian.

NATALIE DUDDINGTON.

SELECT BIBLIOGRAPHY

Pushkin made his first appearance in the press in June 1814 with a poem in the magazine *Messenger of Europe*. For the next six years he wrote lyrics, but in 1820 appeared his first narrative poem, *Ruslan and Lyudmila*. He was next chiefly occupied in producing narrative poems (*The Prisoner of the Caucasus*, 1821; *The Fountain of Bahchisaray*, 1822; *Gipsies*, 1824; *Poltava*, 1828), culminating in *Eugeni Onegin* (1825-32). His later poems include the *Fairy Tales* (1832-5), of which 'The Golden Cockerel' is one, and *The Bronze Horseman* (1841), usually reckoned to be his poetical masterpiece. In 1825 he had written the tragedy *Boris Godunov* (published in 1831). This was followed by four smaller plays, his last dramatic effort being *The Rusalka* (begun in 1832 and published in 1841).

Pushkin's earliest published prose appeared in 1825 in the form of critical articles. His first story was *Peter the Great's Negro* (1828-41), which was followed by *Tales of Belkin* (1831), containing five stories of which 'The Station-master' was one. His other fiction is *The History of the Manor of Goryukhino* (1857), *Dubrovsky* (1841), *The Queen of Spades* (1834), *Kirdjali* (1834), *The Captain's Daughter* (1836), *The Egyptian Nights* (1841).

His miscellaneous prose is made up of an historical study, *The History of the Pugachev Rebellion* (1834); a travel book, *A Voyage to Arzrum* (1836); and a collection of anecdotes given the English title of *Table Talk* (1857). He also left a small journal of the years 1833-5, and a mass of correspondence which was not published until 1906-8.

See Prince Mirsky, *Pushkin*, 1926; J. Cleugh, *Prelude to Parnassus*, 1936; J. Lavrin, *Pushkin and Russian Literature*, 1947; H. Troyat, *Pushkin* (trans.), 1951; W. N. Vickery, *Pushkin: Death of a Poet*, 1968; J. Bayley, *Pushkin: A Comparative Commentary*, 1971; Henri Troyat, *Pushkin: A Biography*, 1974.

CONTENTS

THE CAPTAIN'S DAUGHTER

CHAPTER I

A SERGEANT OF THE GUARDS

Watch over your honour while you are young.
A Proverb.

He would have been a Captain in the Guards to-morrow.
'I do not care for that; a common soldier let him be.'
A splendid thing to say! He'll have much sorrow . . .

Who is his father, then?

Kniazhnin.

My father, Andrey Petrovitch Grinyov, had in his youth served under Count Münnich and retired with the rank of first Major in 17—. From that time onwards he lived on his estate in the province of Simbirsk, where he married Avdotya Vassilyevna U., daughter of a poor landowner of the district. There had been nine of us. All my brothers and sisters died in infancy. Through the kindness of Prince B., our near relative, who was a major of the Guards, I was registered as sergeant in the Semyonovsky regiment. I was supposed to be on leave until I had completed my studies. Our bringing-up in those days was very different from what it is now. At the age of five I was entrusted to the groom Savelyitch, who was told off to look after me, as a reward for the sobriety of his behaviour. Under his supervision I had learned, by the age of twelve, to read and write Russian, and could judge very soundly the points of a borzoi dog. At that time my father hired for me a Frenchman, Monsieur Beaupré, who was fetched from Moscow together with the yearly supply of wine and olive oil. Savelyitch very much disliked his coming.

'The child, thank heaven, has his face washed and his hair combed, and his food given him,' he grumbled to him-

3

self. 'Much good it is to spend money on the Frenchman, as though there weren't enough servants on the estate!'

In his native land Beaupré had been a hairdresser; afterwards he was a soldier in Prussia, and then came to Russia *pour être outchitel,*[1] without clearly understanding the meaning of that word. He was a good fellow, but extremely thoughtless and flighty. His chief weakness was his passion for the fair sex; his attentions were often rewarded by blows, which made him groan for hours. Besides, 'he was not an enemy of the bottle', as he put it; that is, he liked to take a drop too much. But since wine was only served in our house at dinner, and then only one glass to each person, and the tutor was generally passed over, my Beaupré soon grew accustomed to the Russian home-made brandy and, indeed, came to prefer it to the wines of his own country as being far better for the digestion. We made friends at once, and although he was supposed by the agreement to teach me 'French, German, and all subjects', he preferred to pick up some Russian from me and, after that, we each followed our own pursuits. We got on together capitally. I wished for no other mentor. But fate soon parted us, and this was how it happened.

The laundress, Palashka, a stout pock-marked girl, and the dairymaid, one-eyed Akulka, had agreed to throw themselves together at my mother's feet, confessing their culpable weakness and tearfully complaining of the *mossoo* who had seduced their innocence. My mother did not like to trifle with such things and complained to my father. My father was not one to lose time. He sent at once for that rascal, the Frenchman. They told him *mossoo* was giving me my lesson. My father went to my room. At that time Beaupré was sleeping the sleep of innocence on the bed; I was usefully employed. I ought to mention that a map of the world had been ordered for me from Moscow. It hung on the wall; no use was made of it, and I had long felt tempted by its width and thickness. I decided to make a kite of it and, taking advantage of Beaupré's slumbers, set to work upon it. My father came in just at the moment when I was fixing a tail of tow to the Cape of Good Hope. Seeing my exercises in geography, my father pulled me by

[1] To be a teacher.—TRANSLATOR'S NOTE.

the ear, then ran up to Beaupré, roused him none too gently, and overwhelmed him with reproaches. Covered with confusion, Beaupré tried to get up but could not: the unfortunate Frenchman was dead drunk. He paid all scores at once: my father lifted him off the bed by the collar, kicked him out of the room, and sent him away that same day, to the indescribable joy of Savelyitch. This was the end of my education.

I grew up without any tuition, and spent my time chasing pigeons and playing leap-frog with the boys on the estate. Meanwhile I had turned sixteen. Then there came a change in my life.

One autumn day my mother was making jam with honey in the drawing-room, and I licked my lips as I looked at the boiling scum. My father sat by the window reading the *Court Calendar*, which he received every year. This book always had a great effect on him: he never read it without agitation, and the perusal of it invariably stirred his bile. My mother, who knew all his ways by heart, always tried to stow away the unfortunate book as far as possible, and sometimes the *Court Calendar* did not catch his eye for months. When, however, he did chance to find it, he would not let it out of his hands for hours. And so my father was reading the *Court Calendar*, shrugging his shoulders from time to time and saying in an undertone:

'Lieutenant-General! . . . He was a sergeant in my company . . . a Companion of two Russian Orders! . . . And it isn't long since he and I . . .'

At last my father threw the *Calendar* on the sofa, and sank into a thoughtfulness which boded nothing good.

He suddenly turned to my mother:

'Avdotya Vassilyevna, how old is Petrusha?'

'He will soon be seventeen,' my mother answered. 'Petrusha was born in the very year when Auntie Nastasya Gerasimovna lost her eye and when . . .'

'Very well,' my father interrupted her; 'it is time he went into the Service. He has been climbing dovecots long enough.'

My mother was so overwhelmed at the thought of parting from me that she dropped the spoon into the saucepan and tears flowed down her cheeks. My delight, however, could hardly be described. The idea of military service was connected in my mind with thoughts of freedom and of the pleasures of Petersburg life. I imagined myself as an officer of the Guards which, to my mind, was the height of human bliss.

My father did not like to change his plans or to put them off. The day for my departure was fixed. On the eve of it my father said that he intended sending with me a letter to my future chief and asked for paper and a pen.

'Don't forget, Andrey Petrovitch, to send my greetings to Prince B.,' said my mother, 'and to tell him that I hope he will be kind to Petrusha.'

'What nonsense!' my father answered, with a frown; 'why should I write to Prince B.?'

'Why, you said you were going to write to Petrusha's chief?'

'Well, what of it?'

'But Petrusha's chief is Prince B., to be sure. Petrusha is registered in the Semyonovsky regiment.'

'Registered! What do I care about it? Petrusha is not going to Petersburg. What would he learn if he did his service there? To be a spendthrift and a rake? No, let him serve in the army and learn the routine of it, and know the smell of powder and be a soldier and not a fop in the Guards! Where is his passport? Give it me.'

My mother found my passport, which she kept put away in a chest together with my christening robe, and, with a trembling hand, gave it to my father. My father read it attentively, put it before him on the table, and began his letter.

I was consumed by curiosity. Where was I being sent if not to Petersburg? I did not take my eyes off my father's pen, which moved rather slowly. At last he finished, sealed the letter in the same envelope with the passport, took off his spectacles, called me and said:

'Here is a letter for you to Andrey Karlovitch R., my old friend and comrade. You are going to Orenburg to serve under him.'

And so all my brilliant hopes were dashed to the ground! Instead of the gay Petersburg life, boredom in a distant and wild part of the country awaited me. Going into the army, of which I had thought with such delight only a moment before, now seemed to me a dreadful misfortune. But it was no use protesting! Next morning a travelling-chaise drove up to the house; my bag, a box with tea-things, and bundles of pies and rolls, the last tokens of family affection, were packed into it. My parents blessed me. My father said to me:

'Good-bye, Pyotr. Carry out faithfully your oath of allegiance; obey your superiors; don't seek their favour; don't put yourself forward, and do not shirk your duty; remember the saying: "Watch over your clothes while they are new, and over your honour while you are young".'

My mother admonished me with tears to take care of myself, and bade Savelyitch look after 'the child'. They dressed me in a hare-skin jacket and a fox-fur coat over it. I stepped into the chaise with Savelyitch and set off on my journey weeping bitterly.

In the evening I arrived at Simbirsk, where I was to spend the next day in order to buy the things I needed; Savelyitch was entrusted with the purchase of them. I put up at an inn. Savelyitch went out shopping early in the morning. Bored with looking out of the window into the dirty street, I wandered about the inn. Coming into the billiard-room I saw a tall man of about thirty-five, with a long black moustache, in a dressing-gown, a billiard-cue in his hand, and a pipe in his mouth. He was playing with the marker, who drank a glass of vodka on winning and crawled under the billiard-table on all fours when he lost. I watched their game. The longer it continued, the oftener the marker had to go on all fours, till at last he remained under the table altogether. The gentleman pronounced some expressive sentences by the way of a funeral oration and asked me to have a game. I refused, saying I could not play. This seemed to strike him as strange. He looked at me with something like pity; nevertheless, we entered into conversation. I learned that his name was Ivan Ivanovitch Zurin, that he was captain of a Hussar regiment, that he had come to Simbirsk to receive recruits, and was staying at the inn. Zurin invited me to share his dinner, such as it was, like a fellow-soldier. I readily agreed. We sat down to dinner.

Zurin drank a great deal and treated me, saying that I must get used to army ways; he told me military anecdotes, which made me rock with laughter, and we got up from table on the best of terms. Then he offered to teach me to play billiards.

'It is quite essential to us soldiers,' he said. 'On a march, for instance, one comes to some wretched little place by the western frontier; what is one to do? One can't be always beating Jews, you know. So there is nothing for it but to go to the inn and play billiards; and to do that one must be able to play!'

He convinced me completely and I set to work very diligently. Zurin encouraged me loudly, marvelled at the rapid progress I was making, and after several lessons suggested we should play for money, with three-farthings stakes, not for the sake of gain, but simply so as not to play for nothing, which, he said, was a most objectionable habit. I agreed to this, too, and Zurin ordered some punch and persuaded me to try it, repeating that I must get used to army life; what would the army be without punch! I did as he told me. We went on playing. The oftener I sipped from my glass, the more reckless I grew. My balls flew beyond the boundary every minute; I grew excited, abused the marker who did not know how to count, kept raising the stakes—in short, behaved like a silly boy who was having his first taste of freedom. I did not notice how the time passed. Zurin looked at the clock, put down his cue, and told me that I had lost a hundred roubles. I was somewhat taken aback. My money was with Savelyitch; I began to apologize; Zurin interrupted me:

'Please do not trouble, it does not matter at all. I can wait; and meanwhile let us go and see Arinushka.'

What can I say? I finished the day as recklessly as I had begun it. We had supper at Arinushka's. Zurin kept filling my glass and repeating that I ought to get used to army ways. I could hardly stand when we got up from the table; at midnight Zurin drove me back to the inn.

Savelyitch met us on the steps. He cried out when he saw the unmistakable signs of my zeal for the Service.

'What has come over you, sir?' he said in a shaking voice 'wherever did you get yourself into such a state? Good

Lord! Such a dreadful thing has never happened to you before!'

'Be quiet, you old dodderer!' I mumbled. 'You must be drunk; go and lie down . . . and put me to bed.'

Next day I woke up with a headache, vaguely recalling the events of the day before. My reflections were interrupted by Savelyitch, who came in to me with a cup of tea.

'It's early you have taken to drinking, Pyotr Andreyitch,' he said to me, shaking his head, 'much too early. And whom do you get it from? Neither your father nor your grandfather were drunkards; and your mother, it goes without saying, never tastes anything stronger than kvass. And who is at the bottom of it all? That damned Frenchman. He kept running to Antipyevna: "Madame, shu voo pree vodka". Here's a fine "shu voo pree" for you! There is no gainsaying it, he has taught you some good, the cur! And much need there was to hire an infidel for a tutor! As though master had not enough servants of his own!'

I was ashamed. I turned away and said to him: 'Leave me, Savelyitch, I don't want any tea'. But it was not easy to stop Savelyitch once he began sermonizing.

'You see now what it is to take too much, Pyotr Andreyitch. Your head is heavy, and you have no appetite. A man who drinks is no good for anything. . . . Have some cucumber-water with honey or, better still, half a glass of home-made brandy. Shall I bring you some?'

At that moment a servant-boy came in and gave me a note from Zurin.

DEAR PYOTR ANDREYITCH,

Please send me by the boy the hundred roubles you lost to me at billiards yesterday. I am in urgent need of money.

Always at your service,

IVAN ZURIN.

There was nothing for it. Assuming an air of indifference I turned to Savelyitch, who had charge of my money, my clothes, and all my affairs, and told him to give the boy a hundred roubles.

'What! Why should I give it him?'

'I owe it to him,' I answered, as coolly as possible.

'Owe it!' repeated Savelyitch, growing more and more

amazed; 'but when did you have time to contract a debt, sir? There's something wrong about this. You may say what you like, but I won't give the money.'

I thought that if at that decisive moment I did not get the better of the obstinate old man it would be difficult for me in the future to free myself from his tutelage, and so I said, looking at him haughtily:

'I am your master, and you are my servant. The money is mine. I lost it at billiards because it was my pleasure to do so; and I advise you not to argue, but to do as you are told.'

Savelyitch was so struck by my words that he clasped his hands and remained motionless.

'Well, why don't you go?' I cried angrily.

Savelyitch began to weep.

'My dear Pyotr Andreyitch,' he said, in a shaking voice, 'do not make me die of grief. My darling, do as I tell you, old man that I am; write to that brigand that it was all a joke, and that we have no such sum. A hundred roubles! Good Lord! Tell him that your parents have strictly forbidden you to play unless it be for nuts! . . .'

'That will do,' I interrupted him sternly; 'give me the money or I will turn you out.'

Savelyitch looked at me with profound grief and went to fetch the money. I was sorry for the poor old man, but I wanted to assert my independence and to prove that I was no longer a child.

The money was sent to Zurin. Savelyitch hastened to get me out of the accursed inn. He came to tell me that horses were ready. I left Simbirsk with an uneasy conscience and silent remorse, not saying good-bye to my teacher and not expecting ever to meet him again.

CHAPTER II

THE GUIDE

Thou distant land, land unknown to me!
Not of my will have I come to thee,
Nor was it my steed that brought me here.
I 've been led to thee by my recklessness,
By my courage and youth and my love for drink.

An Old Song.

My reflections on the journey were not particularly pleasant. The sum I had lost was considerable according to the standards of that time. I could not help confessing to myself that I had behaved stupidly at the Simbirsk inn, and I felt that I had been in the wrong with Savelyitch. It all made me wretched. The old man sat gloomily on the coach-box, his head turned away from me; occasionally he cleared his throat but said nothing. I was determined to make peace with him, but did not know how to begin. At last I said to him:

'There, there, Savelyitch, let us make it up! I am sorry; I see myself I was to blame. I got into mischief yesterday and offended you for nothing. I promise you I will be more sensible now and do as you tell me. There, don't be cross; let us make peace.'

'Ah, my dear Pyotr Andreyitch,' he answered, with a deep sigh, 'I am cross with myself—it was all my fault. How could I have left you alone at the inn! There it is— I yielded to temptation: I thought I would call on the deacon's wife, an old friend of mine. It 's just as the proverb says—you go and see your friends and in jail your visit ends. It is simply dreadful! How shall I show myself before my master and mistress? What will they say when they hear that the child gambles and drinks?'

To comfort poor Savelyitch I gave him my word not to dispose of a single farthing without his consent in the future. He calmed down after a time, though now and again he still muttered to himself, shaking his head: 'A hundred roubles! It 's no joke!'

I was approaching the place of my destination. A desolate plain intersected by hills and ravines stretched around. All was covered with snow . . . the sun was setting. The chaise was going along a narrow road, or, rather, a track made by peasant sledges. Suddenly the driver began looking anxiously at the horizon, and at last, taking off his cap, he turned to me and said:

'Hadn't we better turn back, sir?'

'What for?'

'The weather is uncertain: the wind is rising; see how it raises the snow.'

'But what of it?'

'Do you see that?'

The driver pointed with the whip to the east.

'I see nothing but the white steppe and a clear sky.'

'Why, that little cloud there.'

I certainly did see at the edge of the sky a white cloud which I had taken at first for a small hill in the distance. The driver explained to me that the cloud betokened a snowstorm.

I had heard about snowstorms in those parts, and knew that whole transports were sometimes buried by them. Savelyitch, like the driver, thought that we ought to turn back. But the wind did not seem to me strong; I hoped to arrive in time at the next station, and told the man to drive faster.

The driver set the horses at a gallop but still kept glancing eastwards. The horses went well. Meanwhile the wind grew stronger and stronger every hour. The little cloud grew bigger and rose heavily, gradually enveloping the sky. Fine snow began to fall, and then suddenly came down in big flakes. The wind howled, the snowstorm burst upon us. In a single moment the dark sky melted into the sea of snow. Everything was lost to sight.

'It's a bad look out, sir,' the driver shouted. 'Snowstorm!' I peeped out of the chaise: darkness and whirlwind were around us. The wind howled with such ferocious expressiveness that it seemed alive; Savelyitch and I were covered with snow; the horses walked on slowly and soon stopped altogether.

'Why don't you go on?' I asked the driver impatiently.

'What's the good?' he answered, jumping off the box 'I don't know where we are as it is; there is no road and it is dark.'

I began scolding him, but Savelyitch took his side.

'Why ever didn't you take his advice?' he said angrily; 'you would have returned to the inn, had some tea and slept in comfort till the morning, and have gone on when the storm stopped. And what's the hurry? We aren't going to a wedding.'

Savelyitch was right. There was nothing to be done. Snow was falling fast. A great drift of it was being heaped by the chaise. The horses stood with their heads towards the ground and shuddered from time to time. The driver walked round them setting the harness to rights for the sake of something to do. Savelyitch was grumbling; I was looking around in the hope of seeing some sign of a homestead or of the road, but I could distinguish nothing in the opaque whirlwind of snow. Suddenly I caught sight of something black.

'Hey, driver!' I cried. 'Look, what is that black thing over there?'

The driver stared into the distance.

'Heaven only knows, sir,' he said, climbing back on to the box; 'it's not a wagon and not a tree, and it seems to be moving. It must be a wolf or a man.'

I told him to go towards the unknown object, which immediately began moving towards us. In two minutes we came upon a man.

'Hey, there, good man,' the driver shouted to him, 'do you know where the road is?'

'The road is here,' the wayfarer answered. 'I am standing on hard ground, but what's the good?'

'I say, my good fellow, do you know these parts?' I asked him. 'Could you guide us to a night's lodging?'

'I know the country well enough,' the wayfarer answered. 'I should think I have trodden every inch of it. But you see what the weather is: we should be sure to lose our way. Better stop here and wait; maybe the snowstorm will stop and when the sky is clear we can find our bearings by the stars.'

His coolness gave me courage. I decided to trust to

Providence and spend the night in the steppe, when the wayfarer suddenly jumped on to the box and said to the driver:

'Thank God, there's a village close by; turn to the right and make straight for it.'

'And why should I go to the right?' the driver asked with annoyance; 'where do you see the road? It's easy enough to drive other people's horses.'

The driver seemed to me to be right.

'Indeed, how do you know that we are close to a village?' I asked the man.

'Because the wind has brought a smell of smoke from over there,' he answered, 'so a village must be near.'

His quickness and keenness of smell astonished me. I told the driver to go on. The horses stepped with difficulty in the deep snow. The chaise moved slowly, now going into a snowdrift, now dipping into a ravine and swaying from side to side. It was like being on a ship in a stormy sea. Savelyitch groaned as he kept jolting against me. I put down the front curtain, wrapped my fur coat round me and dozed, lulled to sleep by the singing of the storm and the slow swaying motion of the chaise.

I had a dream which I could never since forget and in which I still see a kind of prophecy when I reflect upon the strange vicissitudes of my life. The reader will forgive me, probably knowing from experience how natural it is for man to indulge in superstition, however great his contempt for all vain imaginings may be.

I was in that state of mind and feeling when reality gives way to dreams and merges into them in the shadowy visions of oncoming sleep. It seemed to me the storm was still raging and we were still wandering in the snowy desert. . . . Suddenly I saw a gateway and drove into the court-yard of our estate. My first thought was fear lest my father should be angry with me for my involuntary return and regard it as an intentional disobedience. Anxious, I jumped down from the chaise and saw my mother who came out to meet me on the steps, with an air of profound grief.

'Don't make any noise,' she said. 'Your father is ill; he is dying and wants to say good-bye to you.'

Terror-stricken, I followed her to the bedroom. It was dimly lighted; people with sad-looking faces were standing by the bed. I approached the bed quietly; my mother lifted the bed-curtains and said: 'Andrey Petrovitch! Petrusha has come; he returned when he heard of your illness; bless him'. I knelt down and looked at the sick man. But what did I see? Instead of my father a black-bearded peasant lay on the bed looking at me merrily. I turned to my mother in perplexity, and said to her: 'What does it mean? This is not my father. And why should I ask this peasant's blessing?'—'Never mind, Petrusha,' my mother answered, 'he takes your father's place for the wedding; kiss his hand and he will bless you. . . .' I would not do it. Then the peasant jumped off the bed, seized an axe from behind his back, and began waving it about. I wanted to run away and could not; the room was full of dead bodies; I stumbled against them and slipped in the pools of blood. . . . The terrible peasant called to me kindly, saying: 'Don't be afraid, come and let me bless you'. Terror and confusion possessed me. . . . At that moment I woke up. The horses were standing; Savelyitch held me by the hand, saying:

'Come out, sir; we have arrived.'

'Where?' I asked, rubbing my eyes.

'At the inn. With the Lord's help we stumbled right against the fence. Make haste, come and warm yourself, sir.'

I stepped out of the chaise. The snowstorm was still raging though with less violence. It was pitch-dark. The landlord met us at the gate, holding a lantern under the skirt of his coat, and led us into a room that was small but clean enough; it was lighted by a burning splinter. A rifle and a tall Cossack cap hung on the wall.

The landlord, a Yaïk Cossack, was a man of about sixty, active and well preserved. Savelyitch brought in the box with the tea-things and asked for a fire so that he could make tea, which had never seemed to me so welcome. The landlord went to look after things.

'Where is our guide?' I asked Savelyitch.

'Here, your honour,' answered a voice above me.

I looked up and on the shelf by the stove saw a black beard and two glittering eyes.

'You must have got chilled, brother?'

'I should think I did with nothing but a thin jerkin on! I did have a sheepskin coat, but I confess I pawned it yesterday in a tavern; the frost did not seem to be bad.'

At that moment the landlord came in with a boiling samovar; I offered our guide a cup of tea; he climbed down from the shelf. His appearance, I thought, was striking. He was about forty, of medium height, lean and broad-shouldered. Grey was beginning to show in his black beard; his big, lively eyes were never still. His face had a pleasant but crafty expression. His hair was cropped like a peasant's; he wore a ragged jerkin and Turkish trousers. I handed him a cup of tea; he tasted it and made a grimace.

'Be so kind, your honour . . . tell them to give me a glass of vodka; tea is not a Cossack drink.'

I readily complied with his wish. The landlord took a glass and bottle out of the cupboard, came up to the man, and said, glancing into his face:

'Aha! you are in our parts again! Where do you come from?'

My guide winked significantly and answered in riddles:

'I flew about the kitchen-garden, picking hemp seed; granny threw a flint but missed me. And how are your fellows getting on?'

'Nothing much to be said of them,' the landlord said, also speaking in metaphors. 'They tried to ring the bells for vespers, but the priest's wife said they must not: the priest is on a visit and the devils are busy.'

'Be quiet, uncle,' the tramp answered; 'if it rains, there will be mushrooms, and if there are mushrooms there will be a basket for them; and now' (he winked again) 'put the axe behind your back: the forester is about. Your honour, here's a health to you!'

With these words he took the glass, crossed himself, and drank it at one gulp; then he bowed to me and returned to the shelf by the stove.

I could not at the time understand anything of this thievish conversation, but later on I guessed they were talking of the affairs of the Yaïk Cossacks, who had just settled down after their rebellion in 1772. Savelyitch listened with an air of thorough disapproval. He looked suspiciously both at the landlord and at our guide. The inn stood in the steppe by itself, far from any village, and looked uncommonly like a robbers' den. But there was nothing else for it. There could be no question of continuing the journey. Savelyitch's anxiety amused me greatly. Meanwhile I made ready for the night and lay down on the bench. Savelyitch decided to sleep on the stove; the landlord lay down on the floor. Soon the room was full of snoring and I dropped fast asleep.

Waking up rather late in the morning I saw that the storm had subsided. The sun was shining. The boundless steppe was wrapped in a covering of dazzling snow. The horses were harnessed. I paid the landlord, who charged us so little that even Savelyitch did not dispute about it or try to beat him down as was his wont; he completely forgot his suspicions of the evening before. I called our guide, thanked him for the help he had given us, and told Savelyitch to give him half a rouble for vodka. Savelyitch frowned.

'Half a rouble!' he said. 'What for? Because you were pleased to give him a lift and bring him to the inn? You may say what you like, sir, we have no half-roubles to spare. If we give tips to every one we shall soon have to starve.'

I could not argue with Savelyitch. I had promised that the money was to be wholly in his charge. I was annoyed however, at not being able to thank the man who had saved me from a very unpleasant situation, if not from actual danger.

'Very well,' I said calmly. 'If you don't want to give him half a rouble, give him something out of my clothes. He is dressed much too lightly. Give him my hareskin jacket.'

'Mercy on us, Pyotr Andreyitch!' Savelyitch cried. 'What is the good of your hareskin jacket to him? He will sell it for drink at the next pot-house, the dog.'

'That's no concern of yours, old fellow, whether I sell it for drink or not,' said the tramp. 'His honour gives me a fur coat of his own; it is your master's pleasure to do so, and your business, as a servant, is to obey and not to argue.'

'You have no fear of God, you brigand!' Savelyitch answered in an angry voice. 'You see the child has no sense as yet and you are only too glad to take advantage of his good nature. What do you want with a gentleman's coat? You can't squeeze your hulking great shoulders into it, however you try!'

'Please don't argue,' I said to the old man; 'bring the jacket at once.'

'Good Lord!' my Savelyitch groaned. 'Why, the jacket is almost new! To give it away, and not to a decent man either, but to a shameless drunkard!'

Nevertheless the hareskin jacket appeared. The peasant immediately tried it on. The jacket that I had slightly outgrown was certainly a little tight for him. He succeeded, however, in getting into it, tearing the seams as he did so. Savelyitch almost howled when he heard the threads breaking. The tramp was extremely pleased with my present. He saw me to the chaise and said, with a low bow:

'Thank you, your honour! May God reward you for your goodness; I shall not forget your kindness so long as I live.'

He went his way and I drove on, taking no notice of Savelyitch, and soon forgot the snowstorm of the day before, my guide, and the hareskin jacket.

Arriving in Orenburg I went straight to the General. I saw a tall man, already bent by age. His long hair was perfectly white. An old and faded uniform reminded one of the soldiers of Empress Anna's time; he spoke with a strong German accent. I gave him my father's letter. When I mentioned my name, he threw a quick glance at me.

'*Du lieber Gott !*' he said. 'It does not seem long since Andrey Petrovitch was your age, and now, see, what a big son he has! Oh, how time flies!'

He opened the letter and began reading it in an undertone, interposing his own remarks: '"My dear Sir, Andrey Karlovitch, I hope that your Excellency" . . . Why so formal? Fie, he should be ashamed of himself! Discipline is, of course, a thing of the first importance, but is this the way to write to an old *Kamerad*? . . . "Your Excellency has not forgotten" . . . H'm . . . "and . . . when . . . the late Field-Marshal Münnich . . . the march . . . and also . . . Carolinchen". . . . Ehe, *Bruder*! so he still remembers our old escapades! "Now to business . . . I am sending my young rascal to you" . . . H'm . . . "hold him in hedgehog gloves" . . . What are hedgehog gloves? It must be a Russian saying. . . . What does it mean?' he asked me.

'That means,' I answered, looking as innocent as possible, 'to treat one kindly, not to be too stern, to give one plenty of freedom.'

'H'm, I see . . . "and not to give him too much rope". No, evidently "hedgehog gloves" means something different. . . . "Herewith his passport" . . . Where is it? Ah, here. . . . "Write to the Semyonovsky regiment". . . . Very good, very good; it shall be done. . . . "Allow me, forgetting your rank, to embrace you like an old friend and comrade" . . . Ah, at last he thought of it . . . and so on and so on. . . .'

'Well, my dear,' he said, having finished the letter and put my passport aside, 'it shall all be done as your father wishes; you will be transferred, with the rank of an officer, to the N. regiment, and, not to lose time, you shall go to-morrow to the Belogorsky fortress to serve under Captain Mironov, a good and honourable man. You will see real service there and learn discipline. There is nothing for you to do at Orenburg; dissipation is bad for a young man. And to-night I shall be pleased to have you dine with me.'

'I am going from bad to worse!' I thought. 'What is the good of my having been a sergeant in the Guards almost before I was born! Where has it brought me? To the N. regiment and a desolate fortress on the border of the Kirghis Steppes!'

I had dinner with Andrey Karlovitch and his old aide-de-camp. Strict German economy reigned at his table, and I think the fear of seeing occasionally an additional visitor at his bachelor meal had something to do with my hasty removal to the garrison. The following day I took leave of the General and set off to my destination.

CHAPTER III

THE FORTRESS

In this fortress fine we live;
Bread and water is our fare.
And when ferocious foes
Come to our table bare,
To a real feast we treat them.
Load the cannon and then beat them.

Soldiers' Song.

Old-fashioned people, sir.

Von Vizin.

THE Belogorsky fortress was twenty-five miles from Oren-burg. The road ran along the steep bank of the Yaïk. The river was not yet frozen and its leaden waves looked dark and mournful between the monotonous banks covered with white snow. Beyond it the Kirghis Steppes stretched into the distance. I was absorbed in reflections, for the most part of a melancholy nature. Life in the fortress did not attract me. I tried to picture Captain Mironov, my future chief, and thought of him as a stern, bad-tempered old man who cared for nothing but discipline and was ready to put me under arrest on a diet of bread and water for the least little trifle. Meanwhile it was growing dusk. We were driving rather fast.

'Is it far to the fortress?' I asked the driver.

'No, not far,' he answered; 'it's over there, you can see it.'

I looked from side to side, expecting to see menacing battlements, towers, and a moat, but saw nothing except a village surrounded by a log fence. On one side of it stood three or four haystacks, half-covered with snow, on another a tumbledown windmill with wings of bark that hung idle.

'But where is the fortress?' I asked in surprise.

'Why here,' answered the driver, pointing to the village, and as he spoke we drove into it.

At the gate I saw an old cannon made of cast iron; the streets were narrow and crooked, the cottages small and, for the most part, with thatched roofs. I told the driver to take me to the Commandant's, and in another minute the chaise stopped before a wooden house built upon rising ground close to a church, also made of wood.

No one came out to meet me. I walked into the entry and opened the door into the next room. An old soldier was sitting on the table, sewing a blue patch on the sleeve of a green uniform. I asked him to announce me.

'Come in, my dear,' he said, 'our people are at home.'

I stepped into a clean little room, furnished in the old-fashioned style. In the corner stood a cupboard full of crockery; an officer's diploma in a frame under glass hung on the wall; coloured prints, representing 'The Taking of Otchakoff and Küstrin', 'The Choosing of a Bride', and 'The Cat's Funeral', made bright patches on each side of it. An elderly lady, dressed in a Russian jacket and with a kerchief on her head, was sitting by the window. She was winding yarn which a one-eyed old man in an officer's uniform held for her on his outstretched hands.

'What is your pleasure, sir?' she asked me, going on with her work.

I answered that I had come to serve in the army, and thought it my duty to present myself to the Captain, and with these words I turned to the one-eyed old man whom I took to be the Commandant, but the lady of the house interrupted the speech I had prepared.

'Ivan Kuzmitch is not at home,' she answered; 'he has gone to see Father Gerasim; but it makes no difference, sir; I am his wife. You are very welcome. Please sit down.'

She called the maid and asked her to call the sergeant. The old man kept looking at me inquisitively with his single eye.

'May I be so bold as to ask in what regiment you have been serving?'

I satisfied his curiosity.

'And may I ask,' he continued, 'why you have been transferred from the Guards to the garrison?'

I answered that such was the decision of my superiors.

'I presume it was for behaviour unseemly in an officer of the Guards?' the persistent old man went on.

'That's enough nonsense,' the Captain's lady interrupted him. 'You see the young man is tired after the journey; he doesn't want to listen to you. . . . Hold your hands straight.'

'And don't you worry, my dear, that you have been banished to these wilds,' she went on, addressing herself to me. 'You are not the first nor the last. You will like it better when you are used to it. Shvabrin, Alexey Ivanitch, was transferred to us five years ago for killing a man. Heaven only knows what possessed him, but, would you believe it, he went out of town with a certain lieutenant and they both took swords and started prodding each other—and Alexey Ivanitch did for the lieutenant, and before two witnesses, too! There it is—one never knows what one may do.'

At that moment the sergeant, a young and well-built Cossack, came into the room.

'Maximitch!' the Captain's lady said to him, 'find a lodging for this gentleman and mind it is clean.'

'Yes, Vasilissa Yegorovna,' the Cossack answered. 'Shall I get rooms for his honour at Ivan Polezhaev's?'

'Certainly not, Maximitch,' said the lady. 'Polezhaev is crowded as it is; besides, he is a friend and always remembers that we are his superiors. Take the gentleman . . . what is your name, sir?'

'Pyotr Andreyitch.'

'Take Pyotr Andreyitch to Semyon Kuzov's. He let his horse into my kitchen-garden, the rascal. Well, Maximitch, is everything in order?'

'All is well, thank God,' the Cossack answered; 'only Corporal Prohorov had a fight in the bath-house with Ustinya Negulina about a bucket of hot water.'

'Ivan Ignatyitch!' said the Captain's lady to the one-eyed old man, 'will you see into it and find out whether Ustinya or Prohorov is to blame. And punish them both! Well, Maximitch, you can go now. Pyotr Andreyitch, Maximitch will take you to your lodging.'

I took leave of her. The Cossack brought me to a cottage that stood on the high bank of the river at the very edge of the village. Half of the cottage was occupied by Semyon Kuzov's family, the other was allotted to me. It consisted of one fairly clean room partitioned into two. Savelyitch began unpacking; I looked out of the narrow window. The melancholy steppe stretched before me. On one side I could see a few cottages; several hens strutted about the street. An old woman stood on the steps with a trough, calling to pigs that answered her with friendly grunting. And this was the place where I was doomed to spend my youth! I suddenly felt wretched; I left the window and went to bed without any supper in spite of Savelyitch's entreaties. He kept repeating in distress:

'Merciful heavens; he won't eat! What will my mistress say if the child is taken ill?'

Next morning I had just begun to dress when the door opened and a young officer, short, swarthy, with a plain but extremely lively face, walked in.

'Excuse me,' he said to me in French, 'for coming without ceremony to make your acquaintance. Yesterday I heard of your arrival: I could not resist the desire to see at last a human face. You will understand this when you have lived here for a time.'

I guessed that this was the officer who had been dismissed from the Guards on account of a duel. We made friends at once. Shvabrin was very intelligent. His conversation was witty and entertaining. He described to me in a most amusing way the Commandant's family, their friends, and the place to which fate had brought him. I was screaming with laughter when the old soldier, whom I had seen mending a uniform at the Commandant's, came in and gave me Vasilissa Yegorovna's invitation to dine with them. Shvabrin said he would go with me.

As we approached the Commandant's house we saw in the square some twenty old garrison soldiers in three-cornered hats and with long plaits of hair at the back. They were standing at attention. The Commandant, a tall, vigorous old man, wearing a night-cap and a cotton dressing-gown, stood facing them. When he saw us, he came up, said a few kind words to me, and went on drilling his men. We stopped to look on, but he asked us to go to his house, promising to come soon after.

'There's nothing here worth looking at,' he added. Vasilissa Yegorovna gave us a kind and homely welcome, treating me as though she had known me all my life. The old pensioner and the maid Palasha were laying the table.

'My Ivan Kuzmitch is late with his drilling to-day,' she said. 'Palasha, call your master to dinner. And where is Masha?'

At that moment a girl of eighteen, with a rosy round face, came in; her fair hair was smoothly combed behind her ears which at that moment were burning with shyness. I did not particularly like her at the first glance. I was prejudiced against her: Shvabrin had described Masha, the Captain's daughter, as quite stupid. Marya Ivanovna sat down in a corner and began sewing. Meanwhile cabbage soup was served. Not seeing her husband, Vasilissa Yegorovna sent Palasha a second time to call him.

'Tell your master that our guests are waiting and the soup will get cold; there is always time for drilling, thank heaven; he can shout to his heart's content later on.'

The Captain soon appeared, accompanied by the one-eyed old man.

'What has come over you, my dear?' his wife said to him. 'Dinner has been served ages ago, and you wouldn't come.'

'But I was busy drilling soldiers, Vasilissa Yegorovna, let me tell you.'

'Come, come,' his wife retorted, 'all this drilling is mere pretence—your soldiers don't learn anything and you are no good at it either. You had much better sit at home and say your prayers. Dear guests, come to the table.'

We sat down to dinner. Vasilissa Yegorovna was never silent for a minute and bombarded me with questions: who were my parents, were they living, where did they live, how big was their estate. When she heard that my father had three hundred serfs she said: 'Just fancy! to think of there being rich people in the world! And we, my dear, have only one maid, Palasha, but we are comfortable enough, thank heaven. The only trouble is Masha ought to be getting married, and all she has by way of dowry is a comb and a broom and a brass farthing. If the right man turns up, all well and good, but, if not, she will die an old maid.'

I glanced at Marya Ivanovna; she flushed crimson and tears dropped into her plate. I felt sorry for her and hastened to change the conversation.

'I have heard,' I said, rather inappropriately, 'that the Bashkirs propose to attack your fortress.'

'From whom have you heard it, my good sir?' Ivan Kuzmitch asked.

'I was told it at Orenburg,' I answered.

'Don't you believe it!' said the Commandant, 'we have not heard anything of it for years. The Bashkirs have been scared and the Kirghis, too, have had their lesson. No fear, they won't attack us; and if they do I will give them such a fright that they will keep quiet for another ten years.'

'And you are not afraid,' I continued, turning to Vasilissa Yegorovna, 'to remain in a fortress subject to such dangers?'

'It's habit, my dear,' she answered. 'Twenty years ago when we were transferred here from the regiment I cannot tell you how I dreaded those accursed infidels! As soon as I saw their lynx caps and heard their squealing, my heart stood still, would you believe it! And now I have grown so used to it that I don't stir when they tell us the villains are prowling round the fortress.'

'Vasilissa Yegorovna is a most courageous lady,' Shvabrin remarked, pompously. 'Ivan Kuzmitch can bear witness to it.'

'Yes; she is not of the timid sort, let me tell you!' Ivan Kuzmitch assented.

'And Marya Ivanovna? Is she as brave as you are?' I asked.

'Is Masha brave?' her mother answered. 'No, Masha is a coward. She can't bear even now to hear a rifle-shot; it makes her all of a tremble. And when, two years ago, Ivan Kuzmitch took it into his head to fire our cannon on my name-day, she nearly died of fright, poor dear. Since then we haven't fired the cursed cannon any more.'

We got up from the table. The Captain and his wife went to lie down, and I went to Shvabrin's and spent the rest of the day with him.

CHAPTER IV

THE DUEL

Oh, very well, take up then your position
And you shall see me pierce your body through.
Kniazhnin.

SEVERAL weeks had passed and my life in the Belogorsky fortress had grown not merely endurable but positively pleasant. I was received in the Commandant's house as one of the family. The husband and wife were most worthy people. Ivan Kuzmitch, who had risen from the ranks to be an officer, was a plain and uneducated man, but most kind and honourable. His wife ruled him, which suited his easy-going disposition. Vasilissa Yegorovna looked upon her husband's military duties as her own concern and managed the fortress as she did her own home. Marya Ivanovna soon lost her shyness with me and we made friends. I found her to be a girl of feeling and good sense. Imperceptibly I grew attached to the kind family, and even to Ivan Ignatyitch, the one-eyed lieutenant of the garrison; Shvabrin had said of him that he was on improper terms with Vasilissa Yegorovna, though there was not a semblance of truth in it; but Shvabrin did not care about that.

I received my commission. My military duties were not strenuous. In our blessed fortress there were no parades, no drills, no sentry duty. Occasionally the Commandant, of his own accord, taught the soldiers, but had not yet succeeded in teaching all of them to know their left hand from their right. Shavbrin had several French books. I began reading and developed a taste for literature. In the mornings I read, practised translating, and sometimes composed verses; I almost always dined at the Commandant's and spent there the rest of the day; in the evenings, Father Gerasim and his wife, Akulina Pamfilovna, the biggest gossip in the neighbourhood, sometimes came there also. Of course I saw Alexey Ivanitch Shvabrin every day, but his

conversation grew more and more distasteful to me as time
went on. I disliked his constant jokes about the Commandant's family and, in particular, his derisive remarks
about Marya Ivanovna. There was no other society in
the fortress; and, indeed, I wished for no other.

In spite of the prophecies, the Bashkirs did not rise. Peace
reigned around our fortress. But the peace was suddenly
disturbed by an internal war.

I have already said that I tried my hand at literature.
Judged by the standards of that period my attempts were
quite creditable, and several years later Alexander Petrovitch
Sumarokov [1] thoroughly approved of them. One day I
succeeded in writing a song that pleased me. Everybody
knows that sometimes under the pretext of seeking advice
writers try to find an appreciative listener. And so, having
copied out my song, I took it to Shvabrin, who was the
only person in the fortress capable of doing justice to the
poet's work. After a few preliminary remarks I took my
note-book out of my pocket and read the following verses
to him:

> 'Thoughts of love I try to banish
> And her beauty to forget,
> And, ah me! avoiding Masha
> Hope I shall my freedom get.
>
> But the eyes that have seduced me
> Are before me night and day,
> To confusion they 've reduced me,
> Driven rest and peace away.
>
> When you hear of my misfortunes
> Pity, Masha, pity me!
> You can see my cruel torments:
> I am captive held by thee.'

'What do you think of it?' I asked Shvabrin, expecting
praise as my rightful due. But to my extreme annoyance
Shvabrin, who was usually a kind critic, declared that my
song was bad.

'Why so?' I asked, concealing my vexation.

'Because such lines are worthy of my teacher, Vassily

[1] Sumarokov (1718-77), an early Russian poet of the pseudo-classical
school.—TRANSLATOR'S NOTE.

Kirillitch Tretyakovsky,[1] and greatly remind me of his love-verses.'

He then took my note-book from me and began mercilessly criticizing every line and every word of the poem, mocking me in a most derisive manner. I could not endure it, snatched the note-book from him, and said I would never show him my verses again. Shvabrin laughed at this threat too.

'We shall see,' he said, 'whether you will keep your word. Poets need a listener as much as Ivan Kuzmitch needs his decanter of vodka before dinner. And who is this Masha to whom you declare your tender passion and love-sickness? Is it Marya Ivanovna by any chance?'

'It's none of your business whoever she may be,' I answered frowning. 'I want neither your opinion nor your conjectures.'

'Oho! A touchy poet and a modest lover!' Shvabrin went on, irritating me more and more. 'But take a friend's advice: if you want to succeed, you must have recourse to something better than songs.'

'What do you mean, sir? Please explain yourself.'

'Willingly. I mean that if you want Masha Mironov to visit you at dusk, present her with a pair of ear-rings instead of tender verses.'

My blood boiled.

'And why have you such an opinion of her?' I asked, hardly able to restrain my indignation.

'Because I know her manners and morals from experience,' he answered, with a fiendish smile.

'It's a lie, you scoundrel,' I cried furiously. 'It's a shameless lie!'

Shvabrin changed colour.

'You'll have to pay for this,' he said, gripping my hand; 'you will give me satisfaction.'

'Certainly—whenever you like,' I answered, with relief. I was ready to tear him to pieces at that moment.

I went at once to Ivan Ignatyitch, whom I found with a needle in his hands threading mushrooms to dry for the winter, at Vasilissa Yegorovna's request.

[1] One of the early Russian writers of poetry, remarkable for his unwearying zeal and utter lack of talent.—TRANSLATOR'S NOTE.

'Ah, Pyotr Andreyitch! Pleased to see you!' he said, when he saw me. 'What good fortune brings you? What business, may I ask?'

I explained to him briefly that I had quarrelled with Alexey Ivanitch and was asking him, Ivan Ignatyitch, to be my second. Ivan Ignatyitch listened to me attentively, staring at me with his solitary eye.

'You are pleased to say,' he answered, 'that you intend to kill Alexey Ivanitch and wish me to witness it? Is that so, may I ask?'

'Quite so.'

'Good heavens, Pyotr Andreyitch! What are you thinking about? You have quarrelled with Alexey Ivanitch? What ever does it matter? Bad words are of no consequence. He abuses you—you swear back at him; he hits you in the face—you hit him on the ear, twice, three times—and then go your own way; and we shall see to it that you make it up later on. But killing a fellow-creature—is that a right thing to do, let me ask you? And, anyway, if you killed him it wouldn't matter so much; I am not very fond of Alexey Ivanitch myself, for the matter of that. But what if he makes a hole in you? What will that be like? Who will be made a fool of then, may I ask?'

The sensible old man's arguments did not shake me. I stuck to my intention.

'As you like,' said Ivan Ignatyitch. 'Do what you think best. But why should I be your witness? What for? Two men fighting each other! What is there worth seeing in it, may I ask? I 've been in the Swedish War and the Turkish, and, believe me, I 've seen fighting enough.'

I tried to explain to him the duties of a second, but Ivan Ignatyitch simply could not understand me.

'You may say what you like,' he said, 'but if I am to take part in this affair it is only to go to Ivan Kuzmitch and tell him, as duty bids me, that a crime contrary to the interests of the State is being planned in the fortress—and to ask if the Commandant would be pleased to take proper measures.'

I was alarmed and begged Ivan Ignatyitch to say nothing to the Commandant. I had difficulty in persuading him, but at last he gave me his word and I left him.

I spent the evening, as usual, at the Commandant's. I

tried to appear cheerful and indifferent so as to escape inquisitive questions, and not give grounds for suspicion, but I confess I could not boast of the indifference which people in my position generally profess to feel. That evening I was inclined to be tender and emotional. Marya Ivanovna attracted me more than ever. The thought that I might be seeing her for the last time made her seem particularly touching to me. Shvabrin was there also. I took him aside and told him of my conversation with Ivan Ignatyitch.

'What do we want with seconds?' he said to me, dryly; 'we will do without them.'

We arranged to fight behind the corn-stacks near the fortress and to meet there the following morning between six and seven. We appeared to be talking so amicably that Ivan Ignatyitch, delighted, let out the secret.

'That's right!' he said to me, looking pleased; 'a bad peace is better than a good quarrel; a damaged name is better than a damaged skin.'

'What's this, what's this, Ivan Ignatyitch?' asked Vasilissa Yegorovna, who was telling fortunes by cards in the corner and had not listened.

Ivan Ignatyitch, seeing my look of annoyance and recalling his promise, was confused and did not know what to say. Shvabrin hastened to his assistance.

'Ivan Ignatyitch approves of our making peace,' he said.

'But with whom had you quarrelled, my dear?'

'I had rather a serious quarrel with Pyotr Andreyitch.'

'What about?'

'About the merest trifle, Vasilissa Yegorovna: a song.'

'That's a queer thing to quarrel about! A song! But how did it happen?'

'Why, this is how it was. Not long ago Pyotr Andreyitch composed a song and to-day he began singing it in my presence, and I struck up my favourite:

"Captain's daughter, I warn you,
    Don't you go for midnight walks."

'There was discord. Pyotr Andreyitch was angry at first, but then he thought better of it, and decided that every one may sing what he likes. And that was the end of it.'

Shvabrin's impudence very nearly incensed me, but no one except me understood his coarse hints, or, at any rate, no one took any notice of them. From songs the conversation turned to poets; the Commandant remarked that they were a bad lot and bitter drunkards, and advised me, as a friend, to give up writing verses, for such an occupation did not accord with military duties and brought one to no good.

Shvabrin's presence was unendurable to me. I soon said good-bye to the Captain and his family; when I came home I examined my sword, felt the point of it, and went to bed, telling Savelyitch to wake me at six o'clock.

The following morning I stood behind the corn-stacks at the appointed hour waiting for my opponent. He arrived soon after me.

'We may be disturbed,' he said. 'We had better be quick.'

We took off our uniforms and, dressed in our jackets only, bared our swords. At that moment Ivan Ignatyitch with five soldiers of the garrison suddenly appeared from behind the stacks. He requested us to go to the Commandant's. We obeyed, vexed as we were; the soldiers surrounded us and we followed Ivan Ignatyitch, who led us in triumph, stepping along with an extraordinary air of importance.

We entered the Commandant's house. Ivan Ignatyitch opened the doors and solemnly proclaimed: 'I have brought them!'

We were met by Vasilissa Yegorovna.

'Goodness me! What ever next? What? How could you? Planning murder in our fortress! Ivan Kuzmitch, put them under arrest at once! Pyotr Andreyitch, Alexey Ivanitch! Give me your swords, give them up, give them up! Palasha, take these swords to the pantry! I did not expect this of you, Pyotr Andreyitch; aren't you ashamed of yourself? It is all very well for Alexey Ivanitch—he has been dismissed from the Guards for killing a man, and he does not believe in God, but fancy you doing a thing like this! Do you want to be like him?'

Ivan Kuzmitch fully agreed with his wife, and kept repeating:

'Vasilissa Yegorovna is quite right; let me tell you duels are explicitly forbidden in the army.'

Meanwhile Palasha took our swords and carried them

to the pantry.   I could not help laughing, Shvabrin retained his composure

'With all my respect for you,' he said coolly, 'I must observe that you give yourself unnecessary trouble in passing judgment upon us.   Leave it to Ivan Kuzmitch—it is his business

'But, my dear sir, aren't husband and wife one flesh and one spirit?' the Commandant's lady retorted. 'Ivan Kuzmitch, what are you thinking of?   Put them under arrest at once in different corners and give them nothing but bread and water till they come to their senses!   And let Father Gerasim set them a penance that they may beg God to forgive them and confess their sin to the people.'

Ivan Kuzmitch did not know what to do.   Marya Ivanovna was extremely pale.   Little by little the storm subsided; Vasilissa Yegorovna calmed down and made us kiss each other.   Palasha brought us back our swords.   We left the Commandant's house apparently reconciled.   Ivan Ignatyitch accompanied us.

'Aren't you ashamed,' I said to him angrily, 'to have betrayed us to the Commandant when you promised me not to?'

'God is my witness, I never said anything to Ivan Kuzmitch,' he answered; 'Vasilissa Yegorovna wormed it all out of me.   And she made all the arrangements without saying a word to Ivan Kuzmitch. . . . But thank Heaven that it has all ended in this way.'

With these words he turned home and Shvabrin and I were left alone.

'We cannot let it end at that,' I said to him.

'Of course not,' Shvabrin answered; 'you will answer me with your blood for your insolence, but I expect we shall be watched.   We shall have to pretend to be friends for a few days.   Good-bye.'

And we parted as though nothing had happened.   Returning to the Commandant's I sat down, as usual, by Marya Ivanovna.   Ivan Kuzmitch was not at home; Vasilissa Yegorovna was busy with household matters.   Marya Ivanovna tenderly reproached me for the anxiety I had caused every one by my quarrel with Shvabrin.

'I was quite overcome,' she said, 'when I heard you were

going to fight. How strange men are! Because of a single word which they would be sure to forget in a week's time they are ready to kill each other and to sacrifice their lives and their conscience and the welfare of those who . . . But I am sure you did not begin the quarrel. Alexey Ivanitch is probably to blame.'

'And why do you think so, Marya Ivanovna?'

'Oh, I don't know . . . he always jeers at people. I don't like Alexey Ivanitch. He repels me and yet, strange to say, I would not, on any account, have him dislike me also. That would worry me dreadfully.'

'And what do you think, Marya Ivanovna? Does he like you?'

Marya Ivanovna stammered and blushed.

'I think . . .' she said, 'I believe he does like me.'

'And why do you believe it?'

'Because he made me an offer of marriage.'

'He made you an offer of marriage? When?'

'Last year. Some two months before you came.'

'And you refused?'

'As you see. Of course, Alexey Ivanitch is clever and rich, and of good family; but when I think that in church I should have to kiss him before all the people . . . not for anything! Nothing would induce me!'

Marya Ivanovna's words opened my eyes and explained a great deal to me. I understood the persistent slander with which he pursued her. The words that gave rise to our quarrel seemed to me all the more vile when, instead of coarse and unseemly mockery, I saw in them deliberate calumny. My desire to punish the impudent slanderer grew more intense, and I waited impatiently for an opportunity.

I did not have to wait long. The following day as I sat composing an elegy, biting my pen as I searched for a rhyme, Shvabrin knocked at my window. I left my pen, picked up my sword, and went out to him.

'Why wait?' Shvabrin said, 'we are not watched. Let us go down to the river. No one will disturb us there.'

We walked in silence. Descending by a steep path we stopped at the river-bank and bared our swords. Shvabrin was more skilled than I, but I was stronger and more daring; Monsieur Beaupré, who had once been a soldier, had given me a few lessons in fencing and I made use of them. Shvabrin had not expected to find in me so formidable an opponent. For a time we could neither of us do the other any harm; at last, observing that Shvabrin was weakening, I began to press him and almost drove him into the river. Suddenly I heard someone loudly calling my name. I turned round and saw Savelyitch running towards me down the steep path . . . at that moment I felt a stab in my breast under the right shoulder, and fell down senseless.

CHAPTER V

LOVE

Ah, you young maiden, you maiden fair!
You must not marry while still so young
You must ask your father and mother first,
Your father and mother and all your kin.
You must grow in wisdom and keen good sense,
Must save up for yourself a rich dowry.

A Folk Song.

If you find one better than me—you'll forget me,
If one who is worse—you'll remember.

A Folk Song.

WHEN I regained consciousness I could not grasp for a few minutes where I was, and what had happened to me. I was lying on a bed in a strange room, feeling very weak. Savelyitch was standing before me with a candle in his hand. Someone was carefully unwrapping the bandages round my chest and shoulder. Gradually my thoughts cleared. I remembered my duel, and understood that I had been wounded. At that moment the door creaked.

'How is he?' whispered a voice which sent a tremor through me.

'Still the same,' Savelyitch answered, with a sigh. 'Still unconscious. It's the fifth day.'

I tried to turn my head, but could not.

'Where am I? Who is here?' I said, with an effort.

Marya Ivanovna came up to my bed and bent over me.

'Well, how do you feel?' she asked.

'God be thanked,' I answered in a weak voice. 'Is it you, Marya Ivanovna? Tell me . . .'

I had not the strength to go on, and broke off. Savelyitch cried out. His face lit up with joy.

'He has come to his senses! Thank God! Well, my dear Pyotr Andreyitch, you have given me a fright! Five days, it 's no joke!'

Marya Ivanovna interrupted him.

'Don't talk to him too much, Savelyitch,' she said, 'he is still weak.' She went out and quietly closed the door.

My thoughts were in a turmoil. And so I was in the Commandant's house: Marya Ivanovna had come in to me. I wanted to ask Savelyitch several questions, but the old man shook his head and stopped his ears. I closed my eyes in vexation and soon dropped asleep.

When I woke up I called Savelyitch, but instead of him I saw Marya Ivanovna before me; her angelic voice greeted me. I cannot express the blissful feeling that possessed me at that moment. I seized her hand and covered it with kisses, wetting it with tears of tenderness. Masha did not withdraw her hand . . . and suddenly her lips touched my cheek and I felt their fresh and ardent kiss. A flame ran through me.

'Dear, kind Marya Ivanovna,' I said to her, 'be my wife, consent to make me happy.'

She regained her self-possession.

'Calm yourself, for heaven's sake,' she said, taking her hand from me, 'you are not out of danger yet—the wound may open. Take care of yourself, if only for my sake.'

With these words she went out, leaving me in an ecstasy of delight. Happiness revived me. She would be mine! She loved me! My whole being was filled with this thought.

From that time onward I grew better every hour. I was treated by the regimental barber, for there was no other doctor in the fortress, and fortunately he did not attempt to be clever. Youth and nature hastened my recovery. The whole of the Commandant's family looked after me. Marya Ivanovna never left my side. Of course, at the first opportunity, I returned to our interrupted explanation, and Marya

Ivanovna heard me out with more patience. Without any affectation she confessed her love for me and said that her parents would certainly be glad of her happiness.

'But think well,' she added, 'won't your parents raise objections?'

I pondered. I had no doubts of my mother's kindness; but knowing my father's views and disposition I felt that my love would not particularly touch him and that he would look upon it as a young man's whim. I candidly admitted this to Marya Ivanovna, but decided to write to my father as eloquently as possible, asking him to give us his blessing. I showed my letter to Marya Ivanovna, who found it so touching and convincing that she never doubted of its success and abandoned herself to the feelings of her tender heart with all the trustfulness of youth and love.

I made peace with Shvabrin in the first days of my convalescence. In reprimanding me for the duel Ivan Kuzmitch had said to me:

'Ah, Pyotr Andreyitch, I ought really to put you under arrest, but you have been punished enough already. Alexey Ivanitch, though, is shut up in the storehouse and Vasilissa Yegorovna has his sword under lock and key. It is just as well he should think things over and repent.'

I was much too happy to retain any hostile feeling in my heart. I interceded for Shvabrin, and the kind Commandant, with his wife's consent, decided to release him. Shvabrin called on me; he expressed a profound regret for what had passed between us; he admitted that he had been entirely to blame and asked me to forget the past. It was not in my nature to harbour malice and I sincerely forgave him both our quarrel and the wound he had inflicted on me. I ascribed his slander to the vexation of wounded vanity and rejected love, and generously excused my unhappy rival.

I was soon quite well again and able to move into my lodgings. I awaited with impatience the answer to my last letter, not daring to hope, and trying to stifle melancholy forebodings. I had not yet declared my intentions to Vasilissa Yegorovna and her husband; but my offer was not likely to surprise them. Neither Marya Ivanovna nor I attempted to conceal our feelings from them, and we were certain of their consent beforehand.

At last, one morning Savelyitch came in to me holding a letter. I seized it with a tremor. The address was written in my father's hand. This prepared me for something important, for as a rule it was my mother who wrote to me and my father only added a few lines at the end of the letter. Several minutes passed before I unsealed the envelope, reading over again and again the solemnly worded address: 'To my son Pyotr Andreyevitch Grinyov, at the Belogorsky fortress in the Province of Orenburg'. I tried to guess from the handwriting in what mood my father wrote the letter; at last I brought myself to open it and saw from the very first lines that all was lost. The letter was as follows:

My Son Pyotr!

On the 15th of this month we received the letter in which you ask for our parental blessing and consent to your marriage with Marya Ivanovna, Mironov's daughter; I do not intend to give you either my blessing or my consent, and, indeed, I mean to get at you and give you a thorough lesson as to a naughty boy for your pranks, not regarding your officer's rank, for you have proved that you are not yet worthy to wear the sword which has been given you to defend your fatherland, and not to fight duels with scapegraces like yourself. I will write at once to Andrey Karlovitch asking him to transfer you from the Belogorsky fortress to some remote place where you can get over your foolishness. When your mother heard of your duel and of your being wounded, she was taken ill with grief and is now in bed. What will become of you? I pray to God that you may be reformed although I dare not hope in His great mercy.

Your father,

A. G.

The perusal of this letter stirred various feelings in me. The cruel expressions, which my father did not stint, wounded me deeply. The contemptuous way in which he referred to Marya Ivanovna appeared to me as unseemly as it was unjust. The thought of my being transferred from the Belogorsky fortress terrified me; but most of all I was grieved by the news of my mother's illness. I felt indignant with Savelyitch, never doubting it was he who had informed my parents of the duel. As I paced up and down my tiny room I stopped before him and said, looking at him angrily:

'So it's not enough for you that I have been wounded

because of you, and lain for a whole month at death's door—
you want to kill my mother as well.'

Savelyitch was thunderstruck.

'Good heavens, sir, what are you saying?' he said, almost
sobbing. 'You have been wounded because of me! God
knows I was running to shield you with my own breast
from Alexey Ivanitch's sword! It was old age, curse it,
that hindered me. But what have I done to your mother?'

'What have you done?' I repeated. 'Who asked you to
betray me? Are you here to spy on me?'

'I betrayed you?' Savelyitch answered with tears. 'O
Lord, King of Heaven! Very well, read then what master
writes to me: you will see how I betrayed you.'

He pulled a letter out of his pocket and read the following:

'You should be ashamed, you old dog, not to have written to
me about my son, Pyotr Andreyevitch, in spite of my strict
orders; strangers have to inform me of his misdoings. So this
is how you carry out your duties and your master's will? I will
send you to look after pigs, you old dog, for concealing the
truth, and conniving with the young man. As soon as you
receive this I command you to write to me at once about his
health, which, I am told, is better, in what place exactly he was
wounded, and whether his wound has healed properly.'

It was obvious that Savelyitch was innocent and I had
insulted him for nothing by my reproaches and suspicion.
I begged his pardon; but the old man was inconsolable.

'This is what I have come to,' he kept repeating; 'this is
the favour my masters show me for my services! I am an
old dog and a swineherd, and I am the cause of your wound!
. . . No, my dear Pyotr Andreyitch, not I, but the damned
Frenchman is at the bottom of it: he taught you to prod
people with iron spits, and to stamp with your feet, as though
prodding and stamping could save one from an evil man!
Much need there was to hire the Frenchman and spend money
for nothing!'

But who, then, had taken the trouble to inform my father
of my conduct? The General? But he did not seem to
show much interest in me, and Ivan Kuzmitch did not think
it necessary to report my duel to him. I was lost in conjectures. My suspicions fixed upon Shvabrin. He alone
could benefit by informing against me and thus causing me,

perhaps, to be removed from the fortress and parted from the Commandant's family. I went to tell it all to Marya Ivanovna. She met me on the steps.

'What is the matter with you?' she said when she saw me. 'How pale you are!'

'All is lost,' I answered, and gave her my father's letter.

She turned pale, too. After reading the letter she returned it to me with a hand that shook, and said in a trembling voice:

'It seems it is not to be. . . . Your parents do not want me in your family. God's will be done! God knows better than we do what is good for us. There is nothing for it. Pyotr Andreyitch, may you at least be happy. . . .'

'This shall not be,' I cried, seizing her hand; 'you love me; I am ready to face any risk. Let us go and throw ourselves at your parents' feet; they are simple-hearted people, not hard and proud . . . they will bless us; we will be married . . . and then in time I am sure we will soften my father's heart; my mother will intercede for us; he will forgive me.'

'No, Pyotr Andreyitch,' Masha answered, 'I will not marry you without your parents' blessing. Without their blessing there can be no happiness for you. Let us submit to God's will. If you find a wife, if you come to love another woman —God be with you, Pyotr Andreyitch; I shall pray for you both. . . .'

She burst into tears and left me; I was about to follow her indoors, but feeling that I could not control myself, returned home.

I was sitting plunged in deep thought when Savelyitch broke in upon my reflections.

'Here, sir,' he said, giving me a piece of paper covered with writing, 'see if I am an informer against my master and if I try to make mischief between father and son.'

I took the paper from his hands: it was Savelyitch's answer to my father's letter. Here it is, word for word:

DEAR SIR, ANDREY PETROVITCH, OUR GRACIOUS FATHER!
I have received your gracious letter, in which you are pleased to be angry with me, your servant, saying that I ought to be ashamed not to obey my master's orders; I am not an old dog but your faithful servant; I obey your orders and have always served you zealously and have lived to be an old man. I have not written anything to you about Pyotr Andreyitch's wound,

so as not to alarm you needlessly, for I hear that, as it is, the mistress, our mother Avdotya Vassilyevna, has been taken ill with fright, and I shall pray for her health. Pyotr Andreyitch was wounded in the chest under the right shoulder, just under the bone, three inches deep, and he lay in the Commandant's house where we carried him from the river-bank, and the local barber, Stepan Paramonov, treated him, and now, thank God, Pyotr Andreyitch is well and there is nothing but good to be said of him. His commanders, I hear, are pleased with him and Vasilissa Yegorovna treats him as though he were her own son. And as to his having got into trouble, that is no disgrace to him: a horse has four legs, and yet it stumbles. And you are pleased to write that you will send me to herd pigs. That is for you to decide as my master. I humbly salute you.

Your faithful serf,

ARHIP SAVELYEV.

I could not help smiling more than once as I read the good old man's epistle. I felt I could not answer my father, and Savelyitch's letter seemed to me sufficient to relieve my mother's anxiety.

From that time my position changed. Marya Ivanovna hardly spoke to me and did her utmost to avoid me. The Commandant's house lost all its attraction for me. I gradually accustomed myself to sit at home by myself. Vasilissa Yegorovna chid me for it at first, but seeing my obstinacy left me in peace. I only saw Ivan Kuzmitch when my duties required it; I seldom met Shvabrin and did so reluctantly, especially as I noticed his secret dislike of me, which confirmed my suspicions. Life became unbearable to me. I sank into despondent brooding, nurtured by idleness and isolation. My love grew more ardent in solitude and oppressed me more and more. I lost the taste for reading and composition. My spirits drooped. I was afraid that I should go out of my mind or take to drink. Unexpected events that had an important influence upon my life as a whole suddenly gave my mind a powerful and beneficial shock.

CHAPTER VI

PUGATCHOV'S REBELLION

Listen now, young men, listen,
To what we old men shall tell you.
A Folk Song.

BEFORE I begin describing the strange events which I witnessed, I must say a few words about the position in the Province of Orenburg at the end of 1773.

This vast and wealthy province was inhabited by a number of half-savage peoples who had but recently acknowledged the sovereignty of the Russian Tsars. Unused to the laws and habits of civilized life, cruel and reckless, they were constantly rising, and the Government had to keep unremitting watch over them. Fortresses had been built in suitable places and settled for the most part with Yaïk Cossacks, who had owned the shores of Yaïk for generations. But the Cossacks who were to guard the peace and safety of the place had themselves for some time past been a source of trouble and danger to the Government. In 1772 a rising took place in their chief town. It was caused by the stern measures adopted by Major-General Traubenberg in order to bring the Cossacks to due submission. The result was the barbarous assassination of Traubenberg, a mutinous change in the administration of the Cossack army, and, finally, the quelling of the mutiny by means of cannon and cruel punishments.

This had happened some time before I came to the Belogorsky fortress. All was quiet or seemed so; the authorities too easily believed the feigned repentance of the perfidious rebels, who concealed their malice and waited for an opportunity to make fresh trouble.

To return to my story.

One evening (it was at the beginning of October 1773) I sat at home alone, listening to the howling of the autumn wind, and watching through the window the clouds that raced past the moon. Someone came to call me to the Commandant's. I went at once. I found there Shvabrin,

Ivan Ignatyitch, and the Cossack sergeant, Maximitch. Neither Vasilissa Yegorovna nor Marya Ivanovna was in the room. The Commandant looked troubled as he greeted me. He closed the doors, made us all sit down except the sergeant, who was standing by the door, pulled a letter out of his pocket and said: 'Important news, gentlemen! Listen to what the General writes.' He put on his spectacles and read the following:

TO THE COMMANDANT OF THE BELOGORSKY FORTRESS,
CAPTAIN MIRONOV

Private.

I inform you herewith that a runaway Don Cossack, an Old Believer, Emelyan Pugatchov, has perpetrated the unpardonable outrage of assuming the name of the deceased Emperor Peter III and, assembling a criminal band, has caused a rising in the Yaïk settlements, and has already taken and sacked several fortresses, committing murders and robberies everywhere. In view of the above, you have, sir, on receipt of this, immediately to take the necessary measures for repulsing the afore-mentioned villain and pretender, and, if possible, for completely destroying him, should he attack the fortress entrusted to your care.

'Take the necessary measures,' said the Commandant, removing his spectacles and folding the paper. 'That's easy enough to say, let me tell you. The villain is evidently strong; and we have only a hundred and thirty men, not counting the Cossacks on whom there is no relying—no offence meant, Maximitch.' (The sergeant smiled.) 'However, there is nothing for it! Carry out your duties scrupulously, arrange for sentry duty and night patrols; in case of attack shut the gates and lead the soldiers afield. And you, Maximitch, keep a strict watch over your Cossacks. The cannon must be seen to and cleaned properly. And, above all, keep the whole thing secret so that no one in the fortress should know as yet.'

Having given us these orders, Ivan Kuzmitch dismissed us. Shvabrin and I walked out together, talking of what we had just heard.

'What will be the end of it, do you think?' I asked him.

'Heaven only knows,' he answered. 'We shall see. So far, I don't think there is much in it. But if . . .'

He sank into thought, and began absent-mindedly whistling a French tune.

In spite of all our precautions the news of Pugatchov soon spread throughout the fortress. Although Ivan Kuzmitch greatly respected his wife, he would not for anything in the world have disclosed to her a military secret entrusted to him. Having received the General's letter, he rather skilfully got rid of Vasilissa Yegorovna by telling her that Father Gerasim had had some startling news from Orenburg, which he was guarding jealously. Vasilissa Yegorovna at once decided to go and call on the priest's wife and, on Ivan Kuzmitch's advice, took Masha with her lest the girl should feel lonely at home.

Finding himself master of the house, Ivan Kuzmitch at once sent for us and locked Palasha in the pantry, so that she should not overhear us.

Vasilissa Yegorovna had not succeeded in gaining any information from the priest's wife and, coming home, she learned that, in her absence, Ivan Kuzmitch had held a council, and that Palasha had been locked up. She guessed that her husband had deceived her and began questioning him. Ivan Kuzmitch, however, had been prepared for attack. He was not in the least abashed and boldly answered his inquisitive consort:

'Our women, my dear, have taken to heating the stoves with straw, let me tell you; and since this may cause a fire I have given strict orders that in the future they should not use straw but wood.'

'Then why did you lock up Palasha?' the Commandant's wife asked. 'What had the poor girl done to have to sit in the pantry till our return?'

Ivan Kuzmitch was not prepared for this question; he was confused and muttered something very incoherent. Vasilissa Yegorovna saw her husband's perfidy, but knowing that she would not succeed in learning anything from him, ceased her questions, and began talking of salted cucumbers, which the priest's wife prepared in some very special way. Vasilissa Yegorovna could not sleep all night, trying to guess what could be in her husband's mind that she was not supposed to know.

The next day returning from Mass she saw Ivan Ignatyitch pulling out of the cannon bits of rag, stones, splinters, dice, and all kinds of rubbish that the children had thrust into it.

'What can these military preparations mean?' the Commandant's wife wondered. 'Are they expecting another Kirghis raid? But surely Ivan Kuzmitch would not conceal such trifles from me!' She hailed Ivan Ignatyitch with the firm intention of discovering from him the secret that tormented her feminine curiosity.

Vasilissa Yegorovna made several remarks to him about housekeeping, just as a magistrate who is cross-examining a prisoner begins with irrelevant questions so as to take him off his guard. Then, after a few moments' silence, she sighed deeply and said, shaking her head:

'Oh dear, oh dear! Just think, what news! What ever will come of it?'

'Don't you worry, madam,' Ivan Ignatyitch answered; 'God willing, all will be well. We have soldiers enough, plenty of gunpowder, and I have cleaned the cannon. We may yet keep Pugatchov at bay. Whom God helps, nobody can harm.'

'And what sort of man is this Pugatchov?' she asked.

Ivan Ignatyitch saw that he had made a slip and tried not to answer. But it was too late. Vasilissa Yegorovna forced him to confess everything, promising not to repeat it to any one.

She kept her promise and did not say a word to any one except to the priest's wife, and that was only because her cow was still grazing in the steppe and might be seized by the rebels.

Soon every one began talking about Pugatchov. The rumours differed. The Commandant sent Maximitch to find out all he could in the neighbouring villages and fortresses. The sergeant returned after two days' absence and said that in the steppe, some forty miles from the fortress, he had seen a lot of lights and had heard from the Bashkirs that an innumerable host was approaching. He could not, however, say anything definite, for he had not ventured to go any farther.

The Cossacks in the fortress were obviously in a state of great agitation; in every street they stood about in groups, whispering together, dispersing as soon as they saw a dragoon or a garrison soldier. Spies were sent among them. Yulai, a Calmuck converted to the Christian faith, brought important information to the Commandant. Yulai said that the sergeant's report was false; on his return, the sly Cossack told his comrades that he had seen the rebels, presented himself to their leader, who gave him his hand to kiss, and held a long conversation with him. The Commandant immediately arrested Maximitch and put Yulai in his place. This step was received with obvious displeasure by the Cossacks. They murmured aloud and Ivan Ignatyitch, who had to carry out the Commandant's order, heard with his own ears how they said: 'You will catch it presently, you garrison rat!' The Commandant had intended to question his prisoner the same day, but Maximitch had escaped, probably with the help of his comrades.

Another thing helped to increase the Commandant's anxiety. A Bashkir was caught carrying seditious papers. On this occasion the Commandant thought of calling his officers together once more and again wanted to send Vasilissa Yegorovna away on some pretext. But since Ivan Kuzmitch was a most truthful and straightforward man, he could think of no other device than the one he had used before.

'I say, Vasilissa Yegorovna,' he began, clearing his throat, 'Father Gerasim, I hear, has received from town . . .'

'Don't you tell stories, Ivan Kuzmitch,' his wife interrupted him. 'I expect you want to call a council to talk about Emelyan Pugatchov without me; but you won't deceive me.'

Ivan Kuzmitch stared at her.

'Well, my dear,' he said, 'if you know all about it already, you may as well stay; we will talk before you.'

'That's better, man,' she answered. 'You are no hand at deception; send for the officers.'

We assembled again. Ivan Kuzmitch read to us, in his wife's presence, Pugatchov's manifesto written by some half-illiterate Cossack. The villain declared his intention to march against our fortress at once, invited the Cossacks and the soldiers to join his band, and exhorted the commanders not to resist him, threatening to put them to death if they did. The manifesto was written in crude but impressive language, and must have produced a strong impression upon the people's mind.

'The rascal!' cried Vasilissa Yegorovna. 'To think of his

daring to make us such offers! We are to go and meet him and lay the banners at his feet! Ah, the dog! Doesn't he know that we've been forty years in the army and have seen a thing or two? Surely no commanders have listened to the brigand?'

'I should not have thought so,' Ivan Kuzmitch answered, 'but it appears the villain has already taken many fortresses.'

'He must really be strong, then,' Shvabrin remarked.

'We are just going to find out his real strength,' said the Commandant. 'Vasilissa Yegorovna, give me the key of the storehouse. Ivan Ignatyitch, bring the Bashkir and tell Yulai to bring the whip.'

'Wait, Ivan Kuzmitch,' said the Commandant's wife, getting up. 'Let me take Masha out of the house; she will be terrified if she hears the screams. And, to tell the truth, I don't care for the business myself. Good luck to you.'

In the old days torture formed so integral a part of the judicial procedure that the beneficent law which abolished it long remained a dead letter. It used to be thought that the criminal's own confession was necessary for convicting him, which is both groundless and wholly opposed to judicial good sense: for if the accused person's denial of the charge is not considered a proof of his innocence, there is still less reason to regard his confession a proof of his guilt. Even now I sometimes hear old judges regretting the abolition of the barbarous custom. But in those days no one doubted the necessity of torture—neither the judges nor the accused. And so the Commandant's order did not surprise or alarm us. Ivan Ignatyitch went to fetch the Bashkir, who was locked up in Vasilissa Yegorovna's storehouse, and a few minutes later the prisoner was led into the entry. The Commandant gave word for him to be brought into the room.

The Bashkir crossed the threshold with difficulty (he was wearing fetters) and, taking off his tall cap, stood by the door. I glanced at him and shuddered. I shall never forget that man. He seemed to be over seventy. He had neither nose nor ears. His head was shaven; instead of a beard he had a few stray hairs; he was small, thin and bent, but his narrow eyes still had a gleam in them.

'Aha!' said the Commandant, recognizing by the terrible marks one of the rebels punished in 1741. 'I see you are an old wolf and have been in our snares. Rebelling must be an old game to you, to judge by the look of your head. Come nearer; tell me, who sent you?'

The old Bashkir was silent and gazed at the Commandant with an utterly senseless expression.

'Why don't you speak?' Ivan Kuzmitch continued. 'Don't you understand Russian? Yulai, ask him in your language who sent him to our fortress?'

Yulai repeated Ivan Kuzmitch's question in Tatar. But the Bashkir looked at him with the same expression and did not answer a word.

'Very well!' the Commandant said. 'I will make you speak! Lads, take off his stupid striped gown and streak his back. Mind you do it thoroughly, Yulai!'

Two pensioners began undressing the Bashkir. The unfortunate man's face expressed anxiety. He looked about him like some wild creature caught by children. But when the old man was made to put his hands round the pensioner's neck and was lifted off the ground and Yulai brandished the whip, the Bashkir groaned in a weak, imploring voice and, nodding his head, opened his mouth in which a short stump could be seen instead of a tongue.

When I recall that this happened in my lifetime and that now I have lived to see the gentle reign of the Emperor Alexander, I cannot but marvel at the rapid progress of enlightenment and the diffusion of humane principles. Young man! If my notes ever fall into your hands, remember that the best and most permanent changes are those due to the softening of manners and morals and not to any violent upheavals.

It was a shock to all of us.

'Well,' said the Commandant, 'we evidently cannot learn much from him. Yulai, take the Bashkir back to the storehouse. We have a few more things to talk over, gentlemen.'

We began discussing our position when suddenly Vasilissa Yegorovna came into the room breathless and looking extremely alarmed.

'What is the matter with you?' the Commandant asked in surprise.

'My dear, dreadful news!' Vasilissa Yegorovna answered. 'The Nizhneozerny fortress was taken this morning. Father

Gerasim's servant has just returned from there. He saw it
being taken. The Commandant and all the officers were
hanged. All the soldiers were taken prisoners. The villains
may be here any minute.'

The unexpected news was a great shock to me. I knew
the Commandant of the Nizhneozerny fortress, a modest and
quiet young man; some two months before he had put up at
Ivan Kuzmitch's on his way from Orenburg with his young
wife. The Nizhneozerny fortress was some fifteen miles
from our fortress. Pugatchov might attack us any moment
now. I vividly imagined Marya Ivanovna's fate and my
heart sank.

'Listen, Ivan Kuzmitch,' I said to the Commandant, 'it is
our duty to defend the fortress to our last breath; this goes
without saying. But we must think of the women's safety.
Send them to Orenburg if the road is still free, or to some
reliable fortress farther away out of the villain's reach.'

Ivan Kuzmitch turned to his wife and said:

'I say, my dear, hadn't I indeed better send you and
Masha away while we settle the rebels?'

'Oh, nonsense!' she replied. 'No fortress is safe from
bullets. What's wrong with the Belogorsky? We have
lived in it for twenty-two years, thank Heaven! We have
seen the Bashkirs and the Kirghis; God willing, Pugatchov
won't harm us either.'

'Well, my dear,' Ivan Kuzmitch replied, 'stay if you like,
since you rely on our fortress. But what are we to do about
Masha? It is all very well if we ward them off or last out till
reinforcements come; but what if the villains take the
fortress?'

'Well, then . . .'

Vasilissa Yegorovna stopped with an air of extreme
agitation.

'No, Vasilissa Yegorovna,' the Commandant continued,
noting that his words had produced an effect perhaps for the
first time in his life, 'it is not fit for Masha to stay here. Let
us send her to Orenburg, to her godmother's: there are plenty
of soldiers there, and enough artillery and a stone wall. And
I would advise you to go with her: you may be an old woman,
but you'll see what they'll do to you, if they take the
fortress.'

'Very well,' said the Commandant's wife, 'so be it, let us send Masha away. But don't you dream of asking me—I won't go; I wouldn't think of parting from you in my old age and seeking a lonely grave far away. Live together, die together.'

'There is something in that,' said the Commandant. 'Well, we must not waste time. You had better get Masha ready for the journey. We will send her at daybreak to-morrow and give her an escort, though we have no men to spare. But where is Masha?'

'At Akulina Pamfilovna's,' the Commandant's wife answered. 'She fainted when she heard about the Nizhne-ozerny being taken; I am afraid of her falling ill.'

Vasilissa Yegorovna went to see about her daughter's departure. The conversation continued, but I took no part in it, and did not listen. Marya Ivanovna came in to supper, pale and with tear-stained eyes. We ate supper in silence and rose from the table sooner than usual; saying good-bye to the family, we went to our lodgings. But I purposely left my sword behind and went back for it; I had a feeling that I should find Marya Ivanovna alone. Indeed, she met me at the door and handed me my sword.

'Good-bye, Pyotr Andreyitch,' she said to me with tears. 'I am being sent to Orenburg. May you live and be happy; perhaps God will grant that we meet again, and if not . . .'

She broke into sobs, I embraced her.

'Good-bye, my angel,' I said, 'good-bye, my sweet, my darling! Whatever happens to me, believe that my last thought and my last prayer will be for you!'

Masha sobbed with her head on my shoulder. I kissed her ardently and hastened out of the room.

CHAPTER VII

THE ATTACK

Oh, my poor head, a soldier's head!
It served the Tsar truly and faithfully
For thirty years and three years more.
It won for itself neither gold nor joy,
No word of praise and no high rank.
All it has won is a gallows high
With a cross-beam made of maple wood
And a noose of twisted silk.

A Folk Song.

I DID not undress or sleep that night. I intended to go at dawn to the fortress gate from which Marya Ivanovna was to start on her journey, and there to say good-bye to her for the last time. I was conscious of a great change in myself; the agitation of my mind was much less oppressive than the gloom in which I had been plunged. The grief of parting was mingled with vague but delicious hope, with eager expectation of danger and a feeling of noble ambition. The night passed imperceptibly. I was on the point of going out when my door opened and the corporal came to tell me that our Cossacks had left the fortress in the night, taking Yulai with them by force, and that strange men were riding outside the fortress. The thought that Marya Ivanovna might not have had time to leave terrified me; I hastily gave a few instructions to the corporal and rushed off to the Commandant's.

It was daybreak. As I ran down the street I heard someone calling me. I stopped.

'Where are you going?' Ivan Ignatyitch asked, catching me up. 'Ivan Kuzmitch is on the rampart and has sent me for you. Pugatchov has come.'

'Has Marya Ivanovna left?' I asked with a sinking heart.

'She has not had time,' Ivan Ignatyitch answered. 'The road to Orenburg is cut off; the fortress is surrounded. It is a bad look out, Pyotr Andreyitch!'

We went to the rampart—a natural rise in the ground reinforced by palisading. All the inhabitants of the fortress were crowding there. The soldiers shouldered their rifles.

The cannon had been moved there the day before. The Commandant was walking up and down in front of his small detachment. The presence of danger inspired the old soldier with extraordinary vigour. Some twenty men on horseback were riding to and fro in the steppe not far from the fortress. They seemed to be Cossacks, but there were Bashkirs among them, easily recognized by their lynx caps and quivers. The Commandant walked through the ranks, saying to the soldiers: 'Well, children, let us stand up for our Empress and prove to all the world that we are brave and loyal men!' The soldiers loudly expressed their zeal. Shvabrin stood next to me, looking intently at the enemy. Noticing the commotion in the fortress, the horsemen in the steppe met together and began talking. The Commandant told Ivan Ignatyitch to aim the cannon at the group and fired it himself. The cannon-ball flew with a buzzing sound over their heads without doing any damage. The horsemen dispersed and instantly galloped away; the steppe was empty.

At that moment Vasilissa Yegorovna appeared on the rampart, followed by Masha who would not leave her.

'Well, what's happening?' the Commandant's wife asked. 'How is the battle going?   Where is the enemy?'

'The enemy is not far,' Ivan Kuzmitch answered.   'God willing, all shall be well.   Well, Masha, aren't you afraid?'

'No, father,' Marya Ivanovna answered.   'It is worse at home by myself.'

She looked at me and made an effort to smile.   I clasped the hilt of my sword, remembering that the day before I had received it from her hands, as though on purpose to defend her.   My heart was glowing, I fancied myself her knight. I longed to prove that I was worthy of her trust and waited impatiently for the decisive hour.

At that moment fresh crowds of horsemen appeared from behind a hill that was less than half a mile from the fortress, and soon the steppe was covered with a multitude of men armed with spears and bows and arrows.   A man in a red coat, with a bare sword in his hand, was riding among them mounted on a white horse: he was Pugatchov.   He stopped; the others surrounded him.   Four men galloped at full speed, evidently at his command, right up to the fortress. We recognized them for our own treacherous Cossacks.   One of them was holding a sheet of paper over his cap; another carried on the point of his spear Yulai's head, which he shook off and threw to us over the palisade. The poor Calmuck's head fell at the Commandant's feet; the traitors shouted:

'Don't shoot, come out to greet the Tsar! the Tsar is here!'

'I'll give it you!' Ivan Kuzmitch shouted. 'Shoot, lads!'

Our soldiers fired a volley. The Cossack who held the letter reeled and fell off his horse; others galloped away. I glanced at Marya Ivanovna. Horrified by the sight of Yulai's blood-stained head and stunned by the volley, she seemed dazed. The Commandant called the corporal and told him to take the paper out of the dead Cossack's hands. The corporal went out into the field and returned leading the dead man's horse by the bridle. He handed the letter to the Commandant. Ivan Kuzmitch read it to himself and then tore it to bits. Meanwhile the rebels were evidently making ready for action. In a few minutes bullets whizzed in our ears, and a few arrows stuck into the ground and the palisade near us.

'Vasilissa Yegorovna,' said the Commandant, 'this is no place for women, take Masha home; you see the girl is more dead than alive.'

Vasilissa Yegorovna, who had grown quiet when the bullets began to fly, glanced at the steppe where a great deal of movement was going on; then she turned to her husband and said:

'Ivan Kuzmitch, life and death are in God's hands; bless Masha. Masha, go to your father!'

Masha, pale and trembling, went up to Ivan Kuzmitch, knelt before him, and bowed down to the ground. The old Commandant made the sign of the cross over her three times, then he raised her and kissing her said in a changed voice:

'Well, Masha, may you be happy. Pray to God; He will not forsake you. If you find a good man, may God give you love and concord. Live as Vasilissa Yegorovna and I have lived. Well, good-bye, Masha. Vasilissa Yegorovna, make haste and take her away!'

Masha flung her arms round his neck and sobbed.

'Let us kiss each other, too,' said the Commandant's wife, bursting into tears. 'Good-bye, my Ivan Kuzmitch. Forgive me if I have vexed you in any way.'

'Good-bye, good-bye, my dear,' said the Commandant, embracing his old wife. 'Well, that will do! Make haste and go home; and, if you have time, dress Masha in a sarafan.'

The Commandant's wife and daughter went away. I followed Marya Ivanovna with my eyes; she looked round and nodded to me. Then Ivan Kuzmitch turned to us and all his attention centred on the enemy. The rebels assembled round their leader and suddenly began dismounting.

'Now, stand firm,' the Commandant said. 'They are going to attack.'

At that moment terrible shouting and yelling was heard; the rebels were running fast towards the fortress. Our cannon was loaded with shot. The Commandant let them come quite near and then fired again. The shot fell right in the middle of the crowd; the rebels scattered and rushed back; their leader alone remained. . . . He waved his sword and seemed to be persuading them. . . . The yelling and shouting that had stopped for a moment began again.

'Well, lads,' the Commandant said, 'now open the gates, beat the drum. Forward, children; come out, follow me!'

The Commandant, Ivan Ignatyitch, and I were instantly beyond the rampart; but the garrison lost their nerve and did not move.

'Why do you stand still, children?' Ivan Kuzmitch shouted. 'If we must die, we must—it's all in the day's work!'

At that moment the rebels ran up to us and rushed into the fortress. The drum stopped; the soldiers threw down their rifles; I was knocked down, but got up again and walked into the fortress together with the rebels. The Commandant, wounded in the head, was surrounded by the villains, who demanded the keys; I rushed to his assistance; several burly Cossacks seized me and bound me with their belts, saying: 'You will catch it presently, you enemies of the Tsar!'

They dragged us along the streets; the townspeople came out of their houses with offerings of bread and salt. Church bells were ringing. Suddenly they shouted in the crowd that the Tsar was awaiting the prisoners in the market-place and receiving the oath of allegiance. The people rushed to the market-place; we were driven there also.

Pugatchov was sitting in an arm-chair on the steps of the Commandant's house. He was wearing a red Cossack coat trimmed with gold braid. A tall sable cap with golden tassels was pushed low over his glittering eyes. His face seemed familiar to me. The Cossack elders surrounded him. Father Gerasim, pale and trembling, was standing by the steps with a cross in his hands and seemed to be silently imploring mercy for future victims. Gallows were being hastily put up in the market-place. As we approached, the Bashkirs dispersed the crowd and brought us before Pugatchov. The bells stopped ringing: there was a profound stillness.

'Which is the Commandant?' the Pretender asked.

Our Cossack sergeant stepped out of the crowd and pointed to Ivan Kuzmitch. Pugatchov looked at the old man menacingly and said to him:

'How did you dare resist me, your Tsar?'

Exhausted by his wound the Commandant mustered his last strength and answered in a firm voice:

'You are not my Tsar; you are a thief and a pretender, let me tell you!'

Pugatchov frowned darkly and waved a white handker-chief. Several Cossacks seized the old Captain and dragged him to the gallows. The old Bashkir, whom we had questioned the night before, was sitting astride on the cross-beam. He was holding a rope and a minute later I saw poor Ivan Kuzmitch swing in the air. Then Ivan Ignatyitch was brought before Pugatchov.

'Take the oath of allegiance to the Tsar Peter III!' Pugatchov said to him.

'You are not our Tsar,' Ivan Ignatyitch answered, repeating his captain's words; 'you are a thief and a pretender, my dear!'

Pugatchov waved his handkerchief again, and the good lieutenant swung by the side of his old chief.

It was my turn next. I boldly looked at Pugatchov, making ready to repeat the answer of my noble comrades. At that moment, to my extreme surprise, I saw Shvabrin among the rebellious Cossacks; he was wearing a Cossack coat and had his hair cropped like theirs. He went up to Pugatchov and whispered something in his ear.

'Hang him!' said Pugatchov, without looking at me.

My head was put through the noose. I began to pray silently, sincerely repenting before God of all my sins and begging Him to save all those dear to my heart. I was dragged under the gallows.

'Never you fear,' the assassins repeated to me, perhaps really wishing to cheer me.

Suddenly I heard a shout: 'Stop, you wretches! Wait!' The hangmen stopped. I saw Savelyitch lying at Pugatchov's feet.

'Dear father,' the poor old man said, 'what would a gentle-born child's death profit you? Let him go; they will give you a ransom for him; and as an example and a warning to others, hang me, if you like—an old man!'

Pugatchov made a sign and they instantly untied me and let go of me.

I cannot say that at that moment I rejoiced at being saved; nor would I say that I regretted it. My feelings were too confused. I was brought before the Pretender once more and made to kneel down. Pugatchov stretched out his sinewy hand to me.

'Kiss his hand, kiss his hand,' people around me said. But I would have preferred the most cruel death to such vile humiliation.

'Pyotr Andreyitch, my dear,' Savelyitch whispered, standing behind me and pushing me forward, 'don't be obstinate! What does it matter? Spit and kiss the vill—. I mean, kiss his hand!'

I did not stir. Pugatchov let his hand drop, saying with a laugh:

'His honour must have gone crazy with joy. Raise him!'

They pulled me up and left me in peace. I began watching the terrible comedy.

The townspeople were swearing allegiance. They came up one after another, kissed the cross and then bowed to the Pretender. The garrison soldiers were there, too. The regimental tailor, armed with his blunt scissors, was cutting off their plaits. Shaking themselves they came to kiss

Pugatchov's hand; he gave them his pardon and enlisted them in his gang. All this went on for about three hours. At last Pugatchov got up from the arm-chair and came down the steps accompanied by his elders. A white horse in a rich harness was brought to him. Two Cossacks took him by the arms and put him on the horse. He announced to Father Gerasim that he would have dinner at his house. At that moment a woman's cry was heard. Several brigands had dragged Vasilissa Yegorovna, naked and dishevelled, on to the steps. One of them had already donned her coat. Others were carrying feather-beds, boxes, crockery, linen, and all sorts of household goods.

'My dears, let me go!' the poor old lady cried. 'Have mercy, let me go to Ivan Kuzmitch!'

Suddenly she saw the gallows and recognized her husband.

'Villains!' she cried in a frenzy. 'What have you done to him! Ivan Kuzmitch, light of my eyes, soldier brave and bold! You came to no harm from Prussian swords, or from Turkish guns; you laid down your life not in a combat fair, but perished from a runaway thief!'

'Silence the old witch!' said Pugatchov.

A young Cossack hit her on the head with his sword and she fell dead on the steps. Pugatchov rode away; the people rushed after him.

CHAPTER VIII

AN UNINVITED GUEST

An uninvited guest is worse than a Tatar.
                                                    A Proverb.

THE market-place was empty. I was still standing there, unable to collect my thoughts, confused by the terrible impressions of the day.

Uncertainty as to Marya Ivanovna's fate tortured me most. Where was she? What had happened to her? Had she had time to hide? Was her shelter secure? Full of anxious thoughts I entered the Commandant's house. All was empty; chairs, tables, boxes had been smashed, crockery broken; everything had been taken. I ran up the short stairway that led to the top floor and for the first time in my life entered Marya Ivanovna's room. I saw her bed pulled to pieces by the brigands; the wardrobe had been broken and pillaged; the sanctuary lamp was still burning before the empty iconstand. The little mirror that hung between the windows had been left, too. . . . Where was the mistress of this humble virginal cell? A terrible thought flashed through my mind: I imagined her in the brigands' hands . . . my heart sank. . . . I wept bitterly and called aloud my beloved's name. . . . At that moment I heard a slight noise and Palasha, pale and trembling, appeared from behind the wardrobe.

'Ah, Pyotr Andreyitch!' she cried, clasping her hands. 'What a day! What horrors!'

'And Marya Ivanovna?' I asked, impatiently. 'What has happened to her?'

'She is alive,' Palasha answered; 'she is hiding in Akulina Pamfilovna's house.'

'At the priest's!' I cried, in horror. 'Good God! Pugatchov is there!'

I dashed out of the room, instantly found myself in the street and ran headlong to the priest's house, not seeing or feeling anything. Shouts, laughter, and songs came from there. . . . Pugatchov was feasting with his comrades. Palasha followed me. I sent her to call out Akulina Pamfilovna without attracting attention. A minute later the priest's wife came into the entry to speak to me with an empty bottle in her hands.

'For God's sake, where is Marya Ivanovna?' I asked, with inexpressible anxiety.

'She is lying on my bed there, behind the partition, poor darling,' the priest's wife answered. 'Well, Pyotr Andreyitch, we very nearly had trouble, but thank God, all passed off well: the villain had just sat down to dinner when she, poor thing, came to herself and groaned. I simply gasped! He heard. "Who is it groaning there, old woman?" he said. I made a deep bow to the thief: "My niece is ill, sire, she has been in bed for a fortnight." "And is your niece young?"

"She is, sire." "Show me your niece, old woman." My
heart sank, but there was nothing for it. "Certainly, sire;
only the girl cannot get up and come into your presence."
—"Never mind, old woman, I will go and have a look at her
myself." And, you know, the wretch did go behind the
partition; what do you think? He drew back the curtain,
glanced at her with hawk's eyes—and nothing happened.
. . . God saved us! But, would you believe it, both my husband and I had prepared to die a martyr's death. Fortunately
the dear girl did not know who he was. Good Lord, what
things we have lived to see! Poor Ivan Kuzmitch! Who
would have thought it! And Vasilissa Yegorovna! And
Ivan Ignatyitch! What did they hang him for? How is it
you were spared? And what do you think of Shvabrin?
You know, he cropped his hair like a Cossack and is sitting
here with them feasting! He is a sharp one, there's no
gainsaying! And when I spoke about my sick niece, his
eyes, would you believe it, went through me like a knife;
but he hasn't betrayed us, and that's something to be
thankful for.'

At that moment the drunken shouts of the guests were
heard, and Father Gerasim's voice. The guests were
clamouring for more drink and the priest was calling his wife.
Akulina Pamfilovna was in a flutter.

'You go home now, Pyotr Andreyitch,' she said. 'I
haven't any time for you; the villains are drinking. It
might be the end of you if they met you now. Good-bye,
Pyotr Andreyitch. What is to be, will be; I hope God will
not forsake us!'

The priest's wife left me. I set off to my lodgings feeling
somewhat calmer. As I passed through the market-place I
saw several Bashkirs, who crowded round the gallows, pulling
the boots off the hanged men's feet; I had difficulty in
suppressing my indignation, but I knew that it would have
been useless to intervene. The brigands were running about
the fortress, plundering the officers' quarters. The shouts
of the drunken rebels resounded everywhere. I reached my
lodgings. Savelyitch met me at the threshold.

'Thank God!' he cried, when he saw me. 'I was afraid the
villains had seized you again. Well, Pyotr Andreyitch, my
dear! Would you believe it, the rascals have robbed us of

everything: clothes, linen, crockery—they have left nothing. But there! Thank God they let you off with your life! Did you recognize their leader, sir?'

'No, I didn't; why, who is he?'

'What, sir? You have forgotten that drunkard who took the hareskin jacket from you at the inn? The coat was as good as new, and the brute tore it along the seams as he struggled into it!'

I was surprised. Indeed, Pugatchov had a striking resemblance to my guide. I felt certain Pugatchov and he were the same person and understood the reason for his sparing me. I could not help marvelling at the strange concatenation of circumstances: a child's coat given to a tramp had saved me from the gallows, and a drunkard who had wandered from inn to inn was besieging fortresses and shaking the foundations of the State!

'Won't you have something to eat?' asked Savelyitch, true to his habit. 'There is nothing at home; I will look about and prepare something for you.'

Left alone, I sank into thought. What was I to do? It was not fitting for an officer to remain in a fortress that belonged to the villain or to follow his gang. It was my duty to go where my services could be of use to my country in the present trying circumstances. . . . But love prompted me to stay by Marya Ivanovna to protect and defend her. Although I had no doubt that things would soon change, I could not help shuddering at the thought of the danger she was in.

My reflections were interrupted by the arrival of a Cossack who had run to tell me that 'the great Tsar was asking for me'.

'Where is he?' I said, making ready to obey.

'In the Commandant's house,' the Cossack answered. 'After dinner our father went to the bath-house and now he is resting. Well, your honour, one can see by everything that he is a person of importance: at dinner he was pleased to eat two roast sucking-pigs, and he likes the bath-house so hot that even Taras Kurochkin could not stand it—he passed on the birch to Fomka Bikbaev, and had to have cold water poured over him. There's no denying it, all his ways are so grand. . . . And they say, in the bath-house, he showed them the royal marks on his breast: on one side the two-headed eagle, the size of a penny, and on the other his own likeness.'

I did not think it necessary to dispute the Cossack's opinion and, together with him, went to the Commandant's house, trying to picture my meeting with Pugatchov and wondering how it would end. The reader may well guess that I was not altogether calm.

It was growing dusk when I reached the Commandant's house. The gallows, with its victims, loomed menacingly in the dark. Poor Vasilissa Yegorovna's body was still lying at the bottom of the steps, where two Cossacks were mounting guard. The Cossack who had brought me went to announce me and, returning at once, led me into the room where the night before I had taken such tender leave of Marya Ivanovna.

A curious scene was before me. Pugatchov and a dozen Cossack elders, wearing coloured shirts and caps, were sitting round a table covered with a cloth and littered with bottles and glasses; their faces were flushed with drink and their eyes glittered. Neither Shvabrin nor our sergeant—the freshly recruited traitors—were among them.

'Ah, your honour!' said Pugatchov, when he saw me, 'come and be my guest; here is a place for you, you are very welcome.'

The company made room for me. I sat down at the end of the table without speaking. My neighbour, a slim and good-looking young Cossack, poured out a glass of vodka for me, which I did not touch. I looked at my companions with curiosity. Pugatchov sat in the place of honour leaning on the table, his black beard propped up with his broad fist. His features, regular and rather pleasant, had nothing ferocious about them. He often turned to a man of fifty, addressing him sometimes as Count, sometimes as Timofeitch, and occasionally calling him uncle. They all treated one another as comrades and showed no particular deference to their leader. They talked of the morning's attack, of the success of the rising, and of plans for the future. Every one boasted, offered his opinion, and freely argued with Pugatchov. At this strange council of war it was decided to go to Orenburg: a bold move which was very nearly crowned with disastrous success! The march was to begin the following day.

'Well, brothers,' Pugatchov said, 'let us have my favourite song before we go to bed. Tchumakov, strike up!'

My neighbour began in a high-pitched voice a mournful Volga-boatmen's song and all joined in:

> 'Murmur not, mother-forest of rustling green leaves,
> Hinder not a brave lad thinking his thoughts,
> For to-morrow I go before the judgment-seat,
> Before the dreaded judge, our sovereign Tsar,
> And the Tsar, our lord, will ask of me:
> Tell me now, good lad, tell me, peasant's son,
> With whom didst thou go robbing and plundering,
> And how many were thy comrades bold?
> I shall tell thee the whole truth and naught but truth.
> Four in number were my comrades bold:
> My first trusty comrade was the dark night,
> And my second true comrade—my knife of steel,
> And my third one was my faithful steed,
> And the fourth one was my stout bow,
> And my messengers were my arrows sharp.
> Then our Christian Tsar will thus speak to me:
> Well done, good lad, thou peasant's son!
> Thou knowest how to rob and to answer for it,
> And a fine reward is in store for thee—
> A mansion high in the open plain,
> Two pillars and a cross-beam I grant thee.'

I cannot describe how affected I was by this peasant song about the gallows, sung by men doomed to the gallows. Their menacing faces, their tuneful voices, the mournful expression they gave to the words expressive enough in themselves—it all thrilled me with a feeling akin to awe.

The guests drank one more glass, got up from the table, and took leave of Pugatchov. I was about to follow them when Pugatchov said to me:

'Sit still, I want to talk to you.'

We were left alone. We were both silent for a few minutes; Pugatchov was watching me intently, occasionally screwing up his left eye with an extraordinary expression of slyness and mockery. At last he laughed with such unaffected gaiety that, as I looked at him, I laughed, too, without knowing why.

'Well, your honour?' he said to me. 'Confess you had a

bit of a fright when my lads put your head in the noose? I expect the sky seemed no bigger than a sheepskin to you. . . . And you would have certainly swung if it had not been for your servant. I knew the old creature at once. Well, did you think, your honour, that the man who brought you to the inn was the great Tsar himself?' (He assumed an air of mystery and importance.) 'You are very much at fault,' he continued, 'but I have spared you for your kindness, for your having done me a service when I had to hide from my enemies. But this is nothing to what you shall see! It 's not to be compared to the favour I 'll show you when I obtain my kingdom! Do you promise to serve me zealously?'

The rascal's question and his impudence struck me as so amusing that I could not help smiling.

'What are you smiling at?' he asked with a frown. 'Don't you believe I am the Tsar? Answer me plainly.'

I was confused. I felt I could not acknowledge the tramp as Tsar: to do so seemed to me unpardonable cowardice. To call him a pretender to his face meant certain death; and what I was ready to do under the gallows, in sight of all the people and in the first flush of indignation, now seemed to me useless bravado. I hesitated. Pugatchov gloomily awaited my reply. At last (and to this day I recall that moment with self-satisfaction) the feeling of duty triumphed over human weakness. I said to Pugatchov:

'Listen, I will tell you the whole truth. Think, how can I acknowledge you as Tsar? You are an intelligent man; you would see I was pretending.'

'Who, then, do you think I am?'

'God only knows; but whoever you may be, you are playing a dangerous game.'

Pugatchov glanced at me rapidly.

'So you don't believe,' he said, 'that I am the Tsar Peter III? Very well. But there is such a thing as success for the bold. Didn't Grishka Otrepyev reign in the old days? Think of me what you like, but follow me. What does it matter to you? One master is as good as another. Serve me truly and faithfully and I 'll make you Field-Marshal and Prince. What do you think?'

'No,' I answered, firmly. 'I am a gentleman by birth;

I swore allegiance to the Empress: I cannot serve you. If you really wish me well, let me go to Orenburg.'

Pugatchov was thoughtful.

'And if I let you go,' he said, 'will you promise, at any rate, not to fight against me?'

'How can I promise that?' I answered. 'You know yourself I am not free to do as I like; if they send me against you, I shall go, there is nothing for it. You yourself are a leader now; you require obedience from those who serve under you. What would you call it if I refused to fight when my service was required? My life is in your hands; if you let me go, I will thank you; if you hang me, God be your judge; but I have told you the truth.'

My sincerity impressed Pugatchov.

'So be it,' he said, clapping me on the shoulder. 'I don't do things by halves. Go wherever you like and do what you think best. Come to-morrow to say good-bye to me and now go to bed; I, too, am sleepy.'

I left Pugatchov and went out into the street. The night was still and frosty. The moon and the stars shone brightly, shedding their light on the market-place and the gallows. In the fortress all was dark and quiet. Only the tavern windows were lighted and the shouts of late revellers came from there. I looked at the priest's house. The gates and shutters were closed. All seemed quiet there.

I went home and found Savelyitch grieving for my absence. The news of my freedom delighted him more than I can say.

'Thanks be to God!' he said, crossing himself. 'We shall leave the fortress as soon as it is light and go straight away. I have prepared some supper for you, my dear; have something to eat and then sleep peacefully till morning.'

I followed his advice and having eaten my supper with great relish went to sleep on the bare floor, exhausted both in mind and body.

CHAPTER IX

THE PARTING

Sweet it was, O dear heart,
To meet and learn to love thee.
But sad it was from thee to part—
As though my soul fled from me.

Heraskov.

EARLY in the morning I was wakened by the drum. I went to the market-place. Pugatchov's crowds were already forming into ranks by the gallows, where the victims of the day before were still hanging. The Cossacks were on horseback, the soldiers shouldered their rifles. Banners were flying. Several cannon, among which I recognized ours, were placed on their carriages. All the inhabitants were there, too, waiting for the Pretender. A Cossack stood at the steps of the Commandant's house, holding a beautiful white Kirghis horse by the bridle. I searched with my eyes for Vasilissa Yegorovna's body. It had been moved a little to one side and covered with a tarpaulin. At last Pugatchov appeared in the doorway. The people took off their caps. Pugatchov stood on the steps and greeted them all. One of the elders gave him a bag of coppers and he began throwing them down in handfuls. The crowd rushed to pick them up, shouting; some were hurt in the scramble. Pugatchov was surrounded by his chief confederates. Shvabrin was among them. Our eyes met; he could read contempt in mine, and he turned away with an expression of sincere malice and feigned mockery. Catching sight of me in the crowd, Pugatchov nodded and beckoned to me.

'Listen,' he said to me. 'Go at once to Orenburg and tell the Governor and all his generals from me that they are to expect me in a week. Advise them to meet me with childlike love and obedience, else they will not escape a cruel death. A pleasant journey to you, your honour!'

Then he turned to the people and said, pointing to Shvabrin: 'Here, children, is your new commandant. Obey him

in everything, and he will be answerable to me for you and
the fortress.'

I heard these words with horror; Shvabrin was put in
command of the fortress; Marya Ivanovna would be in his
power! My God! what would become of her? Pugatchov
came down the steps. His horse was brought to him. He
quickly jumped into the saddle without waiting for the
Cossacks to help him. At that moment I saw my Savelyitch
step out of the crowd and hand Pugatchov a sheet of paper.
I could not imagine what this would lead to.

'What is this?' Pugatchov asked, with an air of importance.

'Read and you will see,' Savelyitch answered.

Pugatchov took the paper and gazed at it significantly for
a few moments.

'Why do you write so illegibly?' he said at last. 'Our
bright eyes can make nothing of it. Where is my chief
secretary?'

A young lad in a sergeant's uniform at once ran up to
Pugatchov.

'Read it aloud,' said the Pretender, giving him the paper.
I was extremely curious to know what Savelyitch could have
written to Pugatchov. The chief secretary began reading
aloud, syllable by syllable:

'Two dressing-gowns, one cotton and one striped silk,
worth six roubles.'

'What does this mean?' Pugatchov asked, with a frown.

'Tell him to read on,' Savelyitch answered calmly.

The chief secretary continued:

'A uniform coat of fine green cloth, worth seven roubles.
White cloth trousers, worth five roubles. Twelve fine linen
shirts with frills, worth ten roubles. A tea-set worth two and
a half roubles. . . .'

'What nonsense is this?' Pugatchov interrupted him.
'What do I care about tea-sets and frills and trousers?'

Savelyitch cleared his throat and began explaining:

'Well, you see, sir, this is a list of my master's goods stolen
by the villains. . . .'

'What villains?' Pugatchov said menacingly.

'I am sorry; it was a slip of the tongue,' Savelyitch
answered. 'They are not villains, of course, your men, but
they rummaged about and took these things. Don't be

angry: a horse has four legs and yet it stumbles. Tell him to read to the end anyway.'

'Read on,' Pugatchov said.

The secretary continued:

'A cotton bedspread, a silk eiderdown, worth four roubles. A foxfur coat, covered with red cloth, worth forty roubles. Also a hareskin jacket given to your honour at the inn, worth fifteen roubles. . . .'

'What next!' Pugatchov shouted, with blazing eyes.

I confess I was alarmed for Savelyitch. He was about to give more explanations, but Pugatchov interrupted him.

'How dare you trouble me with such trifles!' he cried, seizing the paper from the secretary's hands and throwing it in Savelyitch's face. 'Stupid old man! They have been robbed—as though it mattered! Why, you old dodderer, you ought to pray for the rest of your life for me and my men, and thank your stars that you and your master are not swinging here together with my rebels. . . . Hareskin jacket, indeed! I'll give you a hareskin jacket! Why, I'll have you flayed alive and make a jacket of your skin!'

'As you please,' Savelyitch answered. 'But I am a bond-man, and have to answer for my master's property.'

Pugatchov was evidently in a generous mood. He turned away and rode off without saying another word. Shvabrin and the Cossack elders followed him. The gang left the fortress in an orderly fashion. The townspeople walked out some distance after Pugatchov. Savelyitch and I were left alone in the market-place. He was holding the paper in his hands, and examining it with an air of deep regret.

Seeing that I was on good terms with Pugatchov, he had decided to take advantage of it; but his wise intention did not meet with success. I tried to scold him for his misplaced zeal, but could not help laughing.

'It's all very well to laugh, sir,' Savelyitch answered. 'It won't be so amusing when we shall have to buy everything afresh!'

I hastened to the priest's house to see Marya Ivanovna. The priest's wife had bad news for me. In the night Marya Ivanovna had developed a fever. She lay unconscious and delirious. Akulina Pamfilovna took me into her room. I walked quietly to the bedside. The change in her face struck me. She did not know me. I stood beside her for some time without listening to Father Gerasim and his kind wife who were, I think, trying to comfort me. Gloomy thoughts tormented me. The condition of the poor defence-less orphan left among the vindictive rebels, and my own helplessness, terrified me. The thought of Shvabrin tortured my imagination more than anything. Given power by the Pretender, put in charge of the fortress where the unhappy girl—the innocent object of his hatred—remained, he might do anything. What was I to do? How could I help her? How could I free her from the villain's hands? There was only one thing left me: I decided to go to Orenburg that very hour and do my utmost to hasten the relief of the Belogorsky fortress. I said good-bye to the priest and to Akulina Pamfilovna, begging them to take care of Marya Ivanovna, whom I already regarded as my wife. I took the poor girl's hand and kissed it, wetting it with my tears.

'Good-bye,' said the priest's wife, taking leave of me, 'good-bye, Pyotr Andreyitch. I hope we shall meet in better times. Don't forget us and write to us often. Poor Marya Ivanovna has now no one to comfort and defend her but you.'

Coming out into the market-place I stopped for a moment to look at the gallows, bowed down before it, and left the fortress by the Orenburg road, accompanied by Savelyitch who kept pace with me.

I walked on occupied with my thoughts, when I suddenly heard the sound of a horse's hoofs behind me. I turned round and saw a Cossack galloping from the fortress; he was leading a Bashkir horse by the bridle and signalling to me from a distance. I stopped and soon recognized our sergeant. Overtaking me he dismounted and said, giving me the reins of the other horse:

'Your honour, our father presents you with a horse and a fur coat of his own' (a sheepskin coat was tied to the saddle), 'and he also presents you'—Maximitch hesitated—'with fifty copecks in money . . . but I lost it on the way; kindly forgive me.'

Savelyitch looked at him askance and grumbled: 'Lost it on the way! And what is this rattling in the breast of your coat? You've got no conscience!'

'What is rattling in the breast of my coat?' replied the

sergeant, not in the least abashed. 'Why, mercy on us, my good man! that's my bridle and not the fifty copecks!'

'Very well,' I said, interrupting the argument. 'Thank from me him who sent you; and on your way back try to pick up the money you dropped and take it for vodka.'

'Thank you very much, your honour,' he answered, turning his horse; 'I shall pray for you as long as I live.'

With these words he galloped back, holding with one hand the breast of his coat, and in another minute was lost to sight. I put on the sheepskin and mounted the horse, making Savelyitch sit behind me.

'You see now, sir,' the old man said, 'it was not for nothing I presented the petition to the rascal; the thief's conscience pricked him. It's true, the long-legged Bashkir nag and the sheepskin coat are not worth half of what they have stolen from us, the rascals, and what you had yourself given him, but it will come in useful; one may as well get a piece of wool off a fierce dog.'

CHAPTER X

THE SIEGE OF THE TOWN

He pitched his camp upon the hills and meadows
And, eagle-like, he gazed upon the city; ·
He had a mound made beyond the camp
Concealing fire, which at night he brought to city walls.

Heraskov.

As we approached Orenburg we saw a crowd of convicts with shaven heads and faces disfigured by the branding iron. They were working at the fortifications under the supervision of garrison soldiers. Some were wheeling away barrels full of rubbish with which the moat had been filled, others were digging; on the ramparts masons were carrying bricks, mending the town wall. At the gates we were stopped by the sentries who asked for our passports. As soon as the sergeant heard that I came from the Belogorsky fortress he took me straight to the General's house.

I found the General in the garden. He was examining the apple-trees already bared by the breath of autumn and, with the help of an old gardener, was carefully wrapping them up in warm straw. His face wore a look of serenity, health, and good nature. He was pleased to see me and began questioning me about the terrible happenings I had witnessed. I told him everything. The old man listened to me attentively as he pruned the trees.

'Poor Mironov!' he said, when I finished my sad story. 'I am sorry for him, he was a fine soldier; and Madam Mironov was an excellent woman and so good at pickling mushrooms! And what has become of Masha, the Captain's daughter?'

I answered that she remained at the fortress, in the charge of the priest's wife.

'Aïe, aïe, aïe!' the General remarked, 'that's bad, very bad. There is certainly no relying on the brigands' discipline. What will become of the poor girl?'

I answered that the Belogorsky fortress was not far and that probably his Excellency would not delay in sending troops to deliver its poor inhabitants. The General shook his head doubtfully. 'We shall see, we shall see,' he said. 'There will be time enough to talk of this. Please come and have a cup of tea with me; I am having a council of war to-day. You can give us exact information about the rascal Pugatchov and his troops. And, meanwhile, go and have a rest!'

I went to the quarters allotted to me, where Savelyitch was already setting things to rights, and awaited impatiently for the appointed hour. The reader may well imagine that I did not fail to appear at the council which was of such importance to my future. At the appointed time I was at the General's.

I found there one of the town officials, the Chief of the Customs, if I remember rightly, a stout, rosy-cheeked old man in a brocade coat. He asked me about the fate of Ivan Kuzmitch with whom he was connected, and often interrupted me with fresh questions and critical remarks which proved, if not his skill in the art of war, at any rate his natural quickness and intelligence. Meanwhile other guests arrived. When all had sat down and cups of tea had been handed round, the General explained at great length and very clearly the nature of the business.

'Now, gentlemen, we must decide how we are to act against the rebels; must we take the offensive or the defensive? Each of these methods has its advantages and disadvantages. The offensive offers more hope of exterminating the enemy in the shortest time; the defensive is safer and more reliable. . . . And so let us take votes in the proper manner; that is, beginning with the youngest in rank. Ensign!' he continued, addressing himself to me, 'please give us your opinion.'

I got up and began by saying a few words about Pugatchov and his gang; I said positively that the impostor had no means of resisting regular troops.

My opinion was received by the the officials with obvious disfavour. They saw in it the defiance and rashness of youth. There was a murmur, and I clearly heard the word 'greenhorn' uttered by someone in an undertone.

The General turned to me and said, with a smile: 'Ensign, the first votes in councils of war are generally in favour of the offensive; this is as it should be. Now let us go on collecting votes. Mr. Collegiate Councillor! tell us your opinion.'

The little old man in the brocade coat hastily finished his third cup of tea, considerably diluted with rum, and said in answer to the General:

'I think, your Excellency, we need not take either the offensive or the defensive.'

'How so, sir?' the General retorted in surprise. 'No other tactics are possible; one must either take the offensive or be on the defensive. . . .'

'Your Excellency, take the way of bribery.'

'Ha! ha! ha! Your suggestion is very reasonable. Bribery is permitted by military tactics and we will follow your advice. We can offer seventy roubles . . . or, perhaps, a hundred for the rascal's head . . . to be paid from the secret sum.'

'And then,' the Chief Customs Officer interrupted, 'may I be a Kirghis sheep and not a collegiate councillor, if those thieves do not surrender their leader to us, bound hand and foot!'

'We will think of it again and talk it over,' the General

answered; 'but we must, in any case, take military measures. Gentlemen, please give your votes in the usual manner!'

All the opinions were opposed to mine. All the officials spoke of troops being unreliable and luck changeable, of caution and such like things. All thought it wiser to remain behind strong walls of stone defended by cannon than venture into the open field. At last, when the General had heard all the opinions, he shook the ashes out of his pipe and made the following speech:

'My dear sirs! I must tell you that for my part I entirely agree with the Ensign's opinion, for it is based upon all the rules of sound military tactics, according to which it is almost always preferable to take up the offensive rather than to remain on the defensive.'

At this point he stopped and began filling his pipe once more. My vanity was gratified. I proudly looked at the officials, who whispered to one another with an air of vexation and anxiety.

'But, my dear sirs,' he continued, letting out, together with a deep sigh, a big whiff of tobacco smoke, 'I dare not take upon myself so great a responsibility when the security of provinces entrusted to me by Her Imperial Majesty, our gracious sovereign, is at stake. And so I agree with the majority, which has decided that it is wiser and safer to remain within the city walls, repulsing the enemy's attacks by artillery and, if possible, by sallies.'

The officials, in their turn, looked mockingly at me. The council dispersed. I could not help regretting the weakness of the venerable soldier who decided against his own conviction to follow the opinion of ignorant and inexperienced men.

Several days after this famous council we learned that Pugatchov, true to his promise, was approaching Orenburg. From the top of the town wall I saw the rebels' army. It seemed to me their numbers had increased tenfold since the last attack which I witnessed. They now had artillery, brought by Pugatchov from the small fortresses he had taken. Recalling the council's decision, I foresaw a prolonged confinement within the town walls and nearly wept with vexation.

I will not describe the siege of Orenburg, which belongs to history, and is not a subject for family memoirs. I will only say that, owing to the carelessness of the local authorities, the siege was terrible for the inhabitants, who suffered from famine and from all sorts of calamities. One may well imagine that life in Orenburg was simply unendurable. All were despondently waiting for their fate to be decided; all complained of the prices, which were, indeed, exorbitant. The inhabitants had grown used to cannon-balls falling into their back-yards; even Pugatchov's assaults no longer excited general interest. I was dying of boredom. Time was passing. I received no letter from the Belogorsky fortress. All the roads were cut off. Separation from Marya Ivanovna was growing unbearable. Uncertainty about her fate tormented me. The sallies were my only distractions; thanks to Pugatchov I had a good horse with which I shared my scanty fare, and I rode it every day to exchange shots with Pugatchov's men. As a rule the advantage in these sallies was on the side of the villains, who were well fed, had plenty to drink, and rode good horses. The starving cavalry of the town could not get the better of them. Sometimes our hungry infantry also went afield, but the thick snow prevented it from acting successfully against the horsemen scattered all over the plain. Artillery thundered in vain from the top of the rampart, and in the field it stuck in the snow and could not move because the horses were too exhausted to pull it along. This is what our military operations were like! And this was what the Orenburg officials called being cautious and sensible.

One day when we succeeded in scattering and driving away a rather thick crowd, I overtook a Cossack who had lagged behind; I was on the point of striking him with my Turkish sword, when he suddenly took off his cap and cried:

'Good morning, Pyotr Andreyitch! How are you getting on?'

I looked at him and recognized our Cossack sergeant. I was overjoyed to see him.

'How do you do, Maximitch,' I said to him. 'Have you been in the Belogorsky lately?'

'Yes, sir,' I was there only yesterday; I have a letter for you, Pyotr Andreyitch.'

'Where is it?' I asked, flushing all over.

'Here,' said Maximitch, thrusting his hand in the breast

of his coat. 'I promised Palasha I would manage somehow to give it to you.'

He gave me a folded paper and galloped away. I opened it and read, with a tremor, the following lines:

It has pleased God to deprive me suddenly of both father and mother; I have no friends or relatives in this world. I appeal to you, knowing that you have always wished me well and that you are ready to help every one. I pray that this letter may reach you! Maximitch has promised to take it to you. Palasha has heard from Maximitch that he often sees you from a distance at the sallies and that you do not take any care of yourself or think of those who pray for you with tears. I have been ill for many weeks, and when I recovered, Alexey Ivanovitch, who is now commandant instead of my father, forced Father Gerasim to give me up to him, threatening him with Pugatchov! I live in our house as a prisoner. Alexey Ivanovitch is forcing me to marry him. He says he saved my life because he did not betray Akulina Pamfilovna when she told the villains I was her niece. And I would rather die than marry a man like Alexey Ivanovitch. He treats me very cruelly and threatens that if I don't change my mind and marry him he will take me to the villains' camp and there the same same thing will happen to me as to Lizaveta Harlova.[1] I have asked Alexey Ivanovitch to give me time to think. He agreed to wait for three more days and if I don't marry him in three days' time he will have no pity on me. Dear Pyotr Andreyitch! You alone are my protector; help me in my distress. Persuade the General and all the commanders to make haste and send a relief party to us, and come yourself if you can. I remain yours obediently,

A poor orphan,
MARYA MIRONOV.

I almost went out of my mind when I read this letter. I galloped back to the town, spurring my poor horse mercilessly. On the way I racked my brain for the means of saving the poor girl, but could think of nothing. When I reached the town I rode straight to the General's and rushed headlong into his house.

The General was walking up and down the room, smoking his pipe. He stopped when he saw me. He must have been struck by my appearance; he inquired with concern about the reason for my coming in such a hurry.

[1] A commandant's daughter whom Pugatchov took for a mistress and afterwards had shot.—TRANSLATOR'S NOTE.

'Your Excellency,' I said to him. 'I appeal to you as to my own father; for God's sake don't refuse me, the happiness of my whole life is at stake.'

'What is it, my dear?' the old man asked in surprise. 'What can I do for you? Tell me.'

'Your Excellency, allow me to have a detachment of soldiers and fifty Cossacks and let me go and clear the Belogorsky fortress.'

The General looked at me attentively, probably thinking that I had gone out of my mind—he was not far wrong.

'How do you mean—to clear the Belogorsky fortress?' he brought out at last.

'I vouch for success,' I said eagerly, 'only let me go.'

'No, young man,' he said, shaking his head; 'at so great a distance the enemy will find it easy to cut off your communication with the main strategic point and to secure a complete victory over you. Once the communication has been cut off. . . .'

I was afraid he would enter upon a military discussion and made haste to interrupt him.

'Captain Mironov's daughter,' I said to him, 'has sent me a letter; she begs for help; Shvabrin is forcing her to marry him.'

'Really? Oh, that Shvabrin is a great *Schelm*, and if he falls into my hands I will have him court-martialled within twenty-four hours and we will shoot him on the fortress wall! But meanwhile you must have patience. . . .'

'Have patience!' I cried, beside myself. 'But meanwhile he will marry Marya Ivanovna!'

'Oh, that won't be so bad,' the General retorted; 'it will be better for her to be Shvabrin's wife for the time being; he will be able to look after her at present, and afterwards, when we shoot him, she will find plenty of suitors, God willing. Charming widows don't remain old maids; I mean a young widow will find a husband sooner than a girl would.'

'I would rather die,' I cried in a rage, 'than give her up to Shvabrin!'

'Oh, I see!' said the old man, 'now I understand. . . . You are evidently in love with Marya Ivanovna. Oh, that's another matter! Poor boy! But all the same, I cannot possibly give you a detachment of soldiers and fifty Cossacks.

Such an expedition would be unreasonable; I cannot take the responsibility for it.'

I bowed my head; I was in despair. Suddenly an idea flashed through my mind. The reader will learn from the following chapter what it was—as the old-fashioned novelists put it.

CHAPTER XI

THE REBELS' CAMP

The lion has just had a meal;
Ferocious as he is, he asked me kindly:
'What brings you to my lair?'

Sumarokov.

I LEFT the General and hastened to my lodgings. Savelyitch met me with his usual admonitions.

'Why ever do you go fighting those drunken brigands, sir? It isn't the thing for a gentleman. You may perish for nothing any day. If at least they were Turks or Swedes— but these wretches are not fit to be mentioned. . . .'

I interrupted him by asking how much money we had.

'We have enough,' he said, with an air of satisfaction; 'the rascals rummaged everywhere, but I have managed to hide it from them.' With these words he took out of his pocket a long knitted purse full of silver.

'Well, Savelyitch,' said I to him, 'give me half of it and take the rest for yourself. I am going to the Belogorsky fortress.'

'My dear Pyotr Andreyitch!' said the kind old man in a shaking voice, 'what are you thinking of! How can you go at a time like this when the brigands are all over the place? Have pity on your parents if you don't care about yourself. How can you go? What for? Wait a little; troops will come and catch the rascals; then go anywhere you like.'

But my decision was firm.

'It is too late to argue,' I answered; 'I must go, I cannot help it. Don't grieve, Savelyitch; God willing, we will meet

again. Now don't be over-scrupulous or stint yourself.
Buy everything you need, even if you have to pay three times
the price. I make you a present of that money. If I don't
return in three days. . . .'

'What, sir!' Savelyitch interrupted me. 'Do you imagine
I would let you go alone? Don't you dream of asking that.
Since you have decided to go, I will follow you; if I have to
walk I won't leave you. To think of my sitting behind a
stone wall without you! I haven't taken leave of my senses
yet. Say what you like, sir, but I will go with you.'

I knew it was useless to argue with Savelyitch and so I
allowed him to prepare for the journey. Half an hour later
I mounted my good horse and Savelyitch a lame and starving
nag which one of the townspeople presented to him, not
having the means to feed it. We rode to the town gates; the
sentries let us pass; we left Orenburg.

It was growing dusk. My way lay through Berda, occupied
by Pugatchov's troops. The main road was covered with
snow-drifts, but traces of horses' hoofs were all over the
steppe, marked afresh each day. I was riding at a quick
trot, Savelyitch could hardly follow me at a distance and kept
shouting:

'Not so fast, sir; for God's sake not so fast! My cursed
nag cannot keep up with your long-legged devil. Where are
you hurrying to? It's not to a feast we are going—more
likely to our funeral! Pyotr Andreyitch! . . . Pyotr Andreyitch, my dear! . . . Good Lord, that child will come
to grief!'

The lights of Berda soon came into sight. We rode up to
the ravines that formed the natural defences of the village.
Savelyitch kept pace with me, never ceasing from his pitiful
entreaties. I was hoping to get round the village when
suddenly I saw before me in the twilight some five peasants
armed with clubs: it was the advance-guard of Pugatchov's
camp. They called to us. Not knowing their password, I
wanted to ride past them without saying anything; but they
immediately surrounded me and one of them seized my horse
by the bridle. I seized my sword and hit the peasant on the
head; his cap saved him, but he staggered and let go the bridle.
The others were confused and ran away; I took advantage of
that moment, spurred my horse and galloped on. The

darkness of the approaching night might have saved me from all danger, when turning round I suddenly saw that Savelyitch was not with me. The poor old man could not ride away from the brigands on his lame horse. What was I to do? After waiting a few minutes and making certain that he had been detained, I turned my horse back and went to his rescue.

As I rode up to the ravine I heard a noise, shouts and my Savelyitch's voice. I rode faster and soon found myself once more among the peasant watchmen who had stopped me a few minutes before. Savelyitch was with them. They had pulled the old man off his nag and were preparing to bind him. My return pleased them. They rushed at me with a shout and instantly pulled me off my horse. One of them, evidently the chief watchman, said that he would take us to the Tsar at once.

'And it is for the Father-Tsar to decide,' he added, 'whether we are to hang you at once or wait till dawn.'

I offered no resistance; Savelyitch followed my example, and the watchmen led us along in triumph.

We crossed the ravine and entered the village. Lights were burning in all the windows. Noise and shouting came from everywhere. We met a number of people in the streets, but in the dark no one noticed us or recognized me for an officer from Orenburg. We were brought straight to a cottage that stood at the cross-roads. There were several wine-barrels and two cannon at the gate.

'Here is the palace,' one of the peasants said. 'I'll go and announce you.'

He went in. I glanced at Savelyitch; the old man was silently repeating a prayer and crossing himself. I waited for many minutes; at last the peasant returned and said to me:

'Walk in, our Father says he will see the officer.'

I went into the cottage or the palace as the peasants called it. It was lighted by two tallow candles and the walls were papered with gold paper; but the benches, the table the washing arrangements, the towel on a nail, the pot-holder in the corner and the stove-shelf covered with pots, were just as in any other cottage. Pugatchov, wearing a red coat and a tall cap, was sitting under the icons with an air of

importance, his arms akimbo. Several of his chief associates
were standing by him with an expression of feigned servility:
news of the arrival of an Orenburg officer had evidently
aroused the rebels' curiosity and they had prepared an
impressive reception for me. Pugatchov recognized me at
the first glance. His assumed air of importance suddenly
disappeared.

'Ah, your honour!' he said genially. 'How are you?
What brings you here?'

I answered that I was travelling on my own business and
that his men had detained me.

'And what is your business?' he asked me.

I did not know what to say. Thinking I did not want to
speak before witnesses, Pugatchov turned to his comrades
and told them to go out of the room. All obeyed except
two who did not stir.

'Speak confidently in their presence,' Pugatchov said to
me, 'I hide nothing from them.'

I threw a sidelong glance at the Pretender's confidants.
One of them, a puny, bent old man with a grey beard, had
nothing remarkable about him except a blue ribbon worn
across the shoulder over a grey peasant coat. But I shall
never forget his comrade. He was tall, stout, and broad-
shouldered, and seemed to be about forty-five. A thick red
beard, grey glittering eyes, a nose without nostrils, and reddish
marks on the forehead and the cheeks gave an indescribable
expression to his broad, pock-marked face. He wore a red
shirt, a Kirghis gown and Cossack trousers. As I learned
later, the first was a runaway corporal, Beloborodov; the
second, Afanasy Sokolov, nicknamed Hlopusha, a convict
who had escaped three times from the Siberian mines. In
spite of the feelings which absorbed me, the company in
which I so unexpectedly found myself strongly appealed to
my imagination. But Pugatchov brought me back to
myself by repeating:

'Tell me on what business have you left Orenburg?'

A strange idea came into my head: it seemed to me that
Providence which had brought me for the second time to
Pugatchov was giving me an opportunity to carry out my
intention. I decided to take advantage of it and, without
stopping to consider my decision, said in answer to Pugatchov:

'I was going to the Belogorsky fortress to rescue an orphan who is being ill-treated there.'

Pugatchov's eyes glittered.

'Which of my men dares to ill-treat an orphan?' he cried. 'He may be as clever as you please, but he won't escape my sentence. Tell me, who is the guilty man?'

'Shvabrin,' I answered. 'He keeps under lock and key the girl whom you saw lying ill at the priest's house, and wants to marry her by force.'

'I'll teach Shvabrin!' said Pugatchov, menacingly. 'I'll show him what it is to take the law into his own hands and to ill-treat people. I will hang him!'

'Allow me to say a word,' Hlopusha said, in a hoarse voice. 'You were in a hurry to put Shvabrin in command of the fortress and now you are in a hurry to hang him. You have already offended the Cossacks by putting a gentleman over them; do not now frighten the gentry by hanging him at the first accusation.'

'One need not pity them nor show them favours!' said the old man with the blue ribbon. 'There is no harm in hanging Shvabrin; but it wouldn't be amiss to question this officer thoroughly, too. Why has he come here? If he doesn't recognize you for Tsar he need not seek justice from you; and if he does acknowledge you, why has he sat till to-day with your enemies in Orenburg? Won't you let me take him to the office and light a fire under his toes? It seems to me his honour has been sent to us by the Orenburg commanders.'

The old villain's logic struck me as rather convincing. A shiver ran down my back when I thought in whose hands I was. Pugatchov noticed my confusion.

'Eh, your honour?' he said to me with a wink. 'I fancy my field-marshal is talking sense. What do you think?'

Pugatchov's mockery gave me back my courage. I calmly answered that I was in his power and that he was free to do what he liked with me.

'Good,' said Pugatchov, 'and now tell me how are things going with you in the town?'

'Thank Heaven, all is well!' I answered.

'All is well?' Pugatchov repeated, 'and people are dying of starvation?' The Pretender was right; but in accordance with my duty I began assuring him that this was an empty rumour and that there were plenty of provisions in Orenburg.

'You see,' the old man chimed in, 'he is deceiving you to your face. All refugees say with one voice that there is famine and pestilence in Orenburg; people eat carcasses and even that is a treat; and his honour assures you they have plenty of everything. If you want to hang Shvabrin, hang this fellow, too, on the same gallows so as to be fair to both!'

The cursed old man's words seemed to have shaken Pugatchov. Fortunately Hlopusha began contradicting his comrade.

'Come, Naumitch,' he said to him, 'you always want to be hanging and murdering. And you are not much of a man to look at—you can hardly keep body and soul together. You have one foot in the grave and yet you are destroying others. Isn't there enough blood on your conscience?'

'You are a fine saint!' Beloborodov retorted. 'Why should you have pity?'

'Of course, I, too, have things on my conscience,' Hlopusha answered, 'and this hand' (he clenched his bony fist and, turning up his sleeve, showed a hairy arm) 'has been guilty of shedding Christian blood. But I destroyed enemies, not guests; on a high road and in the dark forest and not at home behind the stove; with a club and an axe and not with womanish slander.'

The old man turned away and muttered: 'Torn nostrils . . .'

'What are you muttering, you old wretch?' Hlopusha shouted. 'I'll give you "torn nostrils"! Wait a bit, your time will come, too; God willing, you, too, will sniff the hangman's pincers. . . . And, meanwhile, take care I don't pull out your scurvy beard!'

'My Generals!' Pugatchov said pompously, 'that's enough quarrelling! It does not matter if all the Orenburg pack wriggle under the same gallows; but it does matter if our dogs are at one another's throats. There, make peace!'

Hlopusha and Beloborodov did not say a word and looked at each other gloomily. I saw that it was necessary to change the subject of the conversation which might end very badly for me and, turning to Pugatchov, I said to him with a cheerful air:

'Oh, I have forgotten to thank you for the horse and the sheepskin. Had it not been for you I could not have found the road and should have been frozen on the way.'

My ruse succeeded. Pugatchov's good humour was restored.

'One good turn deserves another,' he said, with a wink. 'And tell me now why are you concerned about the girl whom Shvabrin is ill-treating? Is she your sweetheart by any chance?'

'She is my betrothed!' I answered, seeing the favourable change in the weather and not thinking it necessary to conceal the truth.

'Your betrothed!' Pugatchov shouted. 'Why didn't you say so before? Why, we'll have you married and make merry at your wedding!'

Then he turned to Beloborodov and said: 'Listen, Field-marshal! His honour and I are old friends, so let us sit down to supper. Morning is wiser than evening; we shall see to-morrow what we are to do with him'.

I should have been glad to refuse the honour, but there was nothing for it. Two young girls, daughters of the Cossack to whom the hut belonged, spread a white cloth on the table, brought bread, fish-soup, and several bottles of vodka and beer. Once more I found myself at the same table with Pugatchov and his terrible comrades.

The orgy of which I was an involuntary witness lasted far into the night. At last the company were overpowered with drink. Pugatchov dozed; his friends got up and made me a sign to leave him. I went with them out of the room. At Hlopusha's orders the watchman took me into the cottage that served as office; I found Savelyitch there and we were locked up together for the night. The old man was so amazed at all that was happening that he did not ask me a single question. He lay down in the dark and was a long time sighing and groaning; at last he snored, and I gave myself up to thoughts which did not give me a wink of sleep all night.

In the morning Pugatchov sent for me. I went to him. A chaise, drawn by three Tatar horses was standing at his gate. There was a crowd in the street. I met Pugatchov in the entry; he was dressed for the journey in a fur coat and a Kirghis cap. His comrades of the day before surrounded him with an air of servility which little accorded with all that I had seen in the evening. Pugatchov greeted me cheerfully and told me to step into the chaise with him. We took our seats.

'To the Belogorsky fortress!' Pugatchov said to the broad-shouldered Tatar who drove the troika standing.

My heart beat violently. The horses set off, the bell clanged, the chaise flew along . . .

'Stop! Stop!' a familiar voice called out, and I saw Savelyitch running towards us. Pugatchov told the driver to stop.

My dear Pyotr Andreyitch!' Savelyitch cried, 'don't abandon me in my old age among these rascals!'

'Ah, you old creature!' Pugatchov said to him. 'So God has brought us together again. Well, climb on to the box!'

'Thank you, sire, thank you, our father!' said Savelyitch, climbing up. 'May God let you live to be a hundred for your kindness to an old man. I will pray for you as long as I live and will never mention the hareskin jacket again.'

This hareskin jacket might anger Pugatchov in earnest at last. Fortunately he had not heard or took no notice of the inopportune remark. The horses set off at a gallop; the people in the street stopped and bowed. Pugatchov nodded right and left. A minute later we left the village and flew along the smooth road.

One may well imagine what I was feeling at that moment. In a few hours I was to see her whom I had already considered as lost to me. I was picturing the moment of our meeting. . . . I was also thinking of the man in whose hands I was and who was mysteriously connected with me through a strange combination of circumstances. I was recalling the thoughtless cruelty, the bloodthirsty habits of the would-be rescuer of my beloved. Pugatchov did not know that she was Captain Mironov's daughter; Shvabrin in his bitterness might tell him; or Pugatchov might discover the truth in other ways. . . . What would become of Marya Ivanovna then? A shiver ran down my back and my hair stood on end.

Suddenly Pugatchov interrupted my reflections with a question: 'What are you thinking of so deeply, your honour?'

'How can I help thinking,' I answered. 'I am an officer

and a gentleman; only yesterday I was fighting against you and to-day I am driving beside you and the happiness of my whole life depends upon you.'

'Well, are you afraid?' Pugatchov asked.

I answered that since he had spared me once, I was hoping he would do so again and would, indeed, help me.

'And you are right, upon my soul, you are right!' Pugatchov said. 'You saw that my men were looking askance at you; and the old man again insisted this morning that you were a spy and ought to be tortured and hanged; but I did not agree,' he added, lowering his voice so that Savelyitch and the Tatar should not hear him, 'remembering your glass of vodka and the hareskin jacket. You see I am not so bloodthirsty as your people make me out.'

I recalled the taking of the Belogorsky fortress but did not think it necessary to contradict him and did not answer.

'What do they say of me in Orenburg?' Pugatchov asked, after a silence.

'They say it's not easy to deal with you. There's no denying it, you've made your presence felt.'

The Pretender's face assumed an expression of satisfied vanity.

'Yes!' he said cheerfully. 'I am quite a hand at fighting. Do they know at Orenburg about the battle at Yuzeeva? Forty generals were killed, four armies taken captive. What do you think? would the Prussian king be a match for me?'

The brigand's boasting amused me.

'What do you think yourself?' I asked him; 'could you beat Frederick?'

'Why not? I beat your generals and they used to beat him. So far I have been lucky in war. Wait, you'll see even better things when I march on Moscow.'

'Are you thinking of doing that?'

Pugatchov pondered and said in a low voice:

'God only knows. I am cramped; I cannot do as I like. My men are too independent. They are thieves. I have to keep a sharp look out: at the first defeat they will ransom their necks with my head.'

'That's just it!' I said. 'Hadn't you better leave them yourself in good time and appeal to the Empress's mercy?'

Pugatchov smiled bitterly.

'No,' he said; 'it is too late for me to repent. There will be no mercy for me. I will go on as I have begun. Who knows? I may succeed after all! Grishka Otrepyev did reign over Moscow, you know.'

'And do you know what his end was? They threw him out of window, killed him, burned his body and fired a cannon with his ashes.'

'Listen,' Pugatchov said, with a kind of wild inspiration, 'I will tell you a fairy-tale which in my childhood an old Calmuck woman told me. The eagle asked the raven one day: "Tell me, raven-bird, why do you live in the world for three hundred years and I only for thirty-three?"—"Because, father-eagle, you drink living blood," the raven said, "and I feed on things that are dead." The eagle thought "I will try and feed as he does." Very well. The eagle and the raven flew along. They saw the carcass of a horse, came down and perched on it. The raven plucked and praised the food. The eagle took a peck or two, then waved his wing and said: "No, brother raven, rather than feed on dead flesh for three hundred years, I would have one drink of living blood—and leave the rest to God!" What do you think of the Calmuck tale?'

'It is clever,' I answered. 'But to live by murder and brigandage is, to my mind, just what plucking dead flesh means.'

Pugatchov looked at me with surprise and made no answer. We both sank into silence, each absorbed with his own reflections. The Tatar struck up a doleful song; Savelyitch dozed as he sat, rocking to and fro on the box. The chaise flew along the smooth winter road. . . . Suddenly I saw on the steep bank of the Yaïk a village with a palisade round it and a belfry rising above it—and in another quarter of an hour we drove into the Belogorsky fortress.

CHAPTER XII

AN ORPHAN

Our slender young apple-tree
Has no spreading branch nor top to it,
Our tender young bride to be
Has no father nor mother to care for her,
She has no one to see her off,
No one to bestow a blessing on her.

A Wedding Song.

THE chaise drove up to the Commandant's house. The people recognized the sound of Pugatchov's bell and ran after us in a crowd. Shvabrin met the Pretender on the steps. He was dressed like a Cossack and had grown a beard. The traitor helped Pugatchov to step out of the chaise, speaking in servile expressions of his delight and devotion. He was confused when he saw me, but soon recovered and gave me his hand, saying:

'So you, too, are one of us? Time you were!'

I turned away and made no answer.

My heart ached when we came into the familiar room; the certificate of the late Commandant still hung on the wall as a sad epitaph of bygone days. Pugatchov sat down on the sofa where Ivan Kuzmitch used to doze, lulled to sleep by his wife's grumbling. Shvabrin brought him some vodka. Pugatchov drank a glass and said, pointing to me:

'Offer some to his honour, too.'

Shvabrin came up to me with the tray, but I turned away again. He was obviously very uneasy. With his usual quickness he guessed, of course, that Pugatchov was displeased with him; he was afraid, and looked at me with distrust. Pugatchov asked about the state of the fortress, the news of the enemy's troops and such like things, and suddenly asked him:

'Tell me, brother, who is the girl you are keeping prisoner in your house? Show her to me.'

Shvabrin turned white as death.

'Sire,' he said in a shaking voice, 'Sire, she is not a prisoner. She is ill . . . she is upstairs, in bed.'

'Take me to her,' the Pretender said, getting up.

It was impossible to refuse him. Shvabrin led Pugatchov to Marya Ivanovna's room. I followed them.

Shvabrin stopped on the stairs.

'Sire,' he said, 'you may require of me whatever you wish, but do not allow a stranger to enter my wife's bedroom.'

I shuddered.

'So you are married?' I said to Shvabrin, ready to tear him to pieces.

'Keep quiet!' Pugatchov interrupted me. 'It is my affair. And don't you try to be clever,' he went on, addressing Shvabrin, 'or invent excuses; wife or not, I take to her whomsoever I like. Follow me, your honour.'

At Marya Ivanovna's door Shvabrin stopped again and said in a breaking voice:

'Sire, I warn you, she has brain fever and has been raving for the last three days.'

'Open the door!' said Pugatchov.

Shvabrin began searching in his pockets and said he had not brought the key. Pugatchov pushed the door with his foot, the lock fell off, the door opened, and we went in.

I looked—and was aghast. Marya Ivanovna, pale and thin, with dishevelled hair and dressed like a peasant, was sitting on the floor; a jug of water, covered with a piece of bread, stood before her. When she saw me she started and cried out. What I felt then I cannot describe.

Pugatchov looked at Shvabrin and said, with a bitter smile:

'Fine hospital you have here!' Then he went up to Marya Ivanovna and said: 'Tell me, my dear, what is your husband punishing you for? What wrong have you done to him?'

'My husband!' she repeated; 'he is not my husband. I will never be his wife. I would rather die, and I shall die if I am not saved from him.'

Pugatchov looked menacingly at Shvabrin.

'And you dared to deceive me!' he said. 'Do you know what you deserve, you wretch?'

Shvabrin dropped on his knees. . . . At that moment a feeling of contempt outweighed my hatred and anger. I looked with disgust upon a gentleman grovelling at the feet of an escaped convict. Pugatchov was softened.

'I will spare you this time,' he said to Shvabrin, 'but next time you are at fault, this wrong will be remembered against you.'

Then he turned to Marya Ivanovna and said kindly: 'Come away, my pretty maid. I set you free. I am the Tsar!'

Marya Ivanovna glanced at him and understood that her parents' murderer was before her. She buried her face in her hands and fell down senseless. I rushed to her, but at that moment my old friend Palasha very boldly made her way into the room and began attending to her mistress. Pugatchov walked out and the three of us went downstairs.

'Well, your honour,' Pugatchov said, laughing, 'we've delivered the fair maiden! What do you think, hadn't we better send for the priest and tell him to marry you to his niece? I'll give her away if you like, and Shvabrin will be best man; we'll make merry and drink, and give the guests no time to think!'

The very thing that I feared happened. Shvabrin was beside himself when he heard Pugatchov's suggestion.

'Sire!' he cried in a frenzy. 'I am to blame; I have lied to you, but Grinyov, too, is deceiving you. This girl is not the priest's niece; she is the daughter of Captain Mironov who was hanged when the fortress was taken.'

Pugatchov fixed on me his fiery eye.

'What's this?' he asked, in perplexity.

'Shvabrin is right,' I answered firmly.

'You hadn't told me,' remarked Pugatchov, and his face clouded.

'But consider,' I answered him. 'How could I have said in your men's presence that Mironov's daughter was living? They would have torn her to pieces. Nothing would have saved her!'

'That's true enough,' Pugatchov said, laughing. 'My drunkards would not have spared the poor girl. The priest's wife did well to deceive them.'

'Listen,' I said, seeing that he was in a kind mood. 'I do not know what to call you and I don't want to know. . . . But God knows I would gladly pay you with my life for what you have done for me. Only don't ask of me what is against my honour and Christian conscience. You are my benefactor. Finish as you have begun; let me go with the poor orphan whither God may lead us. And whatever happens to you and wherever you may be, we shall pray to Him every day of our lives to save your sinful soul.'

It seemed that Pugatchov's stern heart was touched.

'So be it!' he said. 'I don't believe in stopping half-way, be it in vengeance or in mercy. Take your sweetheart; go with her where you will and God grant you love and concord!'

Then he turned to Shvabrin and told him to give me a pass through all the villages and fortresses subject to his rule.

Shvabrin, utterly overwhelmed, stood like one dumbfounded. Pugatchov went to look at the fortress. Shvabrin accompanied him and I remained behind under the pretext of making ready for the journey.

I ran upstairs. The door was locked. I knocked.

'Who is there?' Palasha asked.

I gave my name. Marya Ivanovna's sweet voice came from behind the door:

'Wait a little, Pyotr Andreyitch; I am changing my dress. Go to Akulina Pamfilovna's. I shall be there directly.'

I obeyed and went to Father Gerasim's house. Both he and his wife ran out to meet me. Savelyitch had already given them the news.

'How do you do, Pyotr Andreyitch?' the priest's wife said. 'God has brought us together again! How are you? We have talked of you every day. Marya Ivanovna has been through a dreadful time without you, poor darling! . . . But tell me, my dear, how did you hit it off with Pugatchov? How is it he hasn't made an end of you? It's something to the villain's credit!'

'That will do, my dear,' Father Gerasim interrupted her. 'Don't blurt out all you know. There is no salvation in speaking overmuch. Please come in, Pyotr Andreyitch! You are very welcome. We haven't seen you for months!'

The priest's wife offered me what food there was and talked incessantly as she did so. She told me how Shvabrin had forced them to give up Marya Ivanovna; how Marya Ivanovna wept and did not want to part from them; how Marya Ivanovna always kept in touch with her through Palasha (a spirited girl who made the sergeant himself dance to her

tune); how she had advised Marya Ivanovna to write a letter
to me, and so on. I, in my turn, briefly told her my story.
The priest and his wife crossed themselves when they heard
that Pugatchov knew of their deception.

'The power of the Holy Cross be with us!' said Akulina
Pamfilovna. 'May the Lord let the storm go by! Fancy
Alexey Ivanitch betraying us! He is a fine one!'

At that moment the door opened and Marya Ivanovna came
in, a smile on her pale face. She had laid aside peasant clothes
and was dressed as before, simply and prettily.

I clasped her hand and for some moments could not utter
a word. Our hearts were too full for speech. Our hosts
felt that we had no thoughts to spare for them and left us.
We were alone. All was forgotten. We talked and talked.
Marya Ivanovna told me all that had happened to her after
the fortress was taken; she described to me the horror of her
position, and all that she had had to endure at the hands of
her vile pursuer. We recalled the bygone happy days. . . .
We were both weeping. . . . At last I put my plans before
her. It was impossible for her to stay in a fortress subject to
Pugatchov and ruled by Shvabrin. It was no use thinking of
Orenburg where the inhabitants were suffering all the horrors
of the siege. She had no one belonging to her in the world.
I offered her to go to my parents' estate. She hesitated at
first; she knew my father's animosity towards her and was
afraid. I reassured her. I knew that my father would be
happy and consider it his duty to welcome the daughter of a
veteran soldier who had died for his country.

'Darling Marya Ivanovna,' I said to her, at last. 'I look
upon you as my wife. Miraculous circumstances have united
us for ever; nothing in the world can part us.'

Marya Ivanovna listened to me without coyness or feigned
reluctance. She felt that her fate was united to mine. But
she repeated that she would only marry me with my parents'
consent. I did not contradict her about it. We kissed each
other sincerely and ardently—and all was settled between us.

An hour later, Maximitch brought me a pass signed with
Pugatchov's hieroglyphics and said that he wanted to see me.
I found him ready for the journey. I cannot express what I
felt on parting from this terrible man, a monster of evil to all
but me. Why not confess the truth? At that moment I

was drawn to him by warm sympathy. I longed to tear him away from the criminals whose leader he was and to save his head before it was too late. Shvabrin and the people who crowded round us prevented me from saying all that was in my heart.

We parted friends. Seeing Akulina Pamfilovna in the crowd Pugatchov shook his finger at her and winked significantly; then he stepped into the chaise, told the driver to go to Berda, and as the horses moved he put out his head from the chaise once more and shouted to me:

'Good-bye, your honour! We may yet meet again.'

We did meet again—but in what circumstances!

Pugatchov drove away. I gazed for some time at the white steppe where his troika was galloping. The crowd dispersed. Shvabrin disappeared. I returned to the priest's house. Everything was ready for our departure. I did not want to delay any longer. All our belongings were packed in the old Commandant's chaise. The drivers harnessed the horses in a trice. Marya Ivanovna went to say good-bye to the graves of her parents, who were buried behind the church. I wanted to accompany her, but she asked me to leave her. She returned in a few minutes, silently weeping quiet tears. The chaise was brought before the house. Father Gerasim and his wife came out on to the steps. The three of us— Marya Ivanovna, Palasha, and I—sat inside the carriage and Savelyitch climbed on the box by the driver.

'Good-bye, Marya Ivanovna, my darling! Good-bye, Pyotr Andreyitch, our bright falcon!' kind Akulina Pamfilovna said to us. 'A happy journey to you, and God grant you happiness!'

We set off. I saw Shvabrin standing at the window in the Commandant's house. His face was expressive of gloomy malice. I did not want to triumph over a defeated enemy and turned my eyes in another direction. At last we drove out of the fortress gates, and left the Belogorsky fortress for ever.

CHAPTER XIII

THE ARREST

'Do not be angry, sire; my duty bids me
To send you off to gaol this very day.'
By all means, I am ready; but I trust
You will first allow me to have my say.

Kniazhnin.

UNITED so unexpectedly to the sweet girl about whom I had
been terribly anxious only that morning, I could not believe
my senses and fancied that all that had happened to me was
an empty dream. Marya Ivanovna gazed thoughtfully now
at me and now at the road: she did not seem to have come to
herself as yet. We were silent. Our hearts were much too
tired. We did not notice how in a couple of hours we found
ourselves at the neighbouring fortress which also was in
Pugatchov's hands. We changed horses there. The quickness with which they were harnessed and the hurried servility
of the bearded Cossack, promoted by Pugatchov to the post
of commandant, proved that, owing to our driver's talkative-
ness, I was being taken for the Tsar's favourite.

We continued our journey. Dusk was falling. We drew
near a small town occupied, according to the bearded commandant, by a strong detachment of Pugatchov's supporters
on their way to join him. We were stopped by the sentries.
To the question, 'Who goes there?' the driver answered, in a
loud voice, 'The Tsar's friend with his lady'. Suddenly a
crowd of hussars surrounded us, swearing fearfully.

'Come out, you devil's friend!' a sergeant, with a big moustache said to me. 'You will get it hot presently, and that girl
of yours, too.'

I stepped out of the chaise and demanded to be taken to
the commanding officer. Seeing my uniform, the soldiers
stopped swearing. The sergeant led me to the colonel.
Savelyitch went with me, muttering to himself: 'There's a
fine Tsar's friend for you! Out of the frying-pan into the
fire. . . . Good Lord, what will the end of it be?' The
chaise followed us at a walking pace. After five minutes'

walk we came to a brilliantly lighted house. The sergeant left me with the sentries and went to announce me. He returned at once, saying that the colonel had not time to see me, but that he ordered that I should be taken to gaol and my lady brought to him.

'What's the meaning of this?' I cried, in a rage. 'Has he gone off his head?'

'I cannot tell, your honour,' the sergeant answered. 'Only his honour said that your honour was to be taken to gaol and her honour brought to his honour.'

I rushed up the steps. The sentries made no attempt to detain me and I ran straight into the room where six officers of the hussars were playing cards. The colonel was dealing. Imagine my surprise when I recognized him for Ivan Ivanovitch Zurin who had won from me at billiards at the Simbirsk inn!

'Is it possible?' I cried. 'Ivan Ivanitch! Is that you?'

'Why, Pyotr Andreyitch! What wind brings you? Where do you come from? Glad to see you, brother. Won't you join the game?'

'Thanks. Better tell them to give me a lodging.'

'What lodging? Stay with me.'

'I cannot; I am not alone.'

'Well, bring your comrade along.'

'It's not a comrade. I am with a lady.'

'A lady! Where did you pick her up? Ehe, brother!' At these words, Zurin whistled so expressively that every one laughed. I was utterly confused.

'Well,' Zurin went on, 'so be it! You shall have a lodging, but it's a pity. . . . We could have had a gay time, as in the old days. . . . Hey, boy! Why don't they bring along Pugatchov's sweetheart? Doesn't she want to come? Tell her she need not fear, the gentleman is very kind and will do her no harm—and give her a good kick to hurry her up.'

'What are you talking about?' I said to Zurin. 'Pugatchov's sweetheart? It is the late Captain Mironov's daughter. I have rescued her and am now seeing her off to my father's estate where I shall leave her.'

'What! So it was you they have just announced? Upon my word! What does it all mean?'

'I will tell you afterwards. And now for heaven's sake reassure the poor girl whom your hussars have frightened.'

Zurin made arrangements at once. He came out into the street to apologize to Marya Ivanovna for the misunderstanding and told the sergeant to give her the best lodging in the town. I was to spend the night with him.

We had supper and when we were left alone I told him my adventures. Zurin listened with great attention. When I had finished, he shook his head and said:

'That's all very good, brother; one thing only is not good: why the devil do you want to be married? I am an honest officer; I would not deceive you; believe me, marriage is a delusion. You don't want to be bothered with a wife and be nursing babies! Throw it up! Do as I tell you: get rid of the Captain's daughter. The road to Simbirsk is safe now; I have cleared it. Send her to-morrow to your parents by herself and you stay in my detachment. There is no need for you to return to Orenburg. If you fall into the rebels' hands once more you may not escape this time. And so the love-foolishness will pass of itself and all will be well.'

I did not altogether agree with him, but I felt that I was in duty bound to remain with the army. I decided to follow Zurin's advice and send Marya Ivanovna to the country while I remained in his detachment.

Savelyitch came to undress me; I told him that he must be ready next day to continue the journey with Marya Ivanovna. He did not want to at first.

'What are you thinking of, sir? How can I leave you? Who will look after you? What will your parents say?'

Knowing Savalyitch's obstinacy I decided to win him by affection and sincerity.

'Arhip Savelyitch, my dear!' I said to him. 'Don't refuse. You will be doing me a great kindness. I shall not need a servant, but I shall not be happy if Marya Ivanovna goes on her journey without you. In serving her you will be serving me, because I am determined to marry her as soon as circumstances allow.'

Savelyitch clasped his hands with an indescribable air of surprise.

'To marry!' he replied. 'The child thinks of marrying! But what will your father say; what will your mother think?'

'They will agree; I am sure they will agree when they know Marya Ivanovna,' I answered. 'I rely on you, too. My father and mother trust you; you will intercede for us, won't you?'

Savelyitch was touched.

'Ah, Pyotr Andreyitch, dear,' he answered, 'though it is much too early for you to think of marrying, Marya Ivanovna is such a good young lady that it would be a sin to miss the opportunity. Have it your own way! I shall go with her, angel that she is, and will tell your parents faithfully that such a bride does not need a dowry.'

I thanked Savelyitch and went to bed in the same room with Zurin. My mind was in a turmoil and I talked and talked. At first Zurin answered me readily, but gradually his words became few and disconnected; at last in answer to a question he gave a snore with a whistle in it. I stopped talking and soon followed his example.

Next morning I went to Marya Ivanovna and told her of my plans. She recognized their reasonableness and agreed with me at once. Zurin's detachment was to leave the town that same day. There was no time to be lost. I said good-bye to Marya Ivanovna there and then, entrusting her to Savelyitch and giving her a letter to my parents. Marya Ivanovna wept.

'Good-bye, Pyotr Andreyitch,' she said, in a low voice. 'God only knows whether we shall meet again; but I will not forget you as long as I live; till death you alone shall remain in my heart.'

I could not answer her. Other people were there. I did not want to abandon myself in their presence to the feelings that agitated me. At last she drove away. I returned to Zurin, sad and silent. He wanted to cheer me; I sought distraction; we spent the day in riotous gaiety and set out on the march in the evening.

It was the end of February. The winter, which had made military operations difficult, was coming to an end, and our generals were preparing for concerted action. Pugatchov was still besieging Orenburg. Meanwhile the army detachments around him were joining forces and approaching the brigands' nest on all sides. Rebellious villages were restored to order at the sight of the soldiers, brigand bands dispersed on our approach, and everything indicated a speedy and successful end of the war.

Soon Prince Golitsin defeated Pugatchov at the Tatishcheva fortress, scattered his hordes, delivered Orenburg and dealt, it seemed, the last and decisive blow to the rebellion. Zurin was at that time sent against a gang of rebellious Bashkirs, who had dispersed before we caught sight of them. Spring found us in a Tatar village. Rivers were in flood and roads impassable. We could do nothing, but comforted ourselves with the thought that the petty and tedious war with brigands and savages would soon be over.

Pugatchov was not caught, however. He appeared at the Siberian foundries, collected there fresh bands of followers and began his evil work once more. Again rumours of his success spread abroad. We heard of the fall of the Siberian fortresses. Soon afterwards, the army leaders, who slumbered care-free in the hope that the contemptible rebel was powerless, were alarmed by the news of his taking Kazan and advancing towards Moscow. Zurin received an order to cross the Volga and hasten to Simbirsk where the flames of insurrection were already burning. I was overjoyed at the thought of being able, perhaps, to call at our estate, embrace my parents and see Marya Ivanovna. I jumped with joy like a child and kept repeating, as I hugged Zurin, 'To Simbirsk! To Simbirsk!' Zurin sighed and said, shrugging his shoulders, 'No, you will come to no good. You will be married and done for!'

We were approaching the banks of the Volga. Our regiment entered the village N. and was to spend the night there. The following morning we were to cross the river. The village foreman told me that all the villages on the other side had rebelled, and that Pugatchov's bands prowled about everywhere. I was very much alarmed at this news.

Impatience possessed me; I could not rest. My father's estate was on the other side of the river, some twenty miles from it. I asked if any one could row me across. All the peasants were fishermen; there were plenty of boats. I went to tell Zurin of my intention.

'Take care,' he said, 'it is dangerous for you to go alone. Wait for the morning. We will be the first to cross and will pay a visit to your parents with fifty hussars in case of emergency.'

I insisted on going. The boat was ready. I stepped into it with two boatmen. They pushed off and plied their oars.

The sky was clear. The moon was shining brightly. The air was still. The Volga flowed calmly and evenly. Swaying rhythmically, the boat glided over the dark waves. Half an hour passed. I sank into dreaming. I thought of the calm of nature and the horrors of civil war; of love, and so on. We reached the middle of the river. . . . Suddenly the boatmen began whispering together.

'What is it?' I asked, coming to myself.

'Heaven only knows; we can't tell,' the boatmen answered, looking into the distance.

I looked in the same direction and saw in the dark something floating down the river. The mysterious object was approaching us. I told the oarsmen to stop and wait.

The moon hid behind a cloud. The floating phantom seemed darker still. It was quite close to me and yet I could not distinguish it.

'Whatever can it be?' the boatmen said. 'It isn't a sail nor a mast.'

Suddenly the moon came out from behind the cloud and lighted a terrible sight. A gallows fixed to a raft was floating towards us. Three corpses were swinging on the cross-bar. A morbid curiosity possessed me. I wanted to look into the hanged men's faces. I told the oarsmen to hold the raft with a boat-hook, and my boat knocked against the floating gallows. I jumped out and found myself between the terrible posts. The full moon lighted the disfigured faces of the unfortunate creatures. . . . One of them was an old Tchuvash,[1] another a Russian peasant boy of about twenty, strong and healthy. I was shocked when I looked at the third and could not refrain from crying out: it was our servant Vanka—poor Vanka, who, in his foolishness, went over to Pugatchov. A black board was nailed over the gallows and had written on it in white letters: 'Thieves and rebels'. The oarsmen waited for me unconcerned, holding the raft with the hook. I stepped into the

[1] The Tchuvashes are a Mongolian tribe settled in Eastern Russia.— TRANSLATOR'S NOTE.

boat. The raft floated down the river. The gallows showed black in the dim night long after we passed it. At last it disappeared and my boat landed at the high and steep bank.

I paid the oarsmen handsomely. One of them took me to the foreman of the village by the landing-stage. We went into the hut together. When the foreman heard that I was asking for horses he spoke to me rather rudely, but my guide whispered something to him and his sternness immediately gave way to hurried obsequiousness. The troika was ready in a minute. I stepped into the carriage and told the driver to take me to our estate.

We galloped along the high road past the sleeping villages. The only thing I feared was being stopped on the way. My night meeting on the Volga proved the presence of rebels in the district, but it also proved strong counteraction on the part of the authorities. To meet all emergencies I had in my pocket the pass given me by Pugatchov and Colonel Zurin's order. But I did not meet any one, and, towards morning, I saw the river and the pine copse behind which lay our village. The driver whipped up the horses and in another quarter of an hour I drove into it. Our house stood at the other end. The horses were going at full speed. Suddenly in the middle of the village street the driver began pulling up.

'What is it?' I asked impatiently.

'A barrier, sir,' the driver answered, bringing with difficulty the fuming horses to a standstill.

Indeed, I saw a barrier fixed across the road and a watchman with a club. The man came up to me and, taking off his hat, asked for my passport.

'What does this mean?' I asked him. 'Why is this barrier here? Whom are you guarding?'

'Why, sir, we are in rebellion,' he answered, scratching himself.

'And where are your masters?' I asked, with a sinking heart.

'Where are our masters?' the peasant repeated. 'Master and mistress are in the granary.'

'In the granary?'

'Why, Andryushka, the foreman, put them in stocks, you see, and wants to take them to our father Tsar.'

'Good heavens! Lift the bar, you blockhead! What are you gaping at?'

The watchman did not move. I jumped out of the carriage, gave him a box on the ear, I am sorry to say, and lifted the bar myself.

The peasant looked at me in stupid perplexity. I took my seat in the carriage once more and told the driver to drive to the house as fast as he could. Two peasants, armed with clubs, were standing by the locked doors of the granary. The carriage drew up just in front of them I jumped out and rushed at them.

'Open the doors!' I said to them.

I must have looked formidable, for they threw down their clubs and ran away. I tried to knock the lock off the door or to pick it, but the doors were of oak and the huge lock was unbreakable. At that moment a young peasant came out of the servants' quarters and haughtily asked me how I dared to make a disturbance.

'Where is Andryushka, the foreman?' I shouted to him. 'Call him to me.'

'I am Andrey Afanasyitch and not Andryushka,' he answered proudly, with his arms akimbo. 'What do you want?'

By way of an answer, I seized him by the collar and dragging him to the granary doors told him to open them. He did not comply at once; but the 'fatherly' chastisement had due effect upon him. He pulled out the key and unlocked the granary. I rushed over the threshold and saw in a dark corner dimly lighted by a narrow skylight my father and mother. Their hands were tied and their feet were in stocks. I flew to embrace them and could not utter a word. They both looked at me with amazement: three years of military life had so altered me that they could not recognize me.

Suddenly I heard the sweet voice I knew: 'Pyotr Andreyitch! It's you?'

I turned round and saw Marya Ivanovna in another corner, also bound hand and foot. I was dumbfounded. My father looked at me in silence, not daring to believe his senses. His face lit up with joy.

'Welcome, Petrusha,' he said, pressing me to his heart. 'Thank God, we have lived to see you!'

My mother cried out and burst into tears.

'Petrusha, my darling!' she said. 'How has the Lord brought you here? Are you well?'

I hastened to cut with my sword the ropes that bound them and to take them out of their prison; but when I came to the door I found that it had been locked again.

'Andryushka, open!' I shouted.

'No fear!' the man answered from behind the door. 'You may as well sit here, too! We'll teach you how to be rowdy and drag the Tsar's officials by the collar!'

I began looking round the granary to see if there was some way of getting out.

'Don't trouble,' my father said to me. 'It's not my way to have granaries into which thieves could find a way.'

My mother, who had rejoiced a moment before at my coming, was overcome with despair at the thought that I, too, would have to perish with the rest of the family. But I was calmer now that I was with them and Marya Ivanovna. I had a sword and two pistols; I could withstand a siege. Zurin was due to arrive in the evening and would set us free. I told all this to my parents and Marya Ivanovna. They gave themselves up completely to the joy of our meeting, and several hours passed for us imperceptibly in expressions of affection and continual conversation.

'Well, Pyotr,' my father said, 'you have been foolish enough, and I was quite angry with you at the time. But it's no use remembering old scores. I hope that you have sown your wild oats and are reformed. I know that you have served as an honest officer should. I thank you; you have comforted me in my old age. If I owe my deliverance to you, life will be doubly pleasant to me.'

I kissed his hand with tears and gazed at Marya Ivanovna, who was so overjoyed at my presence that she seemed quite calm and happy.

About midday we heard extraordinary uproar and shouting. 'What does this mean?' my father said. 'Can it already be your Colonel?'

'Impossible,' I answered. 'He won't come before evening.

The noise increased. The alarm bell was rung. We heard men on horseback galloping across the yard. At that moment Savelyitch's grey head was thrust through the narrow opening cut in the wall and the poor old man said in a pitiful voice:

'Andrey Petrovitch! Pyotr Andreyitch, my dear! Marya Ivanovna! We are lost! The villains have come into the village. And do you know who has brought them, Pyotr Andreyitch? Shvabrin, Alexey Ivanitch, damnation take him!'

When Marya Ivanovna heard the hated name she clasped her hands and remained motionless.

'Listen!' I said to Savelyitch. 'Send someone on horseback to the ferry to meet the hussar regiment and to tell the Colonel of our danger.'

'But whom can I send, sir? All the boys have joined the rebels, and the horses have all been seized. Oh, dear! There they are in the yard! They are coming to the granary.'

As he said this, we heard several voices behind the door. I made a sign to my mother and Marya Ivanovna to move away into a corner, bared my sword, and leaned against the wall just by the door. My father took the pistols, cocked them both, and stood beside me. The lock rattled, the door opened, and Andryushka's head peeped in. I hit it with my sword and he fell, blocking the doorway. At the same moment my father fired the pistol. The crowd that had besieged us ran away, cursing. I dragged the wounded man across the threshold and closed the door.

The courtyard was full of armed men. I recognized Shvabrin among them.

'Don't be afraid,' I said to the women, 'there is hope. And don't you shoot any more, father. Let us save up the last shot.'

My mother was praying silently. Marya Ivanovna stood beside her, waiting with angelic calm for her fate to be decided. Threats, abuse, and curses were heard behind the door. I was standing in the same place ready to hit the first man who dared to show himself. Suddenly the villains subsided. I heard Shvabrin's voice calling me by name.

'I am here. What do you want?'

'Surrender, Grinyov; resistance is impossible. Have pity on your old people. Obstinacy will not save you. I shall get at you!'

'Try, traitor!'

'I am not going to put myself forward for nothing or waste my men; I will set the granary on fire and then we'll see what you will do, Belogorsky Don Quixote. Now it is time to have dinner. Meanwhile you can sit and think it over at leisure. Good-bye! Marya Ivanovna, I do not apologize to you: you are probably not feeling bored with your knight beside you in the dark.'

Shvabrin went away, leaving sentries at the door. We were silent, each of us thinking his own thoughts, not daring to express them to the others. I was picturing to myself all that Shvabrin was capable of doing in his malice. I hardly cared about myself. Must I confess it? Even my parents' fate terrified me less than Marya Ivanovna's. I knew that my mother was adored by the peasants and the house serfs. My father, too, was loved in spite of his sternness, for he was just and knew the true needs of the men he owned. Their rebellion was a delusion, a passing intoxication, and not the expression of their resentment. It was possible that my parents would be spared. But Marya Ivanovna? What did the dissolute and unscrupulous man hold in store for her? I did not dare to dwell upon this awful thought and would have killed her sooner (God forgive me!) than see her fall once more into the hands of the cruel enemy.

Another hour passed. Drunken men could be heard singing in the village. Our sentries envied them, and in their annoyance abused us, threatening us with tortures and death. We were waiting for Shvabrin to carry out his threat. At last there was great commotion in the courtyard and we heard Shvabrin's voice once more.

'Well, have you thought better of it? Do you surrender to me of your own will?'

No one answered.

After waiting a while, Shvabrin ordered his men to bring some straw. In a few minutes flames appeared, lighting the dim granary. Smoke began to rise from under the door.

Then Marya Ivanovna came up to me and, taking me by the hand, said in a low voice:

'Come, Pyotr Andreyitch, don't let both yourself and your parents perish because of me. Shvabrin will listen to me. Let me out!'

'Never!' I cried angrily. 'Do you know what awaits you?'

'I will not survive dishonour,' she answered calmly, 'but perhaps I shall save my deliverer and the family that has so generously sheltered a poor orphan. Good-bye, Andrey Petrovitch! Good-bye, Avdotya Vassilyevna! You have been more than benefactors to me. Bless me! Farewell to you, too, Pyotrr Andreyitch. Believe me that . . . that . . .'

She burst into tears and buried her face in her hands. . . . I was beside myself. My mother was weeping.

'Stop this nonsense, Marya Ivanovna,' said my father. 'Who ever would dream of letting you go alone to the brigands? Sit here and keep quiet. If we must die, we may as well die together. Listen! What is he saying now?'

'Do you surrender?' Shvabrin shouted. 'You see you will be roasted in another five minutes.'

'We won't surrender, you villain!' my father answered firmly.

His vigorous, deeply lined face was wonderfully animated. His eyes sparkled under the grey eyebrows. Turning to me, he said: 'Now's the time!'

He opened the door. The flames rushed in and rose up to the beams whose chinks were stuffed with dry moss. My father fired the pistol, stepped over the burning threshold and shouted 'Follow me!' I took my mother and Marya Ivanovna by the hands and quickly led them out. Shvabrin, shot through by my father's feeble hand, was lying by the threshold. The crowd of brigands who had rushed away at our sudden sally took courage and began closing in upon us. I succeeded in dealing a few more blows; but a well aimed brick hit me right on the chest. I fell down and lost consciousness for a few moments; I was surrounded and disarmed. Coming to myself I saw Shvabrin sitting on the blood-stained grass, with all our family standing before him.

I was supported under the arms. A crowd of peasants, Cossacks, and Bashkirs hemmed us in. Shvabrin was terribly pale. He was pressing one hand to his wounded side. His face expressed malice and pain. He slowly raised his head, glanced at me and said, in a weak, hardly audible voice: •

'Hang him . . . and all of them . . . except her.'

The crowd surrounded us at once and dragged us to the gates. But suddenly they left us and scampered away: Zurin and a whole squadron of hussars, with bared swords, rode into the courtyard.

The rebels were flying as fast as they could. The hussars pursued them, striking right and left with their swords and taking prisoners. Zurin jumped off his horse, bowed to my father and mother, and warmly clasped me by the hand.

'I have come just in time,' he said to me. 'Ah, and here is your betrothed!'

Marya Ivanovna flushed crimson. My father went up to him and thanked him calmly, though he was obviously touched. My mother embraced him, calling him an angel-deliverer.

'Welcome to our home!' my father said to him, and led him towards the house.

Zurin stopped as he passed Shvabrin.

'Who is this?' he asked, looking at the wounded man.

'It is the leader of the gang,' my father answered, with a certain pride that betokened an old soldier. 'God has helped my feeble hand to punish the young villain and to avenge the blood of my son.'

'It is Shvabrin,' I said to Zurin.

'Shvabrin! I am very glad. Hussars, take him! Tell the leech to dress his wound and to take the utmost care of him. Shvabrin must certainly be sent to the Kazan Secret Commission. He is one of the chief criminals and his evidence may be of great importance. . . .'

Shvabrin wearily opened his eyes. His face expressed nothing but physical pain. The hussars carried him away on an outspread cloak.

We went into the house. I looked about me with a tremor, remembering the years of my childhood. Nothing had changed in the house, everything was in its usual place: Shvabrin had not allowed it to be pillaged, preserving in his very degradation an unconscious aversion to base cupidity.

The servants came into the hall. They had taken no part in the rebellion and were genuinely glad of our deliverance. Savelyitch was triumphant. It must be mentioned that during the alarm produced by the brigands' arrival he ran to the stables where Shvabrin's horse had been put, saddled it, led it out quietly and, unnoticed in the confusion, galloped towards the ferry. He met the regiment having a rest this side of the Volga. When Zurin heard from him of our danger, he ordered his men to mount, cried 'Off! Off! Gallop!' and, thank God, arrived in time.

Zurin insisted that the head of Andryushka the foreman should be exposed for a few hours at the top of a pole by the tavern.

The hussars returned from their pursuit bringing several prisoners with them. They were locked in the same granary where we had endured our memorable siege. We all went to our rooms. The old people needed a rest. As I had not slept the whole night, I flung myself on the bed and dropped fast asleep. Zurin went to make his arrangements.

In the evening we all met round the samovar in the drawing-room, talking gaily of the past danger. Marya Ivanovna poured out the tea. I sat down beside her and devoted myself entirely to her. My parents seemed to look with favour upon the tenderness of our relations. That evening lives in my memory to this day. I was happy, completely happy—and are there many such moments in poor human life?

The following day my father was told that the peasants had come to ask his pardon. My father went out on to the steps to talk to them. When the peasants saw him they knelt down.

'Well, you silly fools,' he said to them, 'whatever did you rebel for?'

'We are sorry, master,' they answered like one man.

'Sorry, are you? They get into mischief and then they are sorry! I forgive you for the sake of our family joy— God has allowed me to see my son, Pyotr Andreyitch, again. So be it, a sin confessed is a sin forgiven.'

'We did wrong; of course we did.'

'God has sent fine weather. It is time for haymaking; and what have you been doing for the last three days, you fools? Foreman! send every one to make hay; and mind that by St. John's Day all the hay is in stacks, you red-haired rascal! Begone!'

The peasants bowed and went to work as though nothing had happened.

Shvabrin's wound was not mortal. He was sent under escort to Kazan. I saw from the window how they laid him in the cart. Our eyes met. He bent his head and I made haste to move away from the window; I was afraid of looking as though I were triumphing over a humiliated and unhappy enemy.

Zurin had to go on farther. I decided to join him, in spite of my desire to spend a few more days with my family. On the eve of the march I came to my parents and, in accordance with the custom of the time, bowed down to the ground before them, asking their blessing on my marriage with Marya Ivanovna. The old people lifted me up, and with joyous tears, gave their consent. I brought Marya Ivanovna, pale and trembling, to them. They blessed us. I will not attempt to describe what I was feeling. Those who have been in my position will understand; as to those who have not, I can only pity them and advise them, while there is still time, to fall in love and receive their parents' blessing.

The following day our regiment was ready. Zurin took leave of our family. We were all certain that the military operations would soon be over. I was hoping to be married in another month's time. Marya Ivanovna kissed me in front of all as she said good-bye. I took my seat in the carriage. Savelyitch followed me again and the regiment marched off. As long as I could see it I looked back at the country house that I was leaving once more. A gloomy foreboding tormented me. Something seemed to whisper to me that my misfortunes were not over yet. My heart felt that a storm was ahead.

I will not describe our campaign and the end of the Pugatchov war. We passed through villages pillaged by Pugatchov and could not help taking from the poor inhabitants what the rebels had left them.

The people did not know whom to obey. There was no lawful authority. The landowners were hiding in the forests. Bands of brigands were ransacking the country. The chiefs of separate detachments sent in pursuit of Pugatchov, who was by then retreating towards Astrakhan, arbitrarily punished the guilty and the innocent. The provinces where the conflagration had raged were in a terrible state. God save us from seeing a Russian revolt, meaningless and merciless! Those who are plotting impossible violent changes in Russia are either young and do not know our people, or are hard-hearted men who do not care a straw either about their own lives or those of other people.

Pugatchov was in retreat, pursued by Ivan Ivanovitch Michelson. Soon after we learned that he was utterly defeated. At last Zurin heard that he had been captured and at the same time received an order to halt. The war was over! I could go to my parents at last! The thought of embracing them and of seeing Marya Ivanovna, of whom I had had no news, delighted me. I danced with joy like a child. Zurin laughed and said, shrugging his shoulders, 'No, you'll come to a bad end! You will be married and done for!'

And yet a strange feeling poisoned my joy: I could not help being troubled at the thought of the villain smeared with the blood of so many innocent victims and now awaiting his puhishment. 'Why didn't he fall on a bayonet? or get hit with a cannon-ball?' I thought with vexation. 'He could not have done anything better.' What will you have? I could not think of Pugatchov without remembering how he had spared me at one of the awful moments of my life and saved my betrothed from the vile Shvabrin's hands.

Zurin gave me leave of absence. In a few days I was to be once more with my family and see my Marya Ivanovna. Suddenly an unexpected storm burst upon me.

On the day of my departure, at the very minute when I was to go, Zurin came into my room with a letter in his hand, looking very much troubled. My heart sank. I was frightened without knowing why. He sent out my orderly and said he had something to tell me.

'What is it?' I asked anxiously.

'Something rather unpleasant,' he answered, giving me the letter. 'Read what I have just received.'

I began reading it: it was a secret order to all commanding officers to arrest me wherever they might find me and to send me at once under escort to Kazan, to the Committee of Inquiry into the Pugatchov rising.

The letter almost dropped out of my hands.

'There is nothing for it,' Zurin said; 'my duty is to obey the order. Probably the news of your friendly journeys with Pugatchov has reached the authorities. I hope it will not have any consequences and that you will clear yourself before the Committee. Go, and don't be down-hearted.'

My conscience was clear; I was not afraid of the trial, but the thought of putting off perhaps for several months the sweet moment of reunion, terrified me. The cart was ready. Zurin bade me a friendly good-bye. I stepped into the cart. Two hussars, with bare swords, sat down beside me and we drove along the high road.

CHAPTER XIV

THE TRIAL

Popular rumour is like a sea-wave.

A Proverb.

I WAS certain it was all due to my leaving Orenburg without permission. I could easily justify myself: sallying out against the enemy had never been prohibited and was, indeed, encouraged in every way. I might be accused of too great rashness, but not of disobedience. My friendly relations with Pugatchov, however, could be proved by a number of witnesses and must have seemed highly suspicious, to say the least of it. Throughout the journey I kept thinking of the questions I might be asked and pondering my answers; I decided to tell the plain truth at the trial, believing that this was the simplest and, at the same time, the most certain way of justifying myself.

I arrived at Kazan; it had been devastated and burnt down. Instead of houses there were heaps of cinders in the streets and remnants of charred walls without roofs or windows. Such was the trail left by Pugatchov! I was brought to the fortress that had remained intact in the midst of the burnt city. The hussars passed me on to the officer in charge. He called for the blacksmith. Shackles were put on my feet and soldered together. Then I was taken to the prison and left alone in the dark and narrow cell with nothing in it but bare walls and a window with iron bars.

Such a beginning boded nothing good. I did not, however, lose either hope or courage. I had recourse to the comfort of all the sorrowful and, having tasted for the first time the sweetness of prayer poured out from a pure but bleeding heart, dropped calmly asleep without caring what would happen to me.

The next morning the warder woke me up, saying I was wanted at the Committee. Two soldiers took me across the yard to the Commandant's house; they stopped in the entry and let me go into the inner room by myself.

I walked into a rather large room. Two men were sitting at a table covered with papers: an elderly general who looked cold and forbidding and a young captain of the Guards, a good-looking man of about twenty-eight, with a pleasant and easy manner. A secretary, with a pen behind his ear, sat at a separate table, bending over the paper in readiness to write down my evidence. The examination began. I was asked my name and rank. The General asked whether I was the son of Andrey Petrovitch Grinyov. When I said I was he remarked severely:

'It is a pity that so estimable a man has such an unworthy son!'

I calmly answered that whatever the accusation against me might be, I hoped to clear myself by candidly telling the truth. The General did not like my confidence.

'You are sharp, brother,' he said to me, frowning; 'but we have seen cleverer ones than you!'

Then the young man asked me:

'On what occasion and at what time did you enter Pugatchov's service, and on what commissions did he employ you?'

I answered, with indignation, that as an officer and a gentleman I could not possibly have entered Pugatchov's service or have carried out any commissions of his.

'How was it, then,' my questioner continued, 'that an officer and a gentleman was alone spared by the Pretender, while all his comrades were villainously murdered? How was it that this same officer and gentleman feasted with the rebels, as their friend, and accepted presents from the villain—a sheepskin coat, a horse, and fifty copecks in money? How had such a strange friendship arisen and what could it be based upon except treason or, at any rate, upon base and vile cowardice?'

I was deeply offended by the officer's words and warmly began my defence. I told them how I had first met Pugatchov in the steppe in the snowstorm, and how he recognized and spared me at the taking of the Belogorsky fortress. I admitted that I had not scrupled to accept from the Pretender the horse and the sheepskin coat, but said that I had defended the Belogorsky fortress against him to the last extremity. At last I referred them to my General who could testify to my zealous service during the perilous Orenburg siege.

The stern old man took an unsealed letter from the table and began reading it aloud:

'With regard to your Excellency's inquiry concerning Ensign Grinyov, said to be involved in the present insurrection and to have had relations with the villain, contrary to the military law and to our oath of allegiance, I have the honour to report as follows: The said Ensign Grinyov served at Orenburg from the beginning of October 1773 to 24 February 1774, upon which date he left the city and returned no more to serve under my command. I have heard from refugees that he had been in Pugatchov's camp and went with him to the Belogorsky fortress, where he had served before; as to his conduct, I can . . .'

At this point he interrupted his reading and said to me sternly: 'What can you say for yourself now?'

I wanted to go on as I had begun and to explain my connection with Marya Ivanovna as candidly as all the rest, but I suddenly felt an overwhelming repulsion. It occurred to me that if I mentioned her, she would be summoned by the Committee; and I was so overcome at the awful thought of connecting her name with the vile slanders of the villains, and of her being confronted with them, that I became confused and hesitated.

My judges, who seemed to have been listening to me with favour, were once more prejudiced against me by my confusion. The officer of the Guards asked that I should be faced with the chief informer. The General gave word that

yesterday's villain should be brought in. I turned to the
door with interest, waiting for the appearance of my accuser.
A few minutes later there was a rattle of chains, the door
opened, and Shvabrin walked in. I was surprised at the
change in him. He was terribly pale and thin. His hair
that had a short time ago been black as pitch was now white;
his long beard was unkempt. He repeated his accusations
in a weak, but confident voice. According to him I had
been sent by Pugatchov to Orenburg as a spy; under the
pretext of sallies, I had come out every day to give him
written news of all that was happening in the town; at last
I had openly joined the Pretender, had driven with him
from fortress to fortress, doing my utmost to ruin my fellow-
traitors so as to occupy their posts, and had taken presents
from the Pretender. I heard him out in silence and was
pleased with one thing only: Marya Ivanovna's name had
not been uttered by the base villain, either because his
vanity suffered at the thought of one who had scorned him,
or because there lingered in his heart a spark of the same
feeling which made me keep silent about her. In any case,
the name of the Belogorsky Commandant's daughter was
not mentioned before the Committee. I was more determined than ever not to bring it up, and when the judges
asked me how I could disprove Shvabrin's accusations,
I answered that I adhered to my original explanation and
had nothing more to say in my defence. The General gave
word for us to be led away. We went out together. I
calmly looked at Shvabrin, but did not say a word to him.
He gave a malignant smile and, lifting his chains, quickened
his pace and left me behind. I was taken back to prison and
not called for examination any more.

I have not witnessed the subsequent events of which
I must inform the reader; but I had them told me so often
that the least details are engraved on my memory and I feel
as though I had been invisibly present.

The news of my arrest was a shock to my family. Marya
Ivanovna had told my parents of my strange acquaintance
with Pugatchov so simply that, so far from being troubled
about it, they often laughed at it with whole-hearted amusement. My father refused to believe that I could have been
implicated in vile rebellion the aim of which was to over-

throw the throne and exterminate the gentry. He closely questioned Savelyitch. The old man did not conceal the fact that I had been to see Pugatchov and that the villain had been kind to me; but he swore that he had not heard of any treason. My parents were reassured and waited impatiently for favourable news. Marya Ivanovna was very much alarmed but said nothing, for she was extremely modest and prudent.

Several weeks passed. . . . Suddenly my father received a letter from our relative in Petersburg, Prince B. The Prince wrote about me. After beginning in the usual way he went on to say that, unfortunately, the suspicions about my complicity in the rebels' designs proved to be only too true and that I should have been put to death as an example to others had not the Empress, in consideration of my father's merits and advanced age, decided to spare the criminal son and commuted the shameful death-penalty to a mere exile for life in a remote part of Siberia.

This unexpected blow very nearly killed my father. He lost his habitual self-control, and his grief, usually silent, found expression in bitter complaints.

'What!' he repeated, beside himself. 'My son is an accomplice of Pugatchov's! Merciful heavens, what have I lived to see! The Empress reprieves him! Does that make it any better for me? It's not the death-penalty that is terrible. My great-grandfather died on the scaffold for what was to him a matter of conscience; my father suffered, together with Volynsky [1] and Hrushchov.[1] But for a gentleman to betray his oath of allegiance and join brigands, murderers, and runaway serfs! Shame and disrgace to our name!'

Terrified by his despair, my mother did not dare to weep in his presence and tried to cheer him by talking of the uncertainty of rumour and the small faith to be attached to people's opinions. My father was inconsolable.

Marya Ivanovna suffered most. She was certain that I could have cleared myself if I had chosen to do so, and, guessing the truth, considered herself the cause of my misfortune. She concealed her tears and sorrow from every

---

[1] Leaders of the Russian party against Büren, the German favourite of the Empress Anna.—TRANSLATOR'S NOTE.

one, but was continually thinking of the means to save me.

One evening my father was sitting on the sofa turning over the leaves of the *Court Calendar*, but his thoughts were far away and the reading did not have its usual effect upon him. He was whistling an old march. My mother was knitting a woollen coat in silence, and now and again a tear dropped on her work. Suddenly Marya Ivanovna, who sat by her doing needlework, said that it was necessary for her to go to Petersburg, and asked for the means of travelling there. My mother was very much grieved.

'What do you want in Petersburg?' she said. 'Can it be that you, too, want to leave us, Marya Ivanovna?'

Marya Ivanovna answered that her whole future depended upon this journey and that she was going to seek the help and protection of influential people, as the daughter of a man who had suffered for his loyalty.

My father bent his head: every word that reminded him of his son's alleged crime pained him and seemed to him a bitter reproach.

'Go, my dear,' he said to her, with a sigh. 'We don't want to stand in the way of your happiness. God grant you may have a good man for a husband and not a disgraced traitor.'

He got up and walked out of the room.

Left alone with my mother, Marya Ivanovna partly explained her plan to her. My mother embraced her with tears and prayed for the success of her undertaking. Marya Ivanovna was made ready for the journey, and a few days later she set off with the faithful Palasha and the faithful Savelyitch, who in his enforced parting from me comforted himself with the thought that, at least, he was serving my betrothed.

Marya Ivanovna safely arrived at Sofia and, hearing that the Court was at Tsarkoe Selo, decided to stop there. At the posting-station, a tiny recess behind the partition was assigned to her. The station-master's wife immediately got into conversation with her, said that she was the niece of the man who heated the stoves at the Palace, and initiated her into the mysteries of Court life. She told her at what time the Empress woke up in the morning, took coffee, went for walks; what courtiers were with her at the time; what she had said at dinner the day before; whom she had received in the evening. In short, Anna Vlassyevna's conversation was as good as several pages of historical memoirs and would have been precious for posterity. Marya Ivanovna listened to her attentively. They went into the gardens. Anna Vlassyevna told the history of every avenue and every bridge, and they returned to the station after a long walk, much pleased with each other.

Marya Ivanovna woke up early the next morning, dressed, and slipped out into the gardens. It was a beautiful morning; the sun was lighting the tops of the lime-trees that had already turned yellow under the fresh breath of autumn. The broad lake, without a ripple on it, glittered in the sunlight. The stately swans, just awake, came sailing out from under the bushes that covered the banks. Marya Ivanovna walked along a beautiful meadow where a monument had just been put up in honour of Count Rumyantsev's recent victories. Suddenly a little white dog of English breed ran towards her, barking. Marya Ivanovna was frightened and stood still. At that moment she heard a woman's pleasant voice.

'Don't be afraid, he won't bite.'

And Marya Ivanovna saw a lady sitting on a bench opposite the monument. Marya Ivanovna sat down at the other end of the bench. The lady was looking at her attentively; Marya Ivanovna, in her turn, cast several sidelong glances at her and succeeded in examining her from head to foot. She was wearing a white morning dress, a night-cap, and a Russian jacket. She seemed to be about forty. Her plump and rosy face wore an expression of calm and dignity, her blue eyes and slight smile had an indescribable charm. The lady was the first to break the silence.

'I expect you are a stranger here?' she asked.

'Yes, madam; I came from the country only yesterday.'

'Have you come with your relatives?'

'No, madam; I have come alone.'

'Alone! But you are so young. . . .'

'I have neither father nor mother.'

'You are here on business, of course?'

'Yes, madam. I have come to present a petition to the Empress.'

'You are an orphan; I suppose you are complaining of some wrong or injustice?'

'No, madam. I have come to ask for mercy, not justice.'

'Allow me to ask, What is your name?'

'I am Captain Mironov's daughter.'

'Captain Mironov's! The man who was Commandant in one of the Orenburg fortresses?'

'Yes, madam.'

The lady was evidently touched.

'Excuse me,' she said, still more kindly, 'for interfering in your affairs, but I go to Court sometimes; tell me what your petition is and perhaps I may be able to help you.'

Marya Ivanovna got up and respectfully thanked her.

Everything in the unknown lady instinctively attracted her and inspired her with confidence. Marya Ivanovna took a folded paper out of her pocket and gave it to the lady who began reading it to herself.

At first she read with an attentive and kindly air, but suddenly her expression changed, and Marya Ivanovna, who was watching her every movement, was frightened at the stern look on her face, so calm and pleasant a moment before.

'You are interceding for Grinyov?' the lady said, coldly. 'The Empress cannot forgive him. He joined the Pretender not from ignorance and credulity, but as a dangerous and immoral scoundrel.'

'Oh, it isn't true!' Marya Ivanovna cried.

'How, it isn't true?' the lady repeated, flushing crimson.

'It isn't true; I swear to God it isn't! I know all about it; I will tell you everything. It was solely for my sake that he went through it all. And if he hasn't cleared himself before the judges, it was only because he did not want to implicate me.'

And she told, with great warmth, all that is already known to the reader.

The lady listened to her attentively.

'Where have you put up?' she asked, and hearing that it was at Anna Vlassyevna's, said, with a smile: 'Ah, I know. Good-bye, do not tell any one of our meeting. I hope you will not have long to wait for an answer to your letter.'

With these words, she rose and went into a covered avenue and Marya Ivanovna, full of a joyous hope, returned to Anna Vlassyevna's.

Her landlady chid her for her early walk which, she said, was not good for a young girl's health as it was autumn. She brought the samovar and had just begun, over a cup of tea, her endless stories about the Court, when suddenly a Court carriage stopped at the door and a footman from the Palace came into the room, saying that the Empress invited Miss Mironov to her presence.

Anna Vlassyevna was surprised and flurried.

'Dear me!' she cried. 'The Empress sends for you to come to the Palace! How has she heard of you? And how are you going to appear before the Empress, my dear? I expect you know nothing about Court manners. . . . Hadn't I better go with you? I could warn you about some things, at any rate. And how can you go in your travelling dress? Hadn't we better send to the midwife for her yellow gown?'

The footman announced that it was the Empress's pleasure that Marya Ivanovna should come alone and as she was. There was nothing else for it; Marya Ivanovna stepped into the carriage and drove to the Palace accompanied by Anna Vlassyevna's admonitions and blessings.

Marya Ivanovna felt that our fate was going to be decided; her heart was throbbing. A few minutes later the carriage stopped at the Palace. Marya Ivanovna walked up the stairs, trembling. The doors were flung wide open before her. She walked through a number of deserted, luxuriously furnished rooms; the footman was pointing out the way. At last, coming to a closed door, he said he would go in and announce her, and left her alone.

The thought of seeing the Empress face to face so terrified her that she could hardly keep on her feet. In another minute the door opened and she walked into the Empress's dressing-room.

The Empress was seated in front of her dressing-table. Several courtiers were standing round her, but they respectfully made way for Marya Ivanovna. The Empress turned to her kindly and Marya Ivanovna recognized her as the lady to whom she had been talking so freely not many minutes before.   The Empress called her to her side and said, with a smile:

'I am glad that I have been able to keep my promise to you, and to grant your request.   Your case is settled.   I am convinced that your betrothed is innocent.   Here is a letter which please take yourself to your future father-in-law.'

Marya Ivanovna took the letter with a trembling hand and fell, weeping, at the feet of the Empress, who lifted her up, kissed her and engaged her in conversation.

'I know you are not rich,' she said, 'but I am in debt to Captain Mironov's daughter.   Do not worry about the future.   I will provide for you.'

After saying many kind things to the poor orphan, the Empress dismissed her.   Marya Ivanovna was driven back in the same Court carriage.   Anna Vlassyevna, who had been eagerly awaiting her return, bombarded her with questions, to which Marya Ivanovna answered rather vaguely. Anna Vlassyevna was disappointed at her remembering so little, but ascribed it to provincial shyness and generously excused her.   Marya Ivanovna went back to the country that same day, without troubling to have a look at Petersburg. . . .

.   .   .   .   .   .

The memoirs of Pyotr Andreyitch Grinyov end at this point.   It is known from the family tradition that he was released from confinement at the end of 1774, at the express order of the Empress; that he was present at the execution of Pugatchov, who recognized him in the crowd and nodded to him a minute before his lifeless, bleeding head was held up before the people.   Soon after, Pyotr Andreyitch married Marya Ivanovna.   Their descendants are flourishing in the province of Simbirsk.   Thirty miles from N. there is an estate belonging to ten owners.   In one of the lodges a letter written by Catherine II may be seen in a frame under glass. It is addressed to Pyotr Andreyitch's father; it affirms the innocence of his son and praises the heart and intelligence of Captain Mironov's daughter.

Pyotr Andreyitch Grinyov's memoirs have been given to me by one of his grandchildren who had heard that I was engaged upon a work dealing with the period described by his grandfather. With the relatives' consent, I have decided to publish it separately, prefixing a suitable epigraph to each chapter and taking the liberty to change some of the proper names.

THE EDITOR.

1836.

THE QUEEN OF SPADES

The Queen of Spades means secret hostility.

A New Book on Fortune-telling.

CHAPTER I

In the cold, rain, and sleet
They together would meet
To play.
Lord, forgive them their sin:
Gambling, late to win
They 'd stay.
They won and they lost,
And put down the cost
In chalk.
So on cold autumn days
They wasted no time
In talk.

THEY were playing cards at the house of Narumov, an officer in the Horse Guards. The long winter night passed imperceptibly; it was after four in the morning when they sat down to supper. Those who had won enjoyed their food; the others sat absent-mindedly with empty plates before them. But champagne appeared, the conversation grew livelier, and every one took part in it.

'How have you been doing, Surin?' Narumov asked.

'Losing, as usual. I must confess, I have no luck: I play cautiously, never get excited, never lose my head, and yet I go on losing!'

'And you 've never been carried away? Never risk a high stake? I marvel at your self-control.'

'But look at Hermann!' said one of the visitors, pointing to a young engineer; 'he has never held a card in his hands, never staked a penny on one, and yet he sits with us till five o'clock in the morning watching us play.'

'I am very much interested in cards,' Hermann said, 'but I am not in a position to sacrifice the essential in the hope of acquiring the superfluous.'

'Hermann is a German; he is prudent—that's all!'

Tomsky remarked. 'But the person I really can't understand is my grandmother, Countess Anna Fedorovna.'

'How's that?' the guests cried.

'I cannot conceive why my grandmother does not play,' Tomsky went on.

'But surely there's nothing wonderful in an old lady of eighty not gambling?' Narumov said.

'So you know nothing about her?'

'No! We certainly don't.'

'Oh, then listen! I must tell you that some sixty years ago my grandmother went to Paris and was very popular there.   People ran after her to catch a glimpse of *la Vénus moscovite*; Richelieu paid his addresses to her, and grandmamma assures me that he very nearly shot himself through her cruelty.   In those days ladies used to play faro.   One day at the court she lost a very big sum to the Duke of Orleans.   When she came home she told her husband about her loss while untying her farthingale, and taking off her beauty spots, and ordered him to pay her debt.   My grandfather, so far as I remember, was a kind of butler to my grandmother.   He was terrified of her; and yet when he heard of such a fearful debt he lost his temper, fetched the bills they owed and, proving to her that they had spent half a million in six months, and had neither their Moscow nor their Saratov estate near Paris, flatly refused to pay.   Grandmamma gave him a box on the ear, and went to bed alone as a sign of her displeasure.   The following morning she sent for her husband, hoping that these homely measures had had an effect on him, but found him as firm as ever.   For the first time in her life she went so far as to reason with him and explain; she tried to put him to shame, pointing out with condescension that there were debts and debts, and that there was a difference between a prince and a coach-builder.   But it wasn't a bit of good! Grandpapa was in open revolt.   'No'—and that was the end of it.   Grandmamma did not know what to do.   She counted among her intimate friends a very remarkable man.   You have heard of Count St. Germain, of whom they tell so many marvels.   You know that he claimed to have lived for centuries, to have invented the elixir of life and the philosopher's stone, and so on.   People laughed at him as a charlatan, and Casanova says in his *Memoirs* that he was a spy; but in spite of his mysterious ways St. Germain looked a perfect gentleman, and had a very pleasant manner. Grandmamma is still devoted to him, and gets angry if any one speaks of him with disrespect. Grandmamma knew that St. Germain had plenty of money. She decided to appeal to him, and wrote a note asking him to come to her at once. The eccentric old man came immediately, and found her in terrible distress. She described in the blackest colours her husband's barbarity, and said at last that she rested all her hopes on his friendship and kindness. St. Germain pondered. 'I could provide you with that sum,' he said, 'but I know you wouldn't be happy till you paid me, and I don't like to cause you fresh worry. There's another way: you can win it back.' 'But, dear Count,' grandmamma replied, 'I tell you I have no money at all.' 'It's not a case of money,' St. Germain replied; 'please listen to what I'm going to tell you.' And he revealed to her a secret which every one of us would give a great deal to know. . . .'

The young gamblers redoubled their attention. Tomsky lighted his pipe, and taking a pull at it, continued: 'That very evening grandmamma appeared at Versailles, at the *jeu de la reine*. The Duke of Orleans kept the bank; grandmamma made a slight apology for not having brought the money, and telling some little story to excuse herself, began playing against him. She selected three cards and played them one after the other: all three won, and she retrieved her loss completely.'

'Accident!' said one of the guests.

'A fairy tale,' remarked Hermann.

'Marked cards, perhaps,' a third chimed in.

'I don't think so,' Tomsky replied impressively.

'What!' said Narumov, 'you have a grandmother who can guess three cards in succession and you haven't learnt her secret yet?'

'Learnt it, indeed!' Tomsky replied; 'she had four sons, one of whom was my father; all four were desperate gamblers, but she did not reveal her secret to one of them, though it wouldn't have been a bad thing for them, or even for me. But this is what my Uncle Count Ivan Ilyitch told me, assuring me on his honour that it was true. Tchaplitsky, you know, the one who died a beggar after squandering millions, as a young man once lost three hundred thousand, to Zoritch if I remember rightly. He was in despair. Grandmamma was always severe on young men's follies, but somehow she took pity on Tchaplitsky. She gave him three cards, which he was to play one after another, and made him promise on his honour never to play again. Tchaplitsky went to Zoritch's; they sat down to play. Tchaplitsky staked fifty thousand on his first card and won; doubled his stake and won; did the same again, won back his loss, and had something left him into the bargain. . . .'

'I say, it's time to go to bed; it's a quarter to six.' It was daylight indeed. The young men emptied their glasses and went home.

CHAPTER II

'Il paraît que monsieur est décidément pour les suivantes.'
'Que voulez-vous, madame? Elles sont plus fraîches.'
A Society Conversation.

THE old Countess X. was sitting before a mirror in her dressing-room. Three maids were standing round her. One held a pot of rouge, another a box of hairpins, and the third a tall cap with flame-coloured ribbons. The Countess had not the slightest pretension to beauty—all that had faded long ago—but she preserved all the habits of her youth, followed strictly the fashions of the seventies, and dressed as slowly and carefully as sixty years before. A young lady whom she had brought up from a child was sitting at an embroidery frame by the window.

'Good morning, grand'maman,' said a young officer, coming in. 'Bon jour, mademoiselle Lise. Grand'maman, I have a favour to ask of you.'

'What is it, Paul?'

'Allow me to introduce to you a friend of mine and to bring him to your ball on Friday.'

'Bring him straight to the ball and introduce him to me then. Were you at the N.s' last night?'

'Of course! It was very enjoyable; we danced till five in the morning. Miss Yeletsky looked perfectly charming.'

'Come, my dear! What do you see in her? She isn't a patch on her grandmother, Princess Darya Petrovna! By the way, I expect Darya Petrovna is looking much older, isn't she?'

'How do you mean, looking much older?' Tomsky answered absent-mindedly. 'She's been dead for the last seven years.'

The young lady raised her head and made a sign to the young man. He bit his lip, recalling that they concealed from the Countess the deaths of her old friends. But the Countess heard the news with the utmost indifference.

'Dead! I didn't know,' she said. 'We were maids of honour together, and as we were being presented, the Empress . . .'

And for the hundredth time the Countess told the anecdote to her grandson.

'Well, Paul, now help me to get up,' she said afterwards. 'Lizanka, where is my snuff-box?'

And the Countess went behind the screen with her maids to finish dressing. Tomsky was left with the young lady.

'Whom is it you want to introduce?' Lizaveta Ivanovna asked quietly.

'Narumov. Do you know him?'

'No! Is he in the army?'

'Yes.'

'In the Engineers?'

'No, he is in the Horse Guards. What made you think he was in the Engineers?'

The young lady laughed and made no answer.

'Paul!' the Countess called from behind the screen. 'Send me some new novel, only please not a modern one.'

'How do you mean, grand'maman?'

'I mean, a novel in which the hero does not strangle his father or mother and there are no drowned corpses. I am terribly afraid of them.'

'There are no such novels nowadays. But perhaps you would like a Russian novel?'

'Are there any Russian novels? Send me one, my dear, please do!'

'Excuse me, grand'maman, I am in a hurry. . . . Good-bye, Lizaveta Ivanovna! What made you think, then, that Narumov was in the Engineers?'

And Tomsky went away.

Lizaveta Ivanovna was left alone; she abandoned her work and looked out of the window. Soon a young officer came from behind a corner-house on the other side of the road. Colour came into her cheeks; she took up her work again, bending low over the embroidery. At that moment the Countess came in, fully dressed.

'Order the carriage, Lizanka,' she said, 'and let us go for a drive.'

Liza got up from her embroidery frame and began putting away her work.

'What's the matter with you, my dear? Are you deaf?' the Countess shouted. 'Be quick and order the carriage.'

'Certainly,' the young lady answered quietly, and ran to the hall.

A servant came in, and gave the Countess a parcel of books from Prince Pavel Alexandrovitch.

'Good, thank him,' the Countess said. 'Lizanka, Lizanka, where are you off to?'

'To dress.'

'There's plenty of time, my dear. Stay here. Open the first volume and read to me.'

The girl took the book and read a few lines.

'Louder!' the Countess said. 'What's the matter with you, my dear? Have you lost your voice, or what? Wait a minute . . . give me the footstool. Bring it nearer. . . . Well?'

Lizaveta Ivanovna read two more pages. The Countess yawned.

'Leave off,' she said. 'What rubbish it is! Send the books back to Prince Pavel with my thanks. . . . What about the carriage?'

'The carriage is ready,' said Lizaveta Ivanovna, peeping out into the street.

'And why aren't you dressed?' the Countess said. 'One always has to wait for you. It's too much of a good thing, my dear.'

Liza ran to her room. Two minutes had not passed when the Countess began ringing violently. Three maids rushed in at one door and a footman at the other.

'Why don't you come when you are called?' the Countess said to them. 'Tell Lizaveta Ivanovna that I am waiting.'

Lizaveta Ivanovna came in, wearing a hat and a pelisse.

'At last, my dear!' the Countess said. 'What finery? What is it for? For whose benefit? And what is the weather like? I believe it's windy.'

'No, madam,' the footman replied. 'There's no wind at all.'

'You say anything that comes into your head! Open the window! I thought so: there's a wind, and a very cold wind, too! Unharness the horses! Lizanka, we aren't going: you needn't have dressed after all.'

'And this is my life!' Lizaveta Ivanovna thought.

Indeed, she had a wretched time of it. Bitter is the bread of others, said Dante, and hard the steps of another man's house; and who should know the bitterness of dependence better than a poor orphan brought up by a rich and worldly old woman? The Countess certainly was not bad-hearted, but she was capricious as a woman spoiled by society, stingy, and sunk into cold egoism like all old people who have done with love and are out of touch with the life around them. She took part in all the vanities of the fashionable world; she went to dances, where she sat in a corner, rouged and dressed up in the ancient fashion like some hideous but indispensable ornament of the ball-room. The guests, on arriving, went up to her with low bows, as though carrying out an old-established rite, and after that no one took any notice of her. She received the whole town at her house, observing a strict etiquette and not recognizing any of her guests. Her numerous house-serfs, grown fat and grey in her entrance hall and the maids' room, did what they liked, and vied with one another in robbing the decrepit old woman. Lizaveta Ivanovna was the domestic martyr. She poured out tea and was reprimanded for wasting sugar; she read novels aloud, and was blamed for all the author's mistakes; she accompanied the Countess on her drives—and was responsible for the state of the roads and the weather. She was supposed to receive a salary, which was never paid her in full, and yet she was expected to be as well dressed as every one else—that is, as the very few. She played a most pitiable part in society. Every one knew her and no one noticed her; at balls she danced only when someone was short of a partner, and ladies took her arm each time they wanted to go to the cloak-room to put something right in their attire. She was proud, she keenly felt her position and looked about her waiting impatiently for someone to rescue her; but the young men, vain and calculating in their very frivolity, did not deign to notice her, though Lizaveta Ivanovna was a hundred times more charming than the cold and insolent heiresses on whom they danced attendance. Many times, leaving quietly the dull and sumptuous drawing-room, she went to weep in her humble attic, where there was a paper-covered screen, a chest of drawers, a small mirror, and a painted bedstead, dimly lighted by a tallow candle in a copper candlestick.

One morning, two days after the evening described at the beginning of this story, and a week before the scene that has just been described—one morning Lizaveta Ivanovna, sitting at her embroidery frame by the window had happened to glance into the street. She saw a young officer in the Engineer's uniform who stood gazing at her window. She bent over her work again; five minutes later she looked out once more—the young man was standing on the same spot. Not being in the habit of flirting with passers-by, she looked out no more and worked for a couple of hours without raising her head. Dinner was served. She got up to put away her embroidery frame and, glancing casually into the street, saw the officer again. It struck her as rather strange. After dinner she went up to the window feeling somewhat uneasy, but the officer was no longer there, and she forgot about him. . . .

A couple of days later she saw him again as she was leaving the house with the Countess. He was standing by the front door, his face hidden by his beaver collar; his black eyes gleamed from under his hat. Lizaveta Ivanovna felt alarmed, she did not know why, and stepped into the carriage indescribably agitated.

When she came home she ran to the window—the officer was standing in the same place, his eyes fixed on her; she walked away, consumed with curiosity and excited by a feeling entirely new to her.

Since then not a day had passed without the young man

appearing at a certain hour before the windows of their house. A contact had arisen between them of itself, as it were. Sitting in her usual place at work she felt his approach —and, lifting her head, looked at him longer and longer every day. The young man seemed to be grateful to her for it: with the keen eyes of youth she saw a flush overspread his pale cheeks every time their eyes met. Before the end of the week she had smiled at him.

When Tomsky asked the Countess's permission to introduce a friend of his, the poor girl's heart beat fast. But hearing that Narumov was in the Horse Guards and not in the Engineers, she was sorry, by an indiscreet question, to have betrayed her secret to a thoughtless man like Tomsky.

Hermann was the son of a German who had settled in Russia and left him a small fortune. Firmly convinced that he must secure his independence, Hermann did not touch even the interest, but lived on his pay without indulging in the slightest extravagance. But since he was reserved and ambitious his friends rarely had occasion to laugh at his being too careful with his money. He had strong passions and an ardent imagination, but strength of character saved him from the usual vagaries of youth. Thus, for instance, though a gambler at heart, he never touched cards, having decided that his means did not allow him (as he put it) to sacrifice the essential in the hope of acquiring the superfluous —and yet he spent night after night at the gambling tables watching with a feverish tremor the vicissitudes of the game.

The story about the three cards greatly affected his imagination and haunted his mind all night. 'What if,' he thought the following evening as he wandered about Petersburg, 'what if the old Countess revealed her secret to me? or told me the three winning cards? Why shouldn't I try my luck? . . . be introduced to her, win her favour, become her lover, perhaps; but then all this takes time, and she is eighty-seven, she may die in a week, in a couple of days! And, the story itself . . . is it likely? No! economy, calculation, and hard work—those are my three winning cards, that's what will increase my capital threefold, sevenfold, and secure me leisure and independence!' Arguing in this way he found himself in one of the main streets of

Petersburg in front of a house of old-fashioned architecture The street was crowded with carriages which, one after another, drove up to the lighted porch. Every minute the shapely ankle of a young beauty, a military boot with a clinking spur, or a diplomat's striped stocking and shoe appeared on a carriage step. Fur coats and cloaks flitted past the majestic looking porter. Hermann stopped.

'Whose house is that?' he asked the policeman at the corner.

'Countess X.'s,' the policeman answered.

Hermann shuddered. The marvellous story came into his mind again. He walked up and down the street past the house, thinking of its owner and her wonderful faculty. It was late when he returned to his humble lodgings; he could not go to sleep for hours, and when at last sleep overpowered him he dreamt of cards, of a green-baize-covered table, bundles of notes, and piles of gold. He played card after card, resolutely turning down the corners and won all the time, raking in the gold and stuffing his pockets with notes. Waking up rather late, he sighed at the loss of his fantastic wealth, and, setting out once more to wander about the town, found himself again opposite the Countess's house. It was as though some mysterious power drew him to it. He stopped and gazed at the windows. In one of them he saw a dark-haired girl's head, bent over a book or needle-work. The head was raised. Hermann saw a rosy face and black eyes. That moment decided his fate.

CHAPTER III

Vous m'écrivez, mon ange, des lettres de quatre pages plus vite que je ne puis les lire.

A Correspondence.

THE moment Lizaveta Ivanovna had taken off her hat and mantle, the Countess sent for her and ordered the carriage again. They went out. Just as the two footmen lifted the old lady and put her through the carriage door, Lizaveta Ivanovna saw the officer close to the wheel; he seized her hand; before she had recovered from her fright, the young man had disappeared: a letter was left in her hand. She hid it inside her glove, and heard and saw nothing during the drive. The Countess had the habit of asking every moment while they were out: 'Who was it we met? What is this bridge called? What's written on that signboard?' This time Lizaveta Ivanovna answered inappropriately and at random, so that the Countess was angry.

'What's the matter with you, my dear? Are you asleep? Don't you hear or understand what I'm saying? I speak distinctly enough, thank Heaven, and am not in my dotage yet!'

Lizaveta Ivanovna did not listen. When they came home she ran to her room and pulled the letter out of her glove; it was not sealed. She read it. It contained a declaration of love: it was respectful, tender, and had been taken word for word out of a German novel. But Lizaveta Ivanovna did not know German and was very much pleased with it.

And yet the letter troubled her greatly. It was the first time in her life that she had entered into intimate and secret relations with a young man. His presumption terrified her. She reproached herself for having behaved thoughtlessly and did not know what to do: ought she to give up sitting at the window, and by a show of indifference make the young officer less eager to pursue her? Ought she to return the letter? or to answer him coldly and resolutely? There was no one to advise her: she had neither a governess nor a girl friend. Lizaveta Ivanovna decided to answer the letter.

She sat down to a writing-table, took up a pen and a sheet of paper—and sank into thought. She began the letter more than once, and tore it up: the wording seemed to her either too lenient or too harsh. At last she succeeded in writing a few lines that pleased her. 'I am sure,' she wrote, 'that your intentions are honourable, and that you had no wish to wound me by your thoughtless action; but our acquaintance ought not to have begun in this manner. I return you your letter and hope that in the future I shall have no cause to complain of undeserved disrespect.'

When next day Lizaveta Ivanovna saw Hermann approach she got up from her embroidery frame, went into the next room and, opening the window, threw her letter into the street, trusting to the young officer's agility. Running up,

Hermann picked up the letter, and went into a confectioner's shop. Tearing off the seal he found his own note and Lizaveta Ivanovna's reply. It was just what he had expected, and he returned home very much interested in the affair.

Three days later a sharp-eyed young girl brought Lizaveta Ivanovna a letter from a milliner's shop. Lizaveta Ivanovna opened it anxiously, thinking it was a bill, and suddenly recognized Hermann's handwriting.

'You have made a mistake, my dear,' she said; 'this note is not for me.'

'Yes, it is!' the bold girl answered without concealing a sly smile; 'please read it!'

Lizaveta Ivanovna read the letter. In it Hermann begged her to meet him.

'It cannot be,' said Lizaveta Ivanovna, alarmed at the request coming so soon and at the means of transmitting it. 'I am sure this was not addressed to me.' And she tore the letter into little bits.

'If the letter is not for you why did you tear it?' the shop-assistant said. 'I would have taken it back to the sender.'

'Please, my dear,' said Lizabeta Ivanovna, flushing crimson at her remark, 'don't bring any more letters. And tell him who sent you that he should be ashamed of himself.'

But Hermann would not give in. Every day Lizaveta Ivanovna received a letter from him by one means or another. They were no longer translated from the German. Hermann wrote them inspired by passion, and in the style natural to him: they reflected the intensity of his desires and the disorder of an unbridled imagination. Lizaveta Ivanovna never thought of returning them now: she drank them in eagerly, and took to answering them—and her letters grew longer and more tender every hour. At last she threw out of the window the following note to him:

There is a ball to-night at the N. ambassador's; the Countess will be there. We shall stay till about one o'clock. Here is an opportunity for you to see me alone. As soon as the Countess leaves, the servants will probably go to their quarters; the porter will be left in the hall, but he, too, usually goes to his room. Come at half-past eleven. Walk straight up the stairs. If you meet any one in the hall, ask if the Countess is at home. They will say no—and then there is no help for it, you will have

to go home.   But probably you will not meet any one.   The
maids all sit together in their room.   Turn to the left from the
hall and go straight on till you reach the Countess's bedroom.
In the bedroom, behind the screen, you will see two small doors:
to the right, into the study where the Countess never goes;
and to the left, into the passage with a narrow winding staircase
in it; it leads to my room.'

Hermann waited for the appointed hour like a tiger for its
prey.   At ten in the evening he was already standing by the
Countess's house.   It was a terrible night.   The wind howled,
wet snow fell in big flakes; the street lamps burned dimly;
the streets were empty.   From time to time a sledge driver,
looking out for a belated fare, went slowly by, urging on his
wretched nag.   Hermann stood there without his overcoat,
feeling neither the wind nor the snow.   At last the Countess's
carriage came round.   He saw the old woman in a sable
coat being lifted into the carriage by two footmen: then
Liza in a light cloak, with fresh flowers in her hair, flitted by.
The carriage door banged.   The carriage rolled heavily over
the wet snow.   The porter closed the doors.   The lights in
the windows went out.   Hermann walked up and down the
road by the deserted house; going up to a street lamp he
glanced at his watch: it was twenty past eleven.   He stopped
by the lamp-post, and waited for ten minutes, his eyes fixed
on the hand of the watch.   Precisely at half-past eleven
Hermann walked up the steps of the house and entered the
brightly lit hall.   The porter was not there.   Hermann ran
up the stairs, and opening the nearest door saw a servant
asleep under a lamp in a dirty old-fashioned arm-chair.
Hermann walked past him with a light firm step.   The dark
reception rooms were dimly lit by the lamp in the hall.
Hermann entered the bedroom.   A golden sanctuary lamp
was burning before the ikon-stand filled with ancient ikons.
Arm-chairs upholstered in faded brocade and sofas with down
cushions were ranged with depressing symmetry round the
walls covered with Chinese wall-paper.   Two portraits
painted in Paris by Madame Lebrun hung on the wall.   One
was that of a stout, ruddy-cheeked man of about forty, in a
light-green uniform with a star on his breast; the other was of
a young beauty with an aquiline nose and a rose in her
powdered hair, which was piled high up on her head.   Every

corner was crowded with china shepherdesses, clocks made by the famous Leroy, caskets, roulettes, fans, and various ladies' toys invented at the end of the last century together with Montgolfier's balloon and Mesmer's magnetism. Hermann went behind the screen. A small iron bedstead stood there: to the right was the door into the study, to the left the door into the passage. Opening it Hermann saw a narrow spiral staircase that led to poor Liza's room. But he returned and went into the dark study. The time passed slowly. Everything was quiet. The clock in the drawing-room struck twelve; the clocks in all the other rooms, one after the other, chimed twelve—and all was still again. Hermann stood leaning against the cold stove. He was calm; his heart was beating as evenly as that of a man who is determined on a dangerous but necessary course of action. The clock struck the first and then the second hour of the morning, and he heard the distant rumble of a carriage. In spite of himself he was overcome with agitation. The carriage drove up to the house and stopped. He heard the rattle of the step being lowered. There was commotion in the house. People ran to and fro, voices could be heard, lights were lit. Three old maid-servants ran into the bedroom, and the Countess, tired to death, came in and sank into an arm-chair. Hermann looked through a crack in the door. Lizaveta Ivanovna walked past him. He heard her hurried footsteps on the stairs leading to her room. Something like remorse stirred in his heart, but died down again. He seemed turned to stone. The Countess began undressing in front of the mirror. The maids took off her cap trimmed with roses; they removed the powdered wig from her grey, closely cropped head. Pins fell about her in showers. The silver-embroidered yellow dress fell at her swollen feet. Hermann witnessed the hideous mysteries of her toilet; at last the Countess put on a bed jacket and a nightcap; in that attire, more suited to her age, she seemed less terrible and hideous. Like all old people, the Countess suffered from sleeplessness. Having undressed, she sat down by the window in a big arm-chair and dismissed her maids. They took away the candles; the room was again lighted only by the sanctuary lamp. The Countess sat there, her face quite yellow, her flabby lips moving, her body rocking to and fro.

Her dim eyes showed a complete absence of thought; looking at her one might have imagined that the horrible old woman was moving not of her own will, but under the influence of some hidden galvanic power.

Suddenly an extraordinary change came over that dead face. Her lips ceased moving, her eyes brightened; a stranger was standing before her.

'Don't be alarmed, for Heaven's sake, don't be alarmed!' he said in a low and clear voice. 'I don't mean to do you any harm, I have come to beg a favour of you.'

The old woman stared at him in silence, looking as though she had not heard him. Hermann thought she was deaf, and, bending right over her ear, repeated what he had just said. The old woman said nothing.

'You can bring about my happiness,' Hermann went on, 'and it will cost you nothing. I know you can guess three cards in succession. . . .'

He stopped. The Countess seemed to have grasped what was required of her and was trying to frame her answer.

'It was a joke,' she said at last. 'I swear it was a joke!'

'It's no joking matter,' Hermann answered angrily. 'Think of Tchaplitsky whom you helped to win back his loss.'

The Countess was obviously confused. Her features expressed profound agitation; but she soon relapsed into her former insensibility.

'Will you tell me those three winning cards?' Hermann went on.

The Countess said nothing; Hermann continued:

'For whom do you want to preserve your secret? For your grandchildren? They are rich already, and besides they don't know the value of money. Your three cards would not help a spendthrift. A man who doesn't take care of his inheritance will die a beggar if all the demons in the world take his part. I am not a spendthrift: I know the value of money. Your three cards will not be wasted on me. Well?'

He paused, waiting for her answer with trepidation. The Countess was silent. Hermann knelt down.

'If your heart has ever known the feeling of love,' he said, 'if you remember the delights of it, if you have ever smiled at the cry of your new-born son, if anything human has ever stirred in your breast, I implore you by the feelings of wife, mother, beloved, by all that is holy in life, don't deny me my request, tell me your secret—what does it matter to you? Perhaps the price of it was some terrible sin, the loss of eternal bliss, a compact with the devil. . . . Just think: you are old; you haven't long to live—and I am ready to take your sin upon my soul. Only tell me your secret. Think, a man's happiness is in your hands; not only I, but my children, grandchildren, and great-grandchildren will bless your memory and hold it sacred.' . . .

The old woman did not answer a word.

Hermann got up.

'Old witch!' he said, clenching his teeth; 'I 'll make you speak, then. . . .'

With these words he took a pistol out of his pocket. At the sight of the pistol the Countess once more showed signs of agitation. She nodded her head and raised a hand as though to protect herself, then fell back . . . and remained still.

'Don't be childish,' said Hermann, taking her hand. 'I ask you for the last time—will you name me your three cards? Yes or no?'

The Countess made no answer. Hermann saw that she was dead.

CHAPTER IV

Homme sans mœurs et sans religion.
            A Correspondence.

LIZAVETA IVANOVNA, still wearing her ball dress, sat in her room, plunged in deep thought. On arriving home she had hastened to send away the sleepy maid who had reluctantly offered her services, and, saying she would undress by herself, had gone, trembling, into her room, hoping to find Hermann there and wishing not to find him. The first glance assured her of his absence, and she thanked fate for having prevented their meeting. Without undressing she sat down and began recalling all the circumstances that had led her so far in so short a time. It was not three weeks since she had for the first time seen the young man from the window—and she was carrying on a correspondence with him, and he had already obtained from her a tryst at night! She knew his name simply because some of his letters were signed by it; she had never spoken to him, had never heard his voice, had never heard of him . . . until that evening. It was a strange thing! That very evening, at the ball, Tomsky, vexed with Princess Pauline who, contrary to her habit, flirted with somebody else, decided to revenge himself by a show of indifference: he engaged Lizaveta Ivanovna and danced the endless mazurka with her. He jested all the time about her weakness for officers of the Engineers, assuring her that he knew much more than she could suppose. Some of his jokes were so much to the point that several times Lizaveta Ivanovna thought he must know her secret.

'Who told you all this?' she asked, laughing.

'A friend of the person you know,' Tomsky answered; 'a very remarkable man.'

'And who is this remarkable man?'

'His name is Hermann.'

Lizaveta Ivanovna said nothing, her hands and feet turned ice-cold. . . .

'That Hermann,' Tomsky went on, 'is a truly romantic figure; he has the profile of Napoleon and the soul of Mephistopheles. I think he must have at least three crimes on his conscience. How pale you look!'

'I have a headache. . . . Well, and what did this Hermann . . . or whatever he is called, tell you?'

'Hermann strongly disapproves of his friend; he says he would have acted quite differently in that man's place. . . . I suspect in fact that Hermann has designs upon you himself; at any rate he listens to his friend's ecstatic exclamations with anything but indifference.'

'But where has he seen me?'

'In church, perhaps, or when you were out driving— Heaven only knows! in your own room maybe, while you were asleep; he is quite capable of it.'

Three ladies coming up to them with the question: 'Oubli ou regret?' interrupted the conversation, which was growing painfully interesting to Lizaveta Ivanovna.

The lady chosen by Tomsky proved to be Princess Pauline. She managed to have an explanation with him while dancing an extra turn and flirting for a few minutes before she sat down. Returning to his seat, Tomsky no longer thought of Hermann or Lizaveta Ivanovna. She was very anxious to resume the interrupted conversation, but the mazurka was over, and the old Countess left the ball soon after.

Tomsky's words were just ordinary ball-room chatter, but they sank deep into the romantic girl's heart. The portrait sketched by Tomsky resembled the picture she herself had drawn, and the figure, made commonplace by modern fiction, both terrified and fascinated her. She sat there in her low-cut dress, with her bare arms crossed and her flower-decked head bowed low. . . . Suddenly the door opened and Hermann came in. She shuddered.

'Where have you been?' she asked in a frightened whisper.

'In the old Countess's bedroom,' Hermann answered. 'I have just come from there. The Countess is dead.'

'Good heavens! What are you saying?'

'And I think I was the cause of her death.'

Lizaveta Ivanovna glanced at him, and Tomsky's words re-echoed in her mind: 'That man has at least three crimes on his conscience!' Hermann sat down in the window beside her and told her the whole story.

Lizaveta Ivanovna listened to him with horror. And so those passionate letters and ardent requests, that insolent, relentless persistence—did not mean love! Money—that was what he hungered for! It was not she who could satisfy his desires and make him happy! The poor orphan was merely the blind accomplice of a robber, of her old benefactress's murderer. She wept bitterly in the vain agony of repentance. Hermann looked at her in silence; he too was suffering, but neither the poor girl's tears nor her wonderful charm in her sorrow disturbed his stony heart. He felt no remorse at the thought of the dead woman. One thing horrified him; the irrevocable loss of the secret which was to have brought him wealth.

'You are a monster!' Lizaveta Ivanovna said at last.

'I did not desire her death,' Hermann answered; 'my pistol was not loaded.'

Both were silent.

Morning came. Lizaveta Ivanovna blew out the burnt-down candle. A pale light filled the room. Wiping her

tear-stained eyes, she looked up at Hermann; he was sitting
on the window-sill with his arms folded, a gloomy frown on
his face. In that position he had a remarkable likeness to
a portrait of Napoleon. Even Lizaveta Ivanovna was
struck by the resemblance!

'How will you leave the house? she said at last. 'I had
thought of taking you down the secret staircase, but that
means going past the bedroom, and I am afraid.'

'Tell me how to find this secret staircase; I 'll go out
that way.'

Getting up, Lizaveta Ivanovna took a key out of her chest
of drawers and gave it to Hermann with detailed instructions.
Hermann pressed her cold, irresponsive hand, kissed her
bowed head, and went out.

He walked down the spiral staircase and entered once
more the Countess's bedroom. The dead woman sat as
though turned to stone. Her face wore a look of profound
calm. Stopping before her, Hermann gazed at her for a few
minutes, as though wishing to make sure of the terrible
truth; at last he went into the study and, fumbling for a
door concealed by the wall-paper, descended a dark staircase, disturbed by a strange emotion. 'Maybe at this very
hour sixty years ago,' he thought, 'some happy youth—
long since turned to dust—was stealing into that very
bedroom, in an embroidered jacket, his hair done *à l'oiseau
royal*, pressing his three-cornered hat to his breast; and to-day
the heart of his aged mistress has ceased to beat. . . .'

At the bottom of the stairs Hermann found a door which
he opened with the same key, coming out into a passage that
led into the street.

CHAPTER V

That night the dead Baroness von W. appeared to me. She
was all in white and said: 'How do you do, Mr. Councillor?'
                                        Swedenborg.

THREE days after that fateful night, at nine o'clock in the
morning, Hermann went to the N. monastery where the dead
Countess was to be buried. Though he felt no remorse, he
could not altogether stifle the voice of conscience that kept

repeating to him: 'You are the old woman's murderer!'
Having but little true faith, he had a number of superstitions.
He believed that the dead Countess might have a baneful
influence on his life, and decided to go to her funeral to obtain
her forgiveness.

The church was full. Hermann had difficulty in making
his way through the crowd. The coffin stood on a richly
decorated platform under a dais of velvet. The dead woman
lay with her arms folded on her breast, in a lace cap and a
white satin dress. Members of her household stood around:
servants in black clothes, with ribbons with coats of arms
on their shoulders and lighted candles in their hands; relatives
in deep mourning—children, grandchildren, and great-
grandchildren. No one wept; tears would have been *une
affectation*. The Countess was so old that her death could
not have surprised any one, and her relatives had long
ceased to consider her as one of the living. A young bishop
made a funeral speech. In simple and moving words he
sketched the peaceful end of the saintly woman whose long
life had been a touching and quiet preparation for a Christian
death. 'The angel of death,' he said, 'found her vigilant in
pious thoughts, awaiting the midnight bridegroom.' The
service went on with melancholy solemnity. The relatives
were the first to give the farewell kiss to the deceased. They
were followed by numerous guests who had come to pay the
last homage to one who had for so many years taken part
in their frivolous amusements. After them came the
members of the household. At last the old woman-jester,
of the same age as the Countess, drew near. Two young
girls supported her by the arms. She had not the strength
to bow to the ground—and was the only one to shed a few
tears, kissing her mistress's cold hand. Hermann made up
his mind to go up to the coffin after her. He bowed down
to the ground and lay for a few moments on the cold floor
strewn with pine branches; at last he got up and, pale as the
dead woman herself, went up the steps leading to the coffin
and bowed. . . . At that moment it seemed to him that the
dead woman glanced at him ironically, screwing up one eye.
Hastily drawing back, he missed his footing and crashed
headlong on the floor. They picked him up. At the same
time Lizaveta Ivanovna was carried out of the church in

a swoon. This episode disturbed for a few minutes the solemnity of the mournful rite. There was a dull murmur among the congregation; a thin man in the uniform of a *Kammerherr*, a near relative of the deceased, whispered to an Englishman standing close to him that the young officer was her illegitimate son, to which the Englishman answered coldly: 'Oh?'

Hermann felt greatly troubled the whole of that day. Dining in a quiet little tavern, he drank a great deal, contrary to his habit, in the hope of stifling his inner agitation. But wine excited his imagination all the more. Returning home, he threw himself on his bed without undressing and dropped fast asleep.

It was night when he woke up: his room was flooded with moonlight. He glanced at the clock: it was a quarter to three. He no longer felt sleepy; sitting down on the bed he began thinking of the old Countess's funeral.

At that moment someone peeped in at his window from the street and immediately walked away. Hermann did not pay the slightest attention to this. A minute later he heard the door of the next room being opened. Hermann thought that it was his orderly, drunk as usual, coming home from a night walk. But he heard an unfamiliar footstep: someone was softly shuffling along in slippers. The door opened: a woman in a white dress came in. Hermann took her for his old nurse and wondered what could have brought her at such an hour. But gliding across the floor the white woman suddenly stood before him—and Hermann recognized the Countess!

'I have come to you against my will,' she said in a clear voice, 'but I am commanded to grant your request. Three, seven, and ace will win for you in succession, provided that you stake only one card each day and never in your life play again. I forgive you my death, on condition that you marry my ward, Lizaveta Ivanovna. . . .'

With these words she slowly turned and walked to the door, shuffling with her slippers. Hermann heard the outer door bang and again saw someone peeping in at his window.

It was some time before Hermann could recover. He went into the next room. His orderly was asleep on the floor; Hermann had difficulty in waking him. The orderly was drunk as usual. There was no getting any sense out of him. The outer door was shut. Hermann returned to his room and, lighting a candle, wrote down his vision.

CHAPTER VI

Two fixed ideas cannot coexist in the mind, any more than two physical bodies can occupy the same space. Three, seven, and ace soon made Hermann forget the dead woman. Three, seven, and ace were always in his mind and on his lips. If he saw a young girl he said: 'How graceful she is! A regular three of hearts'. When he was asked: 'What time is it?' he answered: 'Five minutes to a seven'. Every stout man made him think of an ace. Three, seven, and ace pursued him in his dreams, taking all kinds of shapes: the three blossomed before him like a luxurious flower; the seven took the form of a Gothic gateway; the ace, of a big spider. All his thoughts were merged into one—to make use of the secret that had cost him so much. He began to think of resigning his commission and travelling. He wanted to snatch from fortune his magical treasure in the public gambling dens of Paris. An accident saved him the trouble.

A society of rich gamblers was formed in Moscow under the chairmanship of the famous Tchekalinsky, who had spent his life in gambling, and made millions winning I.O.U.s, and paying his losses in cash. His long experience inspired the confidence of his companions, and his hospitality, his excellent cook, his cheerful and friendly manner, won him the respect of the general public. He came to Petersburg. Young men flocked to his house, giving up dances for cards, and preferring the temptations of faro to the delights of flirting. Narumov brought Hermann to him.

They walked through a succession of magnificent rooms full of attentive servants. All the rooms were crowded. Several generals and privy councillors were playing whist; young men lounged about on the brocaded sofas, eating ice-creams and smoking pipes. In the drawing-room some twenty gamblers crowded round a long table, at which

Tchekalinsky was keeping bank. He was a man of about sixty, of the most venerable appearance; his hair was silvery-grey, his full, rosy face had a kindly expression, his sparkling eyes were always smiling. Narumov introduced Hermann to him. Tchekalinsky shook hands with him cordially and, asking him to make himself at home, went on playing.

The game went on for some time. There were more than thirty cards on the table. Tchekalinsky stopped after every round to give the players time to make their arrangements, put down the losses, politely listened to their requests, and still more politely straightened the corner of a card that some careless hand had turned back. At last the game was over. Tchekalinsky shuffled the cards, and made ready to begin another.

'Allow me to have a card,' said Hermann, stretching his hand from behind a stout gentleman who was also playing.

Tchekalinsky smiled and bowed in silence in token of agreement. Narumov, laughing, congratulated Hermann on breaking his long fast and wished him luck.

'Here goes,' said Hermann, chalking the figures over his card.

'How much is it?' Tchekalinsky asked, screwing up his eyes. 'Excuse me, I cannot see.'

'Forty-seven thousand,' Hermann answered.

At these words every head was turned, and all eyes were fixed on Hermann.

'He's gone off his head,' Narumov thought.

'Allow me to point out to you,' Tchekalinsky said with his perpetual smile, 'that you are playing for a very high stake: no one here has staked more than two hundred and seventy-five at a time.'

'Well?' Hermann asked, 'will you accept my card or not?'

Tchekalinsky bowed with the same expression of humble obedience.

'I only meant to inform you,' he said, 'that being honoured with my partners' confidence, I can only play for cash. For my own part I am of course convinced that your word is sufficient, but for the sake of order and our accounts I must ask you to put the money on your card.'

Hermann took a bank-note out of his pocket, and gave it to Tchekalinsky, who glanced at it and put it down on

Hermann's card. The game began. A nine fell on the right, a three on the left.

'Won!' said Hermann, pointing to his card.

There was a murmur among the company. Tchekalinsky frowned, but soon his usual smile appeared on his face.

'Would you like to have it now?' he asked Hermann.

'If you would be so kind.'

Tchekalinsky took a few bank-notes out of his pocket and settled his debt there and then. Hermann took his money and left the table. Narumov could not believe his senses. Hermann drank a glass of lemonade and went home.

The following evening he appeared at Tchekalinsky's again. He walked up to the table; room was immediately made for him. Tchekalinsky, who was keeping the bank, greeted him with a friendly bow. Hermann waited for a break in the game, and played a card, putting over it his original forty-seven thousand and his gain of the day before. Tchekalinsky began dealing. A knave fell on the right, a seven on the left.

Hermann showed his card—it was a seven. Every one cried out. Tchekalinsky was obviously disconcerted. He counted out ninety-four thousand and passed them to Hermann. Hermann coolly accepted the money and instantly withdrew.

The following evening Hermann appeared at the gambling table once more. Every one was waiting for him; generals and privy councillors left their whist to look on at so unusual a game. Young officers jumped off the sofas, and the waiters collected in the drawing-room. All crowded round Hermann. Other gamblers did not put down their cards, eagerly waiting to see what he would do. Hermann stood at the table preparing to play alone against Tchekalinsky, who was pale, but still smiling. Each unsealed a pack of cards. Tchekalinsky shuffled his pack, Hermann cut his and played his card, covering it with a heap of bank-notes. It was like a duel. Deep silence reigned around.

Tchekalinsky began dealing; his hands trembled. A queen fell on the right, an ace on the left.

'The ace has won!' Hermann said, and showed his card.

'Your queen has lost,' Tchekalinsky said kindly.

Hermann shuddered; in fact, instead of an ace there lay

before him a Queen of Spades.   He could not believe his eyes or think how he could have made a mistake.

At that moment it seemed to him that the Queen of Spades screwed up her eyes and gave a meaning smile.   He was struck by the extraordinary likeness. . . .

'The old woman!' he cried in terror.

Tchekalinsky drew the money towards him.   Hermann stood motionless.   When he walked away from the table every one began talking loudly.

'A fine game, that!' the gamblers said.

Tchekalinsky shuffled the cards once more; the game went on as usual.

CONCLUSION

HERMANN lost his reason.   He is in the Obuhovsky hospital, room Number Seventeen; he does not answer any questions, but keeps muttering with astonishing rapidity: 'Three, seven, ace! three, seven, queen!'

Lizaveta Ivanovna married a very amiable young man; he is in the civil service, and is a man of means: he is the son of the old Countess's former steward.   Lizaveta Ivanovna is bringing up a poor cousin.

Tomsky has been promoted captain, and has married Princess Pauline.

DUBROVSKY

CHAPTER I

SEVERAL years ago an old-fashioned Russian landowner, Kiril Petrovitch Troekurov, was living on one of his estates. His wealth, lineage, and connections gave him great weight in the province where the estate was situated. Spoiled by his surroundings, he was used to giving full rein to every impulse of his passionate temperament, and every idea of his somewhat limited intellect. His neighbours were glad to humour his smallest whim; the officials of the province trembled at his very name. Kiril Petrovitch accepted expressions of obsequiousness as his rightful tribute. His house was always full of guests, ready to amuse him in his lordly idleness, and to share his noisy and sometimes riotous pleasures. No one dared refuse his invitations or fail to appear on certain days at Pokrovskoe to pay their respects to him. Kiril Petrovitch was extremely hospitable. In spite of his wonderful constitution, twice a week he suffered from over-eating, and every evening he was slightly tipsy. Few of the serf girls in his household escaped the amorous attentions of this fifty-year-old satyr. In one of the lodges of the house lived sixteen maid-servants engaged in needle-work, as befitted their sex. The lodge windows had wooden gratings, the doors were padlocked, and the keys were in Kiril Petrovitch's keeping. At appointed hours the young recluses came out into the garden and walked there under the supervision of two old women. From time to time Kiril Petrovitch found husbands for some of them, and new ones took the place of those who married. He was harsh and arbitrary with his peasants and house-serfs, but they were loyal to him: they took a pride in their master's renown and wealth and, in their turn, often took advantage of their neighbours, trusting to his powerful protection.

Troekurov spent his time in driving about his extensive

lands, in festive eating and drinking, and in playing practical jokes, freshly invented every day, generally at the expense of some new acquaintance; his old friends were not spared either, with the exception of a certain Andrey Gavrilovitch Dubrovsky. This Dubrovsky, a retired lieutenant in the Guards, was Troekurov's nearest neighbour, and the owner of seventy serfs. Haughty in his dealings with men of the highest rank, Troekurov respected Dubrovsky in spite of his humble position. They had once served in the same regiment, and Troekurov knew by experience what a short-tempered and resolute man Dubrovsky was. The year 1762 of glorious memory [1] parted them for long. Troekurov, a relative of Princess Dashkov's, climbed up; Dubrovsky, having lost most of his property, had to retire and settle on the one estate that remained to him. Hearing of this, Kiril Petrovitch offered him his patronage; but Dubrovsky thanked him and remained poor and independent. A few years later, Troekurov, retired with the rank of general, came to his country seat; the friends met and were glad to see each other. Since then they had met every day, and Kiril Petrovitch, who had never deigned to visit any one, came without ceremony to his old comrade's humble little house. They were of the same age, belonged to the same class by birth, had had the same bringing up, and were to some extent alike in their tastes and temperaments; in some respects their fate was alike too: both had married for love, both had early been left widowers, and each had a child. Dubrovsky's son was being educated in Petersburg, Troekurov's daughter was being brought up under her father's supervision, and Kiril Petrovitch often said to his friend: 'You know, brother Andrey Gavrilovitch, if your Volodya turns out well, I'll marry Masha to him— even though he is poor as a church mouse.' Andrey Petrovitch shook his head and generally said: 'No, Kiril Petrovitch, my Volodya is not a match for Marya Kirilovna. A poor nobleman like him had much better marry a poor girl of good family, and be master in his own house, than be the bailiff of a spoilt young woman.'

Every one envied the harmony that reigned between the haughty Troekurov and his poor neighbour, and marvelled at the latter's courage when at Kiril Petrovitch's table he

[1] Accession of Catherine II to the throne.—TRANSLATOR'S NOTE.

said just what he thought, without troubling whether his opinion was opposed to that of his host. Some tried to follow his example and assert their independence, but Kiril Petrovitch gave them such a lesson that they lost all inclination to try it again; Dubrovsky remained the only exception to the general rule. An accident upset and changed everything.

One day in the early autumn Kiril Petrovitch prepared to go hunting. The kennel-boys and huntsmen were told to be ready by five o'clock the next morning. The kitchen and a tent were sent beforehand to the place where Kiril Petrovitch was to have dinner. He went with his visitors to look at his kennels, where more than five hundred hounds lived in warmth and comfort, singing praises in the canine tongue to Kiril Petrovitch's generosity. There was a hospital for sick dogs supervised by Timoshka, who acted as staff-doctor, and a place set apart for the bitches to have their young and suckle them. Kiril Petrovitch was proud of his beautiful kennels, and never missed an opportunity to boast of them to his friends, each of whom had seen them at least twenty times before. He walked about surrounded by his guests, and accompanied by Timoshka and the chief huntsmen. He stopped in front of certain kennels, inquiring about the sick dogs, making more or less stern and just reprimands or calling to him the dogs he knew, and talking kindly to them His guests considered it their duty to admire Kiril Petrovitch's kennels; Dubrovsky alone frowned and said nothing. He was a passionate sportsman, but he could only afford to keep two hounds and one borzoi bitch. He could not help feeling a certain envy at the sight of this magnificent establishment. 'Why do you frown, brother?' Kiril Petrovitch asked him; 'don't you like my kennels?' 'Yes, they are beautiful kennels,' Dubrovsky answered gloomily; 'I don't suppose your servants are as comfortable as your dogs.' One of the huntsmen was nettled. 'We don't complain of our lot, thanks to God and our master,' he said, 'but it's true enough that many a gentleman might well exchange his house for any of these kennels; he would be warmer here and better fed.' Kiril Petrovitch laughed aloud at his serf's impudent remark, and his guests laughed too, though they felt that the huntsman's joke might refer to them as well.

Dubrovsky turned pale and did not say a word. At that
moment Kiril Petrovitch had some newborn puppies brought
to him in a basket, and he gave his attention to them; he
picked out two and gave word that the others were to be
drowned. Meanwhile Andrey Gavrilovitch had disappeared
unnoticed.

On coming home from the kennels with his guests, Kiril
Petrovitch sat down to supper, and only then missed Dubrovsky. The servants informed him that Andrey Gavrilovitch
had gone home. Troekurov told them to catch him up at
once, and bring him back. He never rode to hounds without
Dubrovsky, a subtle and experienced judge of a dog's points,
and an unerring arbiter in sportsmen's disputes. The
servant dispatched after him returned while the company
were still at table, and reported to his master that Andrey
Gavrilovitch would not obey and refused to return. Kiril
Petrovitch, heated as usual with home-made brandy, lost his
temper, and sent the same servant to tell Andrey Gavrilovitch
that if he did not come at once to spend the night at Pokrovskoe, he, Troekurov, would have nothing more to do with
him. The servant galloped off again. Kiril Petrovitch got
up from the table, and, dismissing his visitors, went to bed.

The first thing he asked in the morning was whether
Andrey Gavrilovitch had come. He was given a letter folded
in a triangle. Kiril Petrovitch told his secretary to read it
aloud, and heard the following:

My Dear Sir,
    I do not intend to come to Pokrovskoe until you send me your
huntsman Paramoshka to ask my pardon; it will be for me to
punish or forgive him; I do not intend to put up with your
serf's jokes, nor with yours either for that matter, because I am
not a clown but a gentleman born. I remain your obedient
servant,
                              Andrey Dubrovsky.

According to the present-day standards of etiquette this
letter would have seemed highly improper; Kiril Petrovitch,
however, was angered not by its peculiar style and its rudeness, but merely by its subject-matter. 'What!' he cried,
jumping off his bed barefoot. 'To send my servants to ask
his pardon! It's for him to forgive or to punish them!
What is he thinking of! He doesn't know his man it strikes

me! I 'll give it him! I 'll make him smart! I 'll teach him what crossing Troekurov means!'

Nevertheless, Kiril Petrovitch dressed and rode out to the hunt with all his customary splendour. But the hunt was not a success: they saw only one hare all that day, and missed it; the dinner in the fields under the tent was not a success, or, anyway, was not to Kiril Petrovitch's taste. He beat the cook, swore at his guests, and on the way back rode on purpose with all his party across Dubrovsky's fields.

CHAPTER II

SEVERAL days had passed, and the hostility between the two neighbours continued. Andrey Gavrilovitch did not return to Pokrovskoe; Kiril Petrovitch was bored without him and vented his vexation by saying the most offensive things which, thanks to the zeal of the local gentry, reached Dubrovsky's ears improved and amplified. A new event destroyed the last hope of peace.

One day Dubrovsky was driving round his small estate; as he neared the birch copse he heard strokes of the axe and, a minute later, the crash of a falling tree. Hastening there, he came upon Troekurov's peasants, who were calmly stealing his wood. Seeing him they set off running; Dubrovsky and his coachman caught two of them and, tying their arms, brought them home with three of the enemy's horses as booty. Dubrovsky was extremely angry; hitherto Troekurov's serfs, notorious rascals, had never dared to do mischief on his estate, knowing of his friendship with their master. Dubrovsky saw that now they were taking advantage of the breach and, contrary to all the conventions of war, decided to punish his prisoners with the twigs they had secured in his own copse, and to send the horses to work in his fields along with his own.

The rumour of this incident reached Kiril Petrovitch the same day. He was beside himself with fury and at first wanted to attack Kistenyovka (that was the name of his neighbour's village) with all his serfs, and, razing it to the ground, besiege the owner in his house; such exploits were not new to him; but soon his thoughts took another turn. Pacing up and down the drawing-room with heavy steps, he happened to glance at the window and see a troika draw up at the front gate; a little man in a leather cap and a woolly coat stepped out of the cart and walked to the steward's lodge. Troekurov recognized Shabashkin, the assessor of the district court, and sent for him. A minute later Shabashkin stood before Kiril Petrovitch, bowing and reverently awaiting his orders.

'Good day . . . let me see, what 's your name?' Troekurov said. 'What have you come for?'

'I was going to town, your Excellency,' Shabashkin answered, 'and I called at Ivan Demyanov's to see if there were any orders from your Excellency.'

'You 've come in the nick of time. . . . What 's your name? I forget. I have something to ask you: have a drink of vodka and listen.'

Such a friendly reception pleasantly surprised the lawyer; he refused the vodka and listened to Kiril Petrovitch with every mark of attention.

'I have a neighbour,' Troekurov said, 'a petty landowner, an impudent man; I want to take his estate from him . . . what do you think about it?'

'Your Excellency, if there are any documents or . . .'

'Nonsense, brother, what do you want with documents? There are ukases for dealing with them. The point is to take away his estate without any regard to law and leave him a beggar. Wait a minute, though! That estate did once belong to us; it was bought from a certain Spitsyn and sold afterwards to Dubrovsky's father. Can we make use of that?'

'It 's difficult, your Excellency; probably the sale was in order.'

'Think well, brother, try to find some way.'

'If, for instance, your Excellency could somehow get from your neighbour the deeds in virtue of which he holds his estate, then, of course . . .'

'Yes, I know, but the trouble is, all his papers were burned during the fire.'

'What, your Excellency? His papers were burned?

Nothing could be better! In that case, you have simply to abide by the law and everything will certainly be settled to your complete satisfaction.'

'You think so? Well, mind then, I rely on you to do your best, and you may be sure I'll thank you well.'

Bowing almost down to the ground, Shabashkin left the room, and that very day set about the business. Thanks to his promptitude, exactly a fortnight later Dubrovsky received a paper from the town asking him to furnish forthwith the necessary explanations in view of a petition filed by his Excellency General Troekurov, alleging that Dubrovsky had no right to the ownership of the village Kistenyovka.

Surprised by this unexpected query, Andrey Gavrilovitch wrote that very day a rather rude reply, saying that he had inherited Kistenyovka from his late father, that he owned it by the right of legacy, that it was none of Troekurov's business, and that any outsider's claim on his property was a fraud and a swindle.

This letter made a very pleasant impression on Shabashkin: he saw, in the first place, that Dubrovsky had little knowledge of legal business, and, in the second, that it would be no difficult matter to put so incautious and hot-tempered a man in a most disadvantageous position.

When Andrey Gavrilovitch considered in cold blood the question that had been put to him, he pondered and saw that it ought to be answered in more detail; he wrote a statement that was very much to the point, but it proved to be insufficient.

Dubrovsky had no experience of litigation. He followed for the most part the dictates of common sense, which is seldom a correct and hardly ever a sufficient guide.

The lawsuit went on. Convinced of the justice of his cause, Andrey Gavrilovitch troubled himself very little about it; he was neither able nor inclined to squander money on bribes, and, though he had often joked about the mercenary conscience of the attorneys, it never occurred to him that he might become the victim of a legal swindle. Troekurev on his side thought equally little about winning his case: Shabashkin was acting for him, using his name, threatening and bribing the judges, and misinterpreting in every possible way all kinds of ukases. In any case, on 9th February

18— Dubrovsky received a summons to appear before the district court to hear the verdict on the dispute between him, Lieutenant Dubrovsky, and General Troekurov about the estate, and to sign his agreement or disagreement with it. Dubrovsky went to the town that very day: on the way he was overtaken by Troekurov; they looked at each other proudly, and Dubrovsky noticed a malignant smile on his adversary's face.

Arriving at the town, Andrey Gavrilovitch put up at the house of a merchant of his acquaintance, spent the night at his house, and the following morning went to the district court. No one took any notice of him. Kiril Petrovitch arrived after him; the clerks stood up, putting their quills behind their ears; the lawyers met him with the greatest obsequiousness and moved up an arm-chair for him out of consideration for his rank, his years, and his corpulence; he sat down. Standing in the open doorway, Andrey Gavrilovitch leaned against the wall. There was a profound stillness in the room, and the secretary began in a high-pitched voice to read the court's decision. We quote it in full, believing that every one will be pleased to learn one of the methods whereby in Russia a man can lose an estate to which he has incontestable rights.[1]

The secretary finished; Shabashkin stood up and with a low bow turned to Troekurov, inviting him to sign the paper; the triumphant Troekurov, taking the pen from him, wrote under the decision of the court that he was completely satisfied with it.

It was Dubrovsky's turn. The secretary handed him the paper, but Dubrovsky stood motionless, hanging his head. The secretary invited him once more 'to sign, expressing his complete and perfect satisfaction or his clear dissatisfaction, should he, by any chance, be honestly convinced that his cause was right and intend to appeal against the court's decision within the appointed time'.

Dubrovsky said nothing. . . . Suddenly he raised his head, his eyes flashed, he stamped, and pushing the secretary so

[1] As can be seen from the rough draft of *Dubrovsky*, Pushkin had intended to insert here an exact copy of the decision of the Kozlov district court which in 1832 by an act of glaring injustice deprived a poor landowner of his property in favour of a rich one.—TRANSLATOR'S NOTE.

violently that the man fell, he seized the inkpot and threw it at Shabashkin. Every one was horror-stricken. Dubrovsky shouted wildly: 'What, to have no respect for the Church of God! Away with you, you offspring of Ham!'—then turning to Kiril Petrovitch he continued: 'It's unheard of, your Excellency! Huntsmen bring dogs into the church of God! Dogs are running about in the church! I'll give it you!'

Hearing the noise the ushers ran in and with some difficulty overpowered Dubrovsky. They took him out and put him in his sledge. Troekurov walked out after him, accompanied by all the officials. Dubrovsky's sudden madness was a great shock to him; it spoiled his triumph. Not deigning to say a kind word to the laywers who had hoped he would thank them, he went straight back to Pokrovskoe, smitten with secret remorse and not altogether satisfied with his vengeance.

Dubrovsky meanwhile was in bed; the district doctor (luckily not quite an ignoramus) bled him, applied leeches and a Spanish fly-blister; towards evening he felt better, and the following day he was taken to Kistenyovka, which now scarcely belonged to him.

CHAPTER III

SOME months had passed, but poor Dubrovsky was still far from well. True, he had had no more attacks of madness, but his strength was obviously failing. He gave up his former occupations, seldom left his room, and sat lost n thought for days together. Yegorovna, a good old woman, who had once nursed his son, now became his nurse too. She looked after him as though he were a child, reminded him about meals and bed-time, gave him food, and put him to sleep. Andrey Gavrilovitch obeyed her, and had nothing to do with any one else. He was not in a fit state to think of his affairs or of estate management, and Yegorovna decided to lay the whole situation before young Dubrovsky, who was an officer in the Foot Guards, and lived in Petersburg. Tearing a leaf out of the account book, she dictated a letter to the cook Hariton, the only man in Kistenyovka who could write, and sent it that same day to be posted in the town.

But it is time to introduce the reader to the real hero of our story. Vladimir Dubrovsky had been brought up in the Cadet Corps, and joined the Guards with the rank of cornet. His father spared nothing to keep him as befitted his position, and the young man received more money from home than he ought to have expected. Careless and ambitious, he indulged in extravagance, played cards, made debts and, little troubling about the future, vaguely thought sometimes that sooner or later he would have to marry a rich wife.

One day, when several fellow-officers sat in his room lounging on the sofas and smoking his amber pipes, his valet Grisha handed him a letter. The seal and the handwriting on the address at once attracted the young man's attention. He opened it hastily and read as follows:

OUR DEAR MASTER VLADIMIR ANDREYEVITCH,

I, your old nurse, venture to inform you of your father's health. He is very bad, and sometimes often wanders in his talk and sits all day long like a foolish child—and life and death are in God's hands—come to us, my bright falcon, we will send the horses to meet you at Pesochnoe. We hear that the district court is going to hand us over to Kiril Petrovitch Troekurov, because they say we belong to him, but we have always belonged to you and have never heard of such a thing. As you live in Petersburg you might tell our Father-Tsar about it, he would be sure to defend us. We have been having rain for the last fortnight and Rodya the shepherd died soon after St. Nicholas' day. I send my maternal blessing to Grisha. Does he serve you well? I remain your faithful servant,

NURSE ARINA YEGOROVNA BUZYREV.

Vladimir Dubrovsky read this rather confused letter over and over with profound emotion. He had lost his mother in early childhood, and knew his father but little, having been brought to Petersburg at the age of eight. Nevertheless he had a romantic affection for him, and loved family life all the more for having had so little time to enjoy its peaceful happiness.

The thought of losing his father pained him deeply, and

the condition of the poor invalid, which he guessed from his old nurse's letter, horrified him. He pictured his father left helpless in an out-of-the-way village in the hands of a foolish old woman and the servants, threatened with some misfortune, and gradually sinking in physical and mental agony. Vladimir reproached himself for criminal neglect. He had had no news of his father for months, but had never thought of inquiring after him, imagining he was away somewhere or busy about the estate. He decided to go to him and to retire from the army, if his father's illness required his presence at home.

Seeing that he was perturbed, his friends went away. Left alone, Vladimir wrote a petition for leave of absence, lighted his pipe, and sank into deep thought. That very day he sent in his petition, and two days later set out for home by stage-coach with his faithful Grisha.

Vladimir was drawing near the station where he had to turn off to Kistenyovka. His heart was full of sad forebodings: he was afraid of finding his father dead; he imagined the melancholy existence awaiting him in the country: a desolate village, no neighbours, poverty, and business responsibilities to which he was an utter stranger. Arriving at the station he went to the station-master and asked if there were any horses for hire. Inquiring where he was going, the station-master said that horses from Kistenyovka had been waiting for him for four days. The old coachman, Anton, who had once looked after his pony, and piloted him round the stables, soon appeared. Tears came into his eyes when he saw Vladimir; he bowed down to the ground before him and, saying that the old master was still alive, ran to harness the horses. Vladimir refused the offer of lunch, anxious to leave at once. Anton drove him along the by-roads, and they fell into conversation.

'Tell me please, Anton, what is this lawsuit between my father and Troekurov?'

'Heaven only knows, Vladimir Andreyevitch, sir. It appears master didn't hit it off with Kiril Petrovitch, and he went to law about it—though often enough he is a law unto himself. It's not the business of us servants to judge our betters, but really it was a pity your father crossed Kiril Petrovitch: it's no use kicking against the pricks.'

'It would seem then this Kiril Petrovitch can do just as he likes with you all?'

'Of course, sir: the Governor hob-nobs with him, he doesn't care a rap for the assessor, they say the police-captain is his errand-boy; the gentry dance attendance on him—but indeed, as the saying is, 'provide a trough and pigs will be sure to come'.

'Is it true that he is taking our estate from us?'

'That's what we have heard, sir, worse luck. The other day the Pokrovskoe sexton was at the christening in our foreman's house and said: 'Your good time is over! Kiril Petrovitch will take you in hand presently!' And Nikita the blacksmith said to him: 'Come, Savelyitch, don't grieve our host and upset the guests! Kiril Petrovitch has his place, Andrey Gavrilovitch has his—and we are all God's and the Tsar's. But you can't shut other people's mouths.'

'So then you don't want Troekurov to take you over?'

'Kiril Petrovitch? God save us and spare us! His own serfs have a bad time of it, and if he gets hold of other people's, he'll not merely fleece but skin them. No, God grant long life to Andrey Gavrilovitch; but if he is taken, we don't want any master but you, my dear. Don't you give us up, and we'll stick up for you.'

With these words Anton brandished his whip, pulled at the reins, and the horses broke into a sharp trot.

Touched by the old coachman's devotion, Dubrovsky was silent and sank into thought. More than an hour passed in this way; suddenly Grisha roused him by exclaiming: 'There's Pokrovskoe!' Dubrovsky raised his head. They were driving along the bank of a wide lake, from which flowed a river winding among the low hills and disappearing in the distance. On one of the hills above the thick verdure of the trees could be seen the green roof and the belvedere of a huge brick house; on another, a church with five cupolas and an ancient belfry; peasant huts, with their wells and kitchen-gardens, were scattered around. Dubrovsky recognized the place; he remembered that he used to play on that very hill with little Masha Troekurov, who was two years younger than he and already at that time promised to be a beauty. He wanted to ask Anton about her, but a kind of shyness restrained him.

As they were driving past the house he saw a white frock
flitting between the trees of the garden. At that moment
Anton struck the horses with the whip and, inspired by the
ambition common both to town cab-drivers and country
coachmen, dashed headlong across the bridge and past the
garden. Leaving the village behind, they drove up a hill,
and Vladimir saw a birch copse, and in an open field to the
left of it a small grey house with a grey roof; his heart beat
faster: Kistenyovka and his father's poor house were
before him.

Ten minutes later he drove into the courtyard. He looked
about him with indescribable emotion: it was twelve years
since he had seen his birthplace. The birch-trees by the
fence that had only just been planted in his time had grown
into big spreading trees. The courtyard, that had once been
adorned by three symmetrical flower-beds with a wide,
carefully swept path between them, had now turned into
a meadow with long grass where a horse was grazing. The
dogs began barking, but, recognizing Anton, subsided and
wagged their shaggy tails. The servants rushed out of their
cottages, and with loud expressions of joy surrounded their
master. Making with some difficulty his way through the
eager crowd, he ran up the rickety steps; Yegorovna met
him in the porch and threw herself weeping on his neck.
'How do you do, how are you, nurse?' he repeated, pressing
the good old woman to his heart. 'How is my father?
Where is he?' At that moment a tall old man in a dressing-
gown and a night-cap, thin and pale, came into the room,
walking with obvious difficulty. 'Where is Volodya?' he
said in a weak voice, and Vladimir warmly embraced his
father. The joy was too great a shock to the invalid; he
felt weak, his legs gave way under him, and he would have
fallen had not his son supported him. 'What ever did you
get up for?' Yegorovna said to him. 'He can hardly keep
on his feet, and yet he must try and do the same as other
people.' The old man was carried to his bedroom. He
wanted to talk to his son, but his thoughts were confused
and there was no coherence in his words. He subsided into
silence and gradually dropped asleep. Vladimir was shocked
by his condition. He had his things brought into his father's
room and asked to be left alone with him. The servants

obeyed, and turned their attentions to Grisha. They took him to the servants' hall and treated him to a good homely meal with every show of hospitality, overwhelming him with questions and greetings.

CHAPTER IV

A coffin stands on the festive board.

A FEW days after his arrival young Dubrovsky wanted to see how matters stood with regard to the estate, but his father was not able to give him the necessary explanations; and Andrey Gavrilovitch had no agent. Sorting out his papers, Vladimir found only the lawyer's first letter and the rough draft of an answer to it. This was not enough to give him a clear idea of the case, and he decided to await developments, trusting to the justice of his cause.

Meanwhile Andrey Gavrilovitch was hourly getting worse. Vladimir saw that the end was not far off, and spent all his time with the old man, who had sunk into complete senility.

Meanwhile the time for lodging an appeal had passed and nothing had been done about it. Kistenyovka belonged to Troekurov. Shabashkin came to him to present his respects and congratulations and to ask when would his Excellency be pleased to take possession of the new estate—and would he do so in person or give someone the power of attorney? Kiril Petrovitch was confused. He was not grasping by nature; his desire for vengeance had carried him too far; his conscience reproached him. He knew what condition his adversary, the old comrade of his youth, was in, and victory did not gladden his heart. He glanced at Shabashkin menacingly, looking for a pretext to abuse him, but finding none said angrily: 'Be off! I have no time for you!' Seeing that he was in a bad humour, Shabashkin bowed and hastened to withdraw. Left alone, Kiril Petrovitch began walking up and down the room, whistling 'Thunder of victory, resound!' which always was with him a sign of extreme mental agitation.

At last he ordered a droshky, put on a warm coat (it was already the end of September), and drove out, taking no coachman with him.

He soon caught sight of Andrey Gavrilovitch's house; conflicting emotions filled his heart. Satisfied vengeance and love of power stifled to some extent his nobler feelings, but the latter triumphed at last. He decided to make peace with his old neighbour and, wiping out every trace of their quarrel, restore his estate to him. Comforting himself by this good intention, Kiril Petrovitch set out at a trot towards his neighbour's house and drove straight into the courtyard.

At that time the sick man was sitting at his bedroom window. He recognized Kiril Petrovitch, and a look of violent agitation came into his face: a flush overspread his pale cheeks, his eyes flashed, he uttered unintelligible sounds. His son, who was sitting in the same room poring over account-books, raised his head and was alarmed at his condition. The invalid was pointing to the courtyard with an expression of horror and anger. At that moment Yegorovna's heavy steps were heard, and she said: 'Master, master! Kiril Petrovitvh has come, Kiril Petrovitch is at the front door!' Suddenly she cried out: 'Good heavens! What is it? What's the matter with him?' The invalid, intending to get up, hurriedly picked up the skirts of his dressing-gown, raised himself a little and suddenly fell down. His son rushed to him: the old man lay senseless, hardly breathing: he had had a stroke.

'Make haste, go to the town for a doctor! Quick!' Vladimir cried.

'Kiril Petrovitch is asking for you,' said a servant, coming in. Vladimir gave him a dreadful look.

'Tell Kiril Petrovitch to be off quick, before I give orders to turn him out—go!' he said.

The servant ran joyfully to carry out his master's bidding. Yegorovna clasped her hands in despair.

'My dear!' she shrieked. 'You've done for yourself! Kiril Petrovitch will be the death of us!'

'Be quiet, nurse!' Vladimir said angrily. 'Make haste and send Anton for the doctor.'

Yegorovna went out. There was no one in the hall: all the servants had run out into the yard to look at Kiril

Petrovitch. She came out on to the steps and heard Grisha give the young master's answer. Kiril Petrovitch heard it sitting in the droshky; his face turned black as night: he smiled contemptuously, gave a menacing look at the servants, and slowly drove along the courtyard. He glanced at the window where Andrey Gavrilovitch had been sitting a moment before, but he was no longer there. The nurse stood on the steps, forgetting the young master's orders. The servants were noisily discussing what had happened. Suddenly Vladimir appeared among them and said sharply: 'No need for a doctor—my father is dead'.

Confusion followed. The servants rushed into the old master's room. He lay in the arm-chair to which Vladimir had carried him; his right arm hung down to the ground, his head was bowed—there was no sign of life in the body, which had not yet grown cold, but was already disfigured by death. Yegorovna set up a wail; the servants surrounded the corpse left to their care; they washed it, and dressing it in the uniform made in 1797, laid it on the very table at which for so many years they had waited on their master.

CHAPTER V

THE funeral took place three days later. The poor old man's body, covered with a shroud and surrounded with lighted candles, lay on the table. The dining-room was full of serfs ready to follow the funeral procession. Vladimir and some of the men lifted the coffin. The priest walked in front, the clerk followed him, singing the burial prayers. The master of Kistenyovka crossed the threshold of his house for the last time. The coffin was carried through the copse—the church was on the other side of it. It was a bright, cold day; autumn leaves were falling. Coming out of the copse they saw the wooden church, and the churchyard overshadowed with old lime-trees. The body of Vladimir's mother rested there; next to her tomb a new grave had been dug the day before. The church was full of the Kistenyovka peasants who had come to render the last homage to their master. Young

Dubrovsky stood in a corner in front; he did not weep or pray, but there was a dreadful look on his face. The sad ceremony came to an end. Vladimir was the first to give the farewell kiss to the dead; members of the household followed him. The women wailed loudly, the men occasionally wiped their eyes with their fists. Vladimir and the same three servants as before carried the coffin to the churchyard, accompanied by the whole village. The coffin was lowered into the grave; each of those present threw a handful of sand into it; the grave was filled up, they bowed before it, and went home. Vladimir walked away hastily and, leaving the others behind, disappeared in the Kistenyovka copse.

Yegorovna, on his behalf, invited the priest and the other clerics to the funeral dinner, saying that the young master did not intend to be present. Father Anton, his wife, and the clerk set out on foot to the house, discussing with Yegorovna the dead man's virtues, and the future that in all probability awaited his heir. (Troekurov's visit and the reception he had had were already known to the whole neighbourhood, and the local politicians deduced important conclusions therefrom.)

'What must be, will be,' the priest's wife said, 'but I shall be sorry if Vladimir Andreyevitch is not our master. There's no denying it, he is a fine fellow.'

'But who else can be our master?' Yegorovna interrupted her. 'Kiril Petrovitch may be as angry as he please, but he's got a tough one to deal with! My young falcon can stand up for himself, and he has friends in high places too. Kiril Petrovitch is much too stuck-up, that's what he is. He did draw in his horns, though, when my Grisha shouted to him: "Go away, you old cur! Be off!"'

'Dear me, Yegorovna!' said the clerk. 'How could Grisha bring himself to say such a thing? I think I'd sooner venture to complain of the bishop than look askance at Kiril Petrovitch. I'm all of a tremble at the very sight of him! And my back bends double of itself before I know where I am.'

'Vanity of vanities!' the priest said; 'they'll sing "eternal memory" to Kiril Petrovitch the same as to Andrey Gavrilovitch to-day; perhaps the funeral will be grander and there will be more visitors—but it's all one to God.'

'Oh, Father, we too wanted to invite all the neighbourhood, but Vladimir Andreyevitch wouldn't have it. We have plenty of everything, no fear, we could have had a good spread . . . but there was nothing for it. At any rate, since there are no other people here, I 'll do my best for you, dear guests.'

This kind promise and the hope of a savoury pie made the guests hasten their steps. They arrived safely at the house, where the table was already set and the vodka served.

Meanwhile Vladimir walked on among the thickets of trees so as to tire himself out, and thus deaden his sorrow. He went on without thinking of the road; branches caught and scratched him every moment, his feet kept sinking in the bog—he noticed nothing. At last he reached a ravine surrounded on all sides by the forest; a brook wound quietly among the trees half bared by the autumn. Vladimir stopped, sat down on the cold grass, and thoughts, each one gloomier than the last, swarmed in his mind. . . . He was painfully conscious of being alone in the world; his future was obscured by menacing storm clouds. His quarrel with Troekurov held the promise of new misfortunes for him. His small property might be taken from him; in that case he would be completely destitute. He sat still for a long time in the same spot, watching the slow motion of the brook carrying away a few faded leaves, and it seemed to him a vivid image of life—such a very true and homely image. He noticed at last that it was growing dusk; getting up he went to look for the road home; after wandering for some time through the unfamiliar wood, he came upon a path that brought him straight to his courtyard gates.

The priest and his party were coming towards him. The thought that it was a bad omen crossed Dubrovsky's mind. Unconsciously he turned aside and hid behind the trees. Engaged in a heated conversation, they failed to notice him.

'Avoid evil and do good,' the priest was saying to his wife. 'We have nothing to fear; it 's nothing to do with you, whatever the end may be.' His wife answered something, but Vladimir could not hear what.

Nearing the house he saw a number of people: peasants and house-serfs were crowding in the yard. Vladimir heard from a distance extraordinary noises and a hubbub of voices. Two troikas stood by the barn. On the front steps several strangers in official uniforms seemed to be talking together. 'What does it mean?' he asked angrily, seeing Anton who was running towards him. 'Who are those people, and what do they want?'

'Ah, Vladimir Andreyevitch, my dear,' the old man answered breathlessly, 'it's the police. They are taking us from you and giving us to Troekurov!'

Vladimir hung his head, his serfs surrounded their luckless master. 'You are our father,' they cried, kissing his hands; 'we don't want any master but you. Give the word, sir, and we'll settle them. We'll stand up for you if we have to die for it.'

Vladimir gazed at them in gloomy agitation. 'Keep quiet,' he said; 'I'll talk to the officers.'

'Do talk to them, sir,' people shouted to him from the crowd; 'bring them to reason, the wretches.'

Vladimir went up to the officials. Shabashkin with his cap on his head stood, arms akimbo, staring haughtily around him. The police-captain, a tall stout man of about fifty, with a red face and a moustache, cleared his throat when he saw Dubrovsky, and said in a hoarse voice:

'And so I repeat what I've said to you already: by the decision of the district court, from this day you belong to Kiril Petrovitch Troekurov, who is represented here by Mr. Shabashkin. Obey him in all things, whatever he may order you; and you, women, love and honour him, for he is very fond of you.'

The police-captain burst out laughing at this witty joke, and Shabashkin and others followed his example. Vladimir was boiling with indignation. 'Allow me to ask, what does this mean?' he asked the merry police-captain, with a show of indifference.

'Why, it means this,' the resourceful official answered, 'that we have come to put Kiril Petrovitch Troekurov in possession of this estate, and to ask other people to get out.'

'But you might, I should have thought, communicate with me and not with my peasants—and tell the owner that his estate no longer belonged to him. . . .'

'The former owner, Andrey, son of Gavril Dubrovsky,

please God, is dead; and who are you?' said Shabashkin
with an insolent stare. 'We don't know you and have no
wish to do so.'

'Your honour, that 's Vladimir Andreyevitch, our young
master,' said a voice in the crowd.

'Who is it dares speak?' the police-captain said menacingly.
'What master? What Vladimir Andreyevitch? Your
master is Kiril Petrovitch Troekurov . . . do you hear,
you fools?'

'Not likely,' said the same voice.

'Why, they are in revolt!' the police-captain shouted.
'Hey, foreman, come here!'

The foreman came forward.

'Find at once the man who dared to speak to me; I 'll
give it him!'

The foreman turned to the crowd, asking who it was had
spoken. But every one was silent. Soon there was a
murmur among those standing farthest away; it grew louder,
and in a minute turned into fearful yells. The police-
captain lowered his voice and thought of persuading them.
. . . 'Don't you mind him!' the peasants cried; 'seize
them, lads!' and the crowd moved forward. Shabashkin
and his companions hastily rushed into the entry and shut
the door behind them. 'Push on, lads,' the same voice
shouted, and the crowd pressed against the door.

'Stop!' Dubrovsky shouted. 'Idiots! What are you
doing? You are ruining both yourselves and me; go home
and leave me in peace. Don't be afraid, the Tsar is merciful.
I will appeal to him—he 'll not wrong us—we are all his
children, but how is he to help you if you behave like
brigands?'

Young Dubrovsky's speech, his resounding voice, and
impressive appearance had the desired effect. The crowd
calmed down and dispersed; the yard grew empty, the
officials remained within doors. Vladimir sadly walked up
the steps. Shabashkin opened the door and began thanking
Dubrovsky for his kind defence, bowing obsequiously.

Vladimir heard him with contempt and made no answer.
'We have decided,' Shabashkin went on, 'to stay the night
here, with your permission; it 's already dark and your
peasants might attack us on the way. Do be so kind, tell

them to spread some hay for us in the drawing-room; we 'll
go home as soon as it is light.'

'Do what you like,' Dubrovsky answered dryly; 'I am no
longer master here.'

With these words he went into his father's room and shut
himself in.

CHAPTER VI

'AND so all is over!' Vladimir said to himself. 'Only this
morning I had a home and was provided for; to-morrow I
shall have to leave the house where I was born. The ground
in which my father is resting will belong to the hateful man
who caused his death and beggared me!' Vladimir clenched
his teeth; his eyes rested on his mother's portrait. She was
painted leaning against the banisters, in a white morning
dress and a rose in her hair. 'This portrait, too, will fall
into our enemy's hands,' Vladimir thought. 'It will be flung
into a lumber room together with some broken chairs or
hang in the hall for his huntsmen to laugh at and comment
upon; and her bedroom, the room where my father died, will
be given to his steward or to the women of his harem. No,
no! He shall not have this house of sad memories from
which he is driving me!' Vladimir clenched his teeth;
terrible thoughts arose in his mind. He heard the officials'
voices; they had made themselves at home and were asking
for this and that, intruding unpleasantly upon his melancholy
reflections. At last all was quiet.

Vladimir opened the chests and drawers and started
sorting out his father's papers. They consisted for the most
part of accounts and business correspondence. He tore
them up without reading them. Among them he found a
packet inscribed: 'My wife's letters'. Vladimir began
reading them with profound emotion: written during the
Turkish campaign, they had been sent from Kistenyovka
to the army. She described to her husband her solitary
life and household occupations, tenderly complained of the

separation, and called him home to the embraces of his devoted wife. In one of the letters she expressed anxiety about little Vladimir's health; in another she pictured a happy and brilliant future for him. He read on, carried away into the world of family happiness, and forgot everything on earth; he did not notice the time passing. The clock on the wall struck eleven. Putting the letters into his pocket, he lighted a candle and came out of the study. The officials were asleep on the drawing-room floor. Empty glasses stood on the table and there was a strong smell of rum in the room. Disgusted, Vladimir walked past them into the entry. It was dark there. Seeing a light, someone dashed into a corner. Turning towards him with a candle, Vladimir recognized Arhip the blacksmith.

'What are you doing here?' he asked in surprise.

'I wanted to . . . I came to see if every one was at home,' Arhip said hesitatingly, in a low voice.

'And what is this axe for?'

'What for? One can't go about without an axe nowadays. Those attorneys are such bullies. They might any moment . . .'

'You are drunk; throw down the axe and go to bed.'

'Drunk? Vladimir Andreyevitch, sir, God is my witness I haven't had a drop . . . is it likely, at a time like this? It's unheard of, attorneys taking possession of us, driving our master out of the house. . . . There they snore, the brutes! Make an end of them, and have done.'

Dubrovsky frowned.

'Look here, Arhip, don't you do anything of the kind,' he said after a pause. 'It's not the attorneys' fault. Light the lantern and follow me.'

Taking the candle out of his master's hand, Arhip found a lantern behind the stove and lit it; both went quietly down the steps and walked along the yard. The watchman's rattle sounded; a dog barked. 'Who is on the watch?' Dubrovsky asked.

'We, sir,' a high-pitched voice answered. 'Vasilissa and Lukerya.'

'Go home.' Dubrovsky said; 'there's no need for you to stay.'

'You've done enough,' Arhip added.

'Thank you, sir,' the women answered, and went home at once.

Dubrovsky walked on. Two men came up to him; they called him; he recognized Anton's and Grisha's voices.

'Why aren't you asleep?' he asked them.

'How could we sleep?' Anton answered. 'To think we have lived to see this! . . .'

'Hush! Dubrovsky interrupted him. 'Where is Yegorovna?'

'In the house, in her room upstairs,' Grisha answered.

'Go and fetch her, and bring all our people out of the house so that not a soul is left there except the lawyers; and you, Anton, have a cart ready.'

Grisha went away, and a minute later appeared with his mother. The old woman had not undressed; no one in the house slept that night except the officials.

'Are you all here?' Dubrovsky asked; 'is there no one left in the house?'

'No one except the attorneys,' Grisha answered.

'Give me some hay or straw,' Dubrovsky said.

The men ran to the stables and returned bringing bundles of hay.

'Put it under the steps. That's right. Now give me a light, lads.'

Arhip opened the lantern, Dubrovsky lighted a splinter.

'Wait a minute,' he said to Arhip. 'I believe in my hurry I shut the door into the entry; run along and open it quick.'

Arhip ran into the entry—the inner door was open. Arhip locked it, muttering to himself: 'Open it, indeed! Not likely!' and returned to Dubrovsky.

Dubrovsky thrust the lighted splinter into the hay; it caught fire and the leaping flames lit the whole courtyard.

'Dear me!' Yegorovna cried pitifully. 'Vladimir Andreyevitch! what are you doing!'

'Be quiet!' Dubrovsky said. 'Well, children, good-bye! I go where God may lead me; be happy with your new owner.'

'Dear master, you are our father,' the men cried. 'We'd rather die than leave you! We'll go with you.'

The horses were ready. Dubrovsky and Grisha stepped into the cart; Anton struck the horses and they drove out of the yard.

In a minute the whole house was in flames. The doors

cracked and gave way; burning beams began to fall; a red smoke rose above the roof; a pitiful scream and cries of 'Help! help!' were heard. 'Not likely,' said Arhip, watching the fire with a malignant smile. 'Arhip dear, save them, the brutes,' Yegorovna said to him; 'God will reward you.' 'Not I,' the blacksmith answered. At that moment the officials appeared at the windows, trying to break the double window-frames. But the roof crashed down—and the screams stopped.

Soon all the house-serfs rushed out into the yard. The women wailed, hastening to save their belongings; the children skipped about admiring the fire. The sparks flew in a fiery whirl; the cottages caught fire. 'Now all is as it should be,' said Arhip; 'it burns well, eh? I expect it looks fine from Pokrovskoe.' At that moment something new attracted his attention: a cat was running about on the roof of the burning barn, not knowing where to jump. Flames were on all sides of it. The poor animal mewed pitifully for help; the little boys screamed with laughter, watching its despair.

'What are you laughing at, you little imps?' the blacksmith said to them angrily. 'You have no fear of God: God's creature is perishing, and you are glad, you sillies!'—and putting a ladder against the burning roof, he climbed up to save the cat. It understood his intention, and with evident gratitude hastily caught at his sleeve. The blacksmith, half scorched, descended with his burden. 'Well, lads, good-bye,' he said to the crowd, which was somewhat abashed, 'there's nothing for me to do here. Good luck to you; don't remember evil against me.'

The blacksmith went away. The fire raged for some time, but subsided at last. Heaps of red-hot embers glowed brightly in the darkness, and the burnt-out inhabitants of Kistenyovka wandered among them.

CHAPTER VII

THE next day the news of the fire spread throughout the neighbourhood. Every one talked of it, making various guesses and surmises. Some said that Dubrovsky's servants, getting drunk at the funeral, set the house on fire through carelessness, others accused the officials, who had had a drop too much in their new home. Some guessed the truth, asserting that Dubrovsky himself, moved by anger and despair, was the cause of the dreadful event; many were certain that he and his servants were burnt also. Troekurov came to the place of the fire the following day, and himself conducted the inquiry. It appeared that the police-captain, the assessor of the district court, and the two clerks, as well as Vladimir Dubrovsky, his nurse Yegorovna, his valet Gregory, the coachman Anton, and the blacksmith Arhip, had disappeared no one knew where. All the servants certified that the officials were burnt when the roof fell on them; their charred bones were found. The women Vasilissa and Lukerya said that they had seen Dubrovsky and Arhip the blacksmith a few minutes before the fire. The blacksmith, according to the general testimony, was still alive, and was probably the chief, if not the only person responsible for the fire. Grave suspicions rested on Dubrovsky. Kiril Petrovitch sent the Governor a detailed description of the events, and again appealed to the law.

Soon there were fresh events to give food to gossip and curiosity. Brigands appeared, spreading terror throughout the neighbourhood. Measures taken against them by the district authorities proved to be insufficient. Robberies, each more daring than the last, followed in rapid succession. There was no safety either in the villages or on the high road. Brigands drove about in broad daylight in troikas all over the province, stopping travellers and the post, coming into villages, robbing the landowners' houses, and setting them on fire. Their chieftain was renowned for his intelligence, courage, and a kind of generosity. People told marvels about him. Dubrovsky's name was on every tongue: all were convinced that he and no other was the leader of the daring villains. The only wonder was that Troekurov's estates had been spared: the robbers had not broken into a single barn, or stopped a single cart belonging to him. With his usual arrogance Troekurov ascribed this chiefly to the fear which he inspired throughout the province, and also to the excellent police he kept in his villages. At first Troekurov's neighbours laughed at his conceit, and expected the uninvited guests to visit Pokrovskoe, where there was plenty for them to loot; but at last they had to agree with him and admit that even robbers treated him with inexplicable respect. Troekurov was triumphant, and at the news of every fresh robbery indulged in reflections upon the Governor, police-captains, and company commanders from whom Dubrovsky always managed to escape unhurt.

Meanwhile, the first of October, the dedication feast of Troekurov's church, was drawing near. But before going on to describe the events that followed, we must introduce the reader to characters that are new to him, or at any rate that have only been briefly mentioned at the beginning of our story.

CHAPTER VIII

THE reader has probably already guessed that Kiril Petrovitch's daughter, of whom so far only a few words have been said, is the heroine of our story. At the period we are describing she was seventeen, and her beauty was in full bloom. Her father loved her excessively, but treated her in his usual arbitrary way, sometimes trying to satisfy her smallest whim, and sometimes frightening her by stern and even cruel treatment. Convinced of her affection, he could never win her confidence; she was used to concealing from him her thoughts and feelings, for she could never be certain of how he would respond to them. She had no friends, and had grown up in solitude. Their neighbours' wives and daughters seldom visited Kiril Petrovitch, whose amusements and conversation usually called for the company of men rather than ladies. Our young beauty seldom appeared among the guests feasting at Kiril Petrovitch's. The huge library, consisting for the most part of the works of the French writers of the eighteenth century, was put at her disposal. Her father, who never read anything except the *Perfect Cook*, could not direct her choice of books, and, having looked through all kinds of works, Masha naturally selected the novels. She was thus completing her education that had begun under the guidance of Mademoiselle Mimi. Kiril Petrovitch had had great confidence in that lady, and had shown her much goodwill; he was obliged at last to send her in secret to another estate when the consequences of their friendship had become too apparent. Mademoiselle Mimi left a rather pleasant memory behind her. She was a kind-hearted girl, and never made a bad use of her influence on Kiril Petrovitch; she differed in that from the other favourites who were constantly superseding one another in his affections. Kiril Petrovitch, too, seemed to be more fond of her than of the others; a black-eyed, lively little boy of about nine, whose face recalled Mademoiselle Mimi's southern features, was being brought up in his house as his son, in spite of the fact that a number of little boys who were the image of Kiril Petrovitch ran about barefoot before his windows, and were regarded as house-serfs. Kiril Petrovitch sent to Moscow for a French tutor for his little Sasha; the tutor arrived at Pokrovskoe during the events we are describing now.

Kiril Petrovitch liked his pleasant appearance and simple manner. He showed Kiril Petrovitch his certificates and a letter from a relative of Troekurov's in whose house he had been tutor for four years. Kiril Petrovitch looked through it all, and the only thing that displeased him was the French-man's youth—not because he thought this amiable defect to be incompatible with patience and experience, so necessary in the wretched calling of a tutor, but for reasons of his own which he decided to put before the young man at once. He sent for Masha (Kiril Petrovitch did not speak French, and she acted as interpreter for him).

'Come here, Masha. Tell this *mossoo* that, so be it, I'll engage him, only he mustn't dare make love to my maids or I'll give it him, the puppy! . . . translate it to him, Masha.'

Masha blushed, and turning to the teacher, said to him in

French that her father trusted to his modesty and good behaviour.

The Frenchman bowed, and said that he hoped to deserve their respect even if they refused him their favour.

Masha translated his answer word for word.

'Very well, very well!' Kiril Petrovitch said. 'He needn't trouble about either respect or favour. His business is to look after Sasha and to teach him grammar and geography . . . translate it to him.'

Masha softened her father's rude expressions in her translation, and Kiril Petrovitch dismissed his Frenchman to the lodge, where a room had been allotted to him.

Masha, brought up in aristocratic prejudices, did not pay the slightest attention to the young Frenchman; a tutor was to her mind a kind of servant or artisan, and a servant or an artisan was not a man in her eyes. She failed to observe the impression she had produced on M. Deforge—his confusion, his agitation, the change in his voice. For a few days in succession she met him fairly often without taking particular notice of him. An unexpected incident gave her quite a new idea of him.

Several bear cubs were generally kept in Kiril Petrovitch's courtyard, providing him with one of his chief amusements. In their early youth the cubs were brought every day to the drawing-room, where Kiril Petrovitch played with them for hours, making them fight cats and puppies. When they grew up they were put on a chain in expectation of a real fight. Sometimes a bear was brought before the manor-house windows, and an empty wine-barrel studded with nails was rolled towards it; the bear sniffed it, then gently touched it, pricked his paws and, getting angry, pushed it more violently—and the pain grew more violent too. Driven to absolute fury, it rushed at the barrel with a roar, until the object of the poor beast's vain fury was taken away from it. Sometimes a couple of bears were harnessed to a cart, visitors—willing and unwilling—were put into it and sent off at a gallop whither chance would take them. But the joke Kiril Petrovitch loved best was as follows.

A hungry bear used to be locked up in an empty room, tied by a rope to a ring in the wall. The rope was almost the length of the room, so that only the opposite corner was safe from the terrible beast's attack. An unsuspecting person was brought to the door of the room and, as if by accident, pushed into it; the door was locked, and the luckless victim was left alone with the shaggy hermit. The poor visitor, with the skirts of his coat torn off and a scratch on his arm, soon discovered the safe corner, but had to stand sometimes for three hours on end, squeezing himself against the wall while the fierce beast, two steps away from him, jumped, reared itself on its hind legs, and growled, striving to reach him. Such were the noble amusements of a Russian country gentleman! A few days after the tutor's arrival Troekurov thought of him and decided to give him a treat in the bear's room. Sending for him one morning, he led him along some dark passages; suddenly a side door opened, and two servants pushed the Frenchman through it, locking it after him. Recovering from his surprise, the tutor saw a bear tied to the wall; the brute began to snort, sniffing his visitor from a distance, and suddenly rearing on its hind legs went straight for him. . . . The Frenchman was not scared, did not run, but waited for the attack. The bear drew near; Deforge took a small pistol out of his pocket and, thrusting it into the ravening beast's ear, let it off. The bear fell. Every one ran up, the door was opened, and Kiril Petrovitch came in, surprised at the result of his joke.

Kiril Petrovitch was determined to get to the bottom of it. Who had warned Deforge about the practical joke that was to be played on him, and why did he carry a loaded pistol in his pocket? He sent for Masha. Masha came running and translated to the Frenchman her father's questions.

'I hadn't heard of the bear,' Deforge answered; 'but I always carry a pistol, for I don't intend to put up with insults for which, in my calling, I cannot demand satisfaction.'

Masha looked at him in amazement and translated his words to Kiril Petrovitch. Kiril Petrovitch made no answer, and gave orders for the bear to be carried out and skinned; then turning to his men he said: 'That's a fine fellow! He wasn't scared, upon my word he wasn't!' From that time he took a fancy to Deforge and never again thought of putting him to the test.

But the incident produced a still greater impression upon Marya Kirilovna. Her imagination was struck by the sight of the dead bear and of Deforge calmly standing beside its body and calmly talking to her. She saw that courage and a proud sense of personal dignity are not the exclusive privilege of one class, and from that day began treating the tutor with a consideration that grew more and more marked as time went on. They were brought into closer relations. Masha had a lovely voice and was very musical; Deforge volunteered to give her lessons. After this, the reader will not find it difficult to guess that Masha fell in love with him without being aware of it.

CHAPTER IX

VISITORS began to arrive on the eve of the festival; some stayed at the manor-house and the lodges, others put up at the bailiff's, at the priest's, and at the richer peasants'; the stables were full of the visitors' horses, the coach-houses and barns were blocked up with carriages of all sorts. At nine o'clock the bells began to ring for Mass, and all set out towards the new brick church that Kiril Petrovitch had built, adding something every year to its decoration. Such a number of gentry had come to Mass that there was no room for the peasants and they had to stand in the porch and outside. Mass had not begun: the priest was waiting for Kiril Petrovitch. He arrived in a carriage drawn by six horses and solemnly walked to his place accompanied by Marya Kirilovna. The eyes of both men and women were turned on her: the first were admiring her beauty, the second scrutinizing her dress. Mass began; a home-trained choir was singing. Kiril Petrovitch, absorbed in prayer and looking neither to the right nor to the left, joined in the singing, and bowed down with proud humility when the deacon prayed in the litany 'for the builder of this temple'.

The Mass was over. Kiril Petrovitch went first to kiss the cross [1]; every one followed him; the neighbours came up

---

[1] At the end of Mass the congregation go up to kiss the crucifix which the priest holds in his hand.—TRANSLATOR'S NOTE.

to him to pay their respects, the ladies surrounded Masha.
As he was leaving the church, Kiril Petrovitch invited every
one to dinner, and stepping into his carriage drove home.
They all followed him.

The rooms were filled with guests; every minute new
visitors appeared, and could hardly make their way to their
host. The ladies, in pearls and diamonds and old-fashioned
costly dresses that had seen better days, sat sedately in a
semicircle; the men crowded round the vodka and the
caviare, talking loudly to one another. In the dining-hall
the table was being set for eighty; the servants bustled about
placing bottles and decanters and arranging the table-cloths.
At last the butler announced that dinner was ready; Kiril
Petrovitch led the way to the table and took his seat; the
married ladies followed him and sat down with dignity,
observing a certain seniority; the young ladies clung together
like a flock of timid gazelles and chose their places next to
one another; the men settled opposite; the tutor sat at the
end of the table next to little Sasha.

The servants served the guests according to their rank; in
cases of uncertainty they acted on Lavater's principles and
hardly ever made a mistake. The clatter of plates and
jingle of spoons mingled with the noise of conversation.
Kiril Petrovitch looked gaily round the table, fully enjoying
the part of the hospitable host. At that moment a carriage
drawn by six horses drove into the yard. 'Who is that?'
Troekurov asked. 'Anton Pafnutyevitch,' several people
answered. The doors were opened and Anton Pafnutyevitch
Spitsyn, a stout man of about fifty with a round, pock-marked
face adorned by a triple chin, came into the dining-room,
bowing, smiling, and apologetic.

'Put another cover here!' Kiril Petrovitch called. 'You
are welcome, Anton Pafnutyevitch! Sit down and tell us
what it means you weren't at my Mass and are late for dinner?
It isn't like you: you are a pious man and you like good fare.'

'I am sorry,' Anton Pafnutyevitch answered, tying a
napkin to the buttonhole of his pea-coloured coat, 'I am
sorry, Kiril Petrovitch, sir; I left home early this morning,
but before I had gone seven miles the tyre of the front wheel
broke in two—so what was I to do? Fortunately we weren't
far from a village, but by the time we had crawled there and

found a blacksmith, and patched up the tyre somehow, three hours had gone—there was nothing for it. I did not venture to go the nearest way, across the Kistenyovka forest, but drove round it.'

'Aha!' Kiril Petrovitch interrupted him, 'you are not over brave, I see. What are you afraid of?'

'What am I afraid of, Kiril Petrovitch, sir? Why, of Dubrovsky: I might fall into his hands any day. He knows what he is about, and no one is safe with him; and me he would fleece doubly.'

'Why should he show you such preference, brother?'

'Why, sir, because of his father, Andrey Gavrilovitch, to be sure. Don't you remember it was I who for your pleasure —that is, in all justice and conscience—testified that the Dubrovskys had no right to Kistenyovka, but owned it solely through your kindness? The dead man, God rest his soul, promised to pay me out, and the son may keep his father's word, perhaps. So far God has spared me. They 've only broken into a barn of mine, but they may get at the house any day.'

'And they 'll have a fine time of it in the house,' Kiril Petrovitch remarked. 'I expect the red cash-box is cram-full.

'Indeed it isn't, Kiril Petrovitch, sir! It was full once, but now it 's quite empty.'

'Don't you tell lies, Anton Pafnutyevitch. I know you. You are not one for spending. You live like a pig, you never entertain, and you fleece your peasants—so you are saving all the time.'

'You are pleased to joke, Kiril Petrovitch,' Anton Pafnutyevitch muttered with a smile, 'but we are ruined, we really are'—and he took a piece of rich pie to take away the taste of his host's gentlemanly joke.

Kiril Petrovitch left him in peace and turned to the new police-captain, who had come to his house for the first time and was sitting at the other end of the table next to the tutor.

'Well, Mr. Police-captain, will you be long catching Dubrovsky?'

The police-captain, all in a flutter, bowed, smiled, and brought out, stammering: 'We 'll do our best, your Excellency'.

'Hm! Do your best! You have long been doing your

best, but it doesn't come to anything. And, indeed, why should you catch him? Dubrovsky's robberies are a perfect godsend to police-captains: you have to go about, conduct inquiries, have travelling expenses—and the money is in your pocket. How could you make an end of your benefactor? Isn't that true, sir?'

'Perfectly true, your Excellency,' the police-captain answered in utter confusion.

The visitors laughed.

'I like this young man's candour!' Kiril Petrovitch said. 'I see I shall have to tackle the business myself without waiting for help from the police. But I regret the loss of our old police-captain, Taras Alexeyevitch: if they hadn't burnt him there would have been less trouble about in the district. And what news of Dubrovsky? Where was he seen last?'

'At my house, Kiril Petrovitch,' a deep feminine voice replied. 'He had dinner with me last Tuesday.'

All eyes were turned on Anna Savvishna Globov, a widow, rather a homely person, loved by every one for her kind and cheerful disposition. All prepared to listen to her story with interest.

'I must tell you that three weeks ago I sent my bailiff to the post with a letter for my Vanyusha. I don't spoil my son, and indeed haven't the means to do so even if I wanted to, but of course an officer in the Guards has to keep up appearances, and I share my income with Vanyusha as best I can. So I sent him two thousand roubles; I did think of Dubrovsky more than once, but I thought it's only five miles to the town, and we might just do it, God willing. And behold, in the evening my bailiff comes home on foot, pale, and his clothes torn! I simply gasped. "What's the matter? What has happened to you?" And he said: "Anna Savvishna dear, highwaymen robbed me and very nearly killed me, too. Dubrovsky himself was there and wanted to hang me, but took pity and let me go; but he robbed me of all I had and took the horse and the cart." I was simply overwhelmed. King of Heaven, what will become of my Vanyusha! There was nothing for it; I wrote another letter to him, told him the whole story, and sent him my blessing without enclosing a penny.

'A week or two passed. Suddenly a carriage drove up to

my house. A general I did not know asked to see me; I said he was welcome. A dark-haired, dark-skinned man with a moustache and beard, a regular portrait of Kulnev, came in. He introduced himself as my husband's friend and colleague, and said that he was passing by and could not resist calling on his comrade's widow, knowing that I lived here. I offered him what food I had in the house, we talked of this and of that and, finally, of Dubrovsky. I told him of my trouble. The general frowned. "That's strange," he said; "I have heard that Dubrovsky doesn't attack every one, but only those who are known to be rich, and even then he doesn't rob them completely, but leaves them half their money. And no one has accused him of murder yet; I wonder if there's some trickery about it. Send for your bailiff, please." They went to fetch the bailiff. He came. When he saw the general he was dumbfounded. "Tell me, brother, how it was Dubrovsky robbed you and wanted to hang you?" My bailiff trembled and fell at the general's feet. "I'm sorry, sir, I did wrong . . . I told a lie." "If so," the general answered, "tell your mistress what happened and I'll listen." The bailiff tried in vain to collect his wits. "Well," the general went on, "tell her, where did you meet Dubrovsky?" "By the two pine-trees, sir, by the two pine-trees." "And what did he say to you?" "He asked me whose servant I was, where I was going, and on what errand." "Well, and then?" "And then he asked me for the letter and the money, and I gave him both." "And he?" "And he . . . sir, I am sorry!" "Well, what did he do?" "He returned me the money and the letter, and said 'Go in peace, take it to the post.'" "Well?" "I am sorry, sir!" "I'll settle you, my man," the general said menacingly. "And you, madam, have that rascal's box searched and give him to me, I'll teach him a lesson. Let me tell you that Dubrovsky has himself been an officer in the Guards and he wouldn't take advantage of a comrade." I guessed who his Excellency was: it was no use my arguing with him. The coachmen tied the bailiff to the box of his carriage. The money was found; the general had dinner with me, and went off immediately after, taking the bailiff with him. The bailiff was found next day in the forest tied to an oak-tree and stripped.'

All listened to Anna Savvishna's story in silence, the young ladies in particular. Many of them secretly sympathized with Dubrovsky, seeing a romantic hero in him, especially Marya Kirilovna, an ardent dreamer, nourished on the mysterious horrors of Mrs. Radcliffe.

'And you think, Anna Savvishna, it was Dubrovsky himself came to see you?' Kiril Petrovitch asked. 'You are very much mistaken. I don't know who your visitor was, but he was certainly not Dubrovsky.'

'How do you mean, not Dubrovsky? Who else would come out on the high road to stop and search passers-by?'

'I can't tell that, but it was not Dubrovsky. I remember him as a child; I don't know if his hair has turned dark— as a boy he had a head of fair, curly hair; but I do know for certain that Dubrovsky is five years older than my Masha, and that means he is not thirty-five but three-and-twenty.'

'Quite so, your Excellency,' the police-captain declared. 'I have in my pocket a description of Vladimir Dubrovsky. It says in it definitely that he is twenty-three.'

'Oh!' Kiril Petrovitch said; 'by the way, read it to us; we'll listen. It's not a bad thing for us to know what he's like: we may come across him, and then he won't escape.'

The police-captain took out of his pocket a rather dirty piece of paper, solemnly unfolded it, and read in a sing-song voice:

'The description of Vladimir Dubrovsky, made from the testimony of his former serfs.

'Age twenty-three, of medium height, a clear skin, no beard, hazel eyes, brown hair, a straight nose. As to special marks, he has none.'

'So that's all!' Kiril Petrovitch said.

'That's all,' the police-captain answered, folding the paper.

'I congratulate you, sir! That's a fine document! You'll have no difficulty in discovering Dubrovsky from this description! As though most people weren't of medium height and hadn't brown hair, hazel eyes, and a straight nose! I bet anything you might be talking for three hours to Dubrovsky himself and not guess who he was. A clever iot you officials are, I must say!'

Humbly putting the document in his pocket, the police-captain tackled in silence the roast goose and cabbage. Meanwhile the servants had gone round the table more than once filling the guests' wine-glasses. Several bottles of Caucasian and Crimean wine were opened with a loud report and favourably received under the name of champagne; cheeks began to glow, conversation grew louder, gayer, and more inconsequent.

'No,' Kiril Petrovitch went on, 'we shall never see another police-captain like Taras Alexeyevitch! He was no wool-gatherer, he knew what he was about. It's a pity he was burned, or not a single man of their band would have escaped him. He would have caught every one of them, and Dubrovsky himself couldn't have dodged him. Taras Alexeyevitch would have taken a bribe from him right enough, but wouldn't have let him off all the same. That was his way. There's nothing for it, it seems I'll have to see to it myself and go for the brigands with my men. To begin with, I'll send a score of them to clear the robbers' wood; they are no cowards, each of them tackles a bear single-handed, and is not likely to turn tail at the sight of brigands.'

'Is your bear well, Kiril Petrovitch?' asked Anton Pafnutyevitch, recalling at these words his shaggy acquaintance, and certain practical jokes of which he had once been victim.

'Misha has departed this life,' answered Kiril Petrovitch; 'he died an honourable death at the hand of an enemy. There is his victor!' Kiril Petrovitch pointed to Deforge 'Get yourself an ikon of my Frenchman's patron saint. He has avenged your . . . if I may say so . . . do you remember?'

'I should think I did!' Anton Pafnutyevitch replied, scratching his head. 'Very much so! So Misha is dead— I am sorry to hear it, I really am! Such an amusing creature he was! So clever! You wouldn't find another like him. But why did *mossoo* kill him?'

Kiril Petrovitch began telling of his Frenchman's exploit with the greatest pleasure, for he had a happy faculty of priding himself on all that in any sense belonged to him. His guests listened attentively to the story of the bear's death, glancing in amazement at Deforge, who calmly sat in his place, occasionally admonishing his lively pupil, and utterly unaware of the fact that his courage was the subject of the conversation.

The dinner, which had lasted about three hours, came to an end; the host put his napkin on the table, every one got up and went to the drawing-room, where coffee and cards were awaiting them, and the drinking, so well begun at dinner, was to continue.

CHAPTER X

ABOUT seven o'clock in the evening some of the guests thought of going home, but Kiril Petrovitch, exhilarated by punch, gave orders to lock the gates, and declared that he would allow no one to go till the morning. Soon the loud strains of a band were heard, the doors into the big hall were thrown open, and dancing began. Troekurov and his cronies sat in a corner drinking glass after glass, watching the young people enjoy themselves. The old ladies were playing cards. There was a shortage of men, as generally happens unless some cavalry brigade is quartered in the neighbourhood; all the men who could dance were recruited for the job. The tutor shone among them; he danced more than any one; all the young ladies chose him by preference and said that he was very easy to waltz with. Several times he danced with Marya Kirilovna, and the young ladies watched them ironically. At last, about midnight, Troekurov felt tired and, stopping the dancing, gave orders for supper to be served while he went to bed.

In Kiril Petrovitch's absence the company felt more lively and at ease; gentlemen ventured to take places next to the ladies; the girls laughed and whispered with their neighbours; the ladies talked loudly across the table. The men drank, argued, and laughed; in short, the supper was extremely pleasant and left many pleasant memories.

One man only took no part in the general enjoyment. Anton Pafnutyevitch sat there gloomy and silent, ate absent-mindedly, and seemed very ill at ease. The conversation about the robbers disturbed his imagination. We shall soon see that he had a good reason to fear them.

In calling God to witness that the red cash-box was empty Anton Pafnutyevitch committed no sin and told no lie; the red cash-box really was empty: the money that had once been kept in it had been transferred to a leather bag which he wore round his neck under his shirt. It was only this precaution that appeased to some extent his continual fear and distrust of every one. Compelled to spend the night in a strange house, he was afraid of being put into some distant room which thieves could enter easily; he looked round for a reliable companion and at last selected Deforge. His strong build and, still more, his courage in tackling the bear, whom poor Anton Pafnutyevitch could not recall without a shudder, decided his choice. When they got up from the table Anton Pafnutyevitch kept close to the young Frenchman, and after some preliminary coughing and clearing his throat, addressed him directly.

'Hm, hm! May I spend the night in your room, *mossoo*, because, you see . . .'

'Que désire monsieur?' asked Deforge with a courteous bow.

'What a nuisance you haven't learnt Russian yet, mossoo! Je veux, moi, chez vous coucher, do you understand?'

'Monsieur, très volontiers,' Deforge answered; 'veuillez donner des ordres en conséquence.'

Very much pleased with his knowledge of the French language, Anton Pafnutyevitch went at once to make the necessary arrangements.

The guests wished each other good night, and each retired to the room appointed to him; Anton Pafnutyevitch went with the tutor to the lodge. The night was dark. The tutor lighted the way with a lantern; Anton Pafnutyevitch followed with a fair amount of confidence, occasionally touching the bag concealed in his bosom to make sure that the money was still in his possession.

When they had come to the lodge, the tutor lit a candle and they both began to undress; meanwhile Anton Pafnut-yevitch walked about the room examining the doors and the windows, and shaking his head at the unsatisfactory state of things. The doors had no lock, but only a latch, and there were no double frames to the windows. He tried to complain of this to Deforge, but his knowledge of French was too limited for so complicated an explanation. The Frenchman failed to understand him, and Anton Pafnut-yevitch had to desist from complaining. Their beds were opposite each other; both lay down, and the Frenchman blew out the candle.

'Pourquoi vous blowez, pourquoi vous blowez?' cried Anton Pafnutyevitch struggling to conjugate the verb 'to blow' in the French manner. 'I cannot *dormir* in the dark.'

Apparently not understanding his exclamation, Deforge wished him good night.

'The wretched infidel!' Spitsyn grumbled, wrapping himself up in the blanket. 'The idea of his blowing out the candle! So much the worse for him, though. I cannot sleep without a light. Mossoo! Mossoo!' he went on, 'je veux avec vous parler'.

But the Frenchman made no answer, and soon began to snore.

'He is snoring, the brute,' Anton Pafnutyevitch thought; 'but there's not much chance of sleep for me: the thieves may come in any moment at the open door or climb in at the window; a cannon wouldn't wake that brute. Mossoo! Mossoo!—the devil take you!'

Anton Pafnutyevitch grew silent; weariness and the wine he had drunk gradually overcame his fears; he began to doze, and soon sank into a profound sleep.

A strange awakening was in store for him. He felt through his sleep that someone was tugging gently at his shirt collar. Anton Pafnutyevitch opened his eyes, and in the pale light of the autumn morning saw Deforge. The Frenchman held a pistol in one hand, and with the other was unfastening the precious bag. Anton Pafnutyevitch turned cold with terror. 'Qu'est-ce que c'est, mossoo, qu'est-ce que c'est?' he brought out in a shaking voice.

'Hush! Be quiet!' the tutor answered in pure Russian. 'Be quiet or you are lost. I am Dubrovsky.'

CHAPTER XI

Now we will ask the reader's permission to explain the last
incidents of our story by referring to circumstances which
we have not yet had time to relate.

In the house of the station-master, whom we have mentioned once before, a traveller sat in a corner with a mild
and patient air that showed him to be a man of humble
origin, or a foreigner—that is, a man who had no rights at
posting stations. His trap stood in the courtyard waiting
to be oiled. It contained a small suit-case—its meagre
dimensions a proof of his lack of means. The traveller
ordered neither tea nor coffee, and kept looking out of the
window and whistling, to the great annoyance of the station-
master's wife who sat behind the partition.

'A regular infliction, that whistler!' she said in an undertone. 'The way he goes on! Plague take him, the cursed
infidel!'

'Why?' the station-master asked. 'What does it matter?
Let him whistle.'

'What does it matter?' his wife retorted angrily; 'don't
you know the saying?'

'What saying? That whistling drives money away?
Nonsense, Pahomovna! Whistling makes no difference to
us—we never have any money anyway.'

'Do let him go, Sidoritch. What's the good of keeping
him here? Give him the horses and let him go to the devil.'

'He can wait, Pahomovna; there are only three troikas
in readiness, the fourth one is resting. Good travellers may
turn up any minute: I don't want to answer for the Frenchman with my own back. Hush! I thought so! There's
somebody driving here! Aha! and how fast! I wonder if
it's some general?'

A carriage drove up to the front steps. The servant
jumped off the box, opened the carriage door, and a minute
later a young man in a military cloak and a white cap came
into the station-master's house; the servant followed, carrying
a box which he put in the window.

'Horses!' the officer said peremptorily.

'Yes, sir,' the station-master answered. 'May I have your pass?'

'I haven't one. I am going off the main track. . . . Don't you know me?'

The station-master, all in a flurry, dashed out of the room to hurry the drivers. The young man paced up and down the room and, going behind the partition, quietly asked the station-master's wife who the other traveller was.

'Heaven only knows,' she answered. 'Some Frenchman; he's been waiting for the horses and whistling for the last five hours. I am dead sick of him, curse him!'

The young man spoke to the traveller in French.

'Where are you going?' he asked him.

'To the nearest town,' the Frenchman answered, 'and from there to a landowner in the district who has engaged me by letter as tutor. I thought I would be there to-day, but Mr. Station-master seems to have decided otherwise. In this country it isn't easy to get horses, Mr. Officer.'

'And which of the local landowners has engaged you?' the officer asked.

'Mr. Troekurov,' the Frenchman answered.

'Troekurov? Who is this Troekurov?'

'*Ma foi*, monsieur, I haven't heard much good about him. They say he is a proud, headstrong man, cruel to his dependants; nobody can get on with him, and all tremble at his very name; he does not stand on ceremony with tutors, and has already flogged two of them to death.'

'Good heavens! And you venture to enter the service of such a monster?'

'But what am I to do, Mr. Officer? He offers me a good salary, three thousand roubles a year and all found. I may be luckier than the others. I have a mother who is no longer young: I'll send her half my salary for her keep, and with the remainder I can save up in five years a small capital —enough to secure my independence—and then *bon soir*, I go to Paris and start a business of my own.'

'Does any one in Troekurov's house know you?' the officer asked.

'No one,' answered the tutor; 'he heard of me through a friend of his in Moscow, whose cook, my fellow-countryman, recommended me. I must tell you that I have been trained as a pastry-cook and not as a teacher, but I was told that in your country being a teacher is far more profitable.'

The officer pondered. 'Look here,' he said, interrupting the Frenchman. 'What if you were offered ten thousand roubles in cash on condition that you went back to Paris at once?'

The Frenchman looked at the officer in surprise, and shook his head with a smile.

'The horses are ready,' the station-master said, coming in. The servant confirmed his words.

'I'm coming,' the officer answered. 'Leave the room for a minute.' The station-master and the servant went out. 'I am not joking,' he went on in French. 'I can give you 10,000 roubles; all I want is your absence and your papers.' With these words he opened the box and took out several bundles of notes.

The Frenchman stared at him. He did not know what to think.

'My absence . . . my papers . . .' he repeated in surprise. 'Here they are, but surely you are joking? What do you want with my papers?'

'That's nothing to do with you. I ask you, do you agree or not?'

Not believing his own ears, the Frenchman handed his papers to the young officer, who quickly looked them over.

'Your passport . . . good; a letter of introduction . . . let's look at it; your birth certificate . . . excellent. Well, here is your money, go back. Good-bye.'

The Frenchman was dumbfounded. The officer turned to him once more.

'I nearly forgot the most important part of it: give me your word of honour that it will all remain between ourselves . . . your word of honour.'

'Yes, certainly,' the Frenchman answered. 'But my papers? What shall I do without them?'

'Say in the first town you come to that you have been robbed by Dubrovsky. They'll believe you and give you the necessary certificate. Good-bye; I hope you will soon be in Paris and find your mother in good health.'

Dubrovsky left the room and, stepping into the carriage, drove off at a gallop.

The station-master was looking out of the window, and when the carriage had gone he turned to his wife and said:

'Pahomovna! do you know what? That was Dubrovsky.'

His wife rushed headlong to the window, but it was too late: Dubrovsky was far away. She began scolding her husband:

'You have no fear of God, Sidoritch! Why didn't you tell me before? I might have had a look at Dubrovsky, and now Heaven only knows when he'll call here again. You have no conscience, that's a fact!'

The Frenchman stood as though rooted to the spot. The money, the pact with the officer—it all seemed to him a dream. But the bundles of notes were there, in his pocket, eloquently confirming the reality of the wonderful event.

He decided to hire horses to take him to the town. The driver went at a snail's pace, and it was night when they arrived.

Before they reached the town-gates, where instead of a sentry there was a tumbledown sentry-box, the Frenchman told the driver to stop. Stepping out of the trap he walked away, explaining by signs that he gave him the trap and the suit-case by way of a tip. The driver was as much surprised by his generosity as the Frenchman himself had been by Dubrovsky's offer. But concluding that the foreign gentleman had gone mad, the driver thanked him with a deep bow and thought it wiser not to go into the town. He drove to a certain place of amusement, the owner of which was a friend of his, and spent the whole night there, going home the following morning with his three horses but no trap and no suit-case, his face swollen and his eyes red.

Having gained possession of the Frenchman's papers, Dubrovsky, as we have seen already, boldly appeared before Troekurov and settled at his house. Whatever his secret intentions may have been (we shall learn about them later), there was nothing reprehensible in his conduct. True, he did not occupy himself much with little Sasha's education; he let the boy do what he liked in his spare time and was not very strict about lessons, which were set to the child merely as a matter of form. On the other hand, however, he followed with much attention Marya Kirilovna's progress in music and often spent hours with her at the piano. Every one liked the young tutor: Kiril Petrovitch for his courage and quickness in the hunting field, Marya Kirilovna for his boundless devotion and deferential attentiveness, Sasha for his leniency, the servants for his kindness and a generosity which seemed out of keeping with his position. He appeared to be fond of the whole family and regarded himself as a member of it.

Nearly a month had passed between the time that he became a tutor and the memorable festival, and no one suspected that the modest young Frenchman was the terrible brigand whose name inspired all the neighbouring landowners with terror. During all that time Dubrovsky had not left Pokrovskoe, but rumours of his robberies never ceased to spread, thanks to the country people's fertile imagination; indeed, his confederates may have gone on with their exploits in their chieftain's absence.

Spending the night in the same room with a man whom he could rightly regard as a personal enemy, largely responsible for his misfortune, Dubrovsky could not resist the temptation. He knew of the precious wallet and decided to gain possession of it. We have seen how greatly he surprised poor Anton Pafnutyevitch by his sudden transformation from a tutor into a brigand.

CHAPTER XII

At nine o'clock in the morning the visitors who had spent the night at Pokrovskoe gathered, one after another, in the drawing-room, where a samovar was already boiling. Marya Kirilovna in a morning gown was sitting before it, and Kiril Petrovitch in a blanket-cloth coat and slippers was drinking tea out of his big cup that looked like a slop-basin. Anton Pafnutyevitch was the last to come in; he looked so pale and distressed that every one was struck by his appearance, and Kiril Petrovitch inquired about his health. Spitsyn answered quite at random, glancing with terror at the tutor, who sat at the table with the others, perfectly unconcerned. A few minutes later a servant came in and told Spitsyn that his carriage was ready. Anton Pafnutyevitch hastily left the room and drove away at once. Troekurov and the visitors could not think what had happened to him; Kiril Petrovitch decided that he had overeaten himself. After the morning tea and a farewell lunch the other visitors left also; soon Pokrovskoe was quiet again and everything went on as usual.

Several days passed and nothing worthy of note happened. Life at Pokrovskoe was uneventful. Kiril Petrovitch rode out hunting every day; reading, walks, and music lessons occupied Marya Kirilovna's time—especially music lessons. She was beginning to understand her own heart, and confessed to herself with vexation that it was not indifferent to the young Frenchman's fine qualities. For his part he never transgressed the bounds of respect and strict decorum, and this soothed her pride and timid doubts. She gave herself up more and more trustfully to the pleasant habit of being with him. She felt dull without him, and, when he was with her, turned to him every minute, wanting to know his opinion on every subject and agreeing with him in everything. Perhaps she was not in love as yet; but at the first obstacle or misfortune that fate might throw in her way the flame of passion was bound to flare up in her heart.

Coming one day into the drawing-room where the tutor was waiting for her, Marya Kirilovna observed with surprise a look of confusion on his pale face. She opened the piano and sang a few notes; but Dubrovsky excused himself, saying that he had a headache and could not go on with the lesson. Closing the book of music, he handed her a note. Marya Kirilovna took it before she had had time to think, and instantly repented; but Dubrovsky was no longer in the room. Marya Kirilovna went to her own room and unfolding the note read as follows:

'Come at seven o'clock to-night to the arbour by the brook; I must speak to you.'

Her curiosity was thoroughly roused. She had long been expecting a declaration, both wishing and fearing it. It pleased her to have a confirmation of what she guessed; but she felt that it would be unseemly for her to hear such an avowal from a man who, owing to his station in life, ought not to hope ever to obtain her hand in marriage. She decided to keep the tryst, but she could not make up her mind whether

she ought to receive the tutor's declaration with aristocratic
indignation, friendly advice, gay jokes, or silent sympathy.
Meanwhile she kept glancing at the clock. It grew dark;
candles were brought in. Kiril Petrovitch sat down to play
boston with some visitors; the clock in the dining-room
struck a quarter to seven; Marya Kirilovna quietly went out
on to the steps, looked about her, and ran into the garden.

The night was dark, the sky was covered with clouds, one
could not see at a distance of two paces, but Marya Kirilovna
walked in the dark along the familiar paths, and was at the
arbour in a minute; she stopped to take breath, so as to
appear before Deforge with a cool and indifferent air. But
Deforge was there already.

'Thank you for not refusing my request,' he said to her in
a low and melancholy voice. 'I would have been in despair
if you hadn't come.'

Marya Kirilovna answered with a phrase she had prepared:
'I hope you will not make me regret it'.

He said nothing, and seemed to be mustering his courage.

'Circumstances require . . . I have to leave you,' he said
at last. 'Soon maybe you 'll hear . . . but I must explain
myself before we part.'

Marya Kirilovna did not answer. She thought his words
were a prelude to the declaration she had been expecting.

'I am not what you suppose,' he went on, bowing his head.
'I am not a Frenchman, and my name is not Deforge—I
am Dubrovsky.'

Marya Kirilovna cried out.

'Don't be afraid, for God's sake! You must not fear my
name. Yes, I am the unfortunate man whom your father
ruined. He drove me out of my parental home and sent me
plundering on the highways. But you need not fear me,
either for yourself or for him. It 's all over . . . I have
forgiven him; listen: you have saved him. His was the
first blood I meant to have shed. I walked round his house
deciding where the fire was to begin, where I was to enter his
bedroom, how I was to cut off all means of escape for him.
At that moment you went past me like a heavenly vision—
and my heart was conquered. I understood that the house
where you lived was sacred, that not a single being related
to you by blood could be the victim of my curse. I renounced

vengeance as madness. For days together I wandered round the Pokrovskoe gardens, hoping to catch a glimpse of your white dress. I followed you in your incautious walks, stealing from bush to bush, happy in the thought that there could be no danger for you where I was secretly present. At last an opportunity offered itself. . . . I settled in your house. These three weeks were days of happiness for me; the memory of them will brighten my melancholy existence. . . . This morning I received news that makes it impossible for me to stay here longer. I am leaving you at once, this very evening. But before going I had to open my heart to you so that you should not curse me or despise me. Think of Dubrovsky sometimes. Believe me that he was born for a different kind of life, that his soul knew how to love you, that never . . .'

At that moment a loud whistle was heard, and Dubrovsky paused. Seizing her hand he pressed it to his burning lips. The whistle was repeated.

'Good-bye,' Dubrovsky said, 'I am being called. A moment's delay may ruin me. . . .'

He walked away. . . . Marya Kirilovna did not move. Dubrovsky came back and took her hand.

'If ever,' said he in a tender and moving voice—'if ever a misfortune befalls you, and there is none to protect and help you, will you promise to appeal to me and ask me to do all in my power to save you? Will you promise not to spurn my devotion?'

Marya Petrovna was weeping in silence. The whistle sounded for the third time.

'You are destroying me!' cried Dubrovsky. 'I will not leave you till you give me an answer: will you promise or not?'

'I promise,' the beautiful creature whispered in distress.

Agitated by her meeting with Dubrovsky, Marya Kirilovna was returning from the garden. It seemed to her that there were many people in the yard; a troika stood at the front steps, the servants were running about, the whole house was in commotion. From some distance she heard Kiril Petrovitch's voice and hastened indoors, afraid lest her absence should be noticed. Kiril Petrovitch met her in the drawing-room; his guests were crowding round the police-captain, pelting him with questions. The police-captain, dressed as for travelling and armed to the teeth, answered them with a mysterious and preoccupied air.

'Where have you been, Masha?' Kiril Petrovitch asked. 'Did you meet Mr. Deforge?'

Masha managed to answer in the negative.

'Would you believe it?' Kiril Petrovitch went on, 'the police-captain has come to arrest him, and assures me that he is Dubrovsky.'

'The description tallies exactly, your Excellency,' the police-captain interrupted respectfully.

'Go to the devil with your description, my dear man. I won't give you my Frenchman till I've seen into the matter myself. One can't take Anton Pafnutyevitch's word for it —he is a liar and a coward: he dreamt that the tutor wanted to rob him. Why didn't he say a word to me about it that morning?'

'The Frenchman threatened him, your Excellency,' the police-captain answered, 'and made him swear he would say nothing.'

'Rubbish!' Kiril Petrovitch decided; 'I'll clear it all up in a minute. Well, where is the tutor?' he asked of a servant who had come into the room.

'He is nowhere to be found, sir,' the servant answered.

'Search for him, then!' shouted Troekurov, beginning to feel doubtful. 'Show me that description you are so proud of,' he said to the police-captain, who handed him the paper at once. 'Hm! Hm! twenty-three years old, and so on. It's all very well, but it proves nothing. Well, where is the tutor?'

'He is not to be found, sir,' was the answer again.

Kiril Petrovitch was growing uneasy; Masha was more dead than alive.

'You are pale, Masha,' her father remarked. 'Did it give you a fright?'

'No, papa,' Masha answered; 'I have a headache.'

'Go to your room, Masha, and don't you worry.'

Masha kissed his hand, and hastened to her room; there she threw herself on her bed and broke into hysterical sobs. The maids ran in, undressed her, and succeeded at last in soothing her with cold water, and all sorts of smelling-salts; they put her to bed, and she went off to sleep.

The Frenchman, meanwhile, was nowhere to be seen. Kiril Petrovitch paced up and down the room, whistling menacingly: 'Thunder of victory, resound!' The visitors whispered among themselves; the police-captain had evidently been fooled: the Frenchman was not to be found. He had probably succeeded in escaping, after being warned. But by whom? How? It remained a mystery.

The clock struck eleven, but no one thought of sleep. At last Kiril Petrovitch said to the police-captain angrily: 'Well? You can't stay here till daylight, my house isn't an inn. You are not quick enough, brother, to catch Dubrovsky —if he really is Dubrovsky. You go home and try to be a bit smarter in the future. And it's time for you to go home too,' he went on, turning to his visitors. 'Order your carriages, I am sleepy.'

Thus ungraciously did Troekurov part with his guests.

CHAPTER XIII

SOME time passed without anything of interest happening. But at the beginning of the following summer many changes took place in Kiril Petrovitch's family life.

Twenty miles from him there was a rich estate belonging to Prince Vereisky. The Prince had lived for many years in foreign parts; his estate was managed by a retired major, and there was no communication whatever between Pokrovskoe and Arbatovo. But at the end of May the Prince returned from abroad, and came to his country-seat which he had never yet seen. Accustomed to dissipation, he could not endure solitude, and on the third day of his arrival went to dine with Troekurov, whom he had known years before.

The Prince was about fifty, but he looked much older. Excesses of all kinds had undermined his health and left their indelible stamp upon him. He was perpetually bored and was in perpetual need of amusement. In spite of that, he had an attractive and distinguished appearance, and the habit of always being in society made his manners amiable, especially with women. Kiril Petrovitch was extremely gratified by his visit, regarding it as a mark of respect from a man who knew the world. True to his habit, he entertained the Prince by showing him various things on the estate and taking him to the kennels. The Prince was nearly choked by the smell of the dogs and hastened to walk out, pressing a scented handkerchief to his nose. The old-fashioned garden with its clipped lime-trees, square pond, and formal avenues did not please him; he liked English parks and so-called nature; but he praised everything and appeared delighted. The servant came to tell them that dinner was on the table. They went in. The Prince was limping slightly, tired with the walk, and was already regretting his visit.

But in the dining-room Marya Kirilovna met them—and the old rake was struck by her beauty. Troekurov put his visitor next to her. Excited by her presence, the Prince was gay, and several times succeeded in attracting her attention by his interesting stories. After dinner Kiril Petrovitch invited him to go for a ride, but the Prince apologized, pointing to his velvet boots and joking about his gout. He suggested going for a drive, so that he need not part from his charming neighbour. The carriage was ordered. The old men and the beautiful girl stepped in and drove along. The conversation never flagged. Marya Kirilovna listened with pleasure to the gay and flattering remarks of a man of the world; suddenly Vereisky asked, turning to Kiril Petrovitch, what were those charred ruins, and did they belong to him? Kiril Petrovitch frowned: the memories that the burnt-down building roused in him were distasteful to him. He answered that the land was his now, but had belonged to Dubrovsky before.

'To Dubrovsky?' Vereisky repeated. 'What, to that famous brigand?'

'To his father,' Troekurov answered. 'And his father was a bit of a brigand too.'

'What has become of our Rinaldo? Has he been caught? Is he living?'

'He is living and is still at large, and so long as we have thieves and villains for police-captains he is not likely to be caught. By the way, Prince, Dubrovsky did pay you a visit at your Arbatovo, didn't he?'

'Yes, I believe last year he burnt something down or broke into some building. Don't you think, Marya Kirilovna, it would be interesting to make a closer acquaintance with this romantic hero?'

'Interesting, indeed!' Troekurov said; 'she knows him already. He taught her music for three weeks, but, thank Heaven, he did not take anything for his lessons.' Kiril Petrovitch began telling the story of the supposed French tutor. Marya Kirilovna felt extremely uncomfortable. Vereisky listened with profound attention and, saying that it all was very strange, changed the subject. When they returned to Pokrovskoe he ordered his carriage and, though Kiril Petrovitch begged him to stay the night, he went home immediately after tea. Before going, however, he asked Kiril Petrovitch to pay him a visit with Marya Kirilovna, and the proud Troekurov promised: for, taking into consideration the princely title, two stars, and three thousand hereditary serfs, he regarded Vereisky as in a sense his equal.

CHAPTER XIV

Two days after Prince Vereisky's visit Kiril Petrovitch and his daughter went to see him. As they neared Arbatovo he could not sufficiently admire the clean and cheerful peasant cottages and the brick manor-house built after the style of an English mansion. In front of the house there was an oval meadow with lush green grass, on which Swiss cows with tinkling bells round their necks were grazing. A large park surrounded the house. Vereisky met his visitors at the steps and offered his arm to the young beauty. They came into a magnificent dining-room where the table had been set for three. The Prince led his visitors to the window, and a lovely view presented itself to them. The Volga flowed in front of the house; loaded barges in full sail glided along it, and the small fishing-boats, so expressively called 'wreckers', flitted to and fro. Hills and meadows stretched beyond the river; several villages added life to the neighbourhood.

Then they went to look at a collection of pictures which the
Prince had purchased abroad. He explained to Marya
Kirilovna the subject of each picture, told the history of the
painters, pointed out the merits and the defects of their
work. He spoke of pictures, not in the conventional language
of a pedantic connoisseur, but with feeling and imagination.
Marya Kirilovna listened to him with pleasure. They went
in to dinner. Troekurov did full justice to his host's wines
and to the art of his cook, and Marya Kirilovna did not feel
the slightest confusion or constraint in talking to a man
whom she was seeing for the second time in her life. After
dinner the Prince invited his visitors into the garden. They
drank coffee in an arbour on the bank of a broad lake dotted
with islands. Suddenly instrumental music was heard, and
a six-oared boat pulled up by the arbour. They were rowed
along the lake, past the islands, visiting some of them: on
one they found a marble statue, on another a solitary cave,
on a third a monument with a mysterious inscription that
aroused Marya Kirilovna's girlish curiosity, which was not
altogether satisfied by the Prince's courteous but incomplete
explanations. The time passed imperceptibly. It began to
grow dusk. The Prince hurried home because of the dew
and evening chill; a samovar was waiting for them. The
Prince asked Marya Kirilovna to play the part of hostess in
an old bachelor's house. She poured out the tea, listening
to the amiable talker's endless stories. Suddenly there was
a shot—and a rocket lighted up the sky. . . . The Prince
handed Marya Kirilovna a shawl and called her and Troekurov
to the balcony. In the darkness many-coloured lights
flared up in front of the house, rising up in sheaves, pouring
down in streams, falling like rain or like shooting stars, going
out and flaring up again. Marya Kirilovna was as happy as
a child. Vereisky enjoyed her delight, and Troekurov was
extremely pleased with the Prince, for he regarded *tous ces
frais* as signs of respect for himself and of a desire to give
him pleasure.

The supper was in no way inferior to the dinner in excel-
lence. The guests retired to the bedrooms allotted to them,
and the following morning parted from their amiable host,
promising to see each other again in the near future.

CHAPTER XV

MARYA KIRILOVNA sat in her room at an embroidery frame by an open window. She did not mix up her silks like Conrad's mistress, who in the absent-mindedness of love embroidered a rose in green silk. Her needle faultlessly reproduced on canvas the design she was copying; but in spite of this, her thoughts did not follow her work—they were far away.

Suddenly a hand was gently thrust in at the window; someone put a letter on the embroidery frame and disappeared before Marya Kirilovna had recovered from her surprise. At that moment a servant came in to her to call her to Kiril Petrovitch. Trembling, she thrust the letter under her fichu and hastened to her father's study.

Kiril Petrovitch was not alone. Prince Vereisky was with him. When Marya Kirilovna came in he got up and bowed to her in silence, with a confusion most unusual for him.

'Come here, Masha,' Kiril Petrovitch said; 'I 'll tell you a piece of news which I hope will please you. Here is your future husband: the Prince makes you an offer of marriage.'

Masha was dumbfounded; a deathly pallor overspread her face. She was silent. The Prince went up to her, and taking her hand, asked in a voice full of feeling whether she would consent to make him a happy man. Masha said nothing.

'Of course she consents,' Kiril Petrovitch said; 'but you know, Prince, a girl finds it hard to say the word. Well, children, kiss each other and may you be happy.'

Masha stood stock-still; the old Prince kissed her hand. Suddenly tears ran down her pale face. The Prince frowned slightly.

'Off with you, off with you!' Kiril Petrovitch said; 'dry your tears and come back to us gay as a lark. They all weep when they are betrothed,' he went on, turning to Vereisky: 'it 's the tradition, you know. Now, Prince, let 's talk of business—that is, of the dowry.'

Marya Kirilovna eagerly took advantage of the permission to withdraw. Running to her room she locked herself in, and gave way to her tears, imagining herself as the old Prince's wife; he suddenly seemed to her hateful, disgusting. . . . To be married to him terrified her like the executioner's axe, like the grave! 'No, no!' she repeated in despair; 'I'd rather die, rather go into a convent, rather marry Dubrovsky. . . .' At this point she recalled the letter and took it out eagerly, guessing that it was from him. And indeed it was written by him, and contained only the following words:

'This evening, at ten o'clock, in the same place.'

The moon was shining; the country night was still; a slight breeze blew up from time to time, raising a rustle in the garden.

Like a fleeting shadow the young beauty drew near the trysting place. She could not see any one; suddenly emerging from behind the arbour, Dubrovsky stood before her.

'I know everything,' he said in a sad and low voice. 'Remember your promise.'

'You offer me your protection?' Masha answered. 'But don't be angry: it frightens me. How could you help me?'

'I could free you from the man you hate.'

'For God's sake don't touch him, don't dare to touch him, if you love me! I don't want to be the cause of anything horrible. . . .'

'I won't touch him: your will is law to me. He owes his life to you. Never shall a murder be committed in your name. You must be pure even in my crimes. But how can I save you from a cruel father?'

'There is still hope: I may touch him by my tears and despair. He is obstinate, but he loves me.'

'Don't hope in vain: he will see in your tears simply the fear and disgust usual in all young girls who marry not for love, but for considerations of prudence. What if he is determined to arrange for your happiness in spite of yourself? What if you are led to the altar by force and given into the power of that old man?'

'Then . . . then there is nothing for it—come for me—I'll be your wife.'

Dubrovsky shuddered; his pale face flushed crimson and then grew paler than before. He paused for a few minutes, hanging his head.

'Muster all your courage, implore your father, throw yourself at his feet; depict to him all the horror of your future, your youth fading beside a decrepit old rake; tell him that riches will not give you even a minute's happiness; luxury comforts only the poor, and even then only for a moment, because they are not used to it; keep on entreating him, don't be afraid of his anger and his threats so long as there is a shadow of hope; for God's sake go on imploring him! But if there is no other means—venture on a cruel explanation: tell him that if he will not give in, you . . . you will find a terrible defender. . . .'

Dubrovsky covered his face with his hands; he seemed to be choking. Masha was weeping.

'My wretched, wretched fate!' he said with a bitter sigh. 'I would give my life for you; to see you from a distance, to touch your hand was a delight to me; and now when I have a chance of pressing you to my throbbing heart and saying, "My angel, let us die together!"—poor me, I have to guard myself from bliss, I must ward it off with all my power! I dare not fall at your feet and thank Heaven for an incredible, undeserved happiness! Oh, how I ought to hate him who . . . but I feel there is now no room for hatred in my heart.'

He put his arm round her slim waist, and gently drew her to his heart. Trustfully she rested her head on the young brigand's shoulder—both were silent. . . .

Time flew. 'I must be going,' Masha said at last. Dubrovsky seemed to wake up from a dream. He took her hand and put a ring on her finger.

'If you decide to ask my help,' he said, 'put the ring into the hollow of this oak-tree; I shall know what to do.'

Dubrovsky kissed her hand and disappeared among the trees.

CHAPTER XVI

PRINCE VEREISKY'S suit was not a secret to the neighbourhood. Kiril Petrovitch was receiving congratulations;
preparations for the wedding were going on. Masha put off
the decisive explanation from day to day. Meanwhile her
manner towards her elderly suitor was cold and constrained.
The Prince did not worry about that: he troubled little about
her love, satisfied with her silent consent.

But time was going on. Masha decided to act at last and
wrote a letter to Prince Vereisky. She tried to rouse a
feeling of generosity in his heart; candidly confessing that
she had not the slightest affection for him, she begged him
to renounce her hand, and to defend her from her father's
power. She slipped the letter into the Prince's hand. He
read it when he was alone—and was not in the least moved
by his betrothed's candour. On the contrary, he saw that
it was necessary to hasten the wedding, and thought it best
to show the letter to his future father-in-law.

Kiril Petrovitch was enraged; the Prince had the greatest
difficulty in persuading him not to let Masha guess that he
knew about her letter. Kiril Petrovitch agreed not to tell
her about it, but decided to waste no time, and fixed the
wedding for the next day but one. The Prince found this
very sensible; he went to Masha and told her that her letter
grieved him very much, but that he hoped to win her affection
in time; that the thought of losing her was too painful to
him, and that he had not the strength to agree to his own
death sentence. Then he respectfully kissed her hand and
went away, not saying a word to her about Kiril Petrovitch's
decision.

But he had no sooner left the house than her father came
in to her and told her straight out to be ready the day after
next. Marya Kirilovna, agitated by her explanation with
Prince Vereisky, burst into tears, and threw herself at her
father's feet. 'Papa!' she cried pitifully, 'papa! don't ruin
me! I don't love the Prince, I don't want to be his wife!'

'What's the meaning of this?' Kiril Petrovitch said
menacingly. 'You've said nothing all this time, and been

quite agreeable, and now, when everything is settled, you suddenly take it into your head to be tiresome and go back on it! Don't be a fool, please; you won't prevail on me in that way.'

'Don't ruin me!' poor Masha repeated; 'why do you drive me away from you and give me to a man I don't love? Have you grown tired of me? I want to stay with you as before. Papa, you'll be sad without me, and still more sad when you know that I am unhappy. Don't force me, papa, I don't want to be married!'

Kiril Petrovitch was touched, but he concealed his emotion, and pushing her away said sternly:

'It's all nonsense; do you hear? I know better than you do what is necessary for your happiness. Tears won't help you; your wedding will be the day after to-morrow.'

'The day after to-morrow!' Masha cried. 'Good heavens! No, no, it's impossible, it shall not be! Papa, listen: if you've decided to ruin me, I'll find a defender of whom you little think: you shall see, you'll be horrified at what you have driven me to!'

'What? What?' Troekurov said. 'You're threatening? Threatening me? Impudent girl! You'll find I'll do to you something you little imagine! You dare threaten me with your defender! We'll see who that defender is going to be!'

'Vladimir Dubrovsky,' Masha answered in despair.

Kiril Petrovitch thought that she had gone out of her mind, and looked at her in amazement.

'Very well,' he said to her after a pause, 'wait for any defender you like, but meanwhile stay in this room—you shall not leave it till your wedding.' With these words Kiril Petrovitch went out and locked the door after him.

The poor girl wept for some time, picturing to herself all that awaited her; but the stormy explanation had lightened her heart and she could reflect more calmly on her future and on what she was to do. The chief thing was to escape the hateful marriage; the fate of a brigand's wife seemed to her a paradise by comparison with the lot that was being prepared for her. She glanced at the ring that Dubrovsky had left her. She passionately longed to see him alone and to talk things over with him before the decisive moment

Her heart told her that in the evening she would find Dubrovsky in the garden by the arbour; she decided to go and wait for him there as soon as it grew dusk. Evening came. Masha prepared to go out, but her door was locked. From behind it the maid told her that Kiril Petrovitch had given orders not to let her out. She was under arrest. Deeply injured, she sat down by the window, and without undressing, remained there motionless till the small hours of the morning, gazing at the dark sky. At daybreak she dozed off; but her light sleep was disturbed by sad visions—and the rays of the rising sun wakened her.

CHAPTER XVII

SHE woke up—and at once the horror of her position rose before her mind. She rang the bell; the maid came in and said in answer to her question that in the evening Kiril Petrovitch had been to X. and came home late; that he had given strict orders not to let her out of the room and to see that no one spoke to her; but that no special preparations for the wedding were being made, except that the priest had been ordered not to leave the village under any pretext whatsoever. After telling her this, the maid left Marya Kirilovna and locked the door once more.

Her words hardened the young prisoner's heart. Her head was on fire, her blood was in a turmoil; she decided to let Dubrovsky know, and began thinking of a way to put the ring into the hollow of the oak-tree. At that moment a pebble struck her window, the glass jingled, and looking out into the yard she saw little Sasha signalling to her. She knew his affection for her and was glad to see him. She opened the window.

'Good morning, Sasha. Why did you call me?'

'I came to ask if you wanted anything. Papa is angry and has forbidden every one to do what you tell them; but give me any order you like and I'll do it for you.'

'Thank you, my dear Sashenka. Look here, do you know the hollow oak-tree by the arbour?'

'Yes, I know.'

'Well, if you love me, make haste and run there and put this ring into the hollow, but mind that nobody sees you.'

With these words she threw the ring to him and shut the window.

The boy picked up the ring and ran with all his might to the oak-tree, which he reached in three minutes. He stopped there, breathless, and looking about him put the ring into the hollow. Having safely accomplished his task he wanted to report it to Marya Kirilovna at once, when suddenly a ragged red-haired boy darted from behind the arbour, and rushing to the oak-tree put his hand into the hollow. Sasha flew at him quicker than a squirrel and seized him with both hands.

'What are you doing here?' he said menacingly.

'It's none of your business,' the boy answered, trying to wrench himself free.

'Let go that ring, you red fox,' Sasha shouted, 'or I'll give you a hiding.'

For answer the boy struck him in the face with his fist; Sasha did not let go, however, but shouted with all his might: 'Thieves! thieves! help!'

The boy tried to free himself. He looked a couple of years older than Sasha and was much stronger; but Sasha was quicker. They struggled for a few minutes. At last the red-haired boy had the better of it. He knocked Sasha down and grasped him by the throat. But at that moment a strong hand seized him by his red bristly hair, and Stepan, the gardener, lifted him a foot from the ground.

'Ah, you red-haired brute,' the gardener said, 'how dare you hit the little gentleman? . . .'

Sasha had had time to jump up and recover.

'You got me under the arms,' he said, 'or else you'd never have forced me down. Give me back the ring at once and clear out.'

'Not likely,' the red-haired boy answered, and suddenly turning round, freed his hair from Stepan's hand. He then started to run, but Sasha overtook him and pushed him in the back; the boy fell headlong on the ground. The gardener seized him again and tied his arms with his belt.

'Give me the ring!' Sasha cried.

'Wait a minute, master,' Stepan said, 'we 'll take him to the bailiff—he 'll deal with him.'

The gardener took the prisoner into the courtyard and Sasha followed, glancing uneasily at his knickers, which were torn and stained with grass. Suddenly all the three found themselves before Kiril Petrovitch, who was going to inspect the stables.

'What 's this?' he asked Stepan.

Stepan shortly described all that had happened.

Kiril Petrovitch listened to him attentively.

'Now, you rascal,' he said, turning to Sasha, 'what did you fight him for?'

'He stole the ring from the hollow, papa; tell him to give me back the ring.'

'What ring? From what hollow?'

'Why, Marya Kirilovna asked . . . that ring . . .'

Sasha was confused and did not know what to say. Kiril Petrovitch frowned and said, shaking his head:

'It 's something to do with Marya Kirilovna. Confess it all, or I 'll give you such a birching that you won't know where you are.'

'But really, papa, I . . . papa . . . Marya Kirilovna did not ask me anything, papa.'

'Stepan! go and cut me a good birch switch.'

'Wait a minute, papa, I 'll tell you everything. I was running about in the yard, and Marya Kirilovna opened her window and I ran up to it, and she dropped a ring, not on purpose, and I hid it in the hollow, and . . . and . . . this red-haired boy wanted to steal the ring.'

'Dropped it not on purpose, you wanted to hide it . . . Stepan, fetch me the switch.'

'Papa, wait a minute, I 'll tell you everything. Marya Kirilovna told me to run to the oak and put the ring into the hollow, so I ran and put it there, and this horrid boy . . .'

Kiril Petrovitch turned to the horrid boy and asked him menacingly: 'Whom do you belong to?'

'I am a house-serf of Mr. Dubrovsky's,' he answered.

Kiril Petrovitch's face darkened.

'You don't seem to acknowledge me as master—very well. And what were you doing in my garden?'

'Stealing raspberries,' the boy answered with great indifference.

'Aha! Like master, like man; and do raspberries grow on my oak-trees? Have you ever heard of that?'

The boy made no answer.

'Papa, tell him to give back the ring,' Sasha said.

'Be quiet, my boy!' Kiril Petrovitch answered. 'Don't forget that I mean to deal with you presently. Go to your room. You seem a sharp lad, you squint-eye; if you make a clean breast of it, I won't whip you, but will give you five copecks. Give back the ring and go.' The boy opened his fist, showing that there was nothing in his hand. 'Or else I'll do to you something you don't expect. Well?'

The boy did not answer a word, and stood with his head bowed, looking a perfect fool.

'Very good,' Kiril Petrovitch said. 'Lock him up somewhere, and see he doesn't run away, or I'll flay the lot of you.'

Stepan took the boy to the dovecot and, locking him in there, told the old poultry-maid Agafya to keep watch on him.

'There's no doubt whatever: she has kept in touch with that cursed Dubrovsky. Can she really have asked his help?' thought Kiril Petrovitch, pacing up and down the room and angrily whistling 'Thunder of victory, resound!' 'Perhaps I am on his track and he won't escape us. We'll take advantage of this opportunity. . . . Hark! a bell! Thank heaven, it's the police-captain. Fetch here the boy who's been caught!'

Meanwhile the trap drove into the courtyard, and the police-captain, whom we have already met, came into the room, covered with dust.

'Good news!' Kiril Petrovitch said; 'I've caught Dubrovsky.'

'Thank Heaven, your Excellency!' said the police-captain with a joyful air. 'Where is he?'

'That is, it isn't Dubrovsky himself, but one of his gang. He'll be brought in directly. He'll help us to catch the chieftain. Here he is.'

The police-captain, was expecting a formidable brigand, was surprised to see a puny boy of thirteen. He turned to Kiril Petrovitch in perplexity, waiting for an explanation. Kiril

Petrovitch told him what had happened in the morning, without mentioning Marya Kirilovna, however.

The police-captain listened to him attentively, glancing every minute at the little rascal, who pretended to be a perfect idiot, and seemed not to take the slightest notice of what was happening around him.

'Allow me to speak to you alone, your Excellency,' the police-captain said at last.

Kiril Petrovitch took him into the next room, shutting the door after him.

In half an hour they came once more into the room where the little prisoner was waiting for his fate to be decided.

'The gentleman wanted to send you to prison, have you whipped, and then deported,' the police-captain said to him; 'but I have interceded for you, and persuaded him to let you off. Untie him!'

The boy was untied.

'Thank the gentleman,' the police-captain said.

The boy went up to Kiril Petrovitch and kissed his hand.

'Go home in peace,' Kiril Petrovitch said to him, 'and don't steal raspberries from oak-trees any more.'

The boy left the room, cheerfully jumped down the front steps, and without looking round ran across the fields to Kistenyovka. Reaching the village he stopped by a tumble-down hut, the first one in the row, and tapped at the window. The pane was lifted, and an old woman looked out.

'Granny, bread!' the boy said. 'I've had nothing to eat all day, and am simply starving.'

'Ah, it's you, Mitya! But where have you been, you little imp?'

'I'll tell you presently, granny; for Heaven's sake, give me some bread.'

'But come indoors.'

'I haven't time, granny; I must run somewhere else first. Give me some bread, for Christ's sake!'

'What a fidget!' the old woman grumbled. 'Well, here's a piece for you,' and she thrust a slice of black bread through the window.

The boy bit into it greedily and, munching, walked farther on.

It was beginning to grow dusk. Mitya was making his

way between barns and kitchen gardens to the Kistenyovka
wood. When he reached the two pine-trees that stood like
sentinels at the entrance to it he stopped, looked about him,
and, giving a short and piercing whistle, stood listening.
A faint and prolonged whistling could be heard in answer;
someone came out of the wood and walked towards him.

CHAPTER XVIII

KIRIL PETROVITCH walked up and down the drawing-room
whistling his favourite tune louder than usual. The whole
house was in commotion: the men-servants ran to and fro,
the maids bustled about; the carriage was being got ready.
There was a crowd of people in the yard. In Marya Kirilovna's room, a lady surrounded by maid-servants was
dressing the pale and listless bride; her head drooped lan-
guidly under the weight of diamonds; she started slightly
when a careless pin pricked her, but said nothing, gazing into
the mirror with unseeing eyes.

'Will you be long?' Kiril Petrovitch's voice asked at the
door.

'One minute,' the lady answered. 'Marya Kirilovna, stand
up and see if everything is right.'

Marya Kirilovna stood up, but made no answer. The
door was opened. 'The bride is ready,' the lady said to
Kiril Petrovitch. 'Tell them to take their seats in the
carriage.'

'In God's name!' Kiril Petrovitch answered. 'Come
closer, Masha,' he said to her in a tone of feeling, taking up
the ikon from the table. 'I bless you . . .'

The poor girl fell at his feet and broke into sobs. 'Papa . . .
papa . . .' she said through her tears in a failing voice.

Kiril Petrovitch hastened to bless her; she was lifted from
the floor, and almost carried to the coach. A lady and a
maid-servant took their seats beside her. They drove to
the church. The bridegroom was waiting for them there.
He came out to meet the bride, and was struck by her pallor

and strange expression. Together they entered the cold,
empty church; the doors were locked behind them. The
priest came towards them and began the ceremony at once.
Marya Kirilovna saw and heard nothing; she had had but
one thought since the morning: she was waiting for Dubrovsky. She did not abandon hope for an instant. When
the priest turned to her with the usual question she shuddered
and turned cold with horror, but still she delayed, still she
was expectant. After waiting in vain for her answer the
priest pronounced the irretrievable words.

The ceremony was over. She felt the cold kiss of the
husband she did not love; she heard the obsequious congratulations of those present, and yet she could not believe
that her life was fettered for ever, that Dubrovsky had not
come to rescue her. The Prince addressed some kind words
to her—she did not understand them; they left the church;
peasants from Pokrovskoe were crowding on the steps. She
threw a rapid glance round them and her eyes assumed their
former apathetic expression. The bride and bridegroom
stepped into a carriage and drove to X.; Kiril Petrovitch
had gone earlier so as to meet them there. Left alone with
his young wife, the Prince was not in the least disconcerted
by her coldness. He did not worry her with mawkish
declarations and ridiculous ecstasies; his remarks were
ordinary and required no answer. They drove in this way
for about seven miles; the horses dashed along the by-roads
and the carriage scarcely jolted on its English springs.
Suddenly shouts of pursuit were heard; the carriage stopped,
and a crowd of armed men surrounded it. A man in a
mask opened the door on the side where the young Princess
was sitting and said to her: 'You are free! Come out!'

'What's the meaning of this?' the Prince shouted. 'Who
are you?'

'It is Dubrovsky,' the Princess said.

Without losing his presence of mind the Prince drew a
travelling pistol out of his side-pocket and shot at the masked
brigand. The Princess screamed and covered her face with
her hands in horror. Dubrovsky was wounded in the
shoulder; the blood flowed. Not losing a moment, the
Prince drew out another pistol. But he was not allowed
to shoot: the carriage doors were opened, several strong

arms pulled him out and seized his pistol. Knives glittered over him.

'Don't touch him!' Dubrovsky cried, and his gloomy confederates drew back. 'You are free,' he continued, turning to the poor Princess.

'No!' she answered. 'It's too late! I am married, I am Prince Vereisky's wife.'

'What are you saying?' Dubrovsky cried in despair. 'No! you are not his wife, you were forced, you could never have given your consent . . .'

'I gave it, I made the vow,' she answered firmly. 'The Prince is my husband. Tell your men to set him free and leave me with him. I haven't deceived you, I was expecting you up to the last moment . . . but now, I tell you, it's too late. Set us free.'

But Dubrovsky heard her no longer; the pain of his wound and his violent emotions overpowered him. He fell down by the wheel; the brigands surrounded him. He succeeded in saying a few words to them; they put him into the saddle. Two men supported him, a third led his horse by the bridle, and they all went off by a side-track, leaving the carriage in the middle of the road, with the horses unharnessed and the servants bound, but not shedding a drop of blood in revenge for their chieftain's wound.

CHAPTER XIX

IN a narrow clearing in the midst of a thick forest there was a small fort consisting of a rampart and a ditch that enclosed several huts and cabins. A number of men, who could at once be recognized as brigands from the way they were dressed and armed, sat on the grass, bareheaded, round a big cauldron, eating their dinner. A sentry squatted on the rampart beside a small cannon. He was putting a patch into a certain garment of his, plying the needle with an art that proved him to be an experienced tailor; at the same time he kept a sharp look out in every direction.

Though the drinking-cup had been passed round several

times, a strange silence reigned in the crowd. The brigands finished their dinner; one after another they got up, offering a silent prayer. Some went to their huts, others wandered off into the forest or lay down to have a nap, after the Russian custom.

The sentry finished his job and, shaking out his patched-up garment, admired his handiwork; then he stuck the needle into his sleeve and sitting astride the cannon sang at the top of his voice the melancholy old song:

> Murmur not, mother-forest of rustling green leaves,
> Hinder not a brave lad thinking his thoughts.

At that moment the door of one of the huts opened and an old woman in a white cap, neatly and carefully dressed, appeared at the door.

'Be quiet, Styopka!' she said angrily. 'Master is resting, and you go on bawling like this! You people have no conscience or pity.'

'I am sorry, Petrovna,' Styopka answered; 'very well, I won't do it any more; let him sleep and get better, bless him.'

The old woman went away, and Styopka began pacing up and down the rampart.

Dubrovsky lay, wounded, on a camp-bed behind a partition in the hut out of which the old woman had appeared. His pistols were on a table in front of him, and his sword hung at the head of the bed. The floor and the walls were covered with rich carpets; a lady's silver dressing-table and a large mirror stood in the corner. Dubrovsky held an open book in his hand, but his eyes were closed. The old woman, who kept glancing at him from behind the partition, could not tell whether he was asleep or merely lost in thought.

Suddenly Dubrovsky started. There was a commotion in the fortress, and Styopka thrust his head in at the window.

'Vladimir Andrevitch, sir!' he shouted, 'our men have signalled: 'we're being tracked.'

Dubrovsky jumped off his bed, seized his sword and the pistols, and came out. The brigands crowded noisily in the yard; when they saw him there was a deep silence.

'Are you all here?' Dubrovsky asked.

'All except those on the road,' they answered.

'Fall in!' Dubrovsky cried, and every one of the brigands went to his appointed place.

At that moment three men who had been stationed on the road ran up to the gate. Dubrovsky went to meet them.

'What is it?' he asked.

'Soldiers are in the forest,' they answered. 'They are surrounding us.'

Dubrovsky ordered them to shut the gate and went to examine the cannon. Voices could be heard in the forest, drawing closer and closer. The brigands waited in silence. Suddenly three or four soldiers appeared out of the forest and immediately drew back again, letting off their muskets as a signal to their comrades.

'Prepare for battle!' Dubrovsky said.

There was a rustle among the crowd; then all was still again. They heard the noise of the approaching enemy; arms glittered among the trees; some hundred and fifty soldiers poured out of the forest and rushed at the rampart with a shout. Dubrovsky lit the fuse; the shot was successful: one soldier had his head blown off, two were wounded. There was a confusion among the troops; but the officer dashed forward, the soldiers followed him and ran down into the ditch. The brigands shot at them out of muskets and pistols, and, with axes in their hands, defended the rampart against the infuriated soldiers who tried to climb it, leaving some twenty wounded comrades in the ditch. A hand-to-hand fight began. The soldiers were on the rampart already, the brigands were losing ground, but Dubrovsky came up to the officer and, thrusting his pistol against the man's breast, shot him. The officer fell on his back; a few soldiers picked him up and hastened to carry him into the forest; having lost their commander, the others stood still. Encouraged by their momentary confusion, the brigands pressed them back into the ditch; the soldiers took to their heels; with loud cries the brigands ran after them. The victory was decisive. Assured that the enemy was completely routed, Dubrovsky called back his men and, giving orders to pick up the wounded, shut himself up in his fortress, doubling the number of the sentries and forbidding any one to leave the place.

These last events drew the attention of the Government to

Dubrovsky's daring robberies. Inquiry was made into his whereabouts. A detachment of soldiers was sent to capture him dead or alive. Several men of his band were caught, but they said that Dubrovsky was no longer among them. Several days after the battle he had called together all his confederates, told them that he was leaving them for ever, and advised them too to change their way of living. 'You have grown rich under my command, every one of you has a passport with which he can safely make his way into some distant province, and spend the rest of his life there in prosperity doing honest work. But you are all rascals and will probably not wish to leave your trade.' After that speech he left them, taking one man with him. No one knew what became of him.

At first the truth of these statements seemed doubtful— the brigands' devotion to their chieftain was well known, and it was thought that they were trying to shield him; but subsequent events justified their words. The terrible raids, incendiarism, and robberies ceased; the roads were safe once more. From other sources it appeared that Dubrovsky had left Russia.

PETER THE GREAT'S NEGRO

CHAPTER I

PETER THE GREAT'S godson, the negro Ibrahim, was among the young men sent by the Tsar to foreign lands to acquire knowledge necessary for a country being so rapidly transformed. Ibrahim studied at the Paris Military School, left it with the rank of a captain of artillery, distinguished himself in the Spanish war and, dangerously wounded, returned to Paris. In the midst of his many labours the Emperor never failed to inquire after his favourite, and always received flattering reports about his progress and conduct. Peter was extremely pleased with him, and more than once called him back to Russia; but Ibrahim was in no hurry. He gave various excuses for not going: now it was his wound, then his wish to improve his education, then lack of money. Peter acceded to his wishes, begged Ibrahim to take care of himself, thanked him for his zeal for learning, and—extremely economical about his own expenses—did not stint money for him, adding to the gold fatherly advice and cautionary admonitions.

According to the testimony of all the historical memoirs, nothing could equal the folly, frivolity, and luxury of the French at that period. The last years of Louis XIV's reign, marked by strict piety, solemnity, and decorum at the Court, had left no trace whatever. The Duke of Orleans, who combined many brilliant qualities with all kinds of vices, had not, unfortunately, a shadow of hypocrisy. The orgies of the Palais-Royal were not a secret in Paris; the example was infectious. About that time John Law made his appearance; greed for money was combined with a thirst for pleasure and

---

¹ Although this story is unfinished it is included in the present volume because it is one of the best known of Pushkin's tales, and also on account of its biographical interest. The negro who was Peter the Great's godson was Pushkin's great-grandfather.—TRANSLATOR'S NOTE.

dissipation; estates were being squandered, moral standards lowered, the French laughed and speculated—and the State was going to ruin to the playful accompaniment of satirical vaudevilles.

Meanwhile the social life of Paris was extremely interesting. Learning and the craving for amusement were drawing together people of all ranks. Fame, wealth, charm, talents, or mere oddity—all that gave food to curiosity or promised pleasure was received with equal favour. Writers, scientists, and philosophers left their quiet pursuits and appeared in high society to do homage to fashion and to dictate to it. Women reigned, but no longer claimed adoration. Superficial politeness replaced the profound respect in which they had been held. The follies of the Duc de Richelieu, the Alcibiades of the modern Athens, belong to history, and give some idea of the morals of the day.

> Temps fortuné, marqué par la licence,
> Où la folie, agitant son grelot,
> D'un pied léger parcourt toute la France,
> Où nul mortel ne daigne être dévot,
> Où l'on fait tout excepté pénitence.

Ibrahim's arrival, his looks, his education, and natural intelligence attracted general attention in Paris. All the ladies wished to see in their houses *le nègre du Czar*, and vied with one another in inviting him. The Regent asked him more than once to his gay evening parties; he attended suppers enlivened by the presence of the young Arouet and the old Chaulieu, by the conversations of Montesquieu and Fontenelle; he did not miss a single ball, a single fête, or first night, and abandoned himself to the general whirlwind with all the ardour of his years and temperament. But it was not only the thought of exchanging this dissipation, these brilliant pleasures for the simplicity of the Petersburg court that terrified Ibrahim; other bonds, stronger than those, attached him to Paris. The young African was in love.

Countess L., no longer in the first flower of youth, was still renowned for her beauty. On leaving the convent at seventeen she was married to a man with whom she had not had time to fall in love, and who made no effort to win her affection afterwards. Gossip ascribed lovers to her but, according to the indulgent convention of society, she had a good reputation, for she could not be reproached with any ridiculous or scandalous adventure. Her house was extremely fashionable, and the best Paris society used to meet there. Ibrahim was introduced to her by Merville, who was generally regarded as her latest lover, and did his best in every way to confirm that idea.

The Countess received Ibrahim courteously, but without any special attention: that flattered him. Usually people regarded the young negro as a marvel and, flocking round him, overwhelmed him with questions and greetings—and their curiosity, although it had an air of friendliness, offended his pride. Women's sweet attention—almost the sole aim of all our efforts—far from delighting him, filled him with bitterness and indignation. He felt that he was for them a kind of rare animal, an alien, peculiar creature, accidentally transported into their world, and having nothing in common with them. He actually envied men who were in no way remarkable, and considered their insignificance a blessing.

The thought that nature had not intended him for the joys of requited passion saved him from self-confidence and pretentious vanity—and this gave a rare charm to his manner with women. His conversation was simple and serious; it pleased Countess L., who was tired of the pompous jokes and subtle insinuations of the French wits. Ibrahim often came to see her. Gradually she grew accustomed to the young negro's appearance, and actually found something pleasing in that curly head showing black among the powdered wigs in her drawing-room. (Ibrahim had been wounded in the head, and wore a bandage instead of a wig.) He was twenty-seven years old; he was tall and well made, and more than one society beauty gazed at him with a feeling more flattering than mere curiosity; but Ibrahim was prejudiced, and either noticed nothing, or put it down to mere coquetry. But when his eyes met the eyes of the Countess, his distrust vanished. Her look expressed such charming good nature, her manner towards him was so simple, so spontaneous that it was impossible to suspect her of the least irony or coquetry.

He did not think of love, but it was already a necessity for him to see the Countess every day. He was always seeking to meet her, and every meeting seemed to him an unexpected gift from Heaven. The Countess divined his feelings sooner than he did.   Whatever people may say, love without hopes or demands is more certain to touch a woman's heart than all the calculations of seduction.   In Ibrahim's presence the Countess watched his every movement, and took in everything he said; without him she brooded and sank into her usual absent-mindedness.   Merville was the first to notice their mutual attraction—and to congratulate Ibrahim. Nothing inflames love more than an encouraging remark from an outsider; love is blind, and, distrusting itself, hastily snatches at every support.

Merville's words roused Ibrahim.   The possibility of possessing the woman he loved had never yet presented itself to his imagination; the light of hope dawned in his soul; he fell madly in love.   Alarmed by the frenzy of his passion, the Countess vainly tried to oppose to it the counsels of friendship and the admonitions of good sense; she was weakening too. . . . Incautious encouragements followed one after another.   At last, carried away by the passion she had inspired, the Countess, succumbing to its power, gave herself to her ecstatic lover.

Nothing can be hidden from the observant eyes of the world. The Countess's new love-affair soon became known to every one.   Some ladies marvelled at her choice; many regarded it as perfectly natural.   Some laughed, others thought it an unpardonable folly on her part.   In the first intoxication of passion Ibrahim and the Countess noticed nothing; but soon men's ambiguous jokes and women's stinging remarks began to reach them.   Hitherto Ibrahim's serious and distant manner had protected him from such attacks; he stood them badly and did not know how to ward them off.   The Countess, accustomed to the respect of society, could not bear to be the object of gossip and derision.   She complained to Ibrahim with tears, reproached him bitterly, or implored him not to try to defend her, so as not to ruin her completely by creating a useless scandal.

A new circumstance complicated their position still further.   The consequence of their imprudent love became apparent.   The Countess told Ibrahim about it with despair. Advice, comfort, suggestions—all was exhausted and rejected. The Countess saw inevitable ruin before her and awaited it in utter misery.

As soon as the Countess's condition became known gossip sprang up afresh; sentimental ladies cried out with horror; men laid wagers as to whether the child would be white or black. There were showers of epigrams at her husband's expense, while he was the only person in the whole of Paris who knew and suspected nothing.

The fateful moment was approaching. The Countess was distracted. Ibrahim came to see her every day. He saw how her spiritual and bodily strength gradually left her. Her horror and her tears were renewed every minute. At last she felt the first pains. Measures were taken hastily. Means were found to send the Count away. The doctor came. Two days before a poor woman had been persuaded to give up her new-born baby; a person of trust had been sent to fetch it. Ibrahim was in the study next to the bedroom where the unfortunate Countess lay. Not daring to breathe, he heard her stifled groans, the maid's whispers, and the doctor's orders. Her agony lasted several hours. Every groan she uttered rent Ibrahim's heart; every interval of silence filled him with horror. . . . Suddenly he heard the feeble wail of an infant—and, unable to contain his delight, rushed into the Countess's bedroom. A black baby lay in the bed at her feet. Ibrahim approached it. His heart was beating violently. With a trembling hand he blessed his son. The Countess gave a languid smile and stretched out a feeble hand to him . . . but the doctor, fearing too much agitation for his patient, drew Ibrahim away from her bed. The new-born infant was put into a covered basket and carried out of the house by a secret staircase. The other baby was brought and put in a cot in the Countess's bedroom. Ibrahim went away feeling somewhat relieved. They were expecting the Count. He came home late and was very pleased to hear that his wife had been safely delivered. Thus the public that had been expecting a scandal was disappointed and had to find its sole comfort in malicious gossip. Everything went on as usual.

But Ibrahim felt that his fate was bound to change and that his affair with the Countess must sooner or later reach her husband's ears. In that case, whatever happened, the Countess's doom would be sealed. Ibraham loved, and was loved, passionately; but the Countess was frivolous and capricious : this was not the first time that she loved.   Disgust and hatred might replace the tenderest feelings in her heart. Ibrahim could already foresee her beginning to grow cold to him.   He had as yet no experience of jealousy, but he had a horrible foreboding of it ; he imagined that the pain of parting would be less agonizing—and he intended to break off his ill-starred love affair, leave Paris, and go to Russia, whither Peter and a vague sense of duty had long been calling him.

CHAPTER II

Days, months passed—and Ibrahim, still in love, could not make up his mind to leave the woman he had seduced.   The Countess grew more attached to him with every hour.   Their son was being brought up in a distant province.   Gossip began to die down, and the lovers enjoyed greater security, silently remembering the past storm and trying not to think of the future.

One day Ibrahim was at the Duke of Orleans's levee. Going past him, the Duke stopped and handed him a letter, telling him to read it at his leisure.   The letter was from Peter I.   Guessing the true cause of his godson's absence, the Tsar wrote to the Duke that he did not intend to put the least pressure on Ibrahim, and left it for him to decide whether he would return to Russia or no ; but that in any case he would never forsake his protégé.   This letter touched Ibrahim to the bottom of his heart.   From that moment his fate was settled.   The next day he told the Regent that he intended to return to Russia at once.

'Think what you are doing,' the Duke said to him: 'Russia is not your native country ; I don't suppose you 'll ever succeed in seeing your tropical fatherland ; but your long stay in France has made you equally a stranger to the climate and customs of half-savage Russia.   You were not born Peter's subject.   Follow my advice : take advantage of his generous permission, remain in France, for which you have already shed your blood, and be sure that your gifts and merits will find their proper reward here also.'

Ibrahim sincerely thanked the Duke, but remained firm in his intention.

'I am sorry,' the Regent said to him, 'but I admit you are right.' He promised to let him leave the army and wrote to the Russian Tsar about it.

Ibrahim soon made ready to go. He spent the evening before his departure at Countess L.'s as usual. She knew nothing. Ibrahim had not the courage to tell her the truth. The Countess was calm and gay. She called him to her side more than once, and joked about his being so preoccupied. After supper all the guests went away. Only the Countess, her husband, and Ibrahim remained in the drawing-room. The unfortunate man would have given anything to be left alone with her; but Count L. seemed to have settled by the fire so comfortably that there was no hope of inducing him to leave the room. All three were silent.

'*Bonne nuit*,' the Countess said at last.

Ibrahim had a pang at his heart and suddenly felt all the horror of parting. He stood stock still.

'*Bonne nuit, messieurs*,' the Countess repeated.

Still he did not move. . . . There was a darkness before his eyes, his head reeled; he was scarcely able to walk out of the room. On arriving home he wrote the following letter, feeling almost delirious:

I am going away, dear Leonora, I am leaving you for ever. I am writing to you because I haven't the courage to tell it you in any other way. My happiness could not have lasted: I enjoyed it in spite of fate, in spite of nature. You were bound to cease loving me; the fascination could not have lasted. This thought haunted me, even at moments when I seemed to forget everything at your feet, revelling in your passionate devotion, in your boundless tenderness. . . . Frivolous society pitilessly persecutes that which it allows in theory: its cold derision would sooner or later have overcome you, would have subdued your ardent heart—and you would have been ashamed of your passion. . . . And what would have become of me then? No, better die, better leave you before that awful moment . . . .

Your peace is more precious to me than anything; you could not enjoy it while society was keeping watch on us. Recall all that you have endured—all the insults to your pride, all the tortures of fear; recall the terrible birth of our son. Think: is it right that I should subject you any longer to the same anxieties and dangers? Why strive to unite the fate of so tender and beautiful a being as yourself with the unhappy lot of a negro, a pitiful creature whom people scarcely deign to recognize as human?

Good-bye, Leonora; good-bye, my precious, my only friend! In leaving you, I leave the first and last joy of my life. I have no fatherland, no kindred; I am going to Russia, where my utter solitude will be a solace to me. Exacting work, to which I shall henceforth devote myself, will stifle, or, at any rate, will distract me from, the agonizing memories of happy, blissful days. Good-bye, Leonora! I tear myself from this letter as though it were from your arms. Good-bye, be happy, and think sometimes of the poor negro, of your faithful Ibrahim.

That same night he set out for Russia. The journey did not seem to him so dreadful as he had expected. His imagination triumphed over reality. The farther he was from Paris, the closer and the more vividly he saw the things that he was leaving for ever.

He scarcely noticed how he reached the Russian frontier. It was the beginning of autumn; but in spite of the bad roads he was driven as fast as the wind. After seventeen days' journey he arrived in the morning at Krasnoe Selo; the main road to Petersburg ran through it in those times.

It was nineteen miles to Petersburg. While the horses were being harnessed, Ibrahim went into the coaching station. In the corner a tall man in a green coat, with a clay pipe in his mouth sat leaning on the table, reading the Hamburg newspapers.

'Aha, Ibrahim!' he cried getting up from the bench. 'How do you do, godson?'

Recognizing Peter, Ibrahim joyfully rushed towards him, but stopped respectfully. The Tsar went up to him and, embracing him, kissed him on the head.

'I have been warned of your coming,' Peter said, 'and am here to meet you. I have been waiting for you here since yesterday.'

Ibrahim could not find words to express his gratitude.

'Tell them,' the Tsar continued, 'to bring your cart along after us, and you come home with me in my carriage.'

The Tsar's carriage was brought; he stepped into it with Ibrahim—and they dashed off. In an hour and a half they arrived in Petersburg. Ibrahim looked with interest at the newborn capital which was rising out of the marsh at the bidding of its Tsar. Rough dams, canals without an embankment, wooden bridges bore witness everywhere to the victory of human will over the reluctant elements. The houses looked as though they had been built in haste. In the whole town there was nothing magnificent except the Neva, which had not yet been framed in granite, but was already covered with war-ships and trading vessels. The Tsar's carriage stopped by the palace, the so-called Tsaritsa's Garden.

A handsome woman of about thirty-five, dressed in the latest Paris fashion, met Peter on the steps. After he had kissed her, Peter took Ibrahim by the hand and said to her:

'Do you recognize my godson, Katinka? Please be kind to him as in the old days.'

Catherine looked at Ibrahim with her penetrating black eyes, and graciously held out her hand to him. Two young beauties, tall, slim, and fresh as roses, were standing behind her; they approached Peter respectfully.

'Liza!' he said to one of them, 'do you remember the little negro who used to steal apples for you from my garden in Oranienbaum? Here he is, let me introduce him to you.'

The Grand-duchess laughed and blushed. They went into the dining-room. The table had been set in expectation of Peter's arrival. He sat down to dinner with all his family, inviting Ibrahim to join them. During the dinner the Tsar talked to him about various subjects, and questioned him about the Spanish war, the state of things in France, and the Regent, whom he liked, though he disapproved of a great deal in him. Ibrahim had a clear and observant mind. Peter was very much pleased with his answers; he recalled several details about Ibrahim's childhood, and told them with such gaiety and good nature that no one could have recognized in the kind and hospitable host the hero of Poltava, the mighty and formidable reformer of Russia.

After dinner the Tsar went to have a rest according to the Russian custom. Ibrahim was left with the Empress and the Grand-duchesses. He tried to satisfy their curiosity by describing the manner of life in Paris, the festivals and capricious fashions. Meanwhile some of the men closely associated with the Tsar came to the palace. Ibrahim recognized the magnificent Menshikov, who, seeing a negro talking to Catherine, gave him a haughty sidelong glance; Prince Yakov Dolgoruki, Peter's stubborn councillor; the learned Bruce, who had the reputation of a Russian Faust among the people; the young Raguzinsky, his former comrade, and others who came to the Tsar to make their reports and receive their orders.

The Tsar appeared in a couple of hours' time.

'Let us see if you have forgotten your old duties,' he said to Ibrahim. 'Take a slate and follow me.'

Peter shut himself up in his study and attended to the affairs of the State. He worked in turn with Bruce, with Prince Dolgoruki, with the chief of police, General Deviere, and dictated several ukases and resolutions to Ibrahim.

Ibrahim could not sufficiently admire the clarity and quickness of his judgment, the flexibility of his mind, his power of concentration, and the wide range of his activities. When Peter had finished work he took out a pocket-book to see whether he had done all that he had intended to do that day. Afterwards, as he was leaving the room, he said to Ibrahim:

'It's late; I expect you are tired; spend the night here as in the old days; to-morrow I'll wake you.'

Remaining alone, Ibrahim could scarcely come to his senses. He was in Petersburg; he was seeing again the great man beside whom, not yet understanding his worth, he had spent his childhood. He confessed to himself almost with remorse that for the first time since their parting Countess L. had not completely occupied his thoughts all through the day. He saw that active and constant occupation and the new manner of life awaiting him might revive his soul, wearied by passions, idleness, and secret melancholy. The thought of being a great man's helper and influencing, together with him, the destiny of a great people aroused in him for the first time the feeling of noble ambition. In that mood he lay down on the camp-bed that had been prepared for him—and then tne familiar dream took him to distant Paris, to the arms of the charming Countess.

CHAPTER III

THE following day Peter woke Ibrahim according to his promise, and conferred on him the rank of lieutenant-captain in the Artillery Company of the Preobrazhensky Regiment, in which Peter himself was captain. The courtiers surrounded Ibrahim, each trying in his own way to be kind to the new favourite. The haughty Prince Menshikov shook hands with him in a friendly way; Sheremetev inquired after his Paris friends, and Golovin invited him to dinner. His example was followed by others, so that Ibrahim received enough invitations to last him at least a month.

Ibrahim's new life was uneventful but busy—consequently he did not suffer from boredom. Every day he grew more and more attached to the Tsar and understood his lofty mind better. To follow a great man's thoughts is the most absorbing of studies. Ibrahim saw Peter at the Senate, arguing with Buturlin and Dolgoruki, dealing with important questions of legislation; he saw him at the Admiralty, laying the foundations of Russia's naval power; he saw him with Bishop Feofan, Gavriil Buzhinsky, and Kopievitch, examining, in his hours of rest, the translations of foreign writers or visiting a factory, a workshop, or a learned man's study. Russia seemed to Ibrahim a huge workshop, where only machines were moving, and every worker was occupied with his job in accordance with a fixed plan. He considered it his duty to carry out his own appointed task, and tried to regret as little as possible the gaieties of Parisian life. He found it more difficult to banish another, a sweet memory: he often thought of Countess L., picturing her just indignation, her tears and dejection. . . . But at times a terrible thought oppressed his heart; the distractions of high society, a new intrigue, another happy lover—he shuddered; jealousy set his African blood on fire—and scalding tears were ready to flow down his black cheeks.

One morning, as he sat in his study surrounded by business papers, he suddenly heard a loud greeting in the French language. Ibrahim turned quickly—and young Korsakov, whom he had left in Paris in the whirl of society life, embraced him with joyful exclamations.

'I have only just arrived,' Korsakov said, 'and have come straight to you. All our Paris friends send you their greetings and are sorry you are not with them. Countess L. said you must come back at all costs, and here is a letter for you from her.'

Ibrahim snatched it with trepidation and gazed at the familiar handwriting on the address, not daring to believe his own eyes.

'How glad I am you haven't yet died of boredom in this barbarous Petersburg!' Korsakov went on. 'What do they do here? How do they spend their time? Who is your tailor? Have you an opera house, at least?'

Ibrahim answered absent-mindedly that the Tsar was probably working now at the Admiralty wharf. Korsakov laughed.

'I see you have no thoughts to spare for me now,' he said. 'We'll talk to our hearts' content some other time; I'll go and present myself to the Tsar.'

With these words he spun round on his heel and ran out of the room.

Left alone, Ibrahim hastily opened the letter. The Countess reproached him tenderly, accusing him of deception and distrust.

'You say,' she wrote, 'that my peace is dearer than anything in the world to you. Ibrahim! if this were true, how could you have caused me the pain that the unexpected news of your departure gave me? You were afraid that I would detain you; believe me that in spite of my love I would have known how to sacrifice it to your welfare and to what you regard as your duty.'

The Countess concluded her letter with passionate assurances of love, and adjured him to write to her sometimes—if there was no hope of their meeting again.

Ibrahim read the letter twenty times over, kissing with delight the precious lines. He was burning with impatience to hear about the Countess, and was preparing to go to the Admiralty in the hope of finding Korsakov still there, when the door opened and Korsakov appeared again. He had already presented himself to the Tsar—and as usual seemed much pleased with himself.

'*Entre nous*,' he said to Ibrahim, 'the Tsar is a most peculiar person; imagine, I found him, dressed in some kind of linen jacket, on the mast of a new ship, where I had to climb up with all my papers. I stood on a rope-ladder and had not enough room to make a decent bow. I was overcome with confusion—a thing which has never happened to me before. However, after reading the papers, the Tsar looked me up and down and was probably pleasantly impressed by my clothes being so smart and in such good taste; anyway, he smiled and invited me to the assembly to-night. But I am simply like a foreigner in Petersburg: during the six years I've been away, I have completely forgotten the customs of the place. Please be my mentor to-day, call for me and introduce me!'

Ibrahim agreed, and hastened to turn the conversation on to a subject that was of more interest to him.

'Well, and how is Countess L.?'

'The Countess? Naturally she was very much grieved by your departure at first; then, of course, she gradually took comfort and found a new lover; do you know whom? The lanky Marquis R. Why do you stare at me like that with your goggle eyes? Do you find it strange, by any chance? Don't you know that it isn't in human nature—especially not in woman's nature—to be grieved for long? Think well about it, and I'll go and rest after my journey; mind you don't forget to call for me.'

What emotions were filling Ibrahim's heart? Jealousy? Fury? Despair? No; but profound, overpowering dejection. He kept repeating to himself: 'I had foreseen it, it was bound to happen'. Then he opened the Countess's letter, read it over again and, hanging his head, wept bitterly. He wept long. Tears lightened his heart. Glancing at the clock he saw that it was time to go. Ibrahim would have been very glad to stay at home, but an assembly was a matter of duty, and the Tsar strictly required his courtiers' presence. He dressed and went to call for Korsakov.

Korsakov sat in his dressing-gown reading a French book.

'So early?' he said when he saw Ibrahim.

'Why, it's half-past five,' Ibrahim answered; 'we shall be late. Make haste and dress, and let us go.'

Korsakov, in a flutter, rang the bell violently; his servants ran in; he began dressing hastily. His French valet brought him shoes with red heels, blue velvet trousers, and a pink jacket embroidered with sequins; in the hall they were hastily powdering a wig. It was brought in; Korsakov thrust his closely cropped head into it, asked for his sword and gloves, and, turning round a dozen times before the mirror, told Ibrahim that he was ready. The footmen brought them bearskin coats, and they drove to the Winter Palace.

Korsakov bombarded Ibrahim with questions: Who was the most beautiful woman in Petersburg? Who was regarded as the best dancer? What dance was in the fashion? Ibrahim satisfied his curiosity very reluctantly. Meanwhile they drove up to the palace. A number of long sledges, old-fashioned carriages, and gilded coaches were already standing in the open space in front. At the steps there was a crowd of liveried coachmen with moustaches; messengers decked with feathers, glittering with gold braid and carrying maces; hussars, pages, clumsy footmen loaded with their masters' fur-coats and muffs—a following which the noblemen of the period considered essential. At the sight of Ibrahim there arose a general murmur among them: 'The negro, the negro, the Tsar's negro!' He made haste to lead Karsakov through this motley crowd. A palace footman flung the doors wide open and they walked into the hall. Korsakov was dumbfounded. . . . In a big room lighted by tallow candles that burned dimly in the clouds of tobacco smoke, noblemen with blue ribbons across the shoulder, ambassadors, foreign merchants, officers of the Guards in green uniforms, and shipbuilders in jackets and striped trousers, moved up and down in a crowd to the continual music of wind instruments. The ladies sat along the walls; the young ones were dressed in all the splendour of fashion. Gold and silver glittered on their gowns; their slender waists rose like the stem of a flower from the huge farthingale; diamonds sparkled in their ears, in their long curls and round their necks. They gaily turned right and left, waiting for the dances to begin and looking for partners. The elderly

ladies had made ingenious attempts to combine the new
fashions with the forbidden old ones; their caps looked like
the sable head-dress of the Tsaritsa Natalya Kirilovna,[1]
and their gowns and mantillas somehow recalled the Russian
sarafan and *dushegreika*. They seemed to feel surprise
rather than pleasure at the newfangled entertainments, and
glanced askance at the Dutch skippers' wives and daughters
in cotton skirts and red bodices who sat there knitting
stockings, laughing and talking among themselves as though
they were at home.

Noticing new guests, a servant came up to them with beer
and glasses on a tray. Korsakov did not know what to think.

'*Que diable est-ce que tout cela?*' he asked Ibrahim in an
undertone.

Ibrahim could not help smiling. The Empress and the
Grand-duchesses, resplendent with beauty and brilliant
attire, walked about among the guests, talking to them
graciously. The Tsar was in the next room. Wishing to show
himself to him, Korsakov could hardly make his way
through the continually moving crowd. The room was
occupied chiefly by foreigners, who sat there, solemnly
smoking their clay pipes and emptying earthenware mugs.
On the tables there were bottles of wine and beer, leather
bags with tobacco, glasses of punch and chess-boards. At
one of the tables Peter was playing draughts with a broad-
shouldered English skipper. They zealously discharged
volleys of tobacco smoke at each other, and the Tsar was so
disconcerted by an unexpected move on his opponent's part
that he failed to notice Korsakov in spite of all the latter's
efforts. At that moment a stout gentleman with a big
bouquet on his breast entered hastily and announced in a
loud voice that dancing had begun; he went out immediately,
and a number of guests, Korsakov among them, followed.

He was greatly surprised by the unexpected scene that he
saw. Ladies and gentlemen stood in two rows facing one
another the whole length of the dancing-hall; to the plaintive
strains of a pitiful band the gentlemen bowed low, the ladies
made deep curtsies, first in the direction they faced, then
turning to the right, then turning to the left, then to the front
again, then to the right, then to the left, and so on. Biting

---

[1] Peter the Great's mother.—TRANSLATOR'S NOTE.

his lips, Korsakov stared open-eyed at this peculiar way of spending time. The bows and curtsies went on for about half an hour; at last they stopped, and the stout gentleman with the bouquet announced that the ceremonial dances were over, and ordered the musicians to play the minuet.

Korsakov was glad and prepared to shine. One of the young lady guests particularly attracted him. She was about sixteen; dressed luxuriously but in good taste, she sat next to an elderly man of a stern and imposing appearance. Korsakov dashed up to her, and asked her to do him the honour of dancing with him. The young beauty looked at him in confusion and seemed at a loss for an answer. The man sitting next to her frowned more than ever. Korsakov was waiting for her decision; but the gentleman with the bouquet came up to him and, taking him to the middle of the hall, said solemnly:

'My dear sir, you are at fault: in the first place, you approached this young lady without making three bows in the proper fashion, and in the second, you took it upon yourself to invite her, while in the minuet this right belongs to the lady and not to the gentleman; in view of this you have to be severely punished, namely, you must drink the goblet of the big eagle.'

Korsakov felt more and more bewildered. The other guests instantly surrounded him, noisily demanding that the sentence should be carried out on the spot. Hearing shouts and laughter, Peter came into the room, for he was very fond of being personally present at such punishments. The crowd made way for him, and he entered the circle, in the middle of which stood the condemned man and the marshal of the assembly with a huge goblet filled with malmsey wine. He was vainly trying to persuade the criminal voluntarily to submit to the law.

'Aha!' said Peter, when he caught sight of Korsakov. 'You are caught, brother. Now you must drink, monsieur, and make no grimaces.'

There was nothing for it: the poor dandy drained the whole goblet without drawing breath, and gave it back to the marshal.

'I say, Korsakov,' Peter said to him, 'you have velvet breeches on, such as even I don't wear, and I am much richer than you. That's extravagance; take care that I don't quarrel with you.'

Having received this reprimand, Korsakov tried to make his way out of the circle, but staggered and nearly fell, to the indescribable delight of the Tsar and the whole merry company. So far from breaking up or spoiling the entertainment, that episode merely served to enliven it. The gentlemen scraped and bowed, and the ladies curtsied and clicked their heels with more zeal than ever, no longer troubling to keep time with the music. Korsakov was not able to take part in the general merriment. The lady whom he had selected went up to Ibrahim by order of her father, Gavril Afanasyevitch Rzhevsky, and casting down her blue eyes, timidly gave him her hand. Ibrahim danced the minuet with her, and took her back to her seat; then, finding Korsakov, he led him out of the room, put him in his carriage, and saw him home. On the way Korsakov at first muttered vaguely: 'That damned assembly! . . . that damned goblet!' . . . but soon dropped sound asleep. He was not conscious of arriving home, of being undressed and put to bed, and woke up the next day with a headache, vaguely recalling the bows, the curtsies, the tobacco smoke, the gentleman with the bouquet, and the 'goblet of the big eagle'.

CHAPTER IV

In olden times the feasts were long;
The silver cups and goblets fine
Went slowly round the merry throng
With foaming beer and heady wine.
                    Russlan and Ludmilla.

Now I must introduce my kind reader to Gavril Afanasyevitch Rzhevsky. He came of an ancient boyar family, had huge estates, was hospitable, loved falconry, and kept a number of servants; in short, he was a true Russian nobleman. He could not endure the German spirit, as he put it, and strove in his domestic life to keep up the old customs that he loved. His daughter was seventeen years old. She had lost her mother while still a child. She had been brought up in the old-fashioned way, surrounded by nurses, playmates, and maid-servants; she embroidered in gold, and could not read or write. In spite of his aversion for everything foreign her father could not oppose her wish to learn foreign dances from a captive Swedish officer who lived in their house. This worthy dancing-master was about fifty years old; his right leg had been shot through in the battle of Narva, and was therefore not very efficient at minuets and sarabandes, but the left made the most difficult steps with extraordinary skill and lightness. His pupil did credit to his efforts. Natalya Gavrilovna was considered the best dancer at the assemblies—which was partly the reason of Korsakov's transgression. He came the day after to apologize to Gavril Afanasyevitch; but the proud old man did not like the smartness and address of the young dandy, whom he wittily nicknamed a French monkey.

It was a holiday. Gavril Afanasyevitch was expecting several friends and relatives. A long table was being set in the old-fashioned hall. Visitors arrived with their wives and daughters, who had been freed at last from domestic seclusion by the ukases of the Tsar and by his own example. Natalya Gavrilovna came up to each guest with a silver tray loaded with golden cups, and each emptied one, regretting that the kiss given in the old days on such occasions was no longer the custom. They sat down to dinner. The place of honour next to the host was taken by his father-in-law, Prince Boris Alexeyevitch Lykov, an old man of seventy; other guests chose their seats according to their families' rank, thus recalling the happy days when seniority was observed in all things. The men sat on one side of the table, the women on the other; the woman-jester in her old-fashioned head-dress and jacket, the dwarf—a prim and wrinkled little woman of thirty, and the captive dancing-master in his worn blue uniform occupied their usual places at the end of the table. The table, laden with a number of dishes, was surrounded by a crowd of busy servants; the butler was conspicuous among them by his stern expression, round belly, and majestic immobility. The first moments of the dinner were exclusively devoted to savouring the old-fashioned Russian dishes; the rattle of plates and the jingle of spoons were the only sounds that disturbed the general silence. At last, seeing that the time had come to occupy his guests with pleasant conversation, Gavril Afanasyevitch looked about him and said:

'Where is Yekimovna? Call her here!'

Several servants dashed away in different directions, but at the same moment an old woman, rouged and powdered, in a low-cut brocade dress, decked with flowers and tinsel, came into the room singing and dancing. Her appearance was greeted with pleasure by every one.

'How do you do, Yekimovna?' Prince Lykov said. 'How are you getting on?'

'Very well, gossip: dancing and singing, and waiting for suitors.'

'Where have you been, fool?' Gavril Afanasyevitch asked.

'I've been dressing up, gossip, for our dear guests and for God's holy day, at the Tsar's command and the boyars' remand, in the German fashion, for good people to laugh at!'

There was a burst of laughter at these words, and the fool took up her usual place behind her master's chair.

'The fool talks nonsense enough, but sometimes she speaks the truth,' said Tatyana Afanasyevna, Rzkevsky's eldest sister, whom he sincerely respected. 'The fashions to-day are indeed for good people to laugh at. If you, good sirs, have shaved your beards and put on skimpy jackets, it's no use talking about women's frippery, of course; but really it's a pity about the *sarafan*, the girls' hair-ribbon, and the women's head-dress! Why, just look at the fine ladies nowadays—one can't help laughing and being sorry for them too: their hair is matted like felt, greased, covered with French flour; their stomachs are so laced in, it's a wonder they don't break in two; their petticoats are stretched out with hoops—they have to sit down in a carriage sideways, to bend when they come through a door; they can neither sit nor stand nor draw breath—regular martyrs, poor dears!'

'Ah, Tatyana Afanasyevna dear!' said Kiril Petrovitch T., who had served as a governor in Ryazan and acquired there, not altogether by fair means, three thousand serfs and a young wife. 'I don't mind what my wife wears—she may look like a country bumpkin or a Chinese doll for aught I care, so long as she doesn't order new gowns every month, and throw away those she has scarcely worn. In the old days, a granddaughter used to inherit her grandmother's *sarafan*, and now—the mistress wears a gown one day and her maid the next. What is one to do? It's ruination for the Russian gentry! Dreadful!'

Saying these words he glanced with a sigh at his wife, Marya Ilyinishna, who did not seem at all pleased with their praising the old customs and disparaging the new. Other ladies shared her discontent, but said nothing, for in those days modesty was considered essential in a young woman.

'And whose fault is it?' said Gavril Afanasyevitch, filling a mug with foaming beer. 'Our own. Young women play the fool, and we encourage them.'

'But what are we to do, if we aren't free in the matter?' Kiril Petrovitch retorted. 'Many a husband would be only too glad to shut up his wife in the women's quarters, but soldiers come beating the drum to fetch her to the assembly; the husband takes up the whip, but the wife is busy dressing. Ah, these assemblies! It's the Lord's punishment for our sins.'

Marya Ilyinishna was on tenterhooks; her tongue simply itched to speak; at last she could restrain herself no longer, and turning to her husband she asked him with a sour smile what harm he saw in the assemblies.

'Why, this harm,' Kiril Petrovitch replied angrily: 'since they've been started, husbands cannot keep their wives in hand; wives have forgotten St. Paul's words: "Wives, reverence your husbands"; they think not of housekeeping but of fine clothes; they try to please, not their husbands, but dashing young officers. And is it seemly, madam, for a Russian noblewoman to be in the same room with tobacco-smoking Germans and their servants? It's unheard of—to dance and talk till nightfall with young men! And it isn't as though they were your relatives—they are perfect strangers!'

'I should like to tell a tale, but the wolf is in the vale,' Gavril Afanasyitch said, frowning. 'I confess, I don't care for those assemblies either—you may at any moment run up against someone who is drunk, or may be made drunk yourself for other people's amusement. You have to look sharp that some scapegrace isn't up to mischief with your daughter, and the young people nowadays are spoiled beyond words. At the last assembly, for instance, young Korsakov made such a to-do over my Natasha that I positively blushed. Next day I saw someone driving right up to my front door; I wondered who it could be—Prince Menshikov, perhaps? Not a bit of it: young Korsakov! He could not, if you please, stop his carriage at the gate and take the trouble to walk across the yard—oh, no! he dashed into the room, scraped his foot, chattered away—Lord help us and save us! Yekimovna mimics him admirably; by the way, fool, act the foreign monkey for us.'

Yekimovna seized the lid off one of the dishes, and taking it under her arm as though it were a hat, began grimacing, scraping with her foot and bowing to all sides, repeating: 'Mossoo . . . mam'zelle . . . assembly . . . pardon.' Prolonged and general laughter showed the guests' appreciation of the performance.

'The very image of Korsakov,' said old Prince Lykov, wiping away tears of laughter, when quiet had been gradually restored. 'But we may well confess, he is not the first or the last to return to Holy Russia from foreign parts changed into a clown. What do our children learn there? To scrape with their feet, to chatter in goodness knows what tongue, to make love to other men's wives, and not to respect their elders. Of all the young men brought up in foreign lands, the Tsar's negro (Lord forgive me!) is more of a man than any.'

'Dear me, prince!' Tatyana Afanasyevna said, 'I have seen him, seen him quite close . . . what an awful-looking face! I was quite scared!'

'Of course,' Gavril Afanasyevitch remarked, 'he is a steady respectable man, not like that scapegrace. . . . Who is this driving in at the gate? Is it that foreign monkey again, I wonder? What are you thinking of, you brutes?' he continued, turning to the servants. 'Run and say I will not receive him; and if ever again . . .'

'Are you raving, you grey-beard?' Yekimovna the fool interrupted him. 'Have you gone blind? It's the Tsar's sledge; the Tsar has come.'

Gavril Afanasyevitch hastily got up from the table; all rushed to the windows and, in fact, saw the Tsar walking up the steps leaning on his orderly's shoulder. There was a commotion. Rzhevsky hastened to meet Peter. The servants ran about like mad; the guests were alarmed, and some of them thought of hurrying home. Suddenly Peter's resounding voice was heard behind the door; all grew still, and the Tsar came in, accompanied by his host, who was overcome with joy.

'Good-day, ladies and gentlemen!' said Peter gaily. All made a low bow. The Tsar's quick eyes found Rzhevsky's young daughter in the crowd; he called her. Natalya Gavrilovna came up to him with some show of courage, though she blushed, not merely to the ears, but to the shoulders.

'You grow prettier every hour,' the Tsar said to her, kissing her on the head as was his habit; then he turned to the guests: 'Well, did I disturb you? Were you having dinner? Please sit down again, and give me some aniseed-vodka, Gavril Afanasyevitch.'

Rzhevsky dashed up to his majestic butler, seized the tray from his hands, and, filling a golden cup, gave it to Peter with a bow. Peter drank the vodka, ate a bread-roll, and once more invited the guests to go on with the dinner. All took their former seats, except the dwarf and the woman-jester, who did not dare to remain at the table graced by the Tsar's presence. Peter sat down next to the host, and asked for some cabbage soup. His orderly gave him a wooden spoon mounted in ivory, and a fork and knife with green bone handles, for Peter always used his own. The dinner that had a minute before been gay with talk and laughter continued in silence and constraint.

Out of respect, as well as from joy, the host ate nothing; the guests also stood on ceremony and listened with reverence to the Tsar talking in German to the Swedish officer about the campaign of 1701. The fool Yekimovna, whom the Tsar addressed more than once, answered with a kind of timid coldness which, by the way, was in no sense a proof of her stupidity. At last the dinner was over. The Tsar got up and the other guests did the same.

'Gavril Afanasyevitch,' he said to Rzhevsky, 'I want to speak to you in private'—and taking him by the arm he led him to the drawing-room, shutting the door after them.

The guests remained in the dining-room, talking in whispers about this unexpected visit and, afraid of being indiscreet, soon went home one after another, without thanking their host for his hospitality. His father-in-law, daughter, and sister saw them quietly off to the door, and remained alone in the dining-room, waiting for the Tsar to come out.

CHAPTER V

HALF an hour later the door opened, and Peter came out. He nodded gravely in answer to the salutations of Prince Lykov, Tatyana Afanasyevna, and Natasha, and walked straight to the entry. Rzhevsky helped him on with his red sheepskin coat, saw him off to the sledge, and on the steps thanked him once more for the honour he had done him.

Peter drove away.

Gavril Afanasyevitch seemed much preoccupied when he returned to the dining-room; he angrily ordered the servants to make haste and clear the table, sent Natasha to her room, and, saying to his sister and his father-in-law that he wanted to talk to them, led them into the bedroom where he generally rested after dinner. The old prince lay down on the oak bedstead; Tatyana Afanasyevna settled in the old brocaded arm-chair, resting her feet on a footstool; Gavril Afanasye-vitch locked all the doors and, sitting down on the bed at Prince Lykov's feet, began in an undertone the following conversation:

'It's not for nothing the Tsar came to see me; guess what he was pleased to say to me.'

'How can we tell, dear brother?' Tatyana Afanasyevna said.

'Has the Tsar appointed you governor of some town?' said his father-in-law. 'High time he did. Or has he offered you to serve in an embassy? Well, it's not only government clerks who are sent to foreign sovereigns, but men of noble birth as well.'

'No,' Rzhevsky answered with a frown. 'I am a man of the old sort, and our service isn't needed now, though perhaps an orthodox Russian gentleman is worth as much as those infidels and newly baked nobles who once sold pies.[1] But that's a different matter.'

'What then did he talk to you about, all that time?' Tatyana Afanasyevna asked. 'Have you got into trouble by any chance? The Lord help us and save us!'

'It isn't exactly trouble, but I confess I was rather disconcerted.'

'What is it, brother? What has happened?'

'It is about Natasha: the Tsar came to make a match for her.'

'Thank Heaven!' Tatyana Afanasyevna said, crossing herself. 'It is time she were married; and like match-maker, like suitor. God give them love and concord; it is a great honour. To whom then does the Tsar wish to marry her?'

'Hm!' Gavril Afanasyevitch cleared his throat. 'To whom? That's just it, to whom?'

'To whom, then?' repeated Prince Lykov, who was beginning to doze.

'How can we guess, dear brother?' the old lady answered. 'There are no end of marriageable men at the court: any one of them would be glad to marry your Natasha. Is it Dolgoruky?'

'No, it isn't.'

'Just as well: he is much too proud. Shagin? Troekurov?'

'No, neither of them.'

'And they are not to my taste, either: they are frivolous, and too much infected with the German spirit. Well, is it Miloslavsky?'

'No, it isn't.'

'And a good thing too: he is rich and stupid. Well? Yeletsky? Lvov? Can it be Raguzinsky? No, I give it up. To whom then does the Tsar want to marry Natasha?'

'To the negro Ibrahim.'

The old lady cried out, clasping her hands. Prince Lykov raised his head from the pillow, and repeated in amazement:

'To the negro Ibrahim?'

'Brother darling,' the old lady said in a tearful voice, 'don't ruin your own child, don't give dear Natasha into the black devil's clutches!'

[1] The reference is to Menshikov.—TRANSLATOR'S NOTE.

'But how am I to refuse the Tsar who, if we agree, promises us his favour, me and all our family?' Gavril Afanasyevitch retorted.

'What!' cried the old prince who was wide awake now. 'To marry my granddaughter to a bought negro slave?'

'He is not a commoner,' Gavril Afanasyevitch said. 'He is the son of the Negro Sultan. Infidels took him prisoner and sold him in Constantinople, and our ambassador rescued him and gave him to the Tsar. Ibrahim's elder brother came to Russia with a big ransom and . . .'

'Gavril Afanasyevitch, dear,' the old lady interrupted him, 'we have heard the fairy tale about Prince Bova and Yeruslan Lazarevitch! You'd better tell us what answer you gave to the Tsar.'

'I said that he was our master, and it was his servants' duty to obey him in all things.'

At that moment there was a noise behind the door. Gavril Afanasyevitch went to open it, but felt that there was something holding it. He gave it a violent push—the door opened, and they saw Natasha lying senseless on the blood-stained floor.

Her heart had sunk when the Tsar shut himself in with her father; she had a foreboding that it had something to do with her. When Gavril Afanasyevitch sent her away, saying that he must speak to her aunt and her grandfather, she could not resist her feminine curiosity and, stealing up quietly through the inner rooms to the bedroom door, did not miss a single word of the awful conversation. When she heard her father's last words the poor girl fainted and, falling, hit her head against the iron-clad box in which her dowry was kept.

Servants ran in. Natasha was lifted, carried to her room, and placed on the bed. After a while she regained consciousness and opened her eyes; but she did not recognize her father or her aunt. She was in a high fever; she raved about the Tsar's negro, about the wedding, and suddenly cried in a pitiful and piercing voice:

'Valeryan, dear Valeryan, my life! save me: here they come, here they come! . . .'

Tatyana Afanasyevna glanced anxiously at her brother, who turned pale, bit his lip, and walked out of the room in silence. He joined the old prince, who had remained on the ground floor, as the stairs were too much for him.

'How is Natasha?' he asked.

'She is bad,' said her father sorrowfully, 'worse than I thought: she is delirious and raves about Valeryan.'

'Who is this Valeryan?' the old man asked anxiously; 'can it be that orphan who was brought up in your house?'

'That's the man, worse luck!' Gavril Afanasyevitch answered; 'his father saved my life during the Streltsi's rebellion, and the devil put it into my head to adopt that damned wolf-cub. When two years ago he was at his own request enrolled in a regiment, Natasha burst into tears as she said good-bye to him, while he stood as though turned to stone. It struck me as suspicious, and I spoke of it to my sister at the time. But up to now Natasha has not mentioned him, and nothing more was heard of him. I thought she had forgotten him, but it seems she hasn't. But it is settled: she shall marry the negro.'

Prince Lykov did not contradict him: that would have been useless; he went home. Tatyana Afanasyevna remained by Natasha's bedside; after sending for the doctor, Gavril Afanasyevitch shut himself up in his room, and his house grew still and gloomy.

.   .   .   .   .   .

The unexpected marriage-offer surprised Ibrahim quite as much as it did Gavril Afanasyevitch, if not more. This was how it happened. Working with Ibrahim, Peter said to him:

'I notice, brother, that you are out of spirits; tell me straight, what's wrong?'

Ibrahim assured the Tsar that he was satisfied with his lot and wished for nothing better.

'Good!' said the Tsar; 'if you are depressed for no reason, I know how to cheer you.'

When they had finished work, Peter asked Ibrahim:

'Do you like the girl with whom you danced the minuet at the last assembly?'

'She is very charming, Sire, and seems to be a good and modest girl.'

'Then I'll help you to know her better. Would you like to marry her?'

'I, Sire?'

'Listen, Ibrahim: you are a lonely man, without kindred, a stranger to every one except me. If I were to die to-day, what would become of you to-morrow, my poor African? You must get settled while there is still time, find support in new ties, be allied to the Russian nobility.'

'Sire, I am happy in your Majesty's favour and patronage. God grant I may not outlive my Tsar and benefactor—I wish nothing more; but even if I did think of marriage, would the girl and her relatives agree? My appearance . . . !'

'Your appearance? What nonsense! There's nothing amiss with you. A young girl must obey her parents, and we shall see what old Gavril Rzhevsky will say when I come myself to ask for his daughter's hand for you.'

With these words the Tsar gave orders for his sledge to be brought and left Ibrahim plunged in deep thought.

'To marry!' thought the African. 'Why not? Can I be doomed to live in loneliness, knowing nothing of the highest joys and the most sacred duties of man, simply because I was born in the tropics? I may not hope to be loved; a childish objection! As though one could believe in love! as though a woman's frivolous heart were capable of it! I've given up for ever those charming delusions, and have chosen more substantial attractions instead. The Tsar is right: I must safeguard my future. Marriage to Rzhevsky's daughter will ally me to the proud Russian nobility and I shall no longer be an alien in my new fatherland. I will not expect love from my wife: I shall be content with her fidelity, and shall win her affection by constant tenderness, trust, and indulgence.'

Ibrahim tried to go on with his work as usual, but his mind was in a turmoil. He left his papers and went for a walk along the Neva embankment. Suddenly he heard Peter's voice; turning round he saw the Tsar who, having dismissed his sledge, walked towards him with a cheerful air.

'It's all settled, brother!' Peter said, taking him by the arm. 'Your marriage is arranged. Go to your future father-in-law to-morrow, but mind you humour his family pride: leave your sledge at the gate and walk across the yard to the front door, talk to him about his merits and his noble lineage—and he will dote on you. Now,' he went on, shaking his stick, 'take me to that rascal Danilitch,[1] I have to pay him out for some fresh tricks of his.

Heartily thanking Peter for his fatherly solicitude about him, Ibrahim escorted him to Prince Menshikov's splendid palace and returned home.

CHAPTER VI

A SANCTUARY lamp was burning with a gentle glow before a glazed ikon-stand in which the old family ikons glittered in their setting of gold and silver. Its flickering flame shed a dim light over the curtained bed and a small table covered with medicine bottles. A servant sat by the stove with her spinning-wheel, and the slight whirr of the spindle was the only sound that disturbed the stillness.

'Who is there?' a weak voice asked.

The maid got up at once and, approaching the bed softly, lifted the curtain.

'Will it soon be daylight?' Natasha asked.

'It is midday,' the maid answered.

'Good heavens, why is it so dark then?'

'The window curtains are drawn, miss.'

'Give me my clothes quick.'

'I can't, miss: doctor's orders.'

'Am I ill? Have I been ill long?'

'It's now a fortnight.'

'Indeed? And I fancied I had gone to bed only yesterday. . . .'

Natasha was silent; she was trying to collect her distracted thoughts: something had happened to her, but what it was she could not think. The maid stood before her waiting for orders. At that moment a dull noise came from below.

'What is it?' the invalid asked.

'Dinner is over,' the maid answered. 'They are getting

[1] Menshikov.—TRANSLATOR'S NOTE.

up from the table. Tatyana Afanasyevna will be here
directly.'

Natasha seemed pleased; with a feeble movement of her
hand she dismissed the servant. The maid drew the bed-
curtains and sat down to her spinning-wheel once more. A
few minutes later a head in a broad white cap with dark
ribbons appeared in the doorway and a voice asked in an
undertone:

'How is Natasha?'

'Good morning, auntie,' the invalid said quietly, and
Tatyana Afanasyevna hastened to her.

'Our young lady has come to herself,' said the maid,
bringing up an arm-chair carefully.

Tatyana Afanasyevna kissed with tears her niece's pale,
languid face and sat down beside her. A German doctor in
a black coat and a wig came in after her and, feeling Natasha's
pulse, declared first in Latin and then in Russian that the
danger was over. Asking for paper and ink, he wrote out
a fresh prescription and went away; the old lady got up
and, kissing Natasha once more, went downstairs to give
the good news to Gavril Afanasyevitch.

The Tsar's negro in full uniform, his sword at his belt, and
his hat in his hands, sat in the drawing-room, talking respectfully to Gavril Afanasyevitch. Lolling on a soft couch,
Korsakov listened to them absent-mindedly, teasing an old
borzoi dog; when he tired of this occupation he went up to
the mirror, the usual refuge of idleness, and saw in it Tatyana
Afanasyevna, who stood in the doorway vainly trying to
attract her brother's attention.

'You are wanted, Gavril Afanasyevitch,' said Korsakov,
turning to him and interrupting Ibrahim.

Gavril Afanasyevitch went to his sister at once, shutting
the door behind him.

'I marvel at your patience!' Korsakov said to Ibrahim.
'You've been listening for a whole hour to all that stuff and
nonsense about the antiquity of the Lykov and the Rzhevsky
families, and contributing moral remarks to it, as well! In
your place *j'aurais planté là* the old humbug and all his
family, including Natalya Gavrilovna who gives herself airs,
pretending to be ill—*une petite santé!* Tell me honestly:
surely you aren't in love with this little *mijaurée?*'

'No,' Ibrahim answered, 'I am marrying her not for love, of course, but for practical reasons, and only if she has no positive aversion for me.'

'Look here, Ibrahim,' said Korsakov, 'follow my advice for once; I assure you, I am more reasonable than I appear. Give up this mad idea—don't marry! It seems to me that your betrothed has no particular liking for you. All sorts of things happen in this world, you know. Here, for instance, am I—fairly good-looking, of course, but it has happened to me to deceive husbands who were in no way inferior to me, I assure you. You yourself . . . you remember our Paris friend, Count L.? One cannot rely on a woman's fidelity, and those who don't bother about it are lucky. But you! . . . Is it for a man of your ardent, brooding, and suspicious disposition, with flat nose, fat lips, and fuzzy hair to expose himself to all the dangers of matrimony?'

'Thank you for your friendly advice,' Ibrahim interrupted him coldly, 'but you know the proverb, "You need not trouble to nurse other people's children".'

'Mind, Ibrahim,' Korsakov answered laughing, 'that you don't have to prove the truth of that proverb in a literal sense.'

But the conversation in the next room was growing heated.

'You will kill her,' the old lady was saying. 'The sight of him will be too much for her.'

'But just consider,' her obstinate brother retorted, 'he's been coming to the house as her betrothed for the last fortnight, and he hasn't seen her yet. He may end by thinking that her illness is a sham, and that we are simply trying to delay the marriage so as to get rid of him. And what will the Tsar say? He has sent three times as it is to inquire after Natasha's health. Say what you will, I don't intend to quarrel with him.'

'Good heavens, what will become of the poor girl!' Tatyana Afanasyevna said. 'Let me go at any rate and prepare her for his visit.'

Gavril Afanasyevitch agreed, and returned to the drawing-room.

'Thank God, the danger is over,' he said to Ibrahim. 'Natalya is much better; if I weren't ashamed to leave our

dear guest alone here, I should take you upstairs to have a
look at your betrothed.'

Korsakov congratulated Gavril Afanasyevitch, asked him
not to worry about him, assured him that he had to go away
at once, and ran out of the room, not allowing his host to see
him off.

Meanwhile Tatyana Afanasyevna hastened to prepare the
invalid for her terrible visitor. She came in and sat down,
breathless, by the girl's bedside; she took Natasha's hand,
but had not had time to say a word before the door opened.
Natasha asked: 'Who is it?' The old lady turned cold with
horror. Gavril Afanasyevitch drew back the curtain, looked
at the invalid coldly, and asked how she was. Natasha tried
to smile at him, but could not. She was struck by her
father's stern expression, and a vague uneasiness possessed
her. At that moment it seemed to her that someone was
standing at the head of her bed. She raised her head with an
effort, and suddenly recognized the Tsar's negro. She
recalled everything, and her future appeared before her in
all its horror. But she was so exhausted that she felt no
violent shock. She let her head sink on the pillow again
and closed her eyes . . . her heart was beating painfully.
Tatyana Afanasyevna made a sign to her brother that the
invalid wanted to sleep, and all left the room quietly, except
the maid-servant, who sat down to the spinning-wheel
once more.

The unhappy girl opened her eyes and, seeing no one by
her bedside, called the maid and sent her for the dwarf.
But at the same moment the fat old dwarf seemed to roll up
to her bed like a ball. Lastochka (that was the dwarf's
name) had run upstairs after Gavril Afanasyevitch and
Ibrahim as fast as her short little legs would carry her and,
true to the curiosity natural to the fair sex, had hidden behind
the door. Seeing her, Natasha sent the maid away, and the
dwarf sat down on a bench at her bedside.

Never did a tiny body contain so much mental energy.
She interfered in everything, knew all there was to know,
busied herself with all things. Her sly and insinuating
intelligence helped her to acquire the affection of her masters
and the hatred of the rest of the household, which she domi-
nated completely. Gavril Afanasyevitch listened to her

tales, complaints, and petty requests; Tatyana Afanasyevna was constantly asking her opinion and following her advice; Natasha had boundless affection for her, and confided to her all the thoughts and feelings of her young heart.

'Do you know, Lastochka,' she said, 'my father is marrying me to the negro.'

The dwarf sighed deeply, and her wrinkled face grew more wrinkled than ever.

'Is there no hope?' Natasha continued. 'Won't my father have pity on me?'

The dwarf shook her head.

'Won't my grandfather or auntie intercede for me?'

'No, miss; during your illness the negro has got round every one. Your father is delighted with him, the prince can talk of no one else, and Tatyana Afanasyevna says: "It's a pity he is a negro, but it would be a sin for us to want a better suitor".'

'My God, my God!' groaned poor Natasha.

'Don't grieve, my beauty,' said the dwarf kissing her listless hand; 'even if you are to marry a negro, you will still be free. Things are not what they used to be: husbands don't shut up their wives. The negro is rich, they say; you'll have a lovely home, and live in comfort and plenty.'

'Poor Valeryan!' said Natasha in a voice so low that the dwarf could only guess and not hear the words.

'That's just it, miss,' she said dropping her voice mysteriously; 'if you had thought less about that youth, you wouldn't have raved about him in your fever, and your father wouldn't have been angry.'

'What?' said Natalya, terrified. 'I talked about Valeryan? My father heard it? He was angry?'

'That's just the trouble,' the dwarf answered. 'If you ask him now not to marry you to the negro he will think it is because of Valeryan. There is nothing for it: submit to your father's will, and what is to be, will be.'

Natasha did not answer a word. The thought that her heart's secret was known to her father greatly affected her imagination. One hope only was left her: to die before the hateful marriage. That thought comforted her. Weak and sad at heart, she resigned herself to her fate.

CHAPTER VII

IN Gavril Afanasyevitch's house, to the right from the entrance hall, there was a tiny room with one window. A plain bed covered with a blanket stood in it; in front of the bed there was a deal table on which a tallow candle was burning and a music-book lay open. An old blue uniform and an equally old three-cornered hat hung on the wall, under a print of Charles XII on horseback, fixed up with three nails. Sounds of a flute came from this humble apartment. Its solitary occupant, the captive dancing-master, in a nightcap and a cotton dressing-gown, sought to relieve the boredom of a winter evening by playing ancient Swedish marches. Having spent two hours at this exercise the Swede took the flute to pieces and, putting it into its case, began to undress.

•   •   •   •   •   •

1827.

THE STATION-MASTER

> Here 's a collegiate registrator,
> Of posting stations the dictator.
>
> *Prince Viazemsky.*

WHO has not cursed the superintendents of posting stations? who has not quarrelled with them? Who in a moment of anger has not demanded from them the fatal book to write in it his useless complaint of injustice, rudeness, and inefficiency? Who does not regard them as human monsters, as bad as the attorneys of the old days or at any rate as the Murom highwaymen? Let us be just, however, let us try to consider their position, and perhaps we shall feel more kindly towards them. What is a station-master? A true martyr, whose low rank in the civil service protects him only from blows, and that not always (I appeal to my readers' conscience). What sort of life has this 'dictator', as Prince Viazemsky jokingly calls him? The life of a galley-slave. He has no rest either by day or by night. Travellers vent upon him all the annoyance accumulated during their tedious journey: the weather is unbearable, the roads are bad, the driver is obstinate, the horses don't go—and it is all the station-master's fault. Coming into his poor dwelling, the traveller looks upon him as an enemy; he is lucky if he can soon get rid of his unwelcome visitor; but if there happen to be no horses? . . . Goodness, what abuse, what threats are showered upon him! In rain and sleet he is forced to run about the village trying to find horses; in the storm, in bitter frost he has to go into the cold entry to have a minute's respite from the angry traveller's shouts and blows. A general arrives; the station-master, trembling, gives him his last troikas, including the one for government messengers. The general drives off without saying: 'Thank you'. Five minutes later a bell is heard—and a government courier throws down his pass on the table! Let us consider all this closely and, instead of indignation, our heart will be filled

with genuine sympathy. A few words more: during twenty
years in succession I have travelled up and down Russia in
all directions; I have been on almost all the posting routes;
I have known several generations of drivers; there are few
station-masters whose faces are not familiar to me and with
whom I have not had something to do; I hope to publish
in the near future an interesting collection of my travelling
impressions; meanwhile I shall only say that the class of
station-masters has been grossly misrepresented to the
public. Those officials, so cruelly maligned, are, generally
speaking, peaceable men, obliging by nature, of sociable
disposition, modest in their ambitions, and not too grasping.
Much that is interesting and instructive may be gathered
from their conversation, which the travellers do wrong to
despise. As for myself, I confess I prefer their talk to
that of some important official travelling on government
business.

It is not difficult to guess that I have friends among the
honourable company of station-masters. In fact, the
memory of one of them is precious to me. Circumstances
drew us together once, and it is of him I now want to tell
my kind readers.

In May 1816 I happened to go through the province of X.
along a posting route that has since been done away with.
Being of low rank in the service I travelled by post-stages
and hired only two horses. In consequence station-masters
did not stand on ceremony with me, and I often had to fight
for what I regarded as my lawful due. Being young and
hot-tempered I felt indignant at the station-master's mean-
ness and cowardice when he gave to some gentleman of
rank the team intended for me. It took me just as long to
get accustomed to being passed over by a discriminating
flunkey handing dishes at a governor's dinner. Now both
the one and the other seem to me in the natural order of
things. What, indeed, would become of us if, instead of
the convenient rule of precedence by rank, some other rule
were introduced such as 'precedence by intelligence'. What
disputes there would be! and who would be first served at
dinner? But I return to my story.

The day was hot. Two miles from the station N. I felt
a few spots of rain; in another minute there was a regular

downpour and I was drenched to the skin. When I arrived at the station the first thing I did was to change my clothes; the second, to ask for some tea.

'Dounia!' the station-master cried, 'heat the samovar and run for some cream.'

At these words a girl of about fourteen came out from behind the partition and ran to the entry. I was struck by her beauty.

'Is that your daughter?' I asked the station-master.

'Yes, sir,' he answered with an air of satisfied pride, 'and such a good girl, and so quick, the very picture of her dear mother.'

Thereupon he began copying out my pass, and I examined the pictures that adorned his humble but clean dwelling. They illustrated the story of the Prodigal Son: in the first, a venerable old man in a night-cap and dressing-gown was saying good-bye to the restless youth, who was hastily receiving his blessing and a purse of gold. Another vividly depicted the young man's dissolute conduct: he was sitting at the table surrounded by false friends and shameless women. Farther on, the young man, in a three-cornered hat and ragged clothes, was herding pigs and sharing their meal; his face expressed profound sorrow and penitence. The last picture showed his return to his father: the kind old man in the same dressing-gown and night-cap was running to meet him; the prodigal son was kneeling; in the background the cook could be seen killing the fatted calf, and the elder brother asking the servants about the reason for such rejoicing. Under each picture I read appropriate German verses. I remember it all to this day, as well as the clarkia in pots, the bed with a gaily coloured curtain, and the other things in the room. I clearly see before me the station-master himself, a vigorous and well-preserved man of about fifty, dressed in a long green coat with three medals attached to faded ribbons. I had scarcely had time to settle with my old driver when Dounia came in with the samovar. The little coquette noticed at the second glance the impression she had made on me; she cast down her big blue eyes; I spoke to her; she answered me without any timidity, like a girl who had seen the world. I offered her father a glass of punch, gave Dounia a cup of tea, and we talked together,

the three of us, as though we had known one another all
our lives.

My horses had long been ready, but still I did not want to
part with the station-master and his daughter.   At last I bid
them good-bye; the father wished me a pleasant journey,
and the daughter saw me off to my vehicle.   In the entry
I stopped and asked if she would allow me to kiss her.
Dounia consented.   I can count many kisses,

Since the day I took up this pursuit,

but not one of them left such a long and pleasant memory
in my mind.

Several years had passed, and circumstances brought me
to the same posting route, to the same neighbourhood, once
more.   I recalled the old station-master's daughter, and was
glad to think that I should see her again.   'But perhaps there
is some other man in the old station-master's place,' I thought;
'Dounia is probably already married.'   The thought that
one or the other of them might have died also crossed my
mind, and I approached the station N. with a sad foreboding.
The horses stopped by the station-house.   Coming into the
room I recognized at once the pictures illustrating the story
of the Prodigal Son; the bed and the table stood in their old
places, but there were no longer flowers in the windows, and
everything around me looked worn and neglected.   The
station-master was sleeping under a sheepskin coat; my
arrival woke him; he got up. . . . It was he, Simeon Vyrin,
indeed; but how he had aged!   While he was preparing to
copy out my pass, I gazed at his grey hair, at the deep lines
of his unshaven face, at his stooping shoulders—and could
not understand how three or four years could have transformed him into a decrepit old man.

'Do you recognize me?' I asked.   'You and I are old
friends.'

'Perhaps,' he answered morosely.   'I live on the high road:
many travellers have passed through my station.'

'How is your Dounia?' I asked.

The old man frowned.   'I really couldn't say,' he answered.

'So then she is married?' I asked.

He pretended not to hear me, and went on reading my pass
in a whisper.   I did not question him any further, but asked

to have a kettle put on the fire. I was beginning to feel curious and hoped that punch would untie my old friend's tongue.

I was not mistaken: the old man did not refuse the glass I offered him. I noticed that rum put him into a better humour. At the second glass he grew talkative; he remembered, or pretended to remember, who I was, and I heard from him a story which interested and touched me greatly at the time.

'So you knew my Dounia?' he began. 'Every one knew her, indeed! Ah, Dounia, Dounia! What a fine girl she was! Whoever went by always praised her, no one found fault with her. Ladies would give her a kerchief and a pair of ear-rings. Gentlemen, driving past, would stop to have dinner or supper simply because they wanted to see more of her. However angry a man might be, he always calmed down when he saw her, and spoke to me kindly. Would you believe it, sir, government messengers and couriers used to stop for half an hour talking to her. She kept the house going: did all the cleaning and cooking, and managed everything. And I, old fool that I was, did nothing but delight in her. How I loved my Dounia, how I cherished her! No girl could have had a happier life. But no, there is no keeping off misfortune; what is to be will be.'

Then he told me the story of his trouble. Three years previously, on a winter night, when he was ruling out a new post book, and his daughter behind the partition was making herself a dress, a troika drove up, and a traveller wrapped up in a rug, wearing a Circassian cap and a military uniform, came into the room asking for horses. There were no horses to be had. On hearing this, the traveller raised his voice and his whip; but Dounia, used to such scenes, ran out from behind the partition and amiably asked the traveller if he would have something to eat. Dounia's appearance produced its usual effect. The traveller's anger cooled; he agreed to wait for the horses and ordered supper. When he had taken off his wet shaggy cap, unwrapped his rug and folded his overcoat, he proved to be a graceful young hussar with a small black moustache. He made himself at home, and began talking cheerfully to the station-master and his daughter. Supper was served. Meanwhile the horses had come back and the station-master gave orders that they were to be harnessed at once, without being fed, to the young man's covered sledge; but on coming back he found the young man lying almost senseless on the bench: he had been suddenly taken ill, his head ached, he could not go. . . . What was to be done? The station-master gave up his bed to him, and it was decided that if the invalid was no better in the morning, they would send to S. for a doctor.

The following day the hussar was worse. His servant rode to the town to fetch a doctor. Dounia tied up his head with a handkerchief soaked in vinegar, and sat down by his bedside with her needlework. While the station-master was in the room the invalid groaned and hardly spoke a word, but he managed to drink two cups of coffee and, groaning, ordered some dinner. Dounia never left his side. He asked for a drink every minute and Dounia gave him the mug of lemonade she had prepared. The invalid moistened his lips in it, and every time he returned the mug he gratefully pressed Dounia's hand with his feeble fingers. The doctor arrived by dinner-time. He felt the invalid's pulse, talked to him in German, and declared in Russian that all he needed was rest, and that in a couple of days he would be able to go on with his journey. The hussar gave him twenty-five roubles for his visit, and invited him to share his dinner; the doctor agreed; both ate with much appetite, drank a bottle of wine, and parted very much pleased with each other.

Another day passed and the hussar recovered completely. He was extremely gay, joked all the time with Dounia and her father, whistled tunes, talked to the travellers, and copied out their passes into the post-book; the good old man took such a liking to him that on the morning of the third day he was quite sorry to part from his amiable lodger. It was a Sunday; Dounia was preparing to go to Mass. The hussar's sledge was brought. He said good-bye to the station-master, paying him generously for his board and lodging; he said good-bye to Dounia too, and offered to drive her as far as the church, which was at the end of the village. Dounia hesitated.

'What are you afraid of?' her father said. 'His honour is not a wolf, he won't eat you—have a lift to the church.'

Dounia sat down in the sledge next to the hussar, the

servant jumped on to the box, the driver whistled, and the horses galloped off.

Poor man, he could not understand how he could have allowed his Dounia to drive away with the hussar: he did not know how he could have been so blind, nor what could have become of his good sense. Before half an hour had passed his heart began to ache, and such anxiety possessed him that he could stand it no longer, and went to Mass himself. Coming up to the church he saw that people were already going home, but Dounia was neither in the church-yard, nor on the steps. He hastily entered the church; the priest was leaving, the sexton was blowing out the candles; two old women were still praying in a corner, but Dounia was not there. Her poor father could scarcely bring himself to ask the sexton whether Dounia had been to Mass. The sexton answered that she had not. The station-master went home more dead than alive. He had one hope left: with the thoughtlessness of youth Dounia might have decided to drive as far as the next station where her godmother lived. He waited in an agony of suspense for the return of the troika in which he had let her go. The driver was late; he returned at last in the evening, by himself, drunk, with the awful news that Dounia had gone on with the hussar from the next station.

The blow was too much for the old man; he was taken ill on the spot, and lay down in the same bed where the night before the young impostor had rested. Later on he guessed, putting all the circumstances together, that the hussar's illness had been a sham. The station-master had brain-fever, and was taken to S., while another man was tem-porarily appointed in his place. The same doctor who had come to the hussar, treated him. He assured the station-master that the young man had been perfectly well; he had guessed his evil intention at the time, but said nothing, fearing the hussar's whip. Whether the German spoke the truth or merely wanted to boast of his foresight, his words were not of the least comfort to the sick man. He had hardly recovered from his illness when he obtained a two months' leave from the S. postmaster and, not saying a word to any one about his intention, set out on foot in search of his daughter. He knew from the hussar's pass that Captain Minsky was travelling from Smolensk to Petersburg; the driver who had taken him said that Dounia wept all the way, though she seemed to have gone of her own will.

'I may bring home my lost lamb,' thought the station-master. With this idea he came to Petersburg, put up at the house of a retired sergeant, an old comrade of his in the service, and began his search. He soon learned that Captain Minsky was in Petersburg and lived in Demoute's Hotel: the station-master decided to go to him.

Early in the morning he came to his door and asked the servant to tell his honour that an old soldier wished to see him. The orderly, who was polishing boots, said that his master was asleep, and could not see any one till eleven o'clock. The station-master went away and came back at the appointed hour. Minsky in a dressing-gown and a red fez came out to him. 'What do you want, brother?' he asked.

The old man's heart brimmed over, tears came into his eyes, and he could only bring out in a shaking voice: 'Your honour! . . . be so kind, I beg you! . . .'

Minsky glanced at him quickly, flushed crimson, and taking him by the hand led him to his study, shutting the door after him.

'Your honour!' the old man went on, 'it 's no use crying over spilt milk, but give me back my poor Dounia. You have had your pleasure; don't ruin her for nothing.'

'What is done cannot be undone,' said the young man in extreme confusion. 'I have wronged you, and am glad to ask your forgiveness; but don't think that I could ever abandon Dounia; she will be happy, I promise you on my honour. What do you want with her? She loves me; she has lost the habit of her old life. Neither you nor she could forget what has happened.'

After that, thrusting something into the cuff of the old man's sleeve, he opened the door, and the station-master did not remember how he found himself in the street.

He stood motionless for some time; then he saw a bundle of papers in the cuff of his sleeve; taking them out he unfolded several crumpled fifty-rouble notes. Tears came into his eyes again—tears of indignation! He crushed the notes into a ball, threw them down, stamped on them, and walked away. . . . After taking a few steps he stood still and thought . . . and went back . . . but the notes were no longer there. A well-dressed young man, catching sight of him, ran up to a cab, stepped in hastily, and shouted to the driver 'Go!' . . . The station-master did not follow him. He decided to go home, to his station, but before doing so he wanted to see his poor Dounia once more. With this end in view he called on Minsky again a couple of days later; but the orderly said to him sternly that his master was not seeing any one, and, almost pushing him out of the entry, banged the door in his face. The old man stood outside for a time and then walked home.

On the evening of that same day, after a service to Our Lady, 'Joy of all the sorrowful', he was walking along the Liteyiny. Suddenly a smart-looking droshky dashed past him, and he recognized Minsky. The droshky stopped at the front door of a house of three stories and the hussar ran up the steps. A happy thought struck the old man. He went back and, going up to the coachman, asked him:

'Whose horse is it? Minsky's, isn't it?'

'Yes, it is,' the coachman answered. 'Why do you ask?'

'Well, it's like this: your master told me to take a note to his Dounia, and as luck would have it, I've forgotten where Dounia lives.'

'Why, here, on the first floor. You are late, brother, with your note; he is with her himself now.'

'Never mind,' the station-master answered with an indescribable feeling in his heart. 'Thank you for telling me, I'll go and deliver the note.' With these words he walked up the stairs.

The door was locked; he rang. He had a few seconds of painful expectation: the key rattled; the door was opened.

'Does Avdotya Simeonovna live here?' he asked. 'Yes,' a young maid-servant answered. 'What do you want her for?'

Without answering the station-master walked into the hall.

'You can't see her!' the maid called after him. 'She has visitors!'

But he walked on, not heeding her. The first two rooms were dark, in the third one there was a light. He walked up to the open door and stopped. Minsky, lost in thought, was sitting in the beautifully furnished room. Dounia, dressed in the height of fashion, sat on the arm of his chair like a rider on a side-saddle. She looked at Minsky tenderly, twisting his black curls round her white fingers. Poor station-master! Never had his daughter seemed to him more beautiful; he could not help admiring her. 'Who is there?' she asked without raising her head. He said nothing. Not receiving an answer, Dounia looked up . . . and fell down on the carpet with a cry. Minsky, terrified, rushed to lift her, but, suddenly seeing her father in the doorway, left Dounia and went up to him shaking with anger. 'What do you want?' he said to him, clenching his teeth. 'Why do you steal after me everywhere like a brigand? Do you want to murder me? Out with you!' and seizing the old man with a strong hand by the collar, he pushed him out on to the stairs.

The station-master walked back to his lodgings; his friend advised him to complain, but on thinking it over he decided to give up the whole thing. Two days later he went back to his station, and took up his duties there. 'It is over two years now,' he concluded, 'that I have lived without Dounia, knowing nothing whatever about her. God only knows whether she is still alive. All sorts of things happen. She is not the first or the last to have been seduced by a passer-by, kept for a while, and then abandoned. There are plenty of those silly girls in Petersburg, wearing satin and velvet one day, and sweeping the streets together with the riff-raff from public-houses the next. When I think sometimes that my Dounia may have gone the same way I can't help wishing she were dead, sinner that I am! . . .'

That was the story that my friend, the old station-master, told me, interrupting it more than once with tears which he picturesquely wiped with the skirt of his coat like the zealous Terentyitch in Dmitriev's beautiful ballad. Those tears were partly excited by punch, of which he drained five glasses in the course of his story—but, anyway, they greatly touched my heart. Long after parting from him I kept thinking of the station-master and of poor Dounia.

Not long ago, passing through the village of X., I remembered my old friend; I heard that the posting station he superintended had been closed. No one could give a satisfactory answer to my question whether the old station-master was still living. I decided to visit the place and, hiring some horses, went on to the village of N.

It was in the autumn. Grey clouds covered the sky; a cold wind blew from the harvested fields, snatching red and yellow leaves from the trees by the roadside. I arrived at the village at sunset, and stopped by the station-house. A fat woman came out into the entry (where poor Dounia had once kissed me); in answer to my questions she said that the station-master had died about a year ago, that the brewer was now living in his house, and that she was the brewer's wife. I regretted my useless journey, and the seven roubles I had spent on it. 'What did he die of?' I asked the woman. 'Of drink, sir,' she answered. 'Where is he buried?' 'Outside the village, next to his wife's grave.' 'Can someone take me there?' 'Why not? Heigh, Vanka! You've played enough with the cat. Take the gentleman to the cemetery, and show him the station-master's grave.'

At these words a ragged little boy, red-haired and blind in one eye, ran up to me and proceeded to take me to the cemetery.

'Did you know the old man?' I asked him on the way.

'Oh yes! He taught me to make whistles. When he went home from the public-house (God rest his soul!) we all ran after him crying, 'Grandad, grandad, give us some nuts!' and he would give some to each one. He was always playing with us.'

'And do the travellers remember him?'

'There aren't many travellers now; the assessor comes sometimes, but he has no thoughts to spare for the dead. But last summer a lady came who did ask for the old station-master, and went to his grave, too.'

'What lady?' I asked with interest.

'A lovely lady!' the boy answered. 'She came in a carriage drawn by six horses, and had three children with her, and a wet-nurse, and a black lapdog, and when she heard that the old station-master was dead, she wept, and said to the children: "You sit still, and I'll go to the cemetery". I offered to take her, but she said: "I know the way", and she gave me five copecks in silver . . . such a kind lady!'

We arrived at the cemetery—a bare field, dotted about

with wooden crosses, with no fence round it, and not a single tree. I never saw a more desolate cemetery.

'This is the old station-master's grave,' said the boy, jumping on to a heap of sand with a black cross that had a brass ikon fixed to it.

'And the lady came here?' I asked.

'Yes, she did,' Vanka answered. 'I watched her from a distance. She threw herself down on the grave and lay here for a long time. And then she walked to the village and called the priest, gave him some money, and went away, and gave me five copecks in silver . . . a good lady!'

I, too, gave the boy five copecks, and no longer regretted my journey and the seven roubles I had spent.

THE SNOWSTORM

Horses gallop through the plain
Trampling down the snow.
Far away, there stands a church
In the vale below.

Zhukovsky.

AT the end of 1811—an epoch memorable to us—there lived
on his estate Nenaradovo kind Gavril Gavrilovitch R. He
was renowned in the district for his friendliness and hospitality; neighbours came to his house at every hour of the day
to have a meal and a drink, to play a game of cards for five
copecks stakes with his wife, and some to have a look at their
daughter, Marya Gavrilovna, a pale and graceful girl of seventeen. She was considered an heiress, and many thought of
her as a good match for themselves or for their sons.

Marya Gavrilovna was brought up on French novels, and
consequently was in love. She selected as the subject of her
affections a poor army lieutenant, staying on leave in his
country place. It is needless to say that the young man was
burning with equal passion, and that the parents of his lady-
love, observing their mutual inclination, forbade their
daughter to think of him, and received him worse than a
retired assessor.

The lovers kept up a correspondence and met alone every
day in the pinewood or by the old wayside chapel. There
they exchanged vows of eternal love, complained of their fate,
and made various plans. In their letters and conversations
they, quite naturally, arrived at the following argument: if we
cannot breathe without each other, and the cruel parents' will
prevents our happiness, couldn't we do without their consent?
Of course this fortunate idea occurred first to the young man,
and strongly appealed to Marya Gavrilovna's romantic
imagination.

Winter came and put a stop to their meetings, but their correspondence grew all the more lively. In every letter

Vladimir Nicolaevitch implored her to trust herself to him,
marry him secretly, remain in hiding for a time, and then fall at
the feet of her parents who would of course be touched by the
lovers' heroic constancy and unhappiness and be sure to say
to them: 'Children, come to our arms!'

Marya Gavrilovna hesitated and delayed; many plans of
elopement were rejected by her. At last she consented: on
the appointed day she was to have no supper and retire to her
room on the pretext of headache. Her maid was in the
conspiracy; they were both to slip by the back door into the
garden, find at the other side of it a sledge waiting for them,
get into it and drive four miles to the village of Zhadrino,
straight to the church, where Vladimir would be waiting for
them.

On the eve of the decisive day Marya Gavrilovna did not
sleep all night; she packed, tied her dresses and linen into
bundles, wrote a long letter to a friend—a young lady of great
sensibility—and another to her parents. She took leave of
them in most touching words, excused her action by the
irresistible force of passion, and finished by saying that the
happiest moment of her life will be the one when she is
allowed to fall at the feet of her beloved parents. Having
sealed both letters with a seal bearing the device of two
flaming hearts and an appropriate inscription, she threw herself on to her bed at daybreak and dozed off, but terrible
dreams woke her up every minute. Sometimes it seemed to
her that just as she was getting into the sledge to go to church
her father stopped her, and dragging her painfully fast over
the snow, threw her into a dark bottomless dungeon . . . she
flew headlong, her heart fluttering desperately. Or she
dreamt of Vladimir lying on the grass, pale and covered with
blood. Dying, he implored her in a piercing voice to make
haste and marry him. . . . Other visions, senseless and
hideous, flitted before her in rapid succession.

At last she got up, paler than usual, and with a genuine
headache. Her father and mother noticed her uneasiness;
their tender solicitude and constant questions 'What is it,
Masha?' 'Are you unwell, Masha?' wrung her heart. She
tried to reassure them, to appear gay, and could not. Evening came. The thought that she was spending it for the last
time in the midst of her family oppressed her. She could

scarcely breathe; she was secretly taking leave of every person and every object around her.

Supper was served; her heart beat violently. In a trembling voice she said that she did not feel like eating and bade good night to her father and mother. They kissed and blessed her as usual: she almost wept. When she came to her room she threw herself into an armchair and burst into tears. Her maid pleaded with her to calm herself and take courage. All was ready. In half an hour Masha was to leave for ever her parental home, her room, her peaceful girlhood. . . . A snowstorm was raging outside, the wind howled, the shutters shook and clattered; everything seemed to her menacing and foreboding. At last all was quiet and asleep in the house. Masha wrapped herself up in a shawl, put on a warm overcoat, took her casket, and came out by the back door. The maid followed her, carrying two bundles. They went down the steps into the garden. The snowstorm did not abate; the wind blew against them as though trying to stop the young criminal. They had a struggle to reach the end of the garden. In the road a sledge was waiting for them. The horses were feeling the cold and could hardly stand still; Vladimir's coachman paced to and fro in front of the shafts, restraining the spirited animals. He helped the young lady and her maid to settle in the sledge with their bundles and the casket, took up the reins, and the horses dashed off. Let us leave the young lady in the care of fate and of the coachman Tereshka's skill, and turn to the young lover.

Vladimir spent the whole day driving from place to place. In the morning he went to see the priest at Zhadrino, and had much difficulty in arranging matters with him; then he went in search of prospective witnesses among the neighbouring landowners. His first call was to a retired cavalry officer, Dravin, a man of forty, who readily consented, saying that this adventure reminded him of the old days and of the hussars' frolics. He persuaded Vladimir to stay to dinner and assured him that there would be no difficulty in finding the two other witnesses. And indeed immediately after dinner two guests arrived: Shmidt, the surveyor, who wore a moustache and spurs, and the police-captain's son, a boy of sixteen recently enlisted in the uhlans. They not only accepted Vladimir's offer, but swore that they were ready to lay down their lives for him. He embraced them enthusiastically and went home to make ready.

Meanwhile dusk had gathered. He sent his faithful Tereshka with the troika to Nenaradovo, giving him detailed and careful instructions, ordered a small sledge with one horse for himself, and set out without a coachman to Zhadrino where in a couple of hours Marya Gavrilovna was to join him. He knew his way, and it was only a twenty minutes' drive.

But no sooner had Vladimir left the village and come into the open country than the wind rose and such a snowstorm blew up that he could not see a thing. The road was instantly buried in snow; everything around disappeared in a thick yellowish haze through which white flakes of snow were flying; the sky was merged with the earth. Vladimir found himself in the open plain and vainly tried to regain the road; his horse moved at random, now climbing a snowdrift, now sinking into a pit; the sledge constantly turned over. All that Vladimir endeavoured to do was not to lose his bearings. But it seemed to him that more than half an hour had passed and he had not yet reached the Zhadrino copse. Another ten minutes passed; the copse was not yet in sight. Vladimir was driving across a plain intersected by deep ravines. The snowstorm did not abate, the sky did not clear. The horse was growing tired, and he was bathed in perspiration, although he constantly sank waist-deep in the snow.

At last he saw that he was going in the wrong direction. He stopped: he began to think, to recall his movements, to consider where he was, and decided that he ought to turn to the right. He went to the right. His horse was scarcely able to walk. He had been more than an hour on his way. Zhadrino must be close by. But he drove on and on, and the plain was endless. It was nothing but snowdrifts and ravines; the sledge turned over every minute and he kept lifting it. Time passed; Vladimir began to feel uneasy.

At last, on one side something showed black in the distance. Vladimir turned in that direction. As he drew near he saw a copse. 'Thank God,' he thought, 'it isn't far now.' He drove alongside the copse, hoping to strike the familiar road at once, or to drive round the copse: Zhadrino lay just behind it. He soon found the road and entered into the darkness under the trees bared by the winter. The wind could not rage here; the road was smooth; the horse rallied, and Vladimir was reassured.

But he went on and on, and Zhadrino was not to be seen; the copse was endless. Vladimir saw with horror that he was in a forest he did not know. Despair possessed him. He struck the horse; the poor animal broke into a trot, but soon began to flag, and quarter of an hour later walked along at foot pace, in spite of all that the unhappy Vladimir did to urge it on.

Gradually the trees began to thin, and Vladimir came out of the forest. There was no Zhadrino in sight. The hour must have been about midnight. Tears gushed from his eyes; he drove on at random. The storm had ceased, the clouds were dispersing; a plain covered with a wavy carpet of snow lay before him. The night was fairly clear. In the near distance he saw a hamlet consisting of four or five homesteads. Vladimir drove up to it. He stopped by the first cottage, ran up to the window, and began knocking. After a few minutes the wooden shutter was lifted and an old man thrust out his grey beard.

'What do you want?'

'Is it far to Zhadrino?'

'To Zhadrino, you say?'

'Yes, yes! Is it far?'

'No, not far; about eight miles.'

At this answer Vladimir remained motionless, clutching at his head like a man condemned to death.

'And where do you come from?' the old man continued.

Vladimir was too dispirited to answer questions.

'Can you procure me some horses, old man, to take me to Zhadrino?'

'Our horses are no good,' the peasant answered.

'Can I at least have a guide? I'll pay him what he likes.'

'Wait,' said the old man, letting down the shutter. 'I'll send you my son; he'll go with you.'

Vladimir waited. In less than a minute he began knocking again. The shutter was raised, the beard poked out.

'What do you want?'

'Is your son coming?'

'He won't be long, he is putting on his snow-boots. Are you cold? Come in and warm yourself.'

'Thank you; tell your son to be quick.'

The gates creaked; a young man with a thick stick came out and walked in front of the sledge, pointing out the road covered by snowdrifts, or looking for it.

'What time is it?' Vladimir asked him.

'It will soon be daybreak,' the young peasant answered.

Vladimir said nothing more.

Cocks were crowing and it was already light when they reached Zhadrino. The church was locked. Vladimir paid his guide and drove to the priest's house. His troika was not in the courtyard. What news awaited him!

But let us return to the good people at Nenaradovo and see what is happening there.

Why, nothing.

The old couple woke up and came into the drawing-room, Gavril Gavrilovitch in a nightcap and a warm jacket, Praskovya Petrovna in a quilted dressing-gown. The samovar was brought in, and Gavril Gavrilovitch sent the little servant girl to inquire how Marya Gavrilovna felt and what sort of night she had had. The girl returned saying that the young lady had had a bad night, but was feeling better now, and would come to the drawing-room directly. Indeed the door opened, and Marya Gavrilovna came in to wish good morning to her father and mother.

'How is your headache, Masha?' asked Gavril Gavrilovitch.

'It's better, papa,' Masha answered.

'I expect it's the charcoal fumes yesterday that gave it you,' said Praskovya Petrovna.

'Very likely, mamma,' Masha answered.

The day passed as usual, but in the night Masha was taken ill. The town doctor was sent for. He arrived towards evening and found the patient delirious. She was in high fever, and for a fortnight the poor girl hovered on the brink of death.

No one in the house knew about the proposed elopement. Masha burnt the letters she had written on the eve of it; her maid did not say a word to anyone, for fear of her masters' anger. The priest, the retired cavalry officer, the moustached surveyor, and the young uhlan were discreet, and with a good reason. The coachman Tereshka never babbled, not even when he was drunk. Thus the secret was preserved by more than half a dozen conspirators. But in her continual delirium Marya Gavrilovna herself gave it away. Her words, however, were so incoherent that her mother, who never left the invalid's bedside, could only gather from them that her daughter was desperately in love with Vladimir Nicolaevitch, and that probably love was the cause of her illness. She consulted her husband and some of their neighbours, and at last all agreed that evidently it was fated, that marriages were made in heaven, that poverty was no vice, that one had to live with a man and not with his money, and so on. Moral proverbs are wonderfully useful in cases when we have little to say in self-justification.

Meanwhile the young lady began to recover. Vladimir had not been seen in Gavril Gavrilovitch's house for weeks. He had been scared away by his usual reception there. It was decided to send for him and announce to him unexpected good fortune: their consent to the marriage. But what was the parents' amazement when in reply to their invitation they received a half-crazy letter from him! He declared that he would never set foot in their house and begged them to forget an unhappy man whose only hope was in death. A few days later they heard that Vladimir had gone to join the army. That was in 1812.

Many days passed before they ventured to tell this to Masha, who was still convalescent. She never mentioned Vladimir. Several months later, finding his name in the casualty lists among those who had distinguished themselves and been dangerously wounded in the battle of Borodino, she fainted, and it was feared that her illness might return. But, thank heaven, the fainting fit had no bad consequences.

She was visited by another sorrow: Gavril Gavrilovitch died, leaving her his sole heiress. But wealth was no comfort to her; she sincerely shared Praskovya Petrovna's grief and vowed never to part from her. They left Nenaradovo—the place of sad memories—and went to live on another estate, in a different province.

There too suitors circled round the rich and charming young lady, but she gave not the slightest encouragement to any of them. Her mother sometimes urged her to select a partner; Marya Gavrilovna shook her head and grew pensive. Vladimir was no more: he died in Moscow, the day before the French entered it. His memory seemed sacred to Masha; at any rate, she treasured everything that could remind her of him: his drawings, the books he had once read, music and verses he had copied out for her. The neighbours, hearing of this, marvelled at her constancy and waited with interest for the hero who would at last triumph over the sad fidelity of this virgin Artemisia.

Meanwhile the war came to a glorious end. Our regiments were returning from abroad. Crowds ran out to meet them. Military bands played the airs won by the victors: *Vive Henri Quatre*, Tyrolese waltzes, and arias from *Joconde*. Officers who had gone to the war as mere boys came back as grown-up men, seasoned in battle and covered with military decorations. Soldiers gaily talked to one another, constantly introducing French and German words into their conversation. An unforgettable time! A time of enthusiasm and glory! How the Russian heart throbbed at the word 'Fatherland'! How sweet were the tears of reunion! How unanimously we combined the feelings of national pride with love for the Tsar! And what a moment it was for him!

Women, Russian women, were at that time beyond compare. Their usual coldness disappeared. Their enthusiasm was truly ravishing, when meeting the victors they shouted *hurrah!*

And threw up their bonnets in the air.

What officer of the period would deny that his best and most precious reward came from Russian women?

At that brilliant epoch Marya Gavrilovna was living with her mother in the —— province and did not see how the two capitals [1] celebrated the army's home-coming. But in country towns and villages the general enthusiasm was perhaps even greater. If an officer arrived there, he was given a triumphal reception, and in his company a lover in civilian dress had a poor time of it.

We have already said that in spite of her coldness Marya Gavrilovna was, as before, surrounded by suitors. But all had to retreat when there appeared in her castle a wounded colonel of the hussars, Burmin, with St. George's Cross on his breast, and 'an interesting pallor,' as the local young ladies

[1] Moscow and Petersburg.—TRANSLATOR'S NOTE.

used to say. He was about twenty-six years old. He came on leave to his estates, which neighboured on Marya Gavrilovna's land. She showed him marked attention. In his presence her usual pensiveness gave way to animation. It could not be said that she flirted with him, but a poet, observing her behaviour, would have said:

Se amor non è, che dunque . . .?

And indeed Burmin was a very attractive young man. He had just the type of intellect which women like: pliant and observant, utterly unpretentious and gaily ironical. He was simple and unconstrained in his manner towards Marya Gavrilovna, but his eyes and his whole mind closely followed everything she said or did. He seemed to be of a quiet and modest disposition, but rumour had it that he had once been a dreadful scapegrace. This did not lower him in Marya Gavrilovna's estimation, for like all young women she readily excused escapades that showed an ardent and fearless temperament.

But more than anything else (more than his tenderness, his pleasant conversation, his 'interesting pallor,' and his band-aged arm), the young hussar's reticence stirred her curiosity and imagination. She could not help admitting that he liked her very much; probably he too, with his intelligence and experience, noticed that she singled him out; how was it then that she had not yet seen him at her feet and heard his avowal? What restrained him? Timidity, inseparable from true love, pride, or the coquetry of a cunning Don Juan? It was a mystery to her. After much thought she came to the conclusion that timidity was the only cause and decided to encourage him by showing him more attention, and even tenderness if need be. She was preparing a most unexpected denouement, and was impatiently waiting for the moment of the romantic explanation. Mystery, of whatever kind, is always irksome to the feminine heart.

Her manœuvres had the desired effect: at any rate, Burmin grew so pensive, and his black eyes gazed at Marya Gavrilovna so ardently, that the decisive moment seemed to be near. The neighbours talked of the wedding as though all had been settled, and good Praskovya Petrovna rejoiced that her daughter had at last found a suitor worthy of her.

One day when the old lady sat alone in the drawing-room, playing patience, Burmin walked in and at once inquired about Marya Gavrilovna. 'She is in the garden,' the old lady answered; 'you go to her, and I'll wait for you here.' Burmin went out, and she crossed herself and thought: 'God grant it may all be decided today.'

Burmin found Marya Gavrilovna by the pond under a willow, in a white dress and with a book in her hands—just like the heroine of a novel. After the first questions Marya Gavrilovna deliberately ceased to keep up the conversation, thus increasing their mutual confusion, which could only be ended by a sudden and decisive explanation. And this indeed was what happened. Conscious of his embarrassment Burmin declared that he had long been seeking an opportunity to open his heart to her, and asked for a minute's attention. Marya Gavrilovna closed the book and lowered her eyes in token of acquiescence.

'I love you,' said Burmin, 'I love you passionately. . . .' (Marya Gavrilovna blushed and bent her head still lower.) 'I acted heedlessly, abandoning myself to the delightful habit —the habit of seeing and hearing you every day.' (Marya Gavrilovna recalled St. Preux's first letter.[1]) 'Now it is too late to struggle against fate; the remembrance of you, your sweet, incomparable image will be my joy and misery for the rest of my life; but I must first carry out a painful duty, reveal a terrible secret, and put an unsurmountable barrier between us——'

'It has always existed,' Marya Gavrilovna interrupted him impetuously. 'I could never be your wife. . . .'

'I know,' he answered gently, 'I know that you loved once, but death and three years of mourning . . . Dear, kind Marya Gavrilovna! do not try to deprive me of my last comfort—of the thought that you would consent to make me happy, if only . . . don't speak, for God's sake, don't say anything. You torture me. Yes, I know, I feel that you would have been mine, but—I am the unhappiest creature . . . I am married!'

Marya Gavrilovna looked at him in astonishment.

'I am married,' Burmin continued. 'I have been married

---

[1] The reference is to J. J. Rousseau's novel *Julie, ou La Nouvelle Héloïse.*—TRANSLATOR'S NOTE.

for the last four years and I do not know who my wife is, and where she is, and whether I shall ever see her!'

'What are you saying?' Marya Gavrilovna exclaimed. 'How very strange! Go on; I'll tell you afterwards . . . but go on, I beg you.'

'At the beginning of 1812,' said Burmin, 'I was hastening to Vilna where our regiment was stationed. One day I arrived at a posting station late in the evening and ordered that the horses should be harnessed at once; but suddenly a terrific snowstorm blew up, and the postmaster and the drivers advised me to wait. I obeyed, but an unaccountable restlessness possessed me; it was as though someone were egging me on. Meanwhile the snowstorm was not abating; I could endure no longer, gave word to harness the horses again and set out in the thick of it. The driver decided to go along the river as this would shorten our journey by nearly three miles. The river banks were buried in snow, and the driver missed the place where one could get on to the road; we thus found ourselves in an unfamiliar part of the country. The storm was still raging; I saw a light in the distance and told the driver to go in that direction. We came to a village; in the church, built of wood, there was a light. The church was open; several sledges stood outside the fence; people were moving about in the porch. "Here, here!" several voices cried. I told the driver to go right up to the church. "Mercy on us, what delayed you?" someone said to me. "The bride has fainted, the priest does not know what to do; we were on the point of going home. Come, be quick!" Without a word I jumped out of the sledge and went into the church, dimly lit by two or three candles. A girl was sitting on a bench in a dark corner of the church; another was rubbing her temples. "Thank heaven you've come at last," said she. "You've nearly killed my young lady." The old priest came up to me with the question: "Am I to begin?"—"Yes, Father, begin," I answered absent-mindedly. They lifted the girl from the bench. She seemed to me rather pretty. . . . Unaccountable, unforgivable folly . . . I took my place beside her before the lectern; the priest was in a hurry; the three men and the maidservant supported the bride and gave her all their attention. We were married. "Kiss each other," said the priest. My wife turned her pale face to me. I was about to kiss her. . . . She cried out: "It isn't he! it isn't he!"—and fell down senseless. The witnesses looked at me in consternation. I turned round, walked out of the church unhindered, jumped into my covered sledge, and called to the driver: "Go on!"'

'Good heavens!' cried Marya Gavrilovna, 'and you do not know what became of your poor wife?'

'I do not know,' Burmin answered. 'I do not know the name of the village where I was married; I do not remember from what station I had set off. At that time I attached so little importance to my criminal prank that after leaving the church I went to sleep and did not wake till the morning, when we had reached the third station. The servant who was with me at the time died during the campaign. I haven't any hope of tracing the girl on whom I played such a cruel joke and who is now so cruelly avenged.'

'Merciful heavens!' said Marya Gavrilovna, seizing his hand, 'so it was you! Don't you recognize me?'

Burmin turned pale . . . and threw himself at her feet.